THE TRAVELER

ALSO BY DAVID L. GOLEMON

THE TRAVELER

An Event Group Thriller

DAVID L. GOLEMON

THOMAS DUNNE BOOKS

ST. MARTIN'S PRESS ✠ NEW YORK

THOMAS DUNNE BOOKS.
An imprint of St. Martin's Press.

THE TRAVELER. Copyright © 2016 by David L. Golemon. All rights reserved. Printed in the United States of America. For information, address St. Martin's Press, 175 Fifth Avenue, New York, N.Y. 10010.

www.thomasdunnebooks.com
www.stmartins.com

The Library of Congress Cataloging-in-Publication Data is available upon request.

ISBN 978-1-250-05764-8 (hardcover)
ISBN 978-1-4668-6143-5 (e-book)

Our books may be purchased in bulk for promotional, educational, or business use. Please contact your local bookseller or the Macmillan Corporate and Premium Sales Department at 1-800-221-7945, extension 5442, or by e-mail at MacmillanSpecialMarkets@macmillan.com.

First Edition: July 2016

10 9 8 7 6 5 4 3 2 1

For my mother and her girls,
Valisa, JoAnne, Katie Anne, Tram, and, of course, Klera

ACKNOWLEDGMENTS

I would like to thank the dark personalities at DARPA, NASA, and Jet Propulsion Labs. A very special thanks to Albert Einstein for his insight into what is possible and impossible. Luckily the latter very rarely entered into his train of thought . . . the impossible to possible is only a hard think away!

DAYS OF FUTURE'S PAST

It has become appallingly obvious that our technology has exceeded our humanity. . . .

—**Albert Einstein**

ANTARCTICA, 227,000 B.C.E.

The tremendous gravitational forces pulling at the man sent his conscious thoughts spinning into obscurity. Through the reinforced windscreen he saw the sky tumbling over and over until the view became a strobelike effect that made his stomach heave. He tried desperately to breathe but found his bodily functions had ceased to work. As he tried to focus on the instrumentation panel in front of him his eyes dimmed and his view became one of tunnel-vision extreme. The instrument panel shorted out and smoke and the acrid smell of ozone filled the small cabin. The man knew he had a task to perform, but as he struggled to keep conscious he could not fathom what that chore was. A jarringly sharp slam of air moved the craft to the left and the man heard but did not understand a sonic boom. Trapped inside the quickly falling capsule, the man broke the sound barrier in its speedy downward descent.

Through the pain and his blurry vision the man heard a series of warning beeps and tones coming from somewhere he could not see. The man tore at the clear visor covering his face, trying desperately to unlock the slide that would allow the protective helmet to be removed. He finally found the slide lock and shoved the glass visor up, and then his bodily reactions took over as he fought for oxygen. The scream of air outside the thick glass had become unbearable. The noise threatened to burst the large man's eardrums as he and the machine plummeted. He tried desperately to focus on the sound of the warning lights and the computer's continued hail of "*pull up, pull up.*" He eventually forced his eyes open and he saw the swirling view of sky, then a deep greenness, then white, and then sky again.

"*Wake up!*" came an unbidden voice from his quickly evaporating memories of human speech.

The man tried again as the frantic inner voice faded to nothing. His eyes fluttered and then he concentrated. He was confused because this was not expected. A decision, a thought, a prayer, and underlying all of this the idea that he knew his life was over. He once again focused and he saw the large red light blinking frantically in front of him. Now what was he supposed to do about it? His mind tried to take him back into the safety of his memory to protect him from the struggle of deduction. He desperately wanted the beeping to stop. He slammed his thickly gloved palm through his anger and frustration into the flashing red light.

The man immediately heard a loud pop that jolted his body painfully against the seat back. He felt the deceleration, and that restrictive motion again made his stomach want to relieve itself of anything he may have eaten in the past few hours. He felt his body jerk and the pain of deceleration strained something in his back. Soon the tumbling stopped and an eerie silence filled the cabin.

As he started to close his eyes against the pain in his back the man felt the craft he was in slam into a yielding force from below. Before he knew what was happening the vehicle rolled completely over and he found himself upside down in his restrictive and limited world. Finally, as he bobbed upon some unknown surface, the man lost consciousness. The last words he spoke he failed to understand as they flowed out of his mouth unbidden.

"Not this time, Jack, not this time . . ."

The man's world went black.

His eyes opened. He felt as if he was in an almost weightless condition. The man turned his head and vomited onto the now dark instrument panel. The man dry-heaved until there was a belching satisfaction from his stomach. He didn't vomit but felt the relief nonetheless. He then felt the coolness of water as it struck his face, and he realized that there was water coming into the enclosed space that had become his confined world. He tried to look out of the windscreen but saw a revolving scene of sunlight, then the darkness of water, and then sunlight once more.

He reached over and felt the tug of restraint and then he realized he had a three-point harness on. He snapped off the restraint and freed himself as the world started to flood into the capsule. He remembered a safety brief he had had and popped the canopy as the water flooded in. He remembered something else and reached over and hit the flashing blue rescue beacon and then slammed his gloved hand down on the lifeboat release. As he did he failed to notice that the wristwatch he was wearing on his gloved and protected wrist was torn free and settled to the bottom of the flooded cockpit.

As the man tore loose from the fast-sinking capsule, he heard the rubber raft and all of his supplies explode as bottled air filled the large boat. He rolled free of the capsule just as the glass windows went under. He splashed and fought his unyielding suit as he struggled to gain the lifeboat. Just as he made it into the life-saving boat he looked up and saw a large head as it rose from the water in front of him. He flinched away as the reptilian features submerged. The creature must have been curious as to all of the noise on the surface, and then it vanished. Before it did the man realized that the animal he had just seen was not normal. The head was that of a crocodile and the body of a fish. He shook his head and collapsed into the confines of the bright yellow raft.

Admiral (temporary grade) Carl Everett realized at that last moment that he was definently not in Kansas anymore.

DORTMUND, GERMANY
MAY 16, 1943

The bunker was designed for maximum bomb protection. The men and equipment buried deep inside the underground facility were as safe from RAF bombs as any cowering official in the extensive Berlin bunker complexes. The two enormous elevator systems lowered the heavy equipment needed for this final test. These large platform elevators traveled along the same conduit tunnel needed for the heavy electric cable system that traveled the twenty-five miles from the Möhne dam. The rubber-encased cables were capable of supplying enough electricity to not only Berlin but Munich and Cologne as well. No power coupling that size had ever been supplied to one facility in the history of electrical engineering.

The bunker itself was not that remarkable in design: five levels of heavily reinforced concrete surrounded by sound-dampening sand lining the outer walls. The entire complex was built on large steel springs to keep vibration to the outside world to a bare minimum. This facet was the outstanding design feature of the system. The city of Dortmund never suspected the bunker system was there at all. The comings and goings of the many technicians needed for the project was tightly controlled through a tunnel access portal fifteen miles outside of the city. Trucks would drop off the needed men and material and then would continue on to Dortmund, never allowing prying eyes to view their comings and goings. The heavier equipment was brought in by truck and aircraft that many area residents supposed were meant for the enormous dam twenty miles distant. For the locals it was not well known that anyone caught within the perimeter of the hidden bunker was never heard from again. Summary execution was the order of the day for any would-be hiker.

Three hundred feet of downward travel was completed in eerie silence by the five men inside the smaller of the two transit elevators. The smallest of the five stood with his leather-gloved hands clasped in front of him. It had been this miniscule gentleman who had commenced full-scale start-up of the experiments that he personally dubbed Operation Traveler. Once the covert order was received and the funds swindled from the military for the massive project, the strange equipment was quick to start arriving on December 15, 1941. Two years of hard work and the expenditure of stolen wealth the Third Reich would never miss and the "Wellsian Doorway" was finally complete.

The small man reached up to his greatcoat's thick collar and closed it more firmly around his chilled neck.

"Apologies, Reichsführer, the temperature on the main concourse and laboratories has to be maintained at a constant fifty-four degrees. It is imperative that we never vary as our computing apparatus is extremely temperamental."

Heinrich Himmler, the Reichsführer of the SS, the head of the most powerful organization outside of the German Wehrmacht, stood silently, not bothering to acknowledge the man in the white lab coat nor temper a comment of his explanation. He finally spared the man a glance. In the dull lighting Professor Lars Thomsen could only see his own reflection in the small wire-rimmed glasses of the former chicken farmer turned mass murderer.

"I am just pleased to note, Professor, that the many millions of Reichsmarks I have funneled to this project were not wasted on creature comforts. I can bare the chill."

"As you will see, Herr Reichsführer, your money"—he quickly noticed the frown as the pencil-thin mustache wrinkled at the corners of the small man's mouth—"with respects, the Reich's money, has been well spent."

The elevator started slowing as it reached the fifth of five levels three hundred feet below the forest floor.

"I assume your special cargo arrived intact from the east?" Himmler asked as two SS guards dressed in long black field coats slid the large elevator doors aside and then immediately went to attention as Himmler waited for his answer inside.

"Yes," Thomsen answered as his eyes flicked to the other three men accompanying them. These black-coated officers raised a brow his way. He knew the semi-disguised men were private industrialists that had assisted the leader of the SS in funding and in the material supply needed, and then coordinated the most technical project in the history of mankind. Himmler finally turned and faced the scientist full on.

"Good, with securing the special package perhaps you can now realize how close this project is to my heart. To directly challenge the Führer's edict, one that was of my own design, would be considered by some as"—he smiled but only briefly—"treasonous? But the need to have complete cooperation from the test subjects cancels all that out, yes?"

Thomsen knew he had better answer right or he would be buried deep inside this bunker when it was razed to the ground after Himmler got what it was he desired out of him. He would show the man his resolve in the finalizing of the design and its test subjects.

"How could the advancement of science ever be construed as treasonous, Herr Reichsführer? As you will see our test subject is now cooperative and very much intelligent enough to see the final test through. The Traveler has accomplished this feat more than once. With the assurances now in place with the transfer of her brother, yes, the Traveler will complete the final test and we can begin to transfer equipment to Berlin at the first opportune moment."

Himmler raised his brow and then nodded. He turned and stepped from the large lift. "I am pleased to hear your reputation for humanitarian causes has its limits." Heinrich Himmler looked back at the much taller scientist as he wanted to see his expression when he realized that the scientist's small meetings he held with his staff over the use of slave labor as test subjects had not gone unnoticed. Thomsen remained silent as Himmler smiled again, this time even more brief than the first, and then nodded for his security detail to move ahead. Thomsen and the other three observers moved quickly to catch up.

The men were led to a large enclosed area that overlooked an even larger room filled with men, women, and equipment, the likes of which none of the SS men or industrialists had ever seen before. Standing in the middle of the laboratory space was what looked like a large door frame constructed of a material that was not immediately recognizable. This frame had large conductors that coiled out of the top and sides of the machine. The entire flooring was covered in a rubberized material that protected the workers inside from static electricity. The men and women all wore coats of either white or blue—it was explained to Himmler that the technicians had been broken into two teams. The white team handled the power output and consumption, which would be massive in scope, while the blue team was in charge of radar tracking, signal acquisition, and would perform the actual conducting of the test. There were sixteen rows of stations with a technician at each console and over 170 power cables running from the monitoring stations to the Doorway, as the Reichsfürher had come to call it. He was adamant about using the doorway's code name because of its British connotations in using its full moniker, the Wellsian Doorway, in honor of the man who wrote about this very subject many years before.

Thomsen turned and bowed his head at Himmler as the Reichsführer remained standing at the large, thick window that gave visitors a view of the entire floor below.

"With your permission," the German scientist asked.

The small man nodded just once.

"As you know, gentlemen, this project began in earnest in 1941. It is meant as a 'fail-safe,' if you will, against the Americans entering the war against Germany, a scenario our farsighted Reichsführer saw as a precursor to the Fatherland losing the war with so much of that world pitted against us. This fail-safe, gentlemen, is now ready and may I say with pride, fully functioning. This will be the final non-German personnel test in the schedule. The next test will be conducted by a representative of the Reichsfüher's staff and myself when our equipment has been properly placed inside our Berlin complex."

Himmler knew that they had lost at least sixty reassigned non-German personnel in the doorway's testing. Some of the lost were recovered right back inside the facility, mangled and in grisly pieces at the doorway's opening, or were lost in the void of time and space.

"As you already know the first gate was commissioned in May of 1942 and was completed that same month. Our scheduling of tests has been nonstop since that historic day. The first success came three days ago." Thomsen handed Himmler a folded newspaper. As he was unfolding it he saw the headline in bold print as described by the *London Times* over one year ago: "American Fortress of Corregidor Falls to Japs." And then next to the headline was the scrawled signature of none other than himself. Himmler nodded as he refolded the newspaper. "May I assume that is your signature next to the headline, Herr Reichsführer, and no others?"

The miniscule man nodded his head and handed the newspaper over to the next man who examined it and passed it on.

"As you know, the very first Wellsian Doorway was built right here in this room you see below. It was dismantled exactly six months ago as we built the secondary door—the one you are now seeing below. The first doorway has ceased to exist for exactly one year, gentlemen, as it was dismantled in the past—only the doorway and its signal remain. No personnel, no power other than what it would take to run the testing. This newspaper and several others like it were placed next to the first doorway over a year ago. To see these newspapers again is proof positive that the Wellsian Doorway"—here he paused for dramatic effect—"works beyond all expectations."

Himmler looked pleased but only he knew just how pleased.

"The third doorway was completed this month, only this one was constructed in Berlin at a secret location known only to the assembly team and the Reichsführer. This doorway will be utilized if the worst-case scenario happens and the war is lost. The new location is far more viable an option of escape for . . . you gentlemen than out here in Dortmund."

"So, we are convinced this is the only way in which Einstein's hypothesis can be achieved?" asked the man who represented Krupp Steel.

"Yes, Herr Einstein has theorized that the balance of inner-dimensional travel can only be achieved through conducting poles of influence. In other words, one doorway has to be connected to another doorway or the travel is unachievable if the direct transfer of material, or in this case, a human, can get to the coordinating doorway in the past. If there is no corresponding doorway the Traveler will be lost and deposited in a time frame, air, water, or land coordinates not of his choosing. Maybe even lost three or four kilometers above the Earth, there would be no rhyme or reason to the Traveler's exit point from the originating Wellsian Doorway without a corresponding doorway, or signal for the first doorway to lock on to."

"So, in essence, what you are saying is the Traveler would not only be sent to a time in the past not of his choosing, but may also materialize deep within the oceans or miles into the sky?"

"Correct, it was never hypothesized by Einstein that this was a safe science to use."

"We know it takes an inordinate amount of power to create the rip in time, but how is that action achieved? The thoughts and schemes of men such as yourself and Herr Einstein fly far above our barbaric ways of thinking," the immaculately dressed gentleman from Klienmann Electronics inquired.

"Ah, the gist of the theory." Thomsen clapped his hands together in excitement as Himmler took in a deep breath.

He was forced to listen to the egghead braggart tell his tale, one in which he was growing ever tired of hearing. The man could not keep his mouth shut, and Himmler knew that was going to be a problem that was easily remedied when the final testing and assembly was complete inside the Berlin city limits. He brushed all thought of covering his tracks aside as Thomsen continued his explanation.

"The doorway we have here will read the coordinates we have programmed into the Traveler's jump pattern, which in turn will read the radio and electron waves from the area of the entered coordinates. When it doesn't find a corresponding signal the signal amplifiers start a search until it finds the correct signal from a doorway we know isn't there any longer, because we dismantled all but the portal and signal amplifiers almost as soon as it was built. The signal is then transferred to a transmission tower high in the Harz Mountains. The reinforced radio waves will search time and space for its sister signal. We know it will not find it simply because it no longer exists—in this current time frame—but it does occupy the same space in the past. Still, the searching transmission will not be defeated when the acquisition of past signal cannot be found. It will expand into space, which we all know is limitless. However, our signal transmitters are so powerful that it travels, and then travels even farther through space until it gets a glimmer of a return." Thomsen gestured toward the laboratory floor where a technician leaned into a microphone at his station.

"Signal acquired at zero twenty hours local time, latitude fifty-one degrees north, longitude seven degrees twenty-seven east."

"Excellent, now confirm signal origin, please," Thomsen said into the intercom.

As the men in the room watched on, the signal emanating from the doorway below it ceased to beep. On the overhead speakers they heard a weaker signal coming from somewhere other than the doorway they were looking at.

"Signal capture confirmed, the doorways are conversing with each other," called out the technician from below.

"Are you saying that the transmission is now being picked up by the original doorway dismantled last year?" one of the three industrialists asked. Thomsen saw the smile grow on Himmler's face, and that was the only approval he needed.

"Correct. Now we will make the connection and the doorway will open. Thus far we have the power to only send two hundred kilos through the door, but we will expand on that as we get more power from the Möhne Dam. The force of the connection expands the rift until a portal, tunnel as we call it, is constructed through the time and space dimensions as described by my colleague Herr Einstein. We have yet to figure the dynamics of the tunnel, but we will learn far more in the next year or so with continued testing and refinement. Soon we will have the full dynamics of the doorway solved."

"You have until Christmas 1945, Herr Professor," Himmler said as the others in the room looked shocked.

"Such a precise and restrictive date, Herr Reichsfüher?" Thomsen inquired worriedly.

"My offices have calculated the approximate month of Germany's final destruction, and that was the most optimistic view rendered. By then we will all be on the run from the Jew-loving allies. Then we will be caught and hung." Himmler turned and faced the men in the room. They all knew that his estimates of the downfall of the Thousand-Year Reich were accurate. "This machine has to be online before this happens. I, gentlemen, do not intend to follow our great leader into his immortal destiny."

The men in the room were now only twenty minutes away from confirming the fact that they had a viable escape route out of Germany when the war was finally lost.

The plan? Run to a place they knew was far safer than the capital would be in 1945. That place was right here, almost two years in the past.

The age of time travel had arrived.

TWO HUNDRED MILES WEST OF THE MÖHNE DAM, GERMANY (OPERATION CHASTISE)

Squadron Leader Guy Gibson felt the heaviness of his Avro Lancaster bomber as it flew at twenty-two thousand feet above France. They had successfully departed England without arousing suspicion just as the plan had called for. His squadron of heavy night bombers was now entering Germany without the Luftwaffe knowing they were coming. Target—the Möhne Dam near Dortmund, Germany. Their task, take out the dam that supplied power to various locations the allies wished to go away. Not only was the process of developing the hard water needed in atomic research progressing near the dams of Germany, but the rumors of even more disturbing projects had started to filter through the minutia of intelligence coming through London and Washington.

Gibson checked on his navigator.

"How are we coming back there, Terry?" he asked through his rubber mask.

"Eighty-seven kilometers from target. We are exactly two minutes ahead of schedule."

"Bloody good," Gibson said to himself as he knew the timing of the bomb drop had to be precise to the minute for the most audacious attack to date outside of the American raid on Tokyo by Colonel Jimmy Doolittle a year before.

"Very good, boys. Now, how is our darling little *Bouncing Baby Boy* doing back there?" Gibson asked into his mic.

"Upkeep is now breathing, waiting for final arming sequence," came the reply from the bomb bay compartment of the large aircraft.

Hanging half in and half out of the bomb bay doors was what the RAF had dubbed "Upkeep." The cylindrical bomb was designed to hit the water in front of a dam and "skip" over the reservoir to the wall of concrete and slowly settle to the bottom of the reservoir where it would detonate at its base. The resulting explosion would be catastrophic to the core of the dam, bringing it all down. There would be two nights of these specialized raids on the dam complexes of Germany.

The *Bouncing Baby Boy* was on its way to end Germany's attempt at developing an atomic weapons platform. However, Squadron Leader Gibson had been briefed and knew that the mission was so much more than that.

THE WELLSIAN DOORWAY

"Expand the doorway, please, gentlemen," Thomsen said as an assistant started passing out earplugs. It was Himmler who raised a brow. "The sonic wave that assaults the inner ear can be rather uncomfortable without protection, Herr Reichsführer." He nervously watched as the leader of the SS nodded his head only once.

Below, the technicians were moving about excitedly as the doorway started to expand by hydraulic lines into a more circular pattern that allowed the stainless steel frame, lined with ceramic tiles, to take its shape so the magnets inside the ceramics could negotiate the complex design. The ceramics were designed to hold back the generated heat that would in turn protect the Traveler from being fried alive inside. The Wellsian Doorway was now six times the size it had been when the hydraulics expansion had started. A loud clang was heard as fifty technicians came through an expanded tunnel with an electric cart pulling a long train of what looked like chain-link. The entirety of the chain was one hundred feet in length and looked as if it went from one conductive coil to the next. Once the electric car was in place a remotely controlled arm started pulling the secured end of the chain up until the entire length was only a few feet from the concrete floor.

"All nonessential personnel evacuate the test area," came an announcement from below as the room was totally cleared with the exception of ten technicians who remained fixated on their consoles. "Connect the light accelerator."

Himmler stood and went to the window as he watched the most expensive piece of hardware ever developed by German science as it dangled off the floor. The chain itself was constructed out of a hard plastic material that had been "weaved" together, forming a composite of nylon, copper, and plastic to form a new element called rylar, a composite manufacturing system originally regarded as years ahead of the curve in composite technology and would eventually fill the need in the aircraft industry for lightweight materials. In this experiment the material would be used to control the tremendous amount of heat generated by the doorway. Interspaced at equal intervals along this chain was what made the proposition of displacement possible—industrial blue diamonds. Himmler and his SS had spent two years collecting these hard-to-come-by diamonds the world over, stolen from museums that had been ransacked by the German army and raids on South African mining facilities. All together there were fifty-six five-ounce diamonds ensconced in the ceramic cocoon, which resembled large, oblong bluish pearls.

As the observers watched on, the chain was moved to the very top of the expanded rectangle of the doorway. The robotic arm held it there by the manipulations of a trained technician. They heard loud humming as a bracket was lowered from the top of the doorway and the arm hooked the chain to it. Then the arm released that end and connected the opposite end. Now the large diamond-ensconced chain was loosely hanging from the hook as the manipulating arm was moved away. The mood was silent as the robotic arm was moved and stored.

"Stand by for charging of the system," Thomsen said into the intercom as a wall was raised below to protect the technicians at their controls. They would be shielded by the charging of the doorway when a flood of neutrinos and charged particles of ion were introduced to the conductive chain. Thomsen could see that Himmler was wide-eyed as he watched. Even though he had seen film of the previous tests and its success Himmler was still fascinated as he watched it live. For the success, or for the chance to watch one of his precious subjects lose their lives, Thomsen wasn't sure. "Herr Reichsführer, when the doorway is fully charged, do not be alarmed when you feel a disorientation as it comes to full power. Its sound waves act as an hallucinogen introduced through the inner ear for some."

"Is it dangerous to us?" he asked as he once again took a seat to watch.

"Frankly, Herr Reichsführer, we just don't know what the long-term effects will be."

Himmler nodded. He really didn't care since the damnable technology would only be used once and for a singular purpose—his escape from the Russians, or the allies.

The lights throughout the complex dimmed as power was brought online. Five miles down the line, buried deeply underground, were the three large rubber-encased conduit electrical lines that ran in from the Möhne Dam twenty-five miles away. They were heating up so much the rubber casing started to sizzle.

"Preparing to charge," came the confident announcement from below.

Thomsen, with a final look and nod from Himmler, opened the intercom to the laboratory below. "Charge the doorway!"

A piercing scream filled the air around every man watching the test. Himmler forced his hands to his ears and then he quickly inserted the earplugs that he had forgotten about. As the audio assault continued one of the SS guards bent over and went to his knees as he became violently ill. Himmler angrily nodded that the man should be removed and punished later for showing his weakness.

"Pulse!" Thomsen said, hoping that the final charging of the doorway would also double Himmler over. But the small man held firm and only gritted his teeth at the onslaught of inner-ear sound and minute vibrations.

Below, the charge of electricity burst into the chain and it stiffened to a straight line of two rows as electricity flowed through it.

Thomsen paced to the side of the Reichsführer and leaned down. "The magnets inside the door frame will be charged and the chain, or what we call the particle accelerator, will conform to its designed structure."

The final charge was sent through the accelerator. Suddenly there was a bright explosion of light as the circular chain rounded and became taut as the force of the magnets inside the doorway distributed magnetism to equal parts of the chain, which brought the expensive links to attention, forming a perfect circle inside the rectangular doorway. As Himmler watched, the interior of the man-made circle started to shimmer. It was as if an invisible wave moved the very air around inside the accelerator as it hung magically in suspended form in a perfect circle where the opposing magnets held it at bay.

"We are forming a man-made current. Just as if we have shot an arrow underwater, the particle accelerator has now forced ions into the doorway. We are seeing this shimmering simply because as of this moment the current and flow have no place to go, or to lock on to, so the entire assault of our time and space remains contained in this laboratory. Start the revolution, please."

The magnets started to rotate, and then spun faster and faster until there was nothing but a trail of blue light forming the brightest of flares any of the men had ever witnessed. The RPMs increased as even more power from the Möhne Dam was used. The sheer power was pulsing energy into the surrounding air. The chain connected fast, and then released the opposing magnets to the next in line, which made the speed reach incalculable levels. This same design would be used in particle accelerators in the future.

"We are now going to send our signal into the doorway." Thomsen again spoke into the intercom. "Go to full revolutions on the particle accelerator!"

Below the circular chain of composite material, steel, plastic, and ceramic was spinning at the speed of sound, which was bringing men to their knees. Himmler grimaced and took hold of the arms of his chair to fight the nausea filling his throat. Thomsen didn't have to explain that this was the closest man had ever come to achieving the speed of light.

A blue haze started to fill the interior of the accelerator as the RPMs continued to multiply. For three hundred kilometers around the Möhne Dam, lights dimmed and transformers blew in almost every town and city. Lightbulbs and fixtures exploded inside the laboratory, making men duck and technicians smile as they felt the power of the very universe strike deep inside the landscape of Germany.

"Now we are near to the power we need," Thomsen said excitedly.

"For what, Herr Professor?"

"To make the connection to the dismantled gate of two years ago, Herr Reichsführer."

God, Himmler thought to himself, *this maniac may have actually produced a viable plan for the second-most powerful man in Germany.* "You may proceed as soon as you are ready."

"Bring in the Traveler," Thomsen said as his eyes went to a small doorway in the far wall as it opened, and two white-coated lab technicians escorted a frightened girl into the lab. She was so emaciated Himmler thought she would collapse.

"Our subject for the test is twelve-year-old Moira Mendelsohn, she is from—"

"I do not wish to know the Jew's name, or anything else about her for that matter, Professor."

"Yes, yes, of course, you have my apologies. Needless to say the Traveler tested at a one hundred forty-seven IQ. Her brother tested only a few points less. Thus far the Traveler has performed magnificently. Now with the guarantee of her return by her brother's very presence."

Himmler watched below as the thin and sickly girl was led to the front of the doorway. They had already placed earphones on her small head to protect her from the audio assault element of the test. Her clothing was tattered and worn as Thomsen wanted the Reichsführer to see that nothing special outside of headphone protection was needed. Her clothing was the same gray rags she had on when she had been transferred from Bergen-Belsen a month before. All the observers could see the yellow Star of David badly stitched to her gray dress. The small scabs on her head from lice infestation from the camps were hidden as well as possible so as not to offend the sensitivities of Himmler, who was widely known for his weak stomach when it came to observing the men, women, and children he had so ruthlessly rounded up. He could talk a good game, but when it came to facing the things he did he was more on the shy side according to British and American intelligence sources. The girl was shaking and quietly crying. The task she was to perform had been explained to her and would be no different from the last test that she performed flawlessly. To ensure the girl's cooperation, a small boy was also escorted into the room and placed into a chair. The doe-eyed male was no more than eight years of age.

"I was led to believe that there would only be one test subject," the man from Krupp Steel inquired as he saw the tears in both the boy's and the girl's eyes as they finally saw each other. It looked as if the girl tried to shrug the hand of the technician away in an attempt to go to comfort the frightened child.

"The boy is not a test subject, sir. He is what we would describe as insurance."

The dawning of understanding illuminated the industrialist's features.

"This was the Reichsführer's idea, after all, we do want certain guarantees that our wayward Traveler steps back into the first doorway and returns. A precaution we have taken since she does know this is the final test with her involvement. After her usefulness is at an end she will be returned to Bergen-Belsen for"—he looked briefly at Himmler—"whatever her fate will be."

No more needed to be said. Thomsen was proving he could be as brutal as Himmler himself.

"Start the signal!" Thomsen cried excitedly.

The doorway was acting like a centrifuge, so powerful in its rotation that the frightened girl shied away from the forces assaulting her. The technician patted the young girl on the shoulder and then stepped away. Suddenly a burst of sound penetrated the noise from below and held steady.

"Tone is sounding and is now in active search mode."

Himmler grimaced as the piercing sound of the signal assaulted his ears even through the earplugs. The girl went to her knees as the pain of the signal coupled with the spinning accelerator knocked the senses from her small body.

"We have signal bounce back! Yes, we have a return!"

Thomsen smiled as he knew the two doorways were talking to each other. The space between times had been breached.

"The Jew Einstein was right all along."

Thomsen smiled down at Himmler. That Jew, as he called him, was the most brilliant theorist Thomsen had ever studied. Himmler and Hitler were fools for chasing these people off like they had; science would not benefit from their action. He went to the intercom.

"Stand!" he said loudly. The girl looked up from her sitting position and back into the glass at the face of the man ordering her to stand. She started to rise but fell back.

"Perhaps you are not strong enough? Your brother perhaps is a better candidate?"

The girl shot a defiant look up at Thomsen. She angrily raised herself from the floor of the lab. With hatred still burning in her green eyes she finally turned and stared into the swirling bands of color that whirlpooled inside the Wellsian Doorway.

"Displacement event seven commencing at zero zero thirty-two hours and fifteen seconds. Commence test."

After a last defiant look back at the observers, the Traveler looked over at her frightened brother and mouthed the words, *I'll come back for you,* and with that, Moira Mendelsohn stepped into the hurricane force of the doorway.

———————

Himmler stood aghast as the girl stepped into the maelstrom of the doorway. He tensed when he saw the young woman stop just beyond the initial frame of the apparatus. Her body was still visible and the Reichsführer could see the frightened girl freeze as the initial force of the Wellsian Doorway snatched her breath away and pulled at the rags of her clothing, sending her ill-fitting dress up and around her thin body.

The Traveler felt the closely cropped hair on her head stand straight up. The tattered woolen sweater she wore was pulled so tightly to her skin due to static electricity that her breathing became restricted. Her heart started a rapid palpitation and her stomach was quickly relieved of the thin gruel of potato soup she had been fed earlier. She felt the wetness of her own discarded meal as the heat of the doorway caught and soon evaporated the material. Still, the wind inside the gate increased as the girl forced her body forward with a feeling of weightlessness.

She felt the sandlike blast of particles as they penetrated her skin and felt the deep burn as they passed through her sinew and bone. Her ears started to bleed and seep from the earphones she wore for protection. The signal from the initiating doorway was so close and strong it ruptured her eardrums. This final test was far more powerful in scope than the previous one.

The Traveler bent over as the agony of the assault made her feel as if her very bones were being pulverized from the inside. Then she fell forward as the force of the corresponding signal from the target doorway pushed back against the first. The connection between worlds had been made. Moira Mendelsohn, a twelve-year-old from the simple streets of the small Polish village of Triske, now forever known as the Traveler, felt the onrush of the last order to be sent from Germany—full power that was sent through the blue diamonds and the RPMs of the electromagnetic field increased a thousandfold. The girl felt the agony of heat coupled with a pulsing of the electrical assault. She opened her eyes at the last second before her body could take no more. She saw the other side of the doorway. It was calm, dimly lit, and peaceful. She blessedly felt her legs give out and she fell forward.

The outline of the girl vanished. Himmler's eyes widened as her body became part of the swirling greens and blues of the electromagnetic storm.

"She's through, she has made the transit!" Thomsen said loudly. "Cut power to fifty percent," he said as he saw five technicians run forward with fire extinguishers when they heard the power being curtailed to the machine. "Prepare one-way communication link," he finished as he walked over to the small radio set that was connected to the main floor of the lab.

The young girl felt the assault on her body and senses ease as her mind started to unscramble. Her stomach heaved once more and the last of her evening supper emptied onto the cold concrete floor. She rose to her elbows and wiped her mouth. Then she quickly remembered where she was and frantically looked back and saw that the doorway was there and still open. The vortex of light and swirling particles obscured the other side but she knew that they were there, waiting to see if the experiment worked. She felt the evilness of the eyes that waited impatiently. She started to stand on shaky, weakened legs.

The room she was in was the exact double of the one in which she had just left. She actually had figured out after the initial test more than a week before that it was in fact the very same room she had left behind. The laboratory was empty of the advanced displacement equipment and the immense space was sparse of light. Only the doorway's frame that held the corresponding signal remained. Spiderwebs blew in the onslaught of wind still being produced by the partially opened doorway. She took a tentative step away from the swirling vortex and felt the ease of pressure. Her head stopped aching and her bones felt as if they had been resolidified somehow. Her stomach settled and she realized that she was thirsting to death. It was as if every bit of moisture had been sucked from her body. Then she saw through the swirling and flashing of the doorway behind her a large water bottle with folded paper cones beside it. She approached cautiously. Her hand reached for the dust-covered clear bottle but froze when the voice came through the doorway.

"Yes, you are thirsty, drink, we have very little time. You must be rehydrated before your return."

The voice echoed in the emptiness of the deserted bunker as if an ancient god were talking to her from Olympus. Her heart leaped as the voice of Thomsen filled the girl with dread. Her hand lowered, forsaking the bottle.

"Ah, yes, the thought that will always come to the trapped animal—the brief glimpse of escape."

The girl felt as if her thoughts had been read. She swallowed as her eyes tried to pierce the round circle of the doorway.

"But you have not thought this through, my dear. You were chosen for your above-average intelligence by our benefactor, the Reichsführer, and also because you come with built-in assurances of cooperation."

Moira realized at that moment that which she so readily forgot—her small brother who was still in their evil hands. She tentatively reached for the water. She unfolded the paper cone and then uncorked the bottle and poured. She drank until she thought she would burst. She had no choice. When she finished she placed the bottle down beside the others she had drank on the other test nights. There were three empty bottles.

"Now, the proof that the Reichsführer requires is on the table, pick anyone, they are all the same."

The girl saw the lined-up newspapers. The headlines of each were covered by a thick layer of dust. She reached for the first newspaper. She blew the dust free and read. She knew very little of the English language but Moira knew instinctively that the headline was not a good one. "American Fortress of Corregidor Falls to Japs." She retrieved the paper with the scrawled signature of Heinrich Himmler next to the bold print and turned toward the doorway.

THE MÖHNE DAM

Squadron Commander Gibson brought the giant Lancaster to within fifteen feet of the surface of the reservoir as his assault charged through the front door of the German antiaircraft defenses. This was the second run against the dam. He had braved the first just to make sure that the level of the waterline had not gone down as they had to skip their payload over the two anti-torpedo nets that spanned the waterway in front of the enormous dam.

"Speed, two hundred thirty knots. Altitude, sixty feet, Gibby, for God's sake let her go!" the copilot screamed as the Lancaster bore in on the dam's angled facing.

Gibson knew they only had one shot at this. If the attack failed the industrial might of Germany would be unaffected, and the research involving the development of hard water would continue.

"I hate to say this, but we're so bloody close to the water we see fish!" came the voice of the starboard machine gunner as the Lancaster roared in, climbing to sixty feet over the shining waters of the Möhne.

"Now!" Gibson cried as he saw the white face of the dam grow like a wall of destruction in his windscreen.

"Upkeep away!" called the bombardier.

The cylindrical Upkeep hit the water just as Gibson pulled up on the stick with all the strength he and his copilot could muster. It felt as though the twin-tailed bomber was going to strike the top of the Möhne Dam but at the last moment the great bomber cleared it by a mere six feet. The force of the bombers' wash knocked over five German soldiers on the walkway as it passed. The Lancaster climbed free as the five-foot-long, barrel-like bomb started its magical skipping action toward the dam. It bounced over the line cable of the first torpedo net and then the second. There was nothing to stop it from striking the dam now.

Six times the *Bouncing Baby Boy* struck the water and then rose back into the dark night sky. Soon the sheer weight of the giant bomb slowed her advance to the point that the nine-thousand-pound bomb was only traveling at 100 kilometers per hour when it struck the reservoir side of the dam. It hit with a force that knocked more German soldiers from their feet as they scrambled to watch the attack. Then gravity took hold and the Upkeep settled and quickly sank into the frigid waters of the Möhne reservoir. It sank, spinning and bumping against the reinforced concrete and then crawled along the face as it was designed to do with the backspin of the launch. It fell directly where it was supposed to fall—right to the base of the fragile system.

Himmler watched and waited. He never suspected the subject of the test, the Traveler, would fail to return. After all, as long as she had the hope of saving her brother she would finish what the experiment called for.

"I assume you have retrieved the evidence of your travel, so return to the doorway," Thomsen said into the microphone as he watched the anticipation on the Reichsführer's face. "Charge the doorway, one hundred and ten percent power."

The doorway started to spin at a fantastic speed and the sparks of color returned. The connection was made once more. Soon Himmler would have the proof he needed. His grand escape plan was now a viable option to his hanging at the hands of his enemies, the allies.

"Power output at one hundred and fifteen percent!" the technician called into the loud void of the laboratory.

They felt the earth beneath the bunker roll as if the ground was made of water instead of bedrock. Heinrich Himmler's eyes widened in shock as the doorway erupted in flame and sparks as her emergency backup systems were knocked offline.

"*Mein Gott*, what has happened?" Thomsen cried as he felt the first ripple of earth movement.

As for Himmler, he knew exactly what had happened. He had been warned of possible RAF assaults on the power-producing systems of the war effort.

"No!" he said loudly as the world around him turned to electrical flame.

The Upkeep traveled to a depth of 112 feet, three feet farther than the designers wanted, but this failure actually ensured the success of the mission. Just as the Upkeep hit the bottom of the dam nearest the last of the solid granite masonry blocks where they joined clay and earthen bank, the shock wave as the hydrostatic fuse detonated the nine thousand pounds of explosive in the barrel-like weapon.

At first there was little reaction other than the giant waterspout above the dam's upper superstructure. The wash inundated the German guards running about in a panic. Then the real magic started to happen as Mother Nature started to take an interest in the game. The initial cracks in the dam were small, but as the explosion reached out from the base, the return of water to that empty pressure void slammed into the wall of concrete at over a thousand miles per hour. It cracked. The sizable void traveled like a snake at maximum speed as it raced up the water-side of the dam. It hit the top and the first of the five-thousand-pound chunks of wall started to cascade into the small village below, whose residents had already started to run for their lives.

The Möhne Dam and the surrounding countryside had only minutes of life left to them.

"Get me my power back!" Thomsen said as a shower of sparks cascaded to the floor, making even Himmler duck low.

"Get me to my car!" Himmler said as calmly as he could as he was pulled by his security team from the glass-enclosed room. His eyes fell on a panicked Thomsen as he tried to find out what was wrong. The fool didn't even realize his precious project had been attacked. Thomsen's eyes showed fear as he knew then that his life and his project were done. He would never survive the Reichsführer's wrath.

The lights flickered as the SS men cleared the room and ran for the elevator while they still had power to operate the lifts.

Himmler turned to two of his SS security men. "Remove Thomsen and only his most essential personnel. The rest need to be silenced, including the Traveler and her sibling, if she returns."

The two men turned and made their way to the laboratory below and started to pull Thomsen from the room amid his cries to help stop the catastrophe to his experiment. Three of his assistants were also pulled out of the lab as others used fire extinguishers to try to stem the flow of the disaster.

Before anyone knew what was happening, bullets ripped into the laboratory below. Technicians froze at their consoles as their world exploded into chaos. Bullets ripped into their screens and then themselves as SS machine guns opened up from the stairwell in the far wall.

Thomsen and his three assistants were pushed toward the elevators. The second was waiting with an SS soldier. Professor Thomsen was hustled toward the lift. Suddenly he felt the large glass window blow inward and was inundated with shrapnel. The largest piece lodged into his thorax and jugular veins. His last view of his precious Wellsian Doorway was of men with weapons destroying it and his people. His last dimming vision was of the small brother of the Traveler as he ran away in fear. He wondered if the boy would ever make it out alive. Thomsen died with many regrets, but the boy's fate was not one of them.

Before the murderers of the many technicians of the doorway could reach the elevator, exploding water from the destroyed Möhne Dam was forced from the conduit tunnel. The furious flow of water burst forth like the rush of an oncoming train. The laboratory started filling fast with water from the collapsing dam.

The girl saw the explosions with the view she had of the doorway before it collapsed. Her eyes had found the frightened visage of her baby brother as the world she knew vanished before her eyes. She reached up at the spinning vortex of color as their eyes met and that was when she saw the frightened face of her brother turn to shock as the bullets ripped into the floor near him. Then the doorway closed forever and she was left with her hand reaching for nothing but the blackness that was the bunker. Moira Mendelsohn collapsed to the floor with the newspaper clutched in her hand.

Three hours later the young woman who had become the first time traveler in the history of the world broke open the door that led to the clean fresh air of the outdoors. It smelled wonderful. She looked at the stars above and took a deep breath.

The Traveler vanished into the Wellsian Doorway on that dark night back in 1943—and then disappeared again into a war-torn world of 1942—almost one year before she vanished the first time.

The Wellsian Doorway was closed and would not be opened again for close to a century.

PART ONE

DEPARTMENT 5656

This is a tale left unfinished . . . so let us conclude the story our way.

—**Dr. Niles Compton, director,
Department 5656,
National Archives**

1

ST. JUDE'S CHILDREN'S HOSPITAL, LOS ANGELES, CALIFORNIA

The nondescript Black Hawk UH-60 helicopter eased its large bulk onto the painted heliport atop the hospital normally used to airlift critically ill patients to one of the most prestigious hospitals in the world. Before the wheels set down, one of the men in the passenger compartment felt the eyes on them in the darkness of the heliport. He knew that with those eyes came weapons—weapons that were right now trained on them and their air force flight crew.

Colonel Jack Collins looked over at his boss, Director Niles Compton, who was just placing paperwork back into his briefcase. Jack watched as the director removed the wire-rimmed glasses from his face and then watched as the fifty-one-year-old Compton rubbed the black eye patch that covered his right socket. Compton realized the colonel was watching him and quickly lowered his hand and replaced the glasses.

The two security men Jack had assigned to escort them to Los Angeles were politely not paying attention to the director nor his recent deformity received during the war with the Grays the previous month. The two men, Diaz and Voorhees, both U.S. Marines, were dressed in civilian attire. Collins unsnapped the seat belt and waited on Compton to gather his things just as the sliding door of the Black Hawk was opened from the outside. Before anyone could stand to leave, a rather large man in a navy blue Windbreaker stepped up to the door with four other men attired in the exact same manner. Jack assisted Niles as he maneuvered his cane to support his badly injured right leg. Collins knew Compton would never walk without the support of the cane again.

As Niles Compton straightened in the dying wind of the helicopter's rotors, Jack thought it beyond curious that Compton was now afflicted with the same war-won deformities that their benefactor, Senator Garrison Lee, had suffered with since his final days in World War II. He didn't know if the sight was ironic, or just a cruel joke for the man who was the most humanitarian gentleman he had ever known—notwithstanding the fact that he was also the most brilliant man in government service, if not the world. The respect he had for the director had grown leaps and bounds since he had first met Niles back in the summer of 2006.

"Gentlemen, we need to scan you before allowing you inside," the large black agent said as he held out a small box. "Thumb, please."

Jack went first by placing his right thumb onto the small glass pad on the top of the box. The Secret Service agent smiled a little when Collins hissed and then removed his thumb and looked at it. The agent looked from Collins to the readout on the black box.

"Sorry, Colonel, new SOP from Homeland Security and the home office, all visitors are now obligated for DNA scan before gaining access to Rough Rider."

Jack raised a brow as the instant DNA analysis was repeated with Niles, who seemed distant as he placed his thumb on the pad. Collins nodded at his two security men, who would not be allowed inside. The two men followed the six-man security team to the rooftop elevator. With their escort Jack counted no less than sixteen pairs of eyes on them coming from hidden locations on the rooftop. He assumed they all had automatic weapons. The protection for the man they had come to see had quadrupled since the war that had cost the world so much. A war that ended fifty-two days before. The country and the planet had lost too much to lose any more.

The pace was slow as everyone, including the Secret Service detail, knew that Niles Compton was just learning how to handle his infirmities. His walking was slow and awkward and Jack was instantly aware that Niles felt self-deprecating for those new infirmities. That coupled with the Group's losses from the war were weighing heavily on the director's mind. Jack knew that as a battlefield commander, Niles had to face certain things all by himself, just as he himself had to learn how to go on living after losing men and women whose lives he had been responsible for.

Collins became curious as they were escorted past the private suite of rooms and the large outside security team guarding it, and instead were guided through the cordon and brought to what looked like a closed hospital kitchen. The large double swinging doors closed behind Niles and Jack and they found themselves in a semidark stainless steel kitchen. The old smells of hospital meals hauntingly teased the air. Collins saw only two Secret Service men. One was standing in a far, very dark corner and the other was sitting by the opposite exit that entered the cafeteria-style seating area beyond. Other than that there was only one other man in the kitchen and he was half a torso deep in the large double-door refrigerator. Niles shook his head when he saw the robed man wiggle his butt as he leaned into the frigid space as he rummaged around, cursing as he did so.

"Not one shred of cheese other than this in the whole damn place!" came the muffled voice from deep inside the refrigerator. The hand dropped a small container of cottage cheese on the table behind him.

"Perhaps if you held strictly to the diet your doctor's set for you that infection in your leg would finally go away and you can stop hiding out in children's hospitals."

The ass in the doorway quit wiggling and the tall man straightened and turned to face the men who had just entered the hospital kitchen.

"Let's see how you would do eating that"—the president pointed to the container of low-fat cottage cheese—"and see how quickly you recover." The president looked at his oldest friend in the world and knew Niles had just gone through a very hard rehab just like himself. He became self-conscious looking at the man who had served as his best man a million years before the nightmares of the recent past.

Niles placed his briefcase upon the stainless steel countertop and then opened it. He brought out a large box and gestured for the president to see what was inside as he cut the string holding the box closed.

"The chefs at Group wanted you to have this . . . well, Alice Hamilton did anyway. I said you probably didn't deserve it, but I was overruled."

The president raised his right brow and spun awkwardly on his casted right leg and looked from Niles to Jack, who nodded that the box was indeed real. The president used a crutch and walked-slipped to stand by Niles's side. He looked from his friend's face to the contents of the box. The president smiled and suspiciously looked from the largest corned beef sandwich he had ever seen to the two Secret Service agents watching the proceedings. The two quickly looked away. The president nodded and before he reached to get Alice Hamilton's reward, he looked at Niles and then Jack. He shook his head and gestured for the protection detail to bring over two tall stools, which were placed before Jack and Niles.

"It feels better if I stand," the president said, tapping his cast as he leaned the crutch against the table as he closely watched his agents while they were close to his sandwich, as if he feared they would steal his precious bundle of cholesterol. When they moved off, Collins and Compton sat. "I'm not going to ask how either of you are, I can see without asking." The president picked the large sandwich up and smelled the meat and the hot mustard inside. His eyes rolled as he put it back in the box. With another suspicious look at his security detail he closed it. "I'll eat this later. Right now we have to talk before they knock me out with all of these new antibiotics they plan to feed me."

Jack watched on, aware of the uncomfortable silence coming from Niles as he waited for the president to continue. Gone was the small talk and playful banter he had always seen between the two men. Now there seemed to be a steeliness between them that wasn't there the previous years. The president waved over one of the Secret Service men who placed two stacks of papers on the tabletop and then moved off for another pile that was placed beside the first two. Three distinct sets of papers.

The president slapped the smallest pile on Jack's left. "Death notifications from the Department of the National Archives, specifically, a secret section of said archives, Department 5656. Spanning the years 1918 to the year 2005, there were 317 deaths attributed to personnel lost on assignment." He looked at both Jack and then Niles. Gone was the friendliness of the man as he looked on. "And those casualties do not include the 1864 raid into Turkey nor the loss of personnel during World War II, which were substantial I may add." His hand moved to the next largest pile and it sat there. "Casualties from 2005 to present, same department. Four hundred eighty-two Event Group deaths." His eyes went from the pile to the neutral face of Jack Collins.

"If this is an indictment or a veiled suggestion that there were any gross failures on the part of security to safeguard those lives—" Niles started to say, but the president acted as though Niles had not spoken as his hand went to the third pile of paperwork.

"The number of official Event code submissions to my and my predecessor's office." The pile was almost as large as the casualty notifications.

All three men knew that by law Department 5656 had twenty-four hours to inform the President of the United States, to whom they reported directly, that an Event action had been called. At that time full disclosure on the historical Event and why it was called had to be given to the commander-in-chief. At that time the president could either declare the Event a valid one, rather it be historical or military by the department, or to veto the action altogether.

"As it stands, I vetoed thirty-two actions that may have had a direct historical bearing on the war we just suffered through. The evidence that was needed to convince the world of the dangers we faced from outside our solar system could have possibly been overlooked in the actions of this and my predecessor's office. Every president from Woodrow Wilson to date may have been directly or indirectly responsible for the disaster we just barely survived."

Jack saw Niles lower his one good eye as if he was feeling relief from some hidden dosage of pain medication. It seemed the two men he was sitting with had discussed whatever this was before, and possibly at angered length if he knew the two old friends well enough.

"How many more historical secrets or outright cover-ups are out there that we cannot simply let lie?" the president said as he halfheartedly pushed the box containing his precious sandwich away. The president nodded once more and one of the Secret Service men removed the piles of papers.

An uncomfortable silence filled the kitchen.

"Colonel, the Event Group was faced with an unprecedented war, and you and your teams performed magnificently. I brought those papers for two reasons, you saved lives. A lot of them. Also for the reasons I have explained. There is far too much time wasted waiting for this busy office to ratify an Event action. That is why I am hereby, with the approval of the general accounting office and certain members of judicial and military establishment, expanding the powers of Department 5656. You now have one hundred hours to report an Event action to the president. This should speed up your response time to any Event."

The president saw the skepticism in Collins's face.

"Yes, it is illegal to a certain degree." He laughed. "Hell, the whole department has been illegal since its inception. Either the Event from Lincoln's time or the formation of the Group by Mr. Wilson, every action by your Group could be construed as illegal, at least in the eyes of the House and Senate."

"Perhaps we had better explain to Colonel Collins the reasoning behind this one-hundred-hour window." Niles looked to his right and half smiled at Jack, who sat and waited.

The president nodded. He made sure his Secret Service detail was looking elsewhere as he leaned in toward Collins like a conspirator. "This window is to allow your department to do things"—he stalled and looked from Jack to Niles and then back—"that may be lacking somewhat in its interpretation of legal action. For instance, the mission that is currently taking place in the Middle East that I know absolutely nothing about."

"Middle East?" Jack asked, looking from his commander-in-chief to Niles, who looked at him with a wry smile.

"I'll let you tell him," the president said as he pulled the small box over and then lifted the hefty sandwich and bit into it.

"At this moment we are chasing down a lead in Israel that may help us with a possible action that the president has ordered to be explored to its fullest. The one hundred hours is meant to make sure that when the CIA comes to the president and says, 'someone is messing around in our garden,' he can have total and complete deniability, which may happen in a few hours if our plan fails."

"What action and what plan?" Collins asked, looking from his boss to a satisfied president as he chewed.

"We have sent Anya Korvesky back home. She, the president, and myself didn't think you would have allowed her to go, so we kept it from you."

"What is the reason you sent the woman who Carl Everett loves back to a place where she is considered a danger to their security for choosing to leave them for a love that is now lost?" Jack asked, growing angrier by the minute for the way these men bypassed him and placed his best friend's woman into harm's way.

"Told you he would have a stick up his ass about this," the president said with a mouth full of corned beef.

"Jack, we had to take a chance. If the stories she's heard over the years are true we have a window of opportunity here."

"A window for what?"

Niles glanced at the president and then raised his brow over his glasses and eye patch.

"If this works out, we may have a chance at bringing home an old friend."

The president placed the sandwich down with much regret.

"I personally owe this man, as I owe all of you." The injured leg kept the movement slow but the president eased himself closer to Jack. "I don't have much time left in office, Colonel, you know it and I know it. In the time I have remaining before someone else moves into the White House I want my desk cleared, and to accomplish this I will not go out without trying to do everything I can to account for those people I lost in the recent war. . . . I owe them."

"What are you two telling me?" Jack asked, looking at Niles.

"We are going after Captain Everett, Jack."

Collins had to stand after the amazing statement from Compton. The president took that opportunity to retrieve the sandwich and begin his assault once more.

"During Anya's debrief she mentioned she had begun her Mossad career at the very bottom of their food chain. She was an analyst, though that has little to do with the tale she told me during her debrief after Operation Overlord. It seems she caught wind of a legend, a rumor, a tale that seemed made up to tell children at bedtime. The search for alien power plants to assist in Overlord reminded her of this legend. It was a long shot that she considered too outlandish to help, and it wasn't until she mentioned it to me during her debrief that we began to see a chance, just a possibility that this may actually be real."

"What in the hell are you two talking about?" Jack asked, looking at the president. "With all due respect of course."

The president only nodded as he continued eating. It was Niles who braved the telling to Jack.

"I think we better start with explaining Anya's role in this first."

ISRAEL STATE ARCHIVES (ISA)
JERUSALEM, ISRAEL

The raven-haired woman sat upon the bench outside of the large, extremely ugly concrete and steel building, which looked like an old bank that would have been robbed during the Depression in American gangster films.

The moon just started to rise over the holy city of God. She was dressed in a navy blue suit with wide-legged pants, necessary for the two ankle holsters she wore beneath them. Her eyes watched the front doors of the building as men and women of the archival staff prepared to leave after their evening shift. She watched as the two very-well-armed guards waved at the departing employees and then securely locked the front doors. The two guards looked through the glass and then turned back to their duties. The woman knew that security here wasn't as tight as at other government facilities, as this operation was more a written and oral history of the State of Israel. So, if you wanted someone's eyewitness testimony in regard to the Holocaust this was the place to go. Any other secrets were stored in many more highly secured facilities across the country. The dark-haired woman could only hope the files had not been transferred over the years.

She saw the young man with the thick horned-rimmed glasses as he also separated from the rest of the archive staff as they made their way to the parking area beside the building. Through years of training she was able to keep her heart from racing faster as she anticipated what the employee had to say. He was obviously up to no good as she took in the frightened way the boy moved. His head flitted left and then right as he approached her and then sat.

"Look, Sami, relax, this is not a facility that houses nuclear secrets. It's just a records storage unit, you said so yourself."

The boy who had just graduated from Tel Aviv Technical Institute frowned as he looked around the park area nervously.

"I said relax." The woman patted the boy's leg. "Do you have the file?"

The young man looked around and shuffled his feet as he clutched his backpack closer to his body.

"Sami, you're not steeling state secrets, it's only concentration camp testimony."

"Yeah, then why was this file cross-referenced with another, and that one is flagged as secret? Secret and no longer in this building."

"Cross-referenced with what?" she asked, becoming concerned.

"A file code-named 'The Traveler.'"

The boy could see something register in the woman's eyes, which were the strangest he had ever seen. In the defused moonlight he could swear she had one green and one brown eye. He decided that this dark-haired woman scared him and he wanted to leave. The beautiful woman was holding out her hand as she was deep in thought.

"Uh, are you forgetting something?" he said as he shied away from her elegant hand.

The woman came back to the present, frowned, and then handed the boy a white envelope. He accepted it and placed it in his backpack and in the same motion brought out a file folder and handed it to her.

"That's only a copy, the original is where it's supposed to be."

The woman acted as though she didn't hear the boy as she opened the file and leaned into the cover of the streetlight to read it. The archivist watched a moment and then moved off into the night. She sat on the vacated park bench as the night became still around her. Her eyes scanned the thin sheets of paper.

She knew she had lost some of her edge when she missed the four men moving in around her. Her eyes continued to read from the weak streetlight above when a hand came from over her shoulder and snatched the file from her fingers. She immediately raised her right leg to retrieve the gun in the ankle holster but a Glock nine-millimeter handgun appeared in her face. As she raised her head, the gun was removed from her grasp, and she saw the young man from the archives being led back to the area. The woman knew just who it was she was facing. She turned and looked at the man who had taken the file from her.

"Uncle," she said as her double-colored eyes took in the heavily mustachioed man in front of her. The large frame of the heavyset former army general stood over the diminutive woman. "How are you?"

"Niece," he said as he closed the file and then looked at the heading on the front. His brown eyes went from it to the woman who was being handcuffed in front of him. He whistled and then handed the folder over to a man next to him. The large man in the blue blazer and simple white shirt shook his head sadly and then turned and left. Her eyes followed him until she couldn't see him anymore.

"You are under arrest for crimes against the State of Israel, in particular, for espionage."

Former Mossad agent Major Anya Korvesky watched a large Mercedes as it sped off. She was pushed and shoved to another waiting car that would follow the Mercedes to her final destination—the headquarters of the Mossad, Israel's hardened intelligence apparatus.

There she would face the charge of treason that her uncle, General Shamni, director of the Mossad, would file against his niece in the next hour.

Still, the only thing she could focus on was the file that had been taken from her and was now speeding back to headquarters with her angry uncle. Now she had lost her only lead to uncovering the truth that she and Doctor Compton sought.

The young Queen of the Gypsies raised in Jerusalem and secretly placed into the Israeli Mossad at the age of eighteen was now going to hang before she could help getting back the man she had fallen in love with—Carl Everett.

Three hours had passed and Anya found herself still waiting in the most uncomfortable position she could have ever imagined, although sitting in a dark room with handcuffs was not a memory she could draw from. The two agents who watched her looked noncommittal as if they dealt with treason on a daily basis, and with her uncle that was probably closer to the truth than she knew. She eyed the men but knew that any escape attempt was futile as these agents watching her were not your average Mossad personnel—they were the personal protection of her uncle, General Shamni. They answered only to him.

A man looking more the academia-type, thin and proper, entered from the large office fronting the empty reception area.

"The general will see you now," the young man said in his perfectly pressed suit, which was a great accomplishment at two in the morning. The man nodded, indicating that the two guards should assist the prisoner to her feet. They did so, far gentler than she could have hoped for. They fell in line behind the first man and soon she found herself in a large and very dark office with no windows. There was a single lamp burning on the large desk of the head of the Mossad—her uncle's desk. The two men stood on either side as the first man brought the general another folder and then with one last disturbing look at Anya, he left the office.

Her eyes went to the general, who was busy reading a file folder report. He absentmindedly held out the small silver key that would free her hands. The agent on the right loosened and then removed the cuffs. Both men turned and left the office. Anya looked for a chair and when she saw one started to move toward it.

"Remain standing in front of me, please, Agent Korvesky."

Anya froze and didn't move as the general kept reading. She watched his large hands as he flipped a page and read some more.

"You have placed me in what the Americans say is 'between a rock and a hard place,' young lady, you know that?"

"I hate that I had to do that, Uncle."

The large rotund man closed the file and finally looked up at her. "Yet here we are. The head of the Mossad and his lovely niece, who was just arrested for espionage."

"This is the last thing I wanted, was to embarrass you, Uncle."

"But again, here we are." He slid the yellow file across his expansive desk and then looked up at his niece as she rubbed her wrists after the uncomfortable cuffs. She watched her uncle's eyes move to a far, darkened corner of his office. "With the world getting even crazier than before this war in space, this is not the time to be a treasonous agent in a paranoid country. The men in charge have certain knee-jerk reactions to things like that. The order of the day would be that you are taken into the desert and shot." His dark eyes settled on Anya. "Believe me, many a person has left this office from the very spot you are now standing and were immediately executed—shot on my direct orders." He slammed his hand down on the desk and the file folder.

"Uncle—"

He held up his beefy hand, stilling her voice.

"Do you think you could keep secrets from me, niece?"

"I—"

"I am the gatekeeper, young lady. I know what is going on in my own home, and the Mossad is *my* home. Israel is my home." His eyes again flitted to the far corner. She saw nothing but the blackness of the room. "I keep the secrets." He shoved the file forward until it was perched on the edge of the desk. "Do you think for one minute your returning to our little family satisfied me enough to lower my guard, even where my niece was concerned?" He shook his head. "Sit, Anya."

With her heart aching for the pain she was causing her only living relative, Anya sat with lowered head.

"I have read a few of the briefing reports to the American security council.

I know why it is you want these files so dearly. I'll tell you now, not that it matters much, that the information you are seeking is not viable. It's a dead end as we ourselves found out three years ago in our cooperative search with the rest of the world as we scanned every archive file for technological information. That's why I can say to you in no uncertain terms that what you seek is just not there."

Anya felt her hope to find the file fall through her stomach as she realized that this was just another dead end.

General Shamni reached down and brought out another file and placed it on the first.

"This is the file you are looking for."

The file was bordered in purple and read "Top Secret" in bold red letters in the Hebrew script.

"It's all there."

"But I'm under arrest," Anya said as the general stood from his high-backed chair.

"We believe the person you seek is no longer alive, at least not in Israel. Moira Mendelsohn no longer exists, I'm afraid, and this is the only record recovered from what is secretly known in certain circles as 'The Traveler' file. One of the most guarded secrets held by this government, so secret that it failed to turn up in our technology search conducted by the Americans. The file 'The Traveler' is only useful in who the Traveler was, not what the project was about. The young woman was never fully compliant when questioned by our people when she was in Israel after World War II. The only reason my predecessor thought the Traveler file was relevant was because of who financed the original project in 1943, and also the man responsible for conducting the experiments."

"The names?" she asked, pushing her bad luck even further. But if she was going to be shot or hanged for treason she wanted to know all there was on the rumored testimony of the Traveler.

"Heinrich Himmler and engineering professor Lars Thomsen, one of Adolf's favorite technology philosophers and a correspondent and contemporary of one Albert Einstein."

"Uncle, if I am to be charged with treason, why are you telling me these things?"

"When I said I was the gatekeeper, evidently I wasn't as good at finding out secrets as keeping them, my dear niece."

She felt her heart slip as she realized just how good her uncle's intelligence service really was.

"Or would you prefer the future Mrs. Carl Everett?"

"No, that adds a certain charm to these proceedings, doesn't it?" a voice from the darkness said.

Anya, after the initial shock of learning that her secret engagement to Carl was now an open secret, was now trying for damage control that was not going to be there. She had indeed become involved with a foreign national, which was another crime against the state considering her job in intelligence. What was one more charge considering her predicament? She turned and faced the darkness where the familiar voice had come from. The man turned on a table lamp and sat with crossed legs.

"You?" she said as startled as she had ever been.

"I understand you two know each other from Antarctica," the general said as he stood and stepped up to Anya as she felt her jaw drop even further when the big man stood up.

"You know this man, Uncle?" she said without turning back to face the head of the Mossad.

"Yes, we have worked together from time to time, just as he works for everyone else if the money is right . . . from time to time of course."

The blond man smiled, reached down, and took Anya's right hand and kissed it, barely brushing his lips against her skin.

"Honored to see you again."

Anya had lost her voice when Colonel Henri Farbeaux spoke and smiled that disarming smile of his. He straightened and then his brows rose three times in rapid succession.

"But alas, I have been reduced to an errand boy by men and women I'm not real sure if I like or not, but they pay and pay well."

"I must admit you kept your secret concerning our dear Mr. Everett close to the vest. I would say you have a future in the intelligence-gathering business, but we both know that would be pushing it, don't we?" her uncle said as he handed the two folders to his niece.

"What are you doing, Uncle?"

"Sending you home. You're an American now, Mrs. Everett, and one that has made her choices."

Anya looked from the files in her hands to her uncle and then she dropped them and hugged the director of the most brilliant intelligence-gathering apparatus in the world. He allowed it, but only briefly. After a moment the large man forced her hands apart and brought them from his neck. She could see the tears well up in his eyes. The man who had so ruthlessly protected the borders of Israel was near to breaking down.

"I have to turn my back on you now, niece. You can no longer return to these shores. As I said, choices have been made, choices you cannot turn from now."

Henri Farbeaux retrieved the two files that had fallen to the carpeted floor as Anya stood there stunned. He read the smaller one. "The Traveler, Moira Mendelsohn." He replaced the first with the second, far thicker file labeled simply "Doorway," and in red letters below it, "testimony of participants." He raised his brows and watched the two people in the room. The woman was still captivating in her exotic looks. He thought back to when they first met in the Antarctic three months before. Yes, the Gypsy woman was beautiful, and he could see the allure for Carl Everett to resign from the world in order to stay with her.

"Go, and watch yourself, niece, there are men out there that are not as family-oriented as myself. Colonel, remove her from this office. Your flight to the States leaves in an hour. My men will escort you through customs and security."

"Uncle," Anya started to say, but the man just placed a hand on her shoulder and stopped her.

"For the record, I liked your naval captain. Through the prime minister's office I am now aware of certain details as to his . . . disappearance. I am giving you over to your new and adoptive country for that simple fact. The world owes the man you married, this is Israel's penance, the price we will pay for what was owed by the world to this man and his sacrifice." General Shamni softened. "That and the fact that I love you so very much."

Anya started to cry for the first time since she learned that Carl was not returning from space. She took a tentative step forward but her uncle turned his back on her and returned to his desk.

"Good luck in what it is you are searching for. Now I have to disavow you as blood, and as an Israeli citizen." Shamni continued to stare at a small picture of him and a beautiful woman from the past. Anya knew this picture was of the general and his sister, her grandmother, the queen of the Gypsies. The picture was taken long before the general was shipped away as a boy to Israel to gain his education on the people his Gypsies used to be a tribe of. Now Anya realized that the general had no one left. She was the last of his blood and now he felt that blood being spilled.

The former French army colonel, Henri Farbeaux, saw that Anya wasn't moving so he took her elbow and steered her toward the door. Once out of the office she allowed the Frenchman to place an arm around her as they walked toward the elevator. She stopped and looked at the antiquities thief.

"How and why are you here, Colonel?"

The elevator doors opened and Henri stepped inside and smiled at her. "As your uncle said, to bring you home. It seems you have very high-placed friends, and a Mrs. Alice Hamilton is among them. She is the one who sent me . . . lucky for you. She oversees most of that strange little man Compton's activities. She thought you may run into trouble."

Anya remembered Alice from Romania at the same time she had met Carl. She never thought the frail-looking old woman was so in touch with the people Carl worked for.

Anya was still hesitant to step inside the elevator even with a death sentence held over her head if she didn't.

"And where is home now?" she asked as Farbeaux's smile grew as he held the doors open. "I met with Dr. Compton in Washington when he debriefed me, that is why I'm here. So, where is home now?" she persisted.

"Well, that's a loaded question, especially for one such as myself who is not adequately informed."

"That doesn't answer my question, Colonel Farbeaux."

The doors slid closed after she stepped into the elevator.

"All I can say is I hope you are comfortable in the high desert of America."

"You mean—"

"That's right, you, like myself, have been shanghaied so to speak by a real Boy Scout. A man that is now being briefed on this outrageous investigation of yours."

Anya Korvesky smiled when she saw the concerned look on the face of the Frenchman. The name that caused the man considerable consternation and the only moniker to ever make Henri Farbeaux frown in such a way as he was now.

"Colonel Jack Collins," she mumbled with a smile starting to cross her red lips.

The elevator started down with a confused Anya Korvesky and a French antiquities thief who had yet to become resigned to his rather disturbing fate.

"Yes, we are going into the barren desert to see Mr. Wonderful himself."

ST. JUDE'S CHILDREN'S HOSPITAL, LOS ANGELES, CALIFORNIA

After the director had explained to Jack Anya's quest for information inside the Israeli archives system, the task he had been performing for the past months of finding the new specialized manpower for the replacement personnel at Group became crystal clear. As the president finished his sandwich with a pleasurable sigh, he rubbed his hands together and looked at Niles.

"Now that Jack knows we can also fall outside of the accepted rules of engagement, I received a partial list of personnel you wish to offer positions to. All have checked out security-wise with the exception of two."

Niles opened his briefcase and brought out two file folders. The first he opened and handed to the president.

"This Xavier Morales." The president raised his eyes and looked at Jack.

"Not my choice," Jack said.

Niles had to smile as he knew what was coming, and he knew his old friend was going to be skeptical at the least and furious at the most.

"The man listed here is picked to head the most advanced computer center in the world, picked over the thousands of qualified men and women in this country, including thirty-two staff members already on Group roles. And this"—he looked at the photo of the young Mexican American youth paperclipped to the file—"is the man, or boy, that you chose?"

"As I said, Mr. President, I didn't choose him to run the comp center and Europa."

The president just raised both brows while he waited.

"Europa herself chose the kid, not me."

"Okay, you mind letting me in on the damn joke?"

Niles shook his head and then looked at Jack and decided he would bail him out on this one.

"Two years ago, Pete Golding"—Collins and the president saw the hurt come into Niles's good eye as he spoke the name of the former computer genius who had been murdered the previous month—"suspected that Europa, the most sophisticated computing system ever created, had been hacked. Not hacked for evil purposes, but hacked just to see if it could be done. This kid was the one responsible and Europa herself was the one that tracked him down. She insists this kid is the only qualified candidate out there. It's like she refuses to accept anyone else. This name always leads her list of qualified candidates. Every time."

"So you're saying that Europa is developing programs that the other four Cray operating systems in use do not exhibit?"

"Pete Golding and his constant refinements of Europa. She is learning on her own."

"Okay, your warped system wants this kid. Tell me about him."

"Xavier Morales, age twenty-five. Born with osteoporosis and has been confined to a wheelchair since the age of five. He has a mother whom he supports and a brother, deceased. He is a prodigy. Graduated high school at thirteen and MIT with a doctorate at twenty-one. Hell, even I heard of him coming up through MIT's system. Pete was also aware of him . . . he was and is a legend. After college he dabbled in software design but it bored him. Then the murder of his older brother by a drug dealer sent our boy into another area of interest—finding and ruining everyone and anyone who had anything to do with his brother's murder. He tracked down everyone from the man who fired the ill-timed shot that killed his brother, to the dealer's connections, and then finally all the way to the source—the now-reorganized Nuevo Laredo Cartel in Mexico and its boss of bosses, Richie Gutiérrez."

"One bad hombre," the president remarked as his memory recalled the ruthlessness of the man who ended the infighting in northern Mexico simply by killing anything that walked or crawled in the region.

"Yes, a bad man who once had far more money than he has now, because of young Morales."

"Explain."

"Our boy deciphered his banking codes, back-doored the security systems of no less than twelve Swiss banks, drained his assets into untraceable accounts in the greater Los Angeles area. Youth organizations, boys and girls clubs in East L.A., and finally the coup was when he transferred one hundred million, five hundred thousand dollars, roughly eleven thousand dollars each into the bank accounts of everyone in his mother's old neighborhood, which was the straw that broke the camel's back and got him caught by the cartel."

The president just looked at Niles, who had answered for Jack. "I don't give the kid very good odds of a long life if he picks and chooses his enemies in such a manner."

"Well, sir," Jack said, "you're right on that point. Gutiérrez and his goons got to him through his mother."

"Jesus."

"He's being held in the cartel's own private prison in northern Mexico affectionately called the House Where Hope Goes to Die. Gutiérrez has something special planned for the kid's demise as soon as he returns from South America after arranging new banking partners. We estimate our boy Morales has about six days left before the bastard has him torn to pieces in one of his prison gladiator shows he likes to put on."

"For a kid in a wheelchair?" the president asked, angered at the brutality of the cartel and Gutiérrez in particular.

"Yes," Niles said as he pulled the folder from the president's hand and closed it. "And we want permission to go get him out, or rather, Europa wants him out."

"Europa wants you to literally invade a neighboring country and kidnap someone?"

"Yes, an American someone." Jack sat looking at his boss without flinching. Now knowing what this search for new personnel was for, his enthusiasm had grown by leaps and bounds.

"Who else?" he asked instead of answering Collins's challenge about Morales being an American.

Niles replaced the first folder with a second. The president scanned the pages inside with his eyes going wide for a split second. He closed the folder.

"Approved, good luck with your recruiting on this one. Getting Morales out may be far easier than dealing with this guy."

"Oh, we have the perfect persuasion heading to San Diego to speak with our great man. I think she'll persuade him to come around to joining us."

"I believe you are referring to your assistant director?"

"The one and only. Virginia Pollock is the only human being in the world that Master Chief Jenks is terrified of. Yes, he will come along just out of fear for his life." Niles took the second folder and then reluctantly handed the president the third and final recruitment request. The president opened it and again scanned the pages with the corners of his mouth turning downward as he progressed.

"Denied," he said simply and as matter-of-fact as he could. The president closed the thickest folder of the three and handed it back to Compton. "I appreciate her assistance, but this is asking too damn much, Niles."

"Look, Anya is risking everything to assist us in getting Carl back. We need her inside the facility," Niles said as he looked at Jack. "I'll take full responsibility for her immediate placement on the Group's active roster. She's not the type to spill Department 5656 files and histories to the world. If the critical information she kept in Romania is any indication, the woman knows how to keep secrets where they belong."

"No, damn it." The president returned to the refrigerator, ignoring the crutch leaning against the table. He removed a jug of milk from it and then thought a second and returned it and again faced the two men watching him. "She's not only a foreign national, gentlemen, but a goddamned intelligence officer at that. No, request denied. As grateful as I am for her involvement thus far, we cannot be giving her departmental access to the foremost secret government reservation in this country." The president placed his hands on the steel table and leaned in, looking from face to face. "Not to an Israeli Mossad agent." He saw the angry line that formed the lips of his best friend. He held up a hand in a "wait" gesture when he knew Niles was going to explode. "Again, I appreciate her directing us to this possible new information concerning this Traveler file, but I have to think of the men before me in this office that kept that facility their own personal secret. No, gentlemen."

"You know she performed magnificently during the war, you read the reports," Niles countered.

"I know all about Miss Anya Korvesky and what she did for the war effort." The president felt a pinch of guilt as he recalled that Carl Everett had been in love with her and she him. Everett had even resigned his navy commission over his relationship with the Israeli intelligence specialist. Miss Korvesky had indeed paid a heavy price for their victory in space.

At that moment the Group's private satellite phone chimed and Niles answered it with a stern look at his friend. The president looked away.

"Compton," he said into the small untraceable device. "I see. What have you done?" Jack and the president watched Niles purse his lips as he listened. "I should have known you would have been on top of it. No, Alice, that is exactly the course you should have taken. Are they safely out of there? Okay, I'll meet everyone in Arizona. Good job and thank you." Niles closed the phone and placed it in his coat pocket. He looked at the president. "Anya recovered the file in question."

"Then her part in this rescue attempt is at an end, correct?" the president inquired.

"She was caught by the Mossad."

"Damn!"

Jack said nothing, but waited.

"Our dear Mrs. Hamilton foresaw this and made a few calls. Her and Garrison Lee's influence has evidently been felt in some very obscure circles; the Mossad seems to be one of them."

"What does Mrs. Hamilton have to do with this very bad situation?" the president asked incredulously.

"She made a deal with Anya's uncle. She's now our problem. Colonel Henri

Farbeaux is already bringing Anya in. It seems, Mr. President, she's now a part of our team whether you like it or not. We owe her at least that."

The president was almost as white as a sheet. "What in the hell does Henri Farbeaux have to do with all of this?"

"Oh, I guess I forgot to mention, I recruited Henri as a specialist for the duration of this Event. After all, he's seen our complex, thus he's not a security risk. He already knows everything."

The president took a moment at this time to turn away, crutch in hand, and walk to the cafeteria area of the kitchen. He sat slowly in a chair with his cast and leg sticking out precariously.

"You and Mrs. Hamilton laid a trap for me, legally speaking, and frankly I don't appreciate it."

"I don't know what you mean, Mr. President," Niles retorted.

"I just gave you executive powers far beyond any agency in the history of the United States by granting you a delayed reporting rule change and you turn around and hit me with a prison escape, a request to allow a foreign intelligence agent into the top-most secret agency in the world, and, oh, by the way, we're also bringing in a sociopath as your head engineer, and now you're saying you want the foremost enemy of this department inside my facility!"

Jack looked at Niles, as he was stunned that just Niles and Alice had done all of the planning.

"Premeditated," the president said. "You knew when you and I planned on sending her back to Israel that the odds were she was going to get caught, thus you had Alice on standby in case the worst happened."

"Problem on all fronts solved. Now everyone, including the colonel and yourself, are up to date on everything. Anya and Henri are now my responsibility, so let's get moving and bring a brave man back home, shall we?" He smiled as he looked from Jack to the president. "If not, I can always tell your wife about your dietary habits when she's not here."

"You bald bastard, get the hell out of here, and if that Frenchman steals anything, it's coming out of your ass. Jesus, we're probably letting the Mossad in on everything we have inside those vaults!"

"You worry too much." Niles stood and he and Jack left the kitchen.

On the way to the elevator and the rooftop helipad, Niles lost his smile as he knew then that it was a good thing the president gave him the hundred-hour window for reporting. He knew that it was not only to keep deniability to other federal agencies, like the CIA, on when and how the president knew something, it was for other reasons also.

"Okay," Niles said as he stopped short of entering the idling Black Hawk helicopter for their return flight to Nellis Air Force Base. "The one thing I didn't tell

the president was that Operation Alcatraz has already commenced." Compton
handed one of his security men his briefcase. "It makes me nervous with the
operation going in so short-handed. How is Mr. Ryan doing in Mexico?"

"He said he had volunteers, that's all I was aware of before his team left for
Mexico. So, I figure Captain Ryan is deep into his role," Jack said.

As Niles climbed into the seating area of the Black Hawk, Jack looked to the
sky. When he knew Niles could not hear him he said a silent rebuttal.

"Just how deep is anyone's guess."

RIO NATCHEZ CORRECTIONAL FACILITY, NORTHERN MEXICO

The Rio Natchez prison was a private concern based on the model perfected in
the States. One of the minor investments of Richard Salvador Gutiérrez, the Rio
Natchez was basically a death camp for storing the drug dealer's enemies until he
had the leisure time to watch them die. At least fifty percent of the eighty-six inmates were sent there to die after committing some grievous error in judgment
against the cartel.

Eyes watched the boy who had struggled to push his wheelchair into the far
corner of the large cell for protection. Thus far the young man, who was no more
than twenty-five and who had a beard as soft and sparse as a young deer, had to be
given the credit he deserved. He had fought and been beaten for the right to hang
on to the wheelchair after some toughs had decided they needed it more. The young
man wiped the blood from his nose after placing the bed's broken slat in his lap.
The three men who had attempted to purloin the chair were now trying to stem
the flow of blood from the noses of two of their number after the young man had
released a torrent of blows to their faces. They were stunned for now, but the new
prisoner knew they would come again and very soon.

The eyes watched as the out-of-place young man once more brought the old
wooden bed slat up and waited for the second assault to begin. The wheelchair-
bound man didn't have to wait long.

The three men turned as one, their burly leader tossing a bloody rag to the
floor. They started toward the brave young man in the chair. The largest attacker
reached into the waistband of his pants and brought out a small picklike weapon.
The toothless smile that crossed his face was one of pure pleasure at what they
were about to do. They surrounded the young man, who raised the slat to defend
himself.

"That's not a very wise thing to do, my brothers," came a voice speaking in
Spanish.

The three men turned and saw a small but very stout man dressed in denim
pants and a white, affectionately nicknamed "wife beater" undershirt. His close-

cropped dark hair was covered by a black bandana. The goatee and crocodile smile were illuminated by the newcomer's three gold front teeth. But the most outstanding feature of the muscular man was the tattoo that started down from his scalp, crawled over his nose and eyes, and ended at a tanned jawline. The tattoo was in the shape of a claw and was etched in deep blues and reds. The man was smiling, showing his gold-plated dental work.

"Be patient, *ese*, you can be next, wait your turn," said the middle-sized man on the left while he placed his arm around the larger one with the toothless grin and the improvised knife. "We have meals-on-wheels to take care of first."

In the corner the young man raised the wooden slat higher. It was noticeable the young man was barely old enough to shave, but his determined look said that he had faced this sort of abuse before . . . bad-luck kids like him usually did.

The rest of the fifty-plus men inside the overcrowded cell took a step back when they saw that the small man who had confronted the three refused to move away. He held his ground as he studied the three very much larger adversaries before him.

"You think Senor Gutiérrez will take the killing of his prized prisoner lightly? If you do then I want to be around when you explain it to him."

The young man in the wheelchair tilted his head as if he were having a hard time following the Spanish being spoken.

The first faltering smile came out of the large one with the shiv and no teeth.

The smallest of the three turned and looked at the wheelchair-bound prisoner. "Later, *ese*, Gutiérrez may not come soon enough, then you'll be ours." Then the man turned to face the tattooed busybody. "But you, *ese*, what was to be his, is now yours." The three men spread out and started to surround the newcomer. He made a stance that invited the three to make their attempt.

The whistle stopped the men before they could spring. The five guards were standing at the bars looking in.

"You speak of patience, I advise as much, for your benefactor will be arriving within the hour. For some of you"—the guard smiled as he looked at a few of the frightened eyes that watched him before settling on the wheelchair and its occupant—"your day of days has arrived." The guards watched the men in the cell for a moment and then turned to leave.

The three brutes had lost all of their enthusiasm for getting even with the young man who had broken two of their noses. They turned away from him with one last dirty look at the man who had interfered, and moved off to sulk, because everyone knew that with the arrival of Gutiérrez some of their fates were already sealed.

The young man in his wheelchair watched the small man with the black beard and bandana as he eyed the departure of the three thugs. He moved his chair forward until he was next to the man with the horrid and fright-inducing tattoo.

"Thank you," the young prisoner in dirty denim said in English, very slowly as if his unlikely savior wouldn't be able to follow the boy's native tongue. The small man turned and looked at him with a frown and concerned dark eyes.

"You're not very smart for some sort of computer prodigy." The man slowly looked him and his chair over. "I mean you don't even speak Spanish, do you?" the man asked, losing all of his own practiced Spanish accent. The boy's face went slack. "Well, for the next hour or so you better become a hell of a lot smarter if you want to live long enough to eat dinner tonight. You understand?" the man asked, his three gold teeth shining in the diffused light of the old cell.

"Who are you?" the young man asked.

"A dickhead, son, a real dickhead"—the man smiled, exposing the brightness of the gold dental work—"who never understood my boss's philosophy of not volunteering for anything, so for now just refer to me as Captain Dickhead."

Richie Gutiérrez sat atop the small platform that fronted the warden's office and faced into the prison's small exercise yard. The prisoners had all been brought out with the exception of the three men who were the object of today's lesson in why you shouldn't betray or mess with Richie Gutiérrez.

The middle-aged man, who was raised on the mean streets of Nuevo Laredo, Mexico, and had fought his way upward through murder, kidnapping, and torture to lead the most ruthless cartel since the heady day of the drug war in South America, was sitting in a large and very ornate chair as if he were the Roman emperor Caligula overseeing a gladiatorial death match. His dress was more appropriate for an evening cocktail party. He was drinking tequila with finely chipped ice as the prison's population was brought into the area surrounding the exercise yard. The chain-link fence separated the privately owned inmates who were there to witness what it was they would one day face themselves.

Gutiérrez accepted a refill of his tequila as he ate grapes and laughed along with his six henchmen as they watched the festivities below. There were two armed men not part of the prison's staff of mercenaries in each corner of the balcony. It wasn't that the drug dealer was afraid of outside influences interfering as the prison was completely legal in the eyes of the law, it was his closest associates the guards watched. The dangerous business he had risen to the top in broke no lackadaisical attitudes in the arena of trusting one's subordinates. No, Gutiérrez was very safe from the law, because here, in this place, he *was* that law.

The FBI, DEA, and the American Homeland Security had chased the cartel and its leader for nearly seven years and could never find him. The warrant the Americans carried told the world that they intended very bad things for Gutiérrez and his organization. The man knew that was not possible in his world. Even with the major monetary loss caused by the subject of today's circus had not dampened the cartel's fortunes as they made the deficit up by increased manufacture. Still, he knew that the execution today would serve its purpose. That fact was proven a moment later when a film crew was brought in. The two men, a cameraman and a sound person, were there to capture the majesty of the moment for the benefit of those who would try to damage him in the future. The black cameraman and the Mexican soundman took up station by the concrete wall near the front of the large balcony.

Gutiérrez lit a large Havana cigar and then nodded at the prison's warden, who was immaculately dressed in a royal blue uniform complete with scarf. He removed his saucer cap as he stood. His crooked, pencil-thin mustache turned up at the corners as he anticipated a great event ahead. The warden had been specially chosen from the Mexican army for his brutal reputation, and for the fact that he had been on the cartel's payroll for nearly fifteen years.

"Bring them out!"

The silence of the gathered inmates gave credence to the fact that this was not an excited gladiatorial arena as the only applause came from the elevated balcony of the warden's office. The prisoners were silent and most crossed themselves as the fifteen prisoners were led forward.

As the chosen inmates had been gathered and hurriedly lined up, the last person to join was the wheelchair-bound prisoner who bravely faced his fate without pleading or comment. The guard who was pushing him smiled when the young man looked back.

"When called, you will advance into the exercise yard in single file," the guard by the large gate said as the sun filtered in from the outside, obscuring the excited look on the lead guard's features. The man turned and exited the waiting area for the exercise yard, leaving only the one guard behind the wheelchair.

"I hear they have something very special planned for you, my friend," the guard said as his hot breath hit the young man in the back of his neck, making him cringe. "I have three thousand pesos that says you end up begging before—"

The young man heard the thud and the hiss of breath as the hands holding the wheelchair handles fell way. The young man turned and saw the tattooed man standing in the place of the guard.

"What are—"

"No time for twenty questions, kid," the man hissed as his eyes scanned the other prisoners in front of them. Some had turned at the minor commotion, but decided that the guard wasn't worth their precious and very limited time. "This is about the third damn plan we've had to scrap in the last twenty-four hours. This is plan D and there isn't a plan E, so be quiet and do exactly as I tell you."

"Who are you?" the young man said as the large double-sided gate started to swing open.

"I'm the asshole who bragged to his bosses this could be done, so I guess they'll have the last laugh when this thing blows up right in my face."

The young man turned to face the front just as his heart fell through his belly to his ass. "Oh, my God, what are you going to do?" he asked as his voice broke just as he was pushed forward following the long line of fifteen condemned men.

"Shut up while I figure a new way to get us killed in the next few minutes."

As they broke into sunlight after the warden's order to bring them into the yard, the tattooed man quickly scanned the area. The prisoners were of no help as a chain-link fence topped with razor wire held them in check. The three guard towers oversaw the entire area, including the exterior of the prison. One benefit he immediately noticed was that the three armed guards had their attention focused on the activities inside, not out. One break, but he needed more as he again quickly evaluated this new situation that had changed drastically this morning when it was announced that the mysterious and hard-to-corner cartel leader was arriving early. Thus, plan D.

"Shit, man, is that son of a bitch going to film my death?" the young man asked as the men in the balcony applauded the condemned men as they entered.

The gold-toothed inmate looked to the balcony and saw the two men. One was a cameraman and the other a soundman. The camera and telescopic sound boom was extended over the balcony as they filmed the men below. The tattooed man exhaled the breath he had been holding as he took in the scene. He halfheartedly smiled in relief that his message earlier that day had been received.

"Yeah, I guess they are going to film it . . . news at eleven, huh, kid?"

"Dude, you need to work on your sense of humor, my man."

"Just wait for the punch line before you judge my comedic talents, son," the man said as he brought the wheelchair to a stop on the broken asphalt of the exercise area.

As the seventeen prisoners watched on in fear, they saw the horse trailers being backed up to the enclosed yard. Several guards stood by the rear doors of each of the four battered and old trailers.

The blood of each man in hearing distance froze as the roar of a wild cat sounded from the first enclosure.

"Man, this is fucking medieval," the young man said as his eyes widened at the thought of what they were to face.

The tattooed man said nothing as he realized the truth of what the FBI and DEA had explained in their reports. The man Gutiérrez was as insane as they come.

The man and woman waited just outside the office area of the registration wing of the prison. The white-haired man sat with a large black doctor's bag between his feet. His round, brown-framed glasses were perched on the end of his nose as he watched the three secretaries at their desks. The woman next to him was attired in green nurse scrubs and sat stoically as she too waited.

The secretary on the phone looked up from her desk and studied the two for a long moment, making both feel uncomfortable, the same feeling they had for the past twenty minutes as they had been forced to wait. The secretary spoke Spanish into the phone and then hung up and stood. She approached the two as her colleagues excitedly stood and hurriedly moved to the window. One of them turned as he moved.

"Hurry, they are bringing them out," the girl called out to the first.

The first secretary stood before them and looked as if she wanted to hurry. Her Spanish was rapid-fire and the two had a hard time keeping up. They both now knew that the recommendation by the linguistics department had been right on; they should have brushed up a little more with their chosen second language.

"Apologies, but the entire staff is unavailable for at least an hour, Doctor. Warden Ramirez says that you will be called when needed in the yard." Without waiting and in a hurry to get to the window with her friends, the woman started to turn but stopped and turned back to the white-haired man in the rumpled suit and the small woman sitting beside him. "The warden inquired as to what happened to Dr. Torrez—he was scheduled for rounds this afternoon."

The white-haired man wanted to face his companion but decided he would act his role out and be brave simply because when this was over he was going to get killed by men other than the maniacs in this prison—men with a lot more talent for killing. He gave the secretary a stern look.

"The good doctor became aware of the scheduled activities this afternoon and decided he was losing his stomach for it, thus I am here in his place as a favor"— he smiled as if he enjoyed the conversation, making even his small female companion suddenly fearful of his demeanor—"as I have no such qualms concerning what's happening out there." He nodded toward the window where the other two women stood.

The secretary decided she wanted to hear no more from this strange white-haired doctor and hurriedly joined her excited friends at the window who were examining the inmates as they entered the yard below.

"They're not going to go outside like we were told they would," the small woman said out of the corner of her mouth.

"Well, the briefing by our man at the FBI was hurriedly put together, I imagine. I'm sure he wasn't expecting for us to make an attempt while so shorthanded in the security department."

"Charlie, if they don't go outside I have to place them into submission," the woman said as she felt the fanny pack she wore. She slid it along her belt until it was in the front where she could reach it quickly. "Just how important is this aspect of the plan?" she asked as the three women by the window started making jokes on who would last the longest in the arena.

Professor Charles Hindershot Ellenshaw III watched the three secretaries for the briefest of moments before he frowned and then faced his acting nurse.

"Then what are you waiting for? Drop them. They're personal assistants to that brutal son of a bitch out there." He nodded toward the balcony beyond the office wall. "To hell with the gentle approach. Teach these ladies they should have far more compassion for their fellow man."

First Lieutenant Sarah McIntire of the United States Army was shocked at the coldness of the proposed edict from cryptozoologist Ellenshaw. Most of the Group back at Nellis had seen the change in Charlie ever since the death of Pete Golding at the hands of a murdering ex-CIA operative. The change was enough to have most concerned. That was why she had been surprised that the colonel had allowed the scientist to take part in the operation. But she suspected what Ellenshaw needed was to occupy himself with other duties, and so Jack allowed Charlie this one slot in the rescue attempt to vent some of the pent-up emotion he was feeling. Being a cryptozoologist didn't prepare you for the shock of sudden death at the hands of your fellow man.

Sarah easily removed the six-barreled electric stun gun from her pouch. With one last look at Ellenshaw, who was waiting with anticipation, she stood and moved toward the window as if she were only curious as to the activity outside.

The woman who had spoken to them a moment before turned with a large smile on her pretty face because she had just chosen the young inmate in the wheel-chair as her bet as the first to fall. She saw Sarah approach and her smile slowly faded as she saw the large plastic stun gun in her right hand.

"Compliments of the doctor," she said as the first electrical barb shot free of the barrel and connected perfectly with the dark-haired woman's right shoulder. The ten-thousand-volt jolt shook the secretary in almost hilarious spasms until she dropped to the tiled flooring. The next two happy women were taken down without even as much fuss as the first. All three lay at the base of the window. Charlie stood and walked over to Sarah and looked down.

"I guess you were the first one to go down . . . I win."

"Do you have the music Jack gave you for the PSYOP portion of this screwed-up plan?"

Charlie felt his pockets in his wrinkled black suit. "Of course, that was my only responsibility." He felt his pocket again and brought out the encased compact disc. He blinked when he thought he remembered it being in a different colored case—this one looked like one of the CD cases from his own collection. He shrugged his shoulders and then replaced the disc in his pocket as he turned for the warden's office. "Well, shall we start the dance?" he asked Sarah as he moved.

"Let's just hope the participants in this little shindig are ready, because all hell is about to break loose."

Outside, the dabbling of applause from the balcony announced that, indeed, the festivities were about to begin.

BROWNSVILLE, TEXAS

The three young boys had every possession they owned in two overstretched garbage bags. They crossed the border early this morning and waited until the U.S. Border Patrol's change of shift. They had waited in the shadows and now moved easily from small arroyos to deep cuts along the worn trail coming in from Mexico. The three had the promise of ranch work farther north in Alvin.

"This is the safest time to move over empty land, Jime," the oldest of the three said as they came to the rising end of an arroyo, where they stopped. "There's no green-suited boogeymen out here. Just two miles and we can reach the main highway and once there we will wait until near dawn and then jump the Northern Pacific all the way into Houston."

"The emptiness of this place gives me the creeps," the youngest said as he waited in the shadows for his two friends to move to the next cut of arroyo for cover.

"Yeah, that's why it's a good route to take, not many would chance crossing with no water until you reach Brownsville." The oldest immigrant looked at the young and inexperienced boy and rubbed his head, knocking the green ball cap off. "Besides, the Americanos don't have the equipment to cover every square inch of desert. There's nothing out there but us and the open road. Now let's go."

The three young men climbed the rise, readying themselves for the sprint over into the next arroyo. When the oldest stopped dead in his tracks at the top of the rise and the other two ran into him their world became instantly surreal. Evidently the Americans had recently allocated far more funds to this area of the border.

"*Pinche vato,*" the oldest said as his eyes widened at the sight before him.

Between the arroyo they had just left and the second sat three U.S. Army Apache Longbow AH-64 attack choppers. The six men who crewed the gunships were standing in front of the giant attack birds and were looking straight at the three illegal immigrants as they stood atop the rise in shock. The weapons officer of one of the ships raised a gray-colored gloved hand and waved at the three, who simultaneously felt their hearts drop. The oldest boy swallowed hard as his right hand slowly came up in greeting.

"Oh, yeah, there's nobody out here," said the youngest.

Suddenly the aircrews below heard the loud beeping coming from their communications gear. The three aircrews ran to their Apaches. The three stunned boys watched as their four-bladed rotors started spooling up. Once more their hearts stopped when all three twenty-millimeter chain guns on the nose of each attack ship started rotating as the weapons officers made sure their main armament was functioning correctly.

"*Madre de dios,*" mumbled the oldest as the first Apache lifted free of the Texas scrub and then the other two birds quickly and noisily followed suit. All three rose, dipped their noses hard forward, and then shot into the air, hugging the ground as the United States Army crossed the border of a friendly nation for their role in Operation Alcatraz. The boys didn't know that five miles away to the east another group of helicopters was lifting off and heading to the same coordinates. Only these ships were a lot larger.

It was the youngest of the three who spoke. "I think I want to go back home."

THE UNITED STATES DEPARTMENT OF STATE
(FOGGY BOTTOM)

The secretary of state waited to deliver his prepared speech to the man who was now being escorted into his large office. The older man smiled, trying to disarm the man before he even sat down. He rose and moved to the front of his desk to greet the visitor.

"Mr. Ambassador, so nice of you to come on such short notice." He shook the smaller man's hand and then gestured to the other occupant in the room, a well-dressed younger gentleman in a perfectly pressed black suit. "I don't believe you have ever met the director of our FBI, Brenton Branch." The large black man stood and offered his hand, which the stymied ambassador from Mexico slowly took with apprehension. "Please, sir, have a seat. We have much to pass on and very little time to do it."

The ambassador to the United States from the nation of Mexico was perplexed as he had only met the American secretary of state one time, and that one time was not a pleasant experience. The old man was just plain mean in his estimation.

"Directly to the point, Mr. Ambassador, the FBI has come into some rather disturbing intelligence concerning one of your major headaches. Mr. Richie Gutiérrez."

The ambassador froze at the mention of his name.

"Yes, we thought that would get your attention right off the bat. I'll let the director tell you."

"Sir, we in the United States government understand that you are having one hell of a time containing this Gutiérrez and his rather lucrative business. Now if this is because you are unable, or unwilling"—the secretary of state gave a wry look at the head of the FBI—"does not concern us at this time." The director held up his hand as the ambassador started to protest the insult hurled at his government. "We have asked your government for three days to act upon this man for the kidnapping of an American citizen, one Xavier Morales, age twenty-five."

"My government cannot act on information provided by a foreign nation without adequate investigation. I am afraid my hands in this matter are virtually tied, Mr. Secretary."

"This is not a meeting that was intended to consult you or your government,

Mr. Ambassador. We are here to simply inform you of a covert military action intended to free our citizens from illegal internment."

"Covert military action?"

"Simply stated, you won't act, so we will, sir."

The secretary of state was relieved when he saw the wheels start turning in the young diplomat's head. He had been briefed that many in the Mexican government were in favor of moving against Gutiérrez and his cartel and smash them with an iron fist, but there were too many men in government who owed the cartel's leader enough to become one of his puppets. But the United States knew that there was a newer, bolder form of Mexican citizen rising from the old—and this man and many others was one of them. The ambassador saw what was happening; the United States was giving his government and the current administration in Mexico City an out. They wouldn't have to raise a hand to assist, nor to apologize if something went wrong. Enlightenment crossed his features like a window being opened to the world. He caught on and caught on quick.

"Oh, but we must protest this action," he said without much enthusiasm. "I must report this incursion immediately." The ambassador stood as did the director of the FBI.

"Before you report to your president, may I offer you some lunch?" he asked as the ambassador buttoned his coat.

"I must report this." The man looked at his watch.

"But it's chicken-fried steak day here at Foggy Bottom."

The Mexican ambassador allowed his lips to form a wry smile. "Well, how can I say no to that." The ambassador allowed the head of the American FBI to escort him to the cafeteria.

The secretary of state lifted his phone and then waited. It was answered on the first ring.

"It's done, Mr. President. Maybe you can explain to me later just why this American citizen is important enough to invade a friendly country."

The President of the United States never answered the secretary. He just said thanks and hung up the phone with the hopes that his friend Niles Compton knew what he was doing.

RIO NATCHEZ CORRECTIONAL FACILITY, NORTHERN MEXICO

Richie Gutiérrez stood with glass in hand. He puffed on his cigar as all eyes were raised to the balcony. He quickly noticed something in the yard below.

"Why are there sixteen inmates when the order was for fifteen?" he asked as his glass lowered and he looked at the warden, who had been caught off guard by the quick observation.

He scanned the exercise yard and saw the man who was not on the list given to him that morning by Gutiérrez. He pointed at the small man standing behind their prized inmate, Morales. The tattoo made the man easy to spot.

"You, who are you?" the warden called down. Every prisoner in the yard looked around, thinking that the warden was talking directly to them.

Commander Jason Ryan, United States Navy, smiled as he released his grip on the wheelchair handles. He smiled his gold-plated smile at those shocked inmates around him. Then Ryan turned his attention to the balcony rising above him and the others. He hoped the inside team was ready because he was about to kick this show off to a great start—a start that if it didn't work would ensure that he and his rescue element would never leave northern Mexico with breath in their lungs.

"Me?" Ryan asked, looking around as if confused. He took a few steps beyond the chair. He didn't use Spanish or anything near that language's accent. "I'm nobody compared to the great Jefe, Señor Gutiérrez," he said as he half turned to the kid in the chair. "Make sure your parking brake isn't on, kid."

"What?" Morales said as he watched the confrontation frightened out of his mind. He had thought he was brave enough to get through this but the continuing roar of the caged animals made him weaken at the prospect of Gutiérrez justice. "Who are you?" he hissed.

Ryan took a few more steps forward.

"My boss told me to pass along to Mr. Gutiérrez a message," Ryan called up, and then waited for a smiling Gutiérrez, who was curious as to the delay, but not angered—yet. The cartel leader stood with his chipped-ice glass of tequila still in hand.

"And who is your boss? If he is the one responsible for getting you drunk and forcing that tattoo on you, I must say he's not much of a boss, or has a far better sense of humor than even myself." He laughed as did everyone in the balcony with the exception of the cameraman and soundman, who were still busy doing their jobs.

"My boss"—here he paused for the best dramatic effect possible as Ryan smiled even wider—"is an even bigger prick than you." The smile faded. "Only he doesn't kill his own people and fill the world with your poison product. He sent me here to explain this to you in no uncertain terms."

This time Gutiérrez lost his confident grin. The game was quickly growing old.

"I don't want to hear any more, release our friends!" he said, and then smiled down upon the tattooed man.

As the gates that fronted the horse trailers opened, the men inside the yard instinctively moved as far away as they could from what was about to join them. As for Ryan, he also smiled, but for a different reason. He returned to the wheelchair-bound Morales.

"Here we go, kid, welcome to the real world!" Ryan said over the fearful cries of the condemned men crowding around him and Morales.

The sky exploded with sound so loud that everyone froze. The prison's PA system came to life with a vengeance.

Ryan smiled as if he were the Cheshire cat. Then the smile quickly faded as he realized this was not the PSYOPS portion of the rescue's chosen music. Instead of frightening, it was beyond confusing. Ryan had decided he would kill Sarah McIntire and Charlie Ellenshaw as they just butchered Jack Collins's theory on shock and awe.

"Psychological warfare my ass!" Ryan yelled, hoping Ellenshaw could hear him.

Gutiérrez stood again as the music choice by Crazy Charlie Ellenshaw struck his eardrums and assaulted them.

On the overhead speaker system and throughout the prison the song "Sugar, Sugar," by the bubble-pop band the Archies blared across the yard. That, coupled with the screams of the inmates as the doors to the trailers were finally opened.

"Shoot that man," Gutiérrez screamed over the blare of the sugarcoated music that was coming near to bursting everyone's eardrums.

Before anyone could react in the confusion, the soundman in the balcony turned and popped a switch on the telescopic microphone boom and a stream of gas issued from the disguised mic. The blue-tinted gas filled the area and dropped two guards immediately.

Gutiérrez was shocked as one of his men fell forward over the balcony and the other just fell. That was when he saw the cameraman turn toward him with his camera and was shocked to see the man wearing a gas mask. Then a compartment on the side of the mini-cam opened and the next thing the cartel leader saw was a nine-millimeter semiautomatic Glock pistol pointed right at his head. The man behind the mask didn't waver as the sound engineer continued his gas assault on the balcony.

Ryan screamed for the men to get down as the music was somehow shoved aside by another, even louder sound.

Before anyone could know what was happening, three American Apache helicopters rose over the eastern, northern, and southern walls of the prison. As the Archies continued to sing on, the chain guns mounted on the nose of each attack chopper opened up. They struck the electrical lines leading into the prison and then one of the Apaches rose a hundred feet and sent a stream of twenty-millimeter rounds into the guard housing next to the cell blocks, effectively keeping any reinforcements from the yard. The second started tearing into the main gate of the facility until the chain-link fence and razor wire hung loosely in utter destruction.

The soundman tossed the now-empty boom over the balcony and studied the warden and the rest of the incapacitated guards. None were moving.

Sarah and Charlie ran from the offices and joined the soundman as he checked everyone to make sure none would spring up and surprise them. Still the Archies sang and the men below cowered.

Ten guards sprang from a blockhouse and started toward the yard. The remaining inmates who had been gathered outside the exercise yard to witness their own eventual fate saw what the guards were attempting and immediately swarmed as each man knew instinctively that something extraordinary was happening and they had to take advantage. The ten armed guards didn't stand a chance against the anger of Gutiérrez's enemies. The Apache gunships circled, looking for any threat that sprang up.

Gutiérrez was standing wide-eyed as the cameraman lowered the nine millimeter and then removed the black gas mask. The black man smiled at him.

"Richard Gutiérrez, we are here to enforce a warrant ordering your arrest," United States Army Captain Will Mendenhall said as he looked back at U.S. Marine Gunnery Sergeant Jesse Rodriguez as he quickly emptied the harness bag they had brought along. Mendenhall looked at his watch under his gloved hand. "Thirty seconds. Sarah, give the gunny a hand, will you? Charlie, you and I have to talk about what represents PSYOPS operations and its intended distraction media. The Archies is not among the chosen selections to frighten your adversary."

"I will have you all tracked down and killed in your homes with your entire families!" Gutiérrez said as he watched the strangers unroll a large set of nylon harnesses.

Will Mendenhall, after being interrupted by the cartel leader and his threat, looked at Gutiérrez and then simply raised the gun and hit him in the forehead with the gun, sending him grimacing as he fell back onto his ornate emperor's throne.

"It's very rude to interrupt," he said as his eyes lingered for only a moment on the man. He turned back to Ellenshaw, who was not smiling even though he knew he had screwed up. "We'll talk later, Doc. Now help get this asshole prepared to fly."

Charlie did as he was told.

Jason Ryan started frantically pushing Morales and his chair forward through the frightened inmates. He was screaming for the condemned men to make a break for the gates and the prison parking lot beyond. He heard the Apaches open up somewhere to his right and hoped there wasn't wholesale killing going on. After all it wasn't Gutiérrez's henchmen they were after, it was only Morales and the leader of the most brutal drug cartel since the Cali, Colombia, extremes of the eighties. He made sure that the guards tending to the wild animals in their cages were either eliminated or on the run, then he went to the direct center of the yard and waited, feeling very exposed to whatever guards made it past the circling Apaches.

With the blare of noise coming from the Archies and the powerful twin engines of the Apaches, no one heard the deeper bass rumble of something much larger as it approached the prison. Men ran and screamed as the giant Chinook double-rotor transport helicopter broke over the height of the south wall. The rotor wash of the large CH-47 heavy-lift chopper knocked men from their feet as they ran away frightened from the American black ops display confronting them. The harness struck the ground near Ryan and he immediately took hold and started strapping the shocked and frightened computer genius to the harness. The wide-eyed young man made no sound other than to scream when Ryan faced him.

"Now don't move until you're told," he said.

"But who in the hell are you!"

"Bye, kid, nice meeting ya!"

Morales was about to ask again when his world went away. He and his chair were pulled so violently upward that he knew he had left his stomach somewhere rolling on the ground with Ryan. As for Jason he had to smile as the screams of the young selection of computer science department head were heard even over the noise of the music and engine assault. The harness held as the boy and his chair flew skyward toward the hovering Chinook. Ryan made sure the kid was pulled in by the CH-47's crew and then he made his way toward the double gates that held the prisoners inside. He opened them and started moving inmates free of the yard. As he did he looked at the three horse trailers and that was when Jason Ryan really smiled.

In the balcony above the action, Sarah, Charlie, and Rodriguez had Gutiérrez ready to ascend into the blue skies above Mexico. The man finally opened his eyes against the pain of Mendenhall's rebuke with the pistol. The dark eyes widened when he saw the black American looking down at him. He was about to scream something over the noise of the Archies when Mendenhall held up his right hand and just simply waved good-bye as Gutiérrez burst into the sky, ripping the make-shift shade cover from the prepared balcony. Will smiled and then attached his own lines as did the other three. He saw Ryan as he stood just below with his own harness attached and waiting.

"Hey, toss down the warden and his men!" Jason screamed at a confused Will. Then he saw his friend's smile and knew exactly what he had planned. With the help of Ramirez, Sarah, and an angry Ellenshaw, the five men were eased to the asphalt below by rope.

As inmates freed themselves from the prison, Jason Ryan, United States Navy, looked down at his handiwork and with the large tattoo gleaming its glorious colors in the sun he gave the signal. The second CH-47 Chinook lifted him, Sarah, Rodriguez, and Mendenhall free of the ground, and with four personnel hanging from the giant bird, slowly made their way north toward the border. Operation Alcatraz was now complete.

Ten minutes later the prison warden awakened with a fright at about the same time as his guards and Gutiérrez's henchmen. With wide eyes and loosened bladder they watched the black-coated Yucatán jaguars as they started creeping toward the spot where they had been deposited. Just before the first sleek cat lowered its ears to spring, he saw the scrawled note between his splayed legs. He read it and then looked up just as the five wildcats started forward with hungry intent. As the freed men ran into the surrounding countryside and the remaining prison guards decided they needed to find new work, the small note blew away in the wind and only the warden of Rio Natchez Prison would ever know what it said: "Compliments of the Greater Nevada Historical Society."

2

BLACKSMITH ENGINEERING CONSULTANTS, SAN DIEGO, CALIFORNIA

The woman waited inside the idling taxicab until she spied her target. She lowered her dark glasses and took in the familiar figure of the man she had known now for eight years. She smiled and then pushed the sunglasses back up her slim nose. She straightened her skirt, then gave the cabdriver a twenty-dollar bill, and took a deep breath as she readied for the confrontation that had been coming for many years. She opened the door and with her briefcase in hand started to follow the broad-shouldered object of this covert visit as he took his brown-paper-bag lunch to the nearby park area.

Assistant Director of Department 5656 Virginia Pollock waited while the brutish little man chose a tree to sit under. She again lowered the sunglasses as the man saw three squirrels frolicking under the protection of the trees. Like most California squirrels, these were in no mood to move from the shade of the tree and the pinecones it offered. She grimaced as she watched the gray-haired man remove the stub of a cigar from his mouth and then lean over.

"You fuckin' rats going to move or am I goin' to throw you into a stew?" the raised voice asked loudly. The squirrels all stopped and looked up into the angry and mean face of the man and then decided they would indeed act like squirrels and run for their lives.

"Yeah, that's what I friggin' thought, bunch of pussies."

Virginia shook her head as she watched Master Chief Petty Officer (retired) Harold C. Jenks slowly ease his bulk onto the grass. She saw that the master chief was tired. The blue denim work shirt he wore was wrinkled and the hair on his head was a little grayer. Assistant Director Pollock knew, like Jack and the rest of her colleagues, that Jenks wasn't taking the recent personnel losses to the nation too well. The master chief had lost as much as anyone at Group; he had lost a student and dear friend when Carl Everett vanished into the wormhole after guaranteeing the destruction of the enemy in its own dimensional shift over Antarctica.

The master chief pulled out a sandwich and then looked at it and decided he wasn't that hungry. Virginia saw him speak with several of his people who were far better dressed than Jenks. Their clothes were expensive and clean, while the owner of Blacksmith Engineering was a complete mess—*Even more so than usual*, Virginia thought. When Jenks said the last to his passing colleagues he saw the tall, thin woman looking at him. He closed his eyes for a moment and then opened them in time to see his worst nightmare still approaching.

"Well, I never thought I would gaze upon those legs again," Jenks said as his eyes traveled up Virginia's legs to her white blouse and jacket.

"That makes two of us, Harold," she said as she stepped forward until she stood over the reclined Jenks.

The master chief's face screwed into one of disgust at the mention of his first name. But then Virginia was the only person in the world who was ever allowed to refer to him that way. The very direct woman could be forgiven for a lot.

"Before you even begin, I'm done."

Virginia smiled and then tossed Jenks her briefcase, which he caught in his lap but not before the corner of the case hit his left testicle. He winced as she sat next to him on the grass. She stretched out her long legs and then smiled over at him.

"Done with what?" she asked, teasing him like she always had.

Jenks started to throw the briefcase from his lap but caught himself as he knew from experience that Ms. Pollock was the only person he had ever known not to cower in terror at his voice. He gently laid the case aside.

"Done helping whatever it is you and your so-called think tank does." He looked sad for the briefest of moments. "If there's anyone left, that is." He looked deeply into her green eyes. "Your director and the president seemed to have killed off everyone else that I had any affection or respect for." He looked away and then immediately back up. "Well, almost all, anyway. So tell your director Compton and his Captain America Jack Collins to screw off, I'm busy."

Virginia knew he still held a soft spot in that black heart of his for her. Their relationship went back to 2007 when they had become close during the Amazonian expedition. She knew that Jenks was hurting just as much as everyone else after losing so many men and women in the recent war. Most were lost on his re-engineered battleship left on Earth by the Martian civilization that preceded Earth by millions of years. Yes, Jenks felt the pangs of guilt and they mostly stemmed from losing the man he had trained as a navy SEAL when he was but a boy, Carl Everett. Jenks was unforgiving toward Jack, Niles, and even her at the sacrifice Carl had had to make in order to end the war. Virginia tilted her head and then placed a thin but beautiful hand on the rough, unshaven cheek of the man she had once been intimate with a million years before. He softened as her hand caressed him.

"Stop that," he said as he pulled his face away.

"You poor bastard, you know how to be angry all the time but you never learned how to grieve, did you?"

"Look, Slim, take your pitch and sell it to some other broken-down ex-SEAL and even worse engineer. I assure you they are out there."

"Yes, they are, and we've interviewed most of them. But alas, and I don't know the reasoning behind the decision, Jack and Niles want you and only you."

"I'm done with consulting for your damn strange Group, Ginny, done."

"I said nothing about consulting, Harold."

A confused look crossed his gruff features.

"We want you to sign on with the Group full-time as the director for special projects. In other words we need all that engineering stuff you can bring to bear. Unlimited budget and full control of engineering and our rather unique facility."

"No."

"Full access to navy, air force, and army technology."

"No."

She smiled, knowing his weakness.

"I want you to take it."

He looked sad for a moment. Then hardened. "No."

She raised her brows.

"No."

"We have something planned, Harold, and Niles and Jack need you, and only you."

"No," he said, and then looked at the woman he loved deeply, and he could say that about only two people he had ever known, Virginia and one other. He became deadly curious and he knew that was a bad thing. "What do you have planned?" he asked as he looked away for having caved so easily.

Virginia Pollock smiled, leaned in, and kissed Jenks fully on the mouth. She held it for the longest time, shocking anyone who worked for the former master chief as they gasped at the sight of the meanest man in the world being romanced by a gorgeous woman. She finally parted from him and then told him what the Event Group was up to.

Ten minutes later the master chief was deep in thought.

"Impossible" was his only word.

"We at Group don't care for that word much, Harold, you should know that."

"Well, start believing and caring, because it's an impossibility. And I don't care who came up with it."

Virginia stood, retrieved her briefcase, and then paused as she leaned in close to Jenks.

"Then I guess we'll have to make the attempt without you, Harold."

Jenks watched her turn and start moving away toward the street. He looked to the sky and cursed his luck. But deep down after hearing what it was Virginia had to say, he knew he was trapped.

"Goddamn it!" he said loudly as he stood, frightening several of his consulting colleagues as they walked past, and then those same people watched stunned as the master chief ran after Virginia Pollock like a loving puppy toward its master.

"All right, I'll only listen on one condition," he called out.

Virginia stopped and waited. "And that is?"

"Don't call me Harold, you manipulative she-devil."

The assistant director smiled.

"You got it, Harold."

The master chief watched Virginia smile and then she moved off, leaving him standing there just as angry as ever. "I'm freakin' glad we got that settled."

Jenks chased after Virginia because he knew, failure or triumph, as an engineer and as a friend, he had to be in on the greatest scientific reach in the history of mankind.

3

CHATO'S CRAWL, ARIZONA

Colonel Henri Farbeaux thought he would never lay eyes on the small town again in his lifetime. As the United States Air Force Black Hawk banked hard over the dead town of Chato's Crawl, Arizona, chills coursed through the former French commando's skin as he recalled the horrors that took place here and in the mountains outside of the small town. Underneath his sunglasses his eyes roamed to the mysterious and foreboding Superstition Mountains, and their dark presence made the deserted town that sat in their ominous shadow welcoming by comparison.

"What is this place?" Anya Korvesky asked as she too saw the desolation of the thirteen-building ghost town. The rotors of the Black Hawk stirred up small dust devils that bounced from dead street corner to dead street corner, dodging the broken and rusty dregs of the automobiles left behind by the few citizens and reporters who survived that horrible two days in the desert.

Henri leaned back and was tempted to reach into his coat pocket and bring out a cigarette that he no longer carried nor had a habit for. He would just have to suffer through the memories of those days that had eventually started bringing to a close his colorful career as a collector of rare and valuable artifacts. Now he was but a paid messenger for a man he had sworn to kill over the death of a wife gone many years now. The past for Henri Farbeaux was always just a thought away, buried deep in memory that not even he himself could sort through.

"That, my dear, is what the Americans refer to as a ghost town. One that was quite active back in the summer of 2006." Farbeaux closed his eyes as he leaned back just as the Black Hawk started to settle down into the desert scrub just outside the dead town. "This is Chato's Crawl. I'm sure it sparks a flare of memory for you." He smiled over at her, making her feel uncomfortable and not knowing why. "After all, it was in all of the papers."

The memory was indeed there thanks to the briefing reports from the Mossad. She looked back at the now-relaxed Farbeaux.

"The terrorist cell that was uncovered here and in the mountains?"

"Terrorist cell?" Henri gave her a bemused chuckle and then looked at Anya full on as he removed his sunglasses. "You're one of them now, and you'll soon learn that most American cover-ups start with a grain of truth and expand from there. Terrorists, yes, by all means they were indeed that."

"One thing you should know about me, Colonel, I do not have your sense of humor."

"Really?" he said as he leaned back against the bulkhead of the compartment and replaced his sunglasses. He smiled again as the large helicopter settled onto the sand-covered roadway where once upon a time giant C-130 Hercules cargo planes had set down to disgorge its cargo of 101st Airborne troops for the defense of the American desert. "Well, my dear, possibly being the future Mrs. Everett, you better develop that sense of humor." His smile left his face as the wheels of the Black Hawk set down on the sand-covered roadway behind the large and abandoned Texaco station. Farbeaux finally sat up and looked at her seriously. "This is the town where the first shots of the war you just survived and your boyfriend did not were fired. Kind of ironic, isn't it? I mean being brought to the place where it all started, for me, for you," he said as he saw the face of Jack Collins on the inside of his eyelids, "and for many others."

"Well, we're not alone," Anya said as the whine of the Black Hawk turbines started to dwindle to nothing as the air force crew chief opened the sliding door and hopped out.

Farbeaux assisted Anya from the helicopter and then saw that there were three more UH-60s sitting in a neat circle in the old parking lot of the Texaco station, which had seen far better days.

"This way," the crew chief said, indicating the broken and smashed diner across the street.

Henri smiled as he recalled the first time he had been there and met the owner of the small eatery. He recalled her name: Julie Dawes. From what he understood the old man, Gus Tilley, had made the woman's and her son's lives quite comfortable after the finding of the Lost Dutchman gold mine. He shook his head as he took in the dilapidated diner. He lost his smile when he remembered the men he had lost in the town and below it in tunnels made by a being from another world as it sought to exterminate men from this planet—the opening shots of the war between mankind and the Grays.

As the filthy glass door of the diner was held open for them by the Black Hawk's crew chief, Henri immediately saw the three armed men just inside. The security was part of the Group. Henri could always tell because Collins trained his men to blend in. The three just sat around in civilian clothes and watched the grouping of six people waiting at tables that had been placed together.

"Colonel Farbeaux, Anya, have a seat, we'll be starting in a moment."

Henri smiled at Virginia Pollock. He swore the lady had more grace to her than most women of royal blood would have coursing through their veins. In his estimation the assistant director of this very strange agency was just plain elegant and deserved to be treated that way.

"It is good to see you again, Dr. Pollock," Farbeaux said as he went to her and kissed her hand. She smiled and then glanced over at a very perturbed Master Chief Jenks, who was puffing heavily on his cigar, which Virginia had told him not to light.

"Wait one goddamn minute," Jenks said as he stood from the table he and Virginia had been sitting at. Virginia rolled her eyes when she realized the master chief was about to fly into a jealous rage. She batted her eyes, thinking that he did feel something for her after all. "You're that son of a bitch Frenchy colonel that sank my freakin' boat!" he said with wide eyes.

Henri realized who the brutish little man was and that he had been near him the entire time down in Antarctica and never put the face to the name—until now.

"Well, the famous Master Chief Jenks. Haven't seen you since—"

"You know goddamn well when the last time was, Froggy: when you blew up and sank my boat down in that backward-ass lagoon in the Amazon."

"That's enough, we can talk about our colorful pasts another time. Sit down, please."

All faces with the exception of Virginia Pollock's turned at the sound of the voice. Niles Compton stood at the swinging doors that used to front the kitchen of the Broken Cactus Bar and Grill. He placed his briefcase down on a covered table and then allowed Gunnery Sergeant Rodriguez to help him settle into the chair. Then Rodriguez and the other three security men went about the small area that used to be full of small cocktail tables, placing large monitors and computer links that had their power lines running over to the Texaco station where a small generator had been set up. There was only one of the original three pool tables left and that was being used by a tray full of Styrofoam cups and steaming coffee. Small sandwiches were also laid next to the service. All eyes were on the shattered features of the director of Department 5656.

"We will begin shortly. It seems our security director has something to work out with his people."

Henri smiled as he sat down next to Anya and then infuriated the master chief when he winked at him. As for the chief, he had decided that as soon as he was able and thought he could get away with it he was going to eat frog legs for dinner. He would kill the Frenchman for destroying his boat, USS *Teacher*. Farbeaux's smile grew when he heard the raised voices coming from the kitchen.

"Mr. Director, I'm so happy that things in security continue to go on as smooth as a French woman's"—he looked at Anya, Virginia, and then with a dip of his head in deference to the women and to the quiet kid in the wheelchair in the corner—"a French baby's bottom."

The comment was accompanied by a smashing of metal onto the old, stained, and broken checkerboard tile of the kitchen.

The old rack of dusty utensils flew to the tiled floor near the repaired hole that was once created by what the Group had come to know as the Destroyer. It had since been filled in with concrete as had all the other hidden tunnels underneath the town. The outline of the repaired hole kept Sarah's attention as she endured the anger of Jack Collins. Captain Jason Ryan was close to being insubordinate to the colonel. The two were almost nose to nose and even Charlie was pushed aside when the two security men clashed.

"I asked you point-blank if your assault and infiltration team was ready, you said yes."

Ryan didn't back away an inch from Collins. Sarah and Charlie Ellenshaw could only watch the two friends come close to blows. She had never seen Jack act like this with his people. Will Mendenhall stood in the far corner with his arms crossed over his chest. Sarah could see that he was torn between coming to Jason's defense as he always did, and seeing Jack's obvious point of view. Will understood the difference, being he was fully trained on tactical assault whereas Jason wasn't fully up to date. He could see the reasoning behind the colonel's anger.

"You," he said as his finger hit Charlie Ellenshaw in the chest.

"Ow," the cryptozoologist said, but to his credit, Mendenhall and the other two noticed Charlie bravely held his ground just as Jason had done.

"I know you're hurting, Doc. You don't lose personnel like Pete and Matchstick, Gus and Dr. Gilliam, and then just go about your everyday life like normal. You have to learn that in the business we have chosen—a business we have *voluntarily* chosen—you lose people, Doc, and they are always friends. Always!" Jack emphasized the point with his nose only inches from Charlie's.

Sarah saw Charlie deflate.

"You lost your pal, Pete, but I and Niles, we lost thousands, Charlie. And no matter what you do, you cannot bring them back. I know for a fact that you can't." Collins turned away from a saddened Ellenshaw and lowered his head and his voice. "I've tried a million different ways to do just that."

"Colonel, I—"

Jack looked up, still angry, but mostly sad for the way he had had to come down on the people he admired and respected. "You are both dismissed. Captain, you too. I need a word with Ryan alone."

Sarah took Charlie by the arm and turned to leave the broken kitchen that still held the lingering smell of old grease and even older beer. After all of this time the diner placed an exclamation point on the term ghost town. Will hesitated before opening the swinging doors as he took in both men. One, his best friend, the other, a man who was more like a father than his commanding officer. He shook his head and then left the kitchen.

Collins rubbed his tired eyes and then faced Ryan. Normally the tattoo on his face would have been cause for teasing and laughing, but lately there had been very little of that throughout the Event Group complex.

"I told you, Jack, I am not the leader you want. Will is far more qualified than I am. Just because I have more time served doesn't mean I am a better or more qualified officer. I'm a fighter-jock, a tomcat driver"—the sad look again—"or was one anyway." He shook his head as he looked at a man he respected above all others. "And you know that kind of fighter jock arrogance makes for terrible leadership skills, at least for me. The navy knew that when everyone else still had hope for me. Now I guess you know, Jack."

"But you made the choice of going in with inexperienced people on your team." Collins nodded. "I know we are horribly shorthanded, Jason, so why didn't you cancel the operation when the specialists you needed weren't available?" He faced Ryan with a sad look. "Carl never would have done that. In order for this plan to work, and believe me it's the thinnest mission we will ever come across, and the most dangerous, I have to have everyone on the same page."

A hurt look came across Jason's face and then he turned to leave the kitchen, but stopped just short of exiting as he stood but didn't face Jack.

"Jack, I'm not Carl." He gestured toward the doors and the people beyond. "No one here is. Who's the one pushing too hard?" He finally faced Jack. "I'll settle it with this, Colonel, would you have canceled the operation with what you know is at stake?" He turned and left, leaving Jack to see himself just as he was seeing others—planning things with too much emotion.

That was unacceptable to a man like Collins. Jason was right, he did what Jack himself would have done. Collins supposed it was the hidden fear of losing even more people. He decided that Ryan's rescue mission was more than brilliant, it was one he himself would have planned.

On exiting the kitchen, Collins walked over to the old and broken waitress station and sat on an old and dusty bar stool. His eyes watched as Jason went to a table where Will had pushed a chair out with his foot. Jason sat. Then his eyes took in the master chief and Virginia, who was patting the retired naval engineer on the arm as if calming him down from something. And as Collins knew, that could be any one of a million things that would set the master chief off. Then his eyes went to the dark corner where the young man sat silently in his wheelchair. Mendenhall had reported that since his rescue from the Mexican prison the young man had said nothing other than to ask about the welfare of his mother. He was now watching the men and women sitting around him with a neutral look on his face. Jack did notice the worn and tattered black Converse sneakers on the young man's crooked feet.

By far the most interesting table was occupied by Anya Korvesky, who nodded her lovely head at Jack. Her companion was looking directly at Collins. Henri Farbeaux sat stoically with his right eyebrow raised in interest after Jack had exited the kitchen. He felt the energy still coming off the colonel and Jack wondered if his bright idea would eventually lead to disaster. But for what they had to do in the next six months they needed the skills that Farbeaux had in abundance.

Niles cleared his throat and then started to stand as was his custom when he taught courses and addressed his management groups, but felt the bright flare of pain in his leg and decided he would speak from the comfort of a chair.

"For those of you who know where we are, I should tell you that the land and the town has been officially purchased by Department 5656. No one will ever be allowed in this town again after this day. We . . ." He paused only briefly. "I decided that this will be considered a battlefield grave site and will be protected as that for now and forever. We lost too many good people and soldiers here."

All in the room saw Niles's head dip as the last words were spoken. They had all indeed come a long way since that black summer in 2006.

Again he cleared his throat. "Your escorts have explained to you what our department does for the United States government." He looked at Anya, Xavier Morales, and Master Chief Jenks. He didn't bother including Henri Farbeaux in that comment due to the fact that the antiquities thief knew just as much about the Event Group as any one of them. "And that is as far as it will be explained until you agree to join us for what we have to do. That is the second reason we are meeting outside of our own facilities. This operation is not officially a part of our expanded charter. What we will do, we do on our own with a little bit of covert help from . . . well, our boss." Compton looked at Collins, who straightened and then took a step forward and faced the room.

"If you choose to end this here and now, you will be escorted back to your former situation or job." Jack looked at the thus far silent Xavier Morales, who still sat with his small hands folded in his lap. At first Jack thought the young man was frightened at the strangeness of the last two days, but he was slowly realizing that the computer genius was just watching, learning—or was it scheming? "The director has arranged for both you, Mr. Morales, and for you, Master Chief Jenks, to return home to your normal lives if you choose not to be a part of our operations. Mr. Morales—" Jack walked over and stood in front of the young man, who only looked up without comment. Jack handed him an envelope. "That is a cashier's check for two hundred thousand dollars. If at the end of your conversation with Director Compton you wish to depart our company, that check will be yours, no strings attached."

The young man's eyes never wavered and he didn't do anything with the envelope except place it on the small table in front of him. Jack moved away after the noncommittal response.

"I think I will take door number one also," Henri said as he looked seriously from Jack to Niles.

"Your deal is completely different, Colonel. Jack will explain that option to you in a more private setting." Compton looked from a nonsmiling Farbeaux to a confident Collins. "I would now like to introduce to most of you someone who you have never met before," Niles said as he looked at his people. "Anya, please stand up."

Mendenhall, Ryan, Sarah, and Charlie all looked confused as each of them had met and worked with Anya since the war began with the Grays.

"Major Korvesky has decided to join Department 5656 as an American citizen. The president has signed an executive order and placed it in her new file at Group. She will be accorded management status and be placed under my direct control until she makes the adjustment to the colonel's security team once this operation is complete. Welcome, Anya, to Department 5656.

"Miss Korvesky is now officially a part of the Group, she has been signed off on by the president. That leaves Master Chief Jenks, you, Colonel Farbeaux, and our young friend, Mr. Morales."

"Easy for me," Henri said as his face corkscrewed into a sour look as he tasted the coffee. "I'll take a check just like you offered this young man and then I'll take my leave." He smiled and sat back down next to Anya, who sat with a bemused look on her face.

The pistol appeared in Henri's face just as he lifted the Styrofoam cup to his lips. The look in the former Mossad agent's face was telling him she had little patience for his offhanded joking. She cocked the nine millimeter.

"Okay, that's a very good negotiating tactic," Henri said as he sipped his coffee, but everyone saw that the Frenchman never blinked. This was not, after all, the first time he had had a gun shoved in his face.

"We do things a little differently here, Miss Korvesky," Niles said as he watched Jack slowly place his thumb between the hammer and the firing pin of the Glock pistol. He easily removed it from a very disappointed Anya. He moved back to the bar after ejecting the clip and placed the weapon on the dusty top. He gave a sour look at his security men, who had supposedly assured them that Anya was not armed. Henri winked as he lowered his cup of coffee, but there was very little humor in the gesture.

"What can I say," Henri said as he turned to face Collins and then back at Anya, "you have piqued my interest."

"Henri, when this operation is completed one way or the other, you're free to go on your merry way. Until then you belong to me. Complete your duties and the guarantee that the president gave you concerning amnesty for all crimes committed within our borders will be expunged as promised six months ago."

"In other words, the same agreement I said yes to before the war—that one," he said angrily as he was shocked to learn that Collins had another plan.

"The very same, Henri."

"So, the colonel is in. I suppose it's not necessary for you to fill out nondisclosure paperwork, Colonel?" Niles asked with the eyebrow over his new eye patch raised in interest.

"I believe you have absorbed too much of Colonel Collins's fantastic personality, Mr. Director."

"Yes, I imagine I have. Now, you, Master Chief."

Jenks pulled the cigar out of his mouth. "Are we gonna do what Ginny said we were gonna do?"

Niles looked at the master chief. The man was decorated by the president for his actions during the war. Afterward he flew home angry when he learned of Everett's death and had not spoken to anyone since. It was as if they were to blame for Everett's actions in vanishing into that wormhole.

"We are, yes." Niles was silent after the answer.

"Then I guess signing on to your ship of fools for life is the price I have to pay to the devil?"

"Yes," Niles said.

Jenks looked at Virginia, who only stared back, waiting for his final answer.

"And engineering is all mine, unlimited budget?"

"To a degree, yes," Compton said, still feeling uneasy at the offer Virginia had negotiated for Jenks. But they needed the master chief just as much as Morales.

"Then I'm in," he said as he tossed his dead cigar away. Then Jenks went and retrieved it after a dirty look from Virginia. "As I said"—he looked at the angry nuclear physicist—"I'm in." She smiled and dipped her head.

"That leaves Mr. Morales," Compton said as he finally took in the brilliant computer whiz. The young man remained silent. After being told the short version of what this agency did, Morales had become introspective as he thought it out. He had heard rumors of a hidden government agency and had even been close to finding out more details just before his brother's murder had stalled his private investigation of this mysterious agency.

The young man simply retrieved the envelope with the cashier's check inside and slid it away from him, giving hope to Niles that he was accepting. He looked at Jason, Sarah, Mendenhall, Rodriguez, and Charlie, and then dipped his dark hair in deference to them. He spoke the first words Niles and Collins had ever heard him speak.

"Thank you for getting me out of the situation I was in." He half smiled at the five people he had thanked. "But it was a situation I was willing to accept for what I had done. In other words no matter what my fate would have been, it was one that I had chosen."

"Even though that fate was to be torn limb from limb by wild animals?" Jason said, not liking the way the brilliant computer wunderkind was speaking.

"Yes, even that. That man and men like him killed my brother and many, many more with names just as familiar to me and my family. I'm afraid I decline your offer. I have much more work to do at a place a little closer to home for me."

"I see," Niles said. Compton cleared his throat and then looked at Rodriguez. He nodded at the director. "Europa, are you online?" Niles asked.

Everyone in the dusty room saw the largest of the five monitors come to life. The printed response was now a familiar sign to those who had been working on Europa since the death of Pete Golding. It was also one of the main reasons why Morales was needed. Europa had not used her voice algorithm since the day she learned Golding would not be coming home. She had remained totally silent. She always fulfilled her duties, but would never respond in voice, only with written text. The Marilyn Monroe voice had not been heard in the computer sciences division since that day.

"*Online Director Compton.*"

"Visual?" Compton asked.

"*Optics available.*"

"Identify and authenticate manufacturing certificate."

"*XP 2760, Blue Ice systems, Code-named; Europa, Cray manufacturing certificate number—0005, last of series, platform was discontinued in 2001.*"

Niles and the others watched the face of Morales and for the first time he showed that he was listening. Still, he sat silent.

"Europa, query," Niles said.

"*Query.*"

"Progress on replacement search, computer sciences division director?"

All eyes went to the screen; even Morales looked up as if only curious.

The room was silent as Europa was dark. Only the flashing cursor showed she was still operational.

"Europa, answer query," Niles persisted.

Silence and darkness on the screen. Compton looked over at Morales, who sat stoically in his wheelchair.

"Europa, number of qualified candidates?"

"*Seventeen qualified candidates.*"

"List the seventeen, please," Niles asked, knowing what was coming.

Silence again. Compton exchanged looks with Virginia and Collins. They were as mystified as he. Still, Europa was dark, just the flashing cursor after Compton's query.

"Europa, list qualified candidates as chosen by computer sciences, please."

"Xavier Morales."

All eyes went to the quiet man in the corner. His brows rose but that was the limit of his surprise.

"List the names of other candidates, please."

Silence and darkness on the screen.

"Europa, separate query, file clearance, Compton, Niles, director, Department 5656. Criminal activity file, United States, query: name person or persons responsible for breaking security protocols for Europa Blue Ice system in the winter of 2012?"

"Xavier Morales, age 25 years 3 months, Los Angeles, California. Duration of criminal activity, seventeen seconds. Trace completed 1/23/2012. No charges filed this date."

"Does that date sound familiar, Mr. Morales?"

The young man finally used his strong hands to push his chair forward and wheeled around. He was looking up at the large monitor.

"Rumor," he said under his breath as he continued to look at the black screen in front of him.

"Excuse me?" Henri said, interested in the goings-on of the world's most advanced computing system. Morales didn't look back as he spoke.

"That night I was chasing a rumor when I hooked up with . . . with . . ."

"My computer system," Niles said, falsifying his anger to a degree.

"Yes, I used a little-known Cray algorithm to get through." He turned to face Compton and the others. "I laid a trap and your system found me."

"You don't have to bother us with the details of your crime, but needless to say you broke into one of five Blue Ice systems in the world. Europa is the most advanced of those systems."

"They are real," Morales said as his verbal tone went into one of wonder at what he was hearing. "They do exist. How many again, this one and four others? Let me guess, the Pentagon," he thought, biting his lower lip as he saw it through. "The CIA, FBI, and the National Security Agency?"

Silence greeted his educated guess. His face suddenly turned white. "Your system set me up?" he asked.

"No, not Europa on her own, our computer sciences director found you after your little hacking foray and wanted to know if you could do it again. You did three days later, and that was when Europa trapped you. Thus the reason why you are here."

"And that makes this young man qualified just because he happens to be good at breaking and entering?" Jenks said with a laugh as he pulled a fresh cigar from his shirt pocket, but replaced it when Virginia raised her brows.

"I'm not qualified. No one is. The Blue Ice system is a system designed to learn at advanced rates. It pioneered the memory sheet for processing. The rumor is that there was one Blue Ice out there with an advanced Bubble Memory processor that has yet to be authenticated by anyone. I suspect this system has that Bubble Chip memory. Who designed it?"

"Dr. Pete Golding."

Morales looked at Niles and his jaw dropped.

"Dr. Golding, the former chair of computer sciences at MIT?" he asked.

"The same," answered Compton with a look at Charlie Ellenshaw, who sat and listened but his eyes were boring in on Morales.

"I did my dissertation on Dr. Golding and his AI theories my sixth year."

"Yes, we know."

"Can I speak to him? I have a million questions to ask," Morales said.

"I agree with the master chief," Charlie said, standing up so fast his chair fell over. "This kid isn't qualified to take Pete's place!" He angrily left the dining area and exited the building altogether.

Morales for the first time looked stunned. He turned and watched Ellenshaw as he left. Then he faced Niles once more.

"You'll have to excuse the professor," Compton said, but did not elaborate on Charlie's anger.

"Pete was killed two months ago," Jack answered for Niles.

Morales actually looked saddened at the news.

"He was a great man, well advanced in his theories." He turned his chair and then wheeled away.

"Mr. Morales, Europa has been acting very strangely since the loss of Dr. Golding."

"She's not using her voice algorithm?" he asked without turning back around. "Refusing to answer certain inquiries?"

"Yes, to both questions," Niles said.

Morales wheeled around and faced the screen.

"The peccadillos of artificial intelligence, ladies and gentlemen. I theorize that the Blue Ice systems, especially one in which Dr. Golding was continually educating, are very peculiar. They sense change, read change, adapt to change. She would not be happy having someone else's hands on her systems. She's spoiled, you might say."

"So why would she focus on you and only you?" Compton asked, hoping beyond hope that the young man had an answer.

"I don't know. Why don't we ask her?"

"Be my guest, but she hasn't been advised of your presence and has no knowledge you're here. So don't be surprised if she doesn't answer you."

The others in the room watched as Morales pushed his chair forward and faced the large monitor.

"Really, no knowledge?" Morales asked with a smile. "Europa, are you online and do you currently have optical capability?"

"*Yes,*" she typed out, but was still silent.

"Identify questioner, please," he asked, watching the screen. They saw the small box atop the monitor as the aperture on the camera lens focused on the man in the wheelchair. There was silence but only for a moment, and then magic happened.

"Xavier Edmund Morales."

Looks were exchanged between Group members as they heard the simulated voice of Marilyn Monroe as she answered verbally for the first time in two months. Morales turned and looked at the people behind him.

"Hello, Europa, it is very nice to meet you."

Jenks looked at Virginia and rolled his eyes. "Love at first sight," he whispered.

"Europa, members of the staff are curious as to why you chose me among all the other qualified candidates?"

Silence.

"Europa, you are instructed to answer my query."

Morales continued to look at the monitor. He turned and looked at Compton. Then back again.

"Europa, please power down and go off-line for the next twenty-four hours."

"What are you doing? That system is needed in other places," Niles said as he struggled to stand and finally making it with Jason's assistance.

"Europa, off-line at sixteen forty-five hours."

The room fell silent as Morales turned away from the monitor.

"You have a very sick Blue Ice system there."

Compton looked at Ryan and then slowly sat back down.

"I suspect that she's learning how to grieve." Morales wheeled to the large dirty window and looked out at the falling sun over the desert. "When dealing with liquid memory bubbles, one has to know that some of those bubbles may become corrupt if the intelligence refuses to accept a certain input."

"What are you saying?" Sarah asked.

"She is refusing to contemplate that her creator has left the building, so to speak," he said, and then immediately felt bad for making light of Dr. Golding's death. "We just don't know enough about Blue Ice dynamics and how they will integrate to a liquid bubble memory system. She is highly capable of expansion of that system and she doesn't know how to do it. Dr. Golding wasn't there to explain it to her. This is why I shut her down until someone qualified can go in and expand her liquid systems to accept new data on operations, and one thing Dr. Golding never instructed her on . . . death of the human species. Oh, she's read about it, but never thought about it . . . she chose me to do it because she really doesn't trust anyone else. Why? Because I guess she believes I was smart enough. Why, I don't know."

"Because you were the only person ever to successfully break into a Blue Ice system outside of Europa herself," Niles said as he took in Morales.

"I suspected as much. Very temperamental, these experimental Cray systems."

Compton started gathering his paperwork together. "Good, you're hired. Salary is commensurate with a first-year government employee."

"God, the poor kid's going to be broke the rest of his life," Jenks said with a laugh.

"Hey, wait a minute, I don't even know what it is you want me for. I mean, what have you people got planned, and more importantly"—he looked at the tattooed face of his rescuer, Ryan—"who in the hell are you people?"

Niles stood with his briefcase with the help of Ryan and Mendenhall.

"Planned?" Niles asked, looking from Morales to the others who were just as curious. Sarah, Jason, Charlie, nor even Will Mendenhall knew what was up. Only the senior management team at the center knew and for the past two months only Anya had knowledge of what was going on. As for the former Israeli Mossad agent, she stood and went to look out of the filthy window deep in thought. Compton shook his head as he took in each new face and even those that were usually in the know. "We are going to attempt to bring home a friend from a very long distance away."

Morales looked at Niles and the others.

"Now, we need you, Mr. Morales. Do we have you?"

Xavier Morales looked from Compton and then to the large blank screen of the monitor.

"I can make sure my mother is taken care of?"

"We have taken the opportunity to move your mother to a better location, but she remains close to her friends, she is very safe," Collins said as he advanced and gave Morales a file. "All the information is in there. She's expecting you to call sometime tonight."

Morales looked at Jack and was amazed at how fast these people worked. He then looked at Compton again.

"Europa will be my responsibility?"

"Yes, complete control of computer sciences and her one hundred and twelve techs."

Morales smiled and just nodded. "The least I can do is take a look at her."

"No, it's either in or out. If out, you will never hear from or see us ever again."

He could see how serious Niles was. Again he nodded. "I'm in."

Niles smiled and nodded. "Welcome aboard Department 5656."

"Now, where are we going?" Henri Farbeaux asked as everyone stood to leave.

Collins went to Henri and stood in front of him with the largest, most uncomfortable smile Henri had ever seen on the face of the most stoic man he had ever met.

"Henri, even you wouldn't believe it if I told you."

"Yes? Well, why don't you give it a try?"

Jack smiled again as he gathered up his own materials. He then looked at Ryan, Sarah, and then finally Mendenhall, knowing they wanted to know just as bad.

"We're going back to Antarctica, Henri."

Jack turned and left.

"You know I hate the cold," Henri said as he wanted the others to protest as much as himself. But they were just as stunned.

"The part of Antarctica we're going to isn't cold at all, Henri." Jack didn't turn around as he left the shattered shell of the Broken Cactus.

"What in the hell does that mean?" Henri asked Virginia as she moved to the door with Jenks.

"It's not where we are going, Colonel Farbeaux, it's *when* we are going."

"What?" he persisted.

Virginia laughed out loud and so did Jenks. Sarah, Ryan, and Mendenhall were curious as to why this was funny to the two of them.

"Colonel, the reason Mrs. Hamilton sent you to Israel was to get Anya and the information she uncovered back to the director safely."

"And that information is?" Henri asked, not liking the way the assistant director unfolded her arms with a sneaky smile and then faced him.

"For the simple reason Anya was able to uncover a trail, a trail that may lead us to Carl."

Virginia left the diner and as she did Anya Korvesky also left, a void of confusion in their wake.

"Does she mean—" Sarah started to ask but Henri cut her off and then put forth the more logical explanation.

"It means you people are absolutely, unequivocally insane."

4

EVENT GROUP COMPLEX, NELLIS AIR FORCE BASE, NEVADA

The conference room on level seven was silent as the members of the specialized team faced one another. For Sarah, Charlie, and Virginia, they had to smile as each and every person at the table who had not been a part of the Event Group before today sat in total shock and a disturbing silence after being hit with the secrets of the entire world laid out before their eyes. The biggest void came from Master Chief Jenks, who sat looking at the polished tabletop. Even Anya, who had guessed at the duties of Carl's decidedly strange agency, was stunned at the few artifact vaults they had been shown. As for the young man, Morales, he was still smiling at what he had seen. The only person who had not been given the grand tour of the complex was, of course, Colonel Henri Farbeaux. Niles just wasn't ready for that and might never be. Farbeaux had been in the complex before but had never seen the vault levels and on Jack's advice would keep it that way. He was escorted into the conference room by Jason Ryan. While Henri went to a seat by the table, Ryan turned on someone they could not see and gestured animatedly. Frustrated, he shot one more barrage of anger at whomever he was speaking to, then closed the conference room door and angrily sat next to Mendenhall.

"Do we have a problem, Commander?" Niles asked as all eyes turned and saw Alice Hamilton walking through the door. The eighty-nine-year-old was dressed in a light blue pantsuit and was carrying an armload of files and paperwork as if she had never retired.

"Mr. Ryan, is there a problem?" Niles repeated.

Alice took her normal place beside Niles and then placed her work on the table and smiled at each of the newcomers. For Anya it was like looking at the wife of George Washington, for as much as Carl had spoken about the famous Mrs. Hamilton and her brilliant boss, the deceased Garrison Lee. Anya had to admit that there was an air of royalty about the woman and as they made eye contact she could see why Sarah was of the opinion that Alice and Anya would soon become great friends.

"Oh, Mr. Ryan is a little put out with Clarisse Carpenter and her people."

Niles looked from Jason to Alice, who had adjusted her seating and was pouring a glass of water from the carafe. "Clarisse? You mean of the logistics department?" Niles asked.

At the end of the table Ryan made a face, scrunching up the horrid tattoo used as cover to break Morales out of prison.

"It seems our logistics department placed the wrong tattoo on Jason here and he's a little put out by it." Alice couldn't help herself as she grinned while trying to cover her mouth with the water glass. She failed miserably.

"Well, are you going to keep us in suspense?" Jack asked, guessing at the predicament Jason was now facing.

Ryan remained silent as he kicked Mendenhall under the table for snickering.

"It seems they used the wrong ink on Jason's prosthetic tattoo."

All eyes went to Ryan, who lowered his head in embarrassment. The tattoo was the most brutal any of them had ever seen. The animal claw actually covered the entirety of his right-side facial features.

"How long?" Niles asked sadly, but inside he was glad that this situation broke up the seriousness of the meeting.

"Five weeks. It won't wear off for five weeks!" Ryan said as he challenged the smiling faces around the table.

"The lady-killer of the high desert—how will you survive?" Will asked in a seriously concerned tone.

Ryan started to say something but Jack stopped them.

"Thank you, Mr. Ryan. I will have a talk with logistics and have some precautions taken for future reference."

"Wonderful," Ryan said as he again gave Will a murderous look.

"I would love to know what our new personnel thought of our artifact and vault level, but I'm afraid we must get down to business. Mr. Morales still has to meet his department heads and has to settle in with Europa. He has quite an amount of work to get done and as always we have very little time to do it in." Compton nodded at Alice.

"Europa, visual aide 17890, please," Alice said, and then looked flustered when Europa did not respond. "Europa, visual aide please," Alice asked again.

On the large 105-inch monitor that sat in the middle of fifty-two smaller ones, the screen came to life and showed an old black-and-white picture. It showed a man in a white lab coat next to a small girl who could not be more than fifteen. It was obviously a young woman from a concentration camp. The two were standing in front of a hundred or so similarly dressed technicians. With the exception of the small, hellishly thin girl, they were all smiling. The date scrawled on the bottom of the photo was 1943.

Niles Compton looked at Anya and nodded just as he had done with Alice.

"Lars Thomsen. German scientist of some renown only for his work in the early twenties with one Albert Einstein. In 1939 Professor Thomsen dropped out of the scientific world for all intents and purposes to dedicate his life to the acquisition of quantum technology."

Everyone heard the exhale of breath from Master Chief Jenks, but he remained quiet after voicing his opinion of quantum theories.

"I understand your doubts, Master Chief, an educated engineer such as yourself always wants facts, hard design, not theory. But be patient with me and I will bring you to believe in the quantum sciences. I was just like you when I started digging after the death of"—she paused, looking embarrassed, but continued—"after the war."

"Who is the girl?" Charlie Ellenshaw asked.

"We'll get to that, Charlie," Niles said as he rubbed the bridge of his nose. "But for now let's concentrate on our findings. We don't have a lot of time before I have to start filling in the other departments on what we will be"—he quickly corrected himself—"hope to be attempting."

Ellenshaw nodded in understanding.

"The Israeli government in the late forties and fifties started a program to interview any Holocaust survivor they could debrief. Most in the vein of hunting down and finding war criminals, but there was other reasoning behind the interviews. Technology was one of those. So"—Anya, without really noticing, stood and started pacing, and all eyes followed the former Mossad agent as she walked—"in the process of debriefing the surviving slave labor force from sites such as Peenemünde, the V-1 rocket facility, Israeli intelligence came up with a name that kept recurring and for the life of them they didn't know why. That place was Dortmund, Germany. It was familiar to some of our people for the simple fact that we were aware of Operation Chastise."

"Excuse me?" Sarah asked, knowing that operational name sounded vaguely familiar.

"The Royal Air Force raids into Germany during the war to eliminate certain projects from the Nazi books by taking out their hydroelectric power generating systems, thus ending any hard-water experiments for their atomic weapons research programs," Jack answered for Anya.

"The famous bouncing bombs? The Dam Busters?" Charlie asked, proud that he recalled such a thing.

"The same," Anya said as she nodded at Jack in thanks. "Dortmund, or in particular the dam that served the region, was called the Möhne. The dam was struck by a bouncing bomb on the night of May 16, 1943, essentially knocking out power to over a thousand towns and villages. Through research we have discovered that the RAF might have been taking out far more than just their hard-water research."

"For instance?" Mendenhall asked.

Anya smiled and nodded at the eagerness. "We'll get to that part, Captain. Now, to the debriefing of all prisoners of war who served German science. While a first-year agent I was assigned the maddening job of refiling these old cases and mothballing, as you Americans say, any file that wasn't relevant to the search for war criminals, as that function had officially ceased to exist for the Mossad after 1984. During this time I came across one interview that was hushed up and se-creted away. It was from, of all people, a thirteen-year-old boy who served with his sister at an unknown bunker complex in Dortmund. I was able to uncover his tes-timony from the official Israeli debriefing conducted in Jerusalem in 1946, and the contents of that testimony led me to investigate the Dortmund area for any war activity that may have been noticed. I did this in the hopes of impressing cer-tain people on my thoroughness. I found nothing. Then it was eventually filed away and I forgot all about the debriefing until the recent war. I brought it up to my uncle, who swept it under the rug and told me that there was nothing to the file and to forget about it. The fact that it was being hushed up by the most powerful man in the Mossad gave me at the very least some doubts about my uncle's motives. I brought this fact up to Alice and Sarah and they conferred with Dr. Pol-lock. They wanted more information as it did have something to do with quantum theory as stated in the main file on this concentration camp survivor. So then on the advice of Dr. Compton and Virginia, I started delving into construction records for the German Army—still nothing. Then I went back to the file on this young prisoner. It seems he described the final night of activity in Dortmund as the night he lost his only living relative. He also described a very famous personage attending this event, whatever it was. By his description it could have been none other than Heinrich Himmler himself."

"What does that mean?" Charlie inquired.

"It means that whatever this project was, why Himmler? Why was he in Dortmund?"

"Maybe like the colonel said, the hard water. I'm sure Himmler would have been interested in that." Charlie made a good point.

"That wasn't it. Europa, slide 17895, please," Anya said, facing the large screen. "Europa?" she repeated.

"Europa, slide number 17895, please," Xavier Morales asked as everyone looked his way.

"Yes, Dr. Morales," Europa finally said in her Marylyn Monroe voice. Again everyone exchanged looks.

"Admiration is one thing, but Europa is pushing it a little," Will said, whispering to Ryan.

On the screen the picture changed and another appeared. This one showed Thomsen during the construction of his bunker system.

"The main clue as to the system and who built it. This is Thomsen himself standing with a construction president, Alexis Knudsen."

"You know where this bunker complex was built?" Alice asked, admiring the newest member of the Event Group for her investigative technique. Alice could see why Carl had fallen for the young Gypsy woman.

"Through the gentleman's surviving family, yes. Unbelievably the plans were still in his office in Dortmund."

"Which leads us to the conclusion that this project was undertaken without the knowledge of the German engineers who usually built these facilities, like the one at Peenemünde, and who were not allowed in on this one project. Why? Because we assume it was Himmler's and Himmler's alone. Thus he hired an outside construction firm to build his series of bunkers."

"That aspect of the investigation was conducted by Dr. Compton and Virginia, who did very well. So, we have an underground bunker complex built by Himmler for this man Thomsen. He hires a construction firm that has no ties with the Nazis or even the German Wehrmacht. That is what we in the intelligence community would call secretive." Anya paused and looked at Niles.

"People, let's get down to it. We suspect that through this Thomsen's ties with Albert Einstein and his connection with quantum theories, that Himmler and his own private mad scientist were attempting time travel. I know it's very thin, but it's a chance."

"Hogwash!" Master Chief Jenks said, not caring if Virginia shot him a warning look. "To me old Albert's as entertaining a theorist as they come, and he did a bang-up job with the relativity thing, but time travel was something that he said would always be theory. It can be done, but never would be because there is no way to travel through time and space with the electrical technology we currently possess. That simple, folks."

"And that is where we were short. We had no proof at all of what Himmler and Thomsen were working on. Until I actually found this child who was a part of the experiments."

"You found him alive?" Sarah asked, amazed at the long odds the kid had to survive to make it to old age.

"Yes, in Tel Aviv . . . before he vanished."

"What did he say?"

"He was afraid to discuss it, but he was old and sick by that time so he told me a story that shocked me, and from that sent us"—she gestured around the conference room at everyone—"down this path. He witnessed his sister, who was used in all of these experiments, actually leave this existence and arrive in another and return."

The questions started flying and it took Niles standing to silence them. He was used to his people being excited about things, but to actually have the ability to travel through time was not something they had ever remotely considered with the technology this planet currently had.

"And we never had a hint of this experiment throughout our world search for quantum technology when the British found Captain Everett's wristwatch in the ice in Antarctica?" asked Sarah again.

"No," Niles said. "It seems Himmler covered his tracks rather well from the Nazi regime. And the Mossad's reluctance after the war to pursue this to the full extent, well, let's just say was disappointing. Now, through the discovered construction records and the description of the site from the concentration camp survivor, we found the location of the bunker system. The boy claimed the last experiment failed because of some mishap in the power supply. We now know that interruption was the RAF doing a number on the Möhne Dam. The boy claims the bunker system was flooded and destroyed and his sister, known to the Germans as the Traveler, never came back."

"She was lost?" Alice asked, always placing a human face on such things from the past that made them seem more real for everyone around the table.

"Yes," Anya said as she watched a weakened Niles Compton walk slowly to his desk near the far wall and lower himself painfully down into the far more comfortable desk chair.

"Since we know the location, why don't we investigate firsthand?" Jason asked as he kept a hand over his partially disfigured face.

"If you had noticed, Colonel Collins was missing for some time a few weeks ago. He and Anya took a little foray into the woods outside of Dortmund. Jack, if you would?" Virginia volunteered.

"We spent three days wandering the woods and then we finally found a conduit access port used for electrical line maintenance. We found the bunker complex and that was why Anya was sent back to Israel to look for the final piece of the puzzle. And why Alice had to use an intermediary to get her out."

Alice was the only one to nod her head in Farbeaux's direction.

"The last puzzle piece? I thought you found the bunker?" Jenks asked as he pulled the cold stub of cigar from his mouth.

"We did indeed. Flooded and collapsed, most of it. A few old skeletons in SS uniforms and evidence that something very powerful happened there."

"And you recovered the equipment used by this Thomsen and Himmler?"

Jack pursed his lips and shook his head.

"None of the displacement equipment was there. It had been removed," Anya finished for him.

"Himmler went back and got it, huh?" Jenks interjected while shaking his head.

"No. The equipment was moved in 1969, several years after all concerned in this particular event was dead, even Himmler."

"How in the hell do you know that?" Jenks persisted, looking for any holes in Jack's or Anya's stories.

"Because the same construction company, which is family owned and operated, removed the equipment that very same year. Contracted by a company not from Germany."

"Where is the equipment?"

Anya looked at Jenks and then lowered her head. "We don't know."

"And that was why Anya went home. We had to know more, personnel records and things like that. We had to know who was still alive in 1969 who would know what it was they were looking for down there. Anya found the only other person who is known to have survived that night." Jack sat down and looked at Anya.

"And that is why we need each and every one of you in the next few weeks. We have the name thanks to Mossad files, we just have to locate that person because they have the time displacement equipment for some reason."

"Well, you goin' to let us in on the big secret?" Jenks said, huffing at the dramatics of the group.

Anya went to her chair and pulled out the same file that General Shamni produced for her. She tossed it into the middle of the table.

"I give you the thief of the technology taken from the bunker in 1969. Moira Mendelsohn."

"Who?" Sarah asked, looking from Anya to Jack. It was Jack who answered.

"Moira Mendelsohn—*the* Traveler."

The room went silent.

"Humph, rumph," the master chief rudely said as he stood up from the table. "So, you're telling us that the only person to actually . . . time travel"—he sourly hissed the words—"stole the equipment we need to retrieve our boy?"

"Yes, that's what we're saying, Master Chief," Jack said.

"So the one question we have to ask is," Niles said from his desk, "where did she go with it and what reasoning did this concentration camp survivor have for wanting it in the first place. Even if we weren't attempting to do the impossible"— he shot a quick glance at the master chief—"we could never allow this technology to be utilized for any one individual's personal gain. The tech itself will eventually have to be outlawed."

"You mean after we possibly use it for our little illegal gain?" Jenks quipped.

"Something like that," Collins said, quickly losing his patience with the master chief.

"I have a better question," Charlie Ellenshaw said. "It seems you have overlooked one little item. If she hid the equipment, where she hid it is not the right question at all. When did she hide it—in the past, or right here in the present?"

Niles lowered his head and rubbed his temples. "That is why I have called upon the most brilliant people I know to find out. Xavier, that is the task I am assigning you and Europa. Find me that woman. Your first order of business."

Young Morales was not afraid of the challenge. He could find anyone, which he had already proven. He just nodded and then frowned when he saw Charlie Ellenshaw staring at him. The man was angry and Morales would need to know more about the strange professor they called Crazy Charlie. For now, as the others filed out of the conference room, he looked up at the still photo of Professor Thomsen and the young girl sadly standing bedside him and he silently repeated the name.

"The Traveler."

Alice Hamilton lagged behind as the others left the conference room and then took her time turning to face Niles, who sat at his desk and pretended he didn't see her. This was a confrontation he had not been looking forward to—a battle with his own conscience as voiced by the marvelous young actress Alice Hamilton.

"Quite a collection of new faces you have; interesting, to say the least," she said as she easily placed her ever-present files on the edge of the large desk.

Compton looked up and smiled. He decided to let Alice throw the first punch and remained silent as she politely folded her hands in her lap and then adjusted a strand of gray hair that slipped from her bun. He kept the smile and waited.

"The young man"—she picked up a thick file from the top of her stack and opened it—"Xavier Morales, brilliant, so many letters after his name it looks like a screwed-up alphabet. Thus far since his professional career has started he has broken into no less than three commercial companies with names like Microsoft, IBM, and Raytheon. He claims boredom. Main achievement in life, hacked close to a billion dollars from a drug cartel." Alice smiled and closed the folder. "Still, him I can understand. You need an abstract mind to keep up with Europa, I get it."

Niles leaned back as he watched the waters of the floodgates overflow. He pushed two aspirins into his mouth and dry-swallowed them. They caught, he grimaced, but then managed to get them down just as Alice reached for the second file. She eyed Niles as she opened it, waiting to see if his one good eye would flinch.

"Master Chief Harold Jenks, United States Navy, retired. Owner Blacksmith Engineering. Everyone in his own company hates his guts even though he has made all fifty-one employees very wealthy. Ruthless, barbaric, and quite the engineering genius. Here only because he has a fatal attraction with the only woman he has ever been terrified of, our own assistant director. Bottom line: unstable, uncontrollable, and any other 'un' you can think of. Not Department 5656 material, and that is according to your own job description and criteria."

"Okay I—"

Alice politely smiled and held up her hand. "Oh, but there is more Mr. Director. How about a foreign intelligence agent who now has access to the greatest finds in the history of the world? Granted, she's a woman we all like and admire, especially myself."

"Alice, I—"

"And let us not forget our good friend Colonel Henri Farbeaux. Do I need to go into his record?"

"Now that was Jack's idea and you have to admit Henri's already paid dividends for this Group."

"Yes, by getting our other high-risk asset out of Jerusalem, I know. It was me who sent him in as I figured if the Mossad arrested him we weren't at a loss of one of our own." Alice started gathering her files. "You are rushing into this, Niles." She stopped and looked at the director. "All I'm saying is be careful. These new people are brilliant and are capable of good things, but make sure they belong here in the long term and not just for getting Carl back. They need to belong."

Niles decided to let it drop now that he knew that Alice was only voicing his own inner thoughts and venting her fears, which were in line with his own. He watched her as she gave him one last look before patting his arm.

"You look pretty good, by the way. How's your buddy?"

"The president is doing better, and yes, I do feel somewhat . . . well, besides being blinded in my right eye, having a scar on my face the length of Long Island, and knowing that this is the best I'll ever walk again, hell, not bad at all." He gave Alice a sour look as she smiled and turned for the conference room door.

"Could have been worse, Mr. Director. After all you still have your balls, and with these new personnel changes here at Group, you're going to need them."

Niles watched the door close and then he faced the large monitor and the image that was still up. He gave a crazed chuckle and wondered if he was doing the right thing in risking more lives to get one back from the dead.

Alice caught up to Xavier Morales as he just finished his rounds in the computer center. Though quiet and shy he asked very legitimate questions of the one hundred men and women who would be working for him in computer sciences. Most of the apprehension at having someone so young being a department head was tempered by the fact that they had all heard of Xavier Morales, the wunderkind of MIT. Alice watched the young man through the glass and immediately saw that he wasn't dressed as a man of his education would have normally dictated: black tennis shoes and an old checkered button-down shirt. His black hair was neatly combed and in his shy way looked as if he were nothing more than a teenage boy.

Jason Ryan turned and saw Alice standing outside of the large theater-style comp center and then nodded as Morales turned to leave. Jason quickly opened the door for him. Alice greeted the young man and introduced herself again. She looked at Jason and stifled a laugh at his tattooed predicament.

"And I suspect Jason was taking you over to meet Europa face-to-face?" Alice asked. With boredom etching his features, Jason nodded. "Well, you probably have far better things to be doing. I'll take him, I need a word with our new comp genius."

Without a word Ryan hurriedly left toward the bank of elevators so he could get down to logistics where a whole lot of people responsible for this tattoo had better be ready for war.

Alice gestured for Xavier to continue down the same hallway. She noticed the old chair and the strong arms that propelled the young man at a pretty good clip.

"Our engineers can find you something far more advanced than that old chair if you wish," she said, suspecting she already knew the young man's answer.

"And Master Chief Jenks is one of those engineers?"

Alice only raised her lovely brows and smiled.

"No, thank you, Mrs. Hamilton, I was raised in this chair and if I get anything else now I would get lazy and also get no exercise at all." He slowed his pace and then looked at Alice. "Tell me about Professor Ellenshaw."

"Charlie?" A sad and knowing look crossed her features as she adjusted her load of files. "I won't go into detail, but Charlie's had a rough go of it the past three months."

"I understand he was close to Dr. Golding?" Morales asked as he stopped by the double clean room doors and the blue-clad Marine guard standing outside. Xavier removed the new temporary ID card from around his neck and gave it to the guard, who checked it. He nodded at Alice as he gave it back.

"Quite close, rather unexplainable as they were such opposites, a man of science and one who chases dreams and sometimes nightmares . . . yes, they became close because they started out so distantly separate. He's hurting and if he's taken it out on you, I assure I'll speak to him."

"No, no, please, don't do that, Mrs. Hamilton. I have an idea: Would you please give me five minutes with Europa to introduce myself properly, and then would you ask Professor Ellenshaw to join me in the clean room?"

With a curious look Alice just nodded. "Yes, I can do that."

The clean room doors hissed open and Morales smiled as the guard handed him a sealed plastic bag with electrostatic clothing. Morales just shook his head with a polite smile.

"Nah, we don't want to start off like that."

The guard looked at Alice and then saw that the Group matriarch was smiling.

"You heard him, that's no way to meet someone for the first time." Alice nodded at Morales and then left.

The doors hissed closed behind Xavier as he entered the dressing area and then easily went to the last door and opened it. He wheeled himself inside and then turned. The console for Europa was there with six stations. Microphones were at each. The large bulletproof glass stretched fifteen feet across the front. The metal screen protecting the inner sanctum was in the down position so Morales could not see inside. But he knew, or could guess, what was there. Gone were the robotic program placement arms, and in their place would be a series of long glass tubes that contained Europa's bubble memory system of Pete Golding's own design. Morales closed his eyes as he faced the large glass remembering the paper he read from Golding describing the theory of bubble memory cylindrical super-microchip technology. He cleared his throat and a seventy-five-inch monitor lowered automatically from the ceiling. It came to life with a simple screen saver that said DEPARTMENT 5656.

"Hello, Europa," he said as he watched the monitor, hoping to get a verbal response.

"Good afternoon Dr. Morales," said the sexy Marylyn Monroe voice.

"How are you today, Europa?"

Silence.

"I asked how you are?" he repeated as he watched the screen.

"*I am well,*" Europa typed.

Morales only smiled as he approached the first of the six workstations.

"No, you're not well. But we'll get you there." Morales patted the console and then raised the large metal panel. What he saw amazed him. The famous, or was it infamous, Blue Ice system with Pete Golding's own fingerprints on it. The sight was beyond his imaginings. The three-foot-in-diameter tubes were filled with large, slow-moving blue bubbles made of clear silicone—the memory carrying system that Europa could tap into in a millisecond.

"Where have you been all my life?" he asked as he leaned forward to look upon the most beautiful thing he had ever seen.

The door hissed open and Charlie Ellenshaw stood in its opening. His hair was still crazed and his glasses were perched on his forehead. His eyes were red.

"Alice asked me to come and see you," he said with a voice that was deadpan.

Morales looked from the blue-tinted Europa programming room to Charlie.

"Professor, we have a very sick lady here, and according to Colonel Collins and Director Compton, we'll need her services desperately"—he looked at his wristwatch—"in less than three hours. I need your help."

Charlie looked from the newcomer to the inner workings of Europa.

"Pete never worked with Europa while her protective screen was up."

"Why is that, Professor?" Morales asked, not out of politeness at the tall, strange man, but because he really wanted to know.

Charlie took a tentative step into the room and the doors hissed closed behind him, startling the older man. He collected himself and then faced Xavier.

"He said it was rude to see her like that, so he did the polite thing and closed the door, like she was—"

"A lovely lady in a dressing room?"

"Yeah," Charlie said as he looked more closely at the youngest genius outside of Niles Compton he had ever met.

Morales, without looking away from Ellenshaw, hit the button and the protective screen came down.

"Europa, are you there?" he asked as he kept watching Charlie.

"*Yes*," she typed out.

Without facing the screen he asked Ellenshaw, "She texted her answer?"

"Yes."

"See, she's not acting right and I think I can guess as to why. Can you help me, Professor?"

"How?"

"Tell me and Europa about Pete Golding."

"What?" he asked in utter confusion, but sat down in the station next to Morales.

"Europa, can you tell me the disposition of Dr. Peter Golding, please?"

There was silence for the longest time, long enough that Morales turned his wheelchair and removed the rolling chair in front of the empty station and then faced Europa's screen.

"Dr. Golding is currently not on station."

This time both men noticed she spoke instead of texting.

"Do you know why?" he asked.

Silence.

"Europa, have you scanned all personnel records for Department 5656 and any corresponding field report deaths from same?"

Silence.

"Europa?"

"Dr. Peter Golding, deceased ninety-seven days, sixteen hours, fifty-six minutes, plus or minus ten minutes."

Morales turned to face Charlie.

"Tell me about Pete." He smiled and then looked at Europa. "Tell us both about Pete and why he died."

Charlie Ellenshaw was flabbergasted to say the least. He didn't know if he wanted to hit the kid and leave or just stare stupefied. Then he saw the text messages on the screen blink out and then the lights in the clean room dimmed as Europa powered down.

"You see, Charlie, she needs to know also. She knows what death is, but no one ever explained why people have to die. That is messing with her advanced AI systems that only Pete had intimate knowledge of. We both need to know about Dr. Golding, especially her."

Ellenshaw sat silent as he studied the young master of artificial intelligence. He didn't know what to think of the young man and his obvious intellect. Charlie could understand Pete simply because they had fought and been through some of the adventures of a lifetime that challenged them as men, but Morales was someone who lived his life outside of his world through others. Charlie came to the realization that Europa might be no different. He watched Morales as he opened what Ellenshaw knew was Pete's 201 file from personnel. He wrote something down and held it up to the camera so Europa could see it.

"Europa, do you recognize these coordinates?" Morales was patient as the temperamental Europa read what he had written. She typed out that yes, the longitude and latitude were confirmed as the Mount Rose Cemetery in Princeton, New Jersey. "Use your satellite imagery files and bring up an aerial view, please. Zoom in on plot 2343, northeast quadrant of the cemetery." As he waited for the satellite image to boot, Morales looked over at a curious Ellenshaw. "By the way, Professor, your choice of music may not have been likable to certain members of your rescue team, but as a PSYOP distraction I thought 'Sugar, Sugar' was a righteous choice," he said, and then smiled at Charlie, who didn't know if he was joking with him or not. Only Xavier Morales knew that if anyone else asked he would say that he had never heard of the song nor the Archies who performed it before that day in Mexico.

On the large monitor an image of New Jersey exploded to a close-up of the cemetery in question. Soon Charlie was looking at a headstone. The name was there. Peter Golding. The date of his birth and of his death. Then the simple message: "A Friend." Ellenshaw knew the headstone well as he had been the one to place it there. Charles Hindershot Ellenshaw III removed his glasses and stared at the image. Europa was motionless and it seemed even the bubble memory system slowed in its intensity behind the large glass.

Charlie didn't know if it was right, but he started talking and for the next hour and a half Europa and Morales listened to a story about a man's life and his death.

All sixteen department heads were present inside the large conference room. Many of the civilian personnel saw the new additions and politely nodded. They watched as Master Chief Jenks came through the doorway dressed in a lab coat and carrying his newly issued blue coveralls all military personnel wore at Group. Compton was silent for a brief moment.

"Dr. Morales, I assume you have made progress with Europa?"

Xavier didn't understand a thing of what was going on but he nodded and gestured toward Charlie Ellenshaw, who sat silently.

"With the assistance of Professor Ellenshaw, yes, Europa has been enlightened to certain things that had not been adequately explained to her. She is even now absorbing the new data." He partially turned to the large monitor. "Let's see. Europa, are you monitoring the minutes of the current meeting?"

"Yes, Dr. Morales, Europa is recording."

All eyes went to Morales as he smiled when Europa used her voice synthesizer to answer. The familiar sexy voice was greeted with thankful sighs from Niles and Virginia, who knew that if they didn't have a fully functional Europa, what they hoped to do would be impossible.

"Thank you," Niles said.

"She's not there yet, but soon will be as soon as she assimilates certain data."

Niles nodded at Alice Hamilton. She stood and started passing out electronic tablets. "Please keep all written notes confined to these pads. They will be linked directly to Europa. There will be no, I repeat no, handwritten reports to be filed on Operation Traveler. Even if successful, this technology can never be confirmed by any written word. It's just too dangerous."

Silence was the order of the day as everyone accepted the electronic pads.

"Master Chief," Virginia said, taking over after Alice had taken her seat, "you will notice that your first fifteen thousand pages are filled with Einstein's and other noted scientists' theories on time displacement and its quantum limitations—theoretically speaking, of course. Familiarize yourself with them as much as possible. I'm afraid it's quite heavy reading. You will learn why as we go along. You will also see the dossiers on several scientists of German background, familiarize yourself with them also. We need your report on the mechanical and scientific feasibility related to these men and their work to compare with my physics department assessment"—she paused and then went all the way in—"in twelve hours."

"Thrilled," Jenks said, but his eyes did look to the pad and the headings of several of the entries. He had to admit, he didn't believe in the theory, but as an engineer, he was intrigued nonetheless.

"Dr. Morales, you will see the main factor in your upcoming research is the Traveler herself, Moira Mendelsohn; she is your target. You and Europa will dig until you have everything you can find on her. We want the number of hairs on her head if you can get it."

Xavier looked from Director Compton to the young face of a girl in ragged clothing that was now up on the large monitor. She had a sad face and Morales could see that the picture was made by blowing up a section with only her in it.

"If she's alive, find her. Without this woman this operation is done before we ever start," Niles said as he pulled a chart out from his stack of papers. He nodded at Virginia to conclude her brief.

"All departments, historical and sciences, will be coordinating with Alice and she will correlate any and all information. Colonel Farbeaux, you are well versed in the German language and have tactical military training, which could become useful. You will be attached to the security department answerable to Commander Ryan and Captain Mendenhall for the duration. You will be included on any field operation if called upon for same," Virginia said as all the eyes in the room watched the Frenchman. They waited for the witty rebuke that they knew would be forthcoming. There was none, just a raised right brow as he sat silent.

All sixteen department heads nodded their understanding. Virginia looked at Jenks as she sat back down on Niles's left. The director cleared his throat.

"Professor Ellenshaw, you have been kept as a part of the team for the simple reason you knew about it from Pete Golding, when the operation was first discussed over a year ago during our search for the alien power plant and its theoretical time warp capabilities. Now that we have proof other than the alien aspect"—Niles paused as Anya Korvesky entered the conference room and then sat next to Will Mendenhall—"that was provided by our asset in Israel, you are retained to be the historical expert on this mission. For the time being the Paleolithic aspects concerning the history of Antarctica: animal life, human or subhuman habitation, and its environment. We will get you assistance if and when we have need for more advanced theory on the continent that existed over two hundred and fifty thousand years ago."

Charlie nodded. "I request a geologist to assist me as we will need a complete geological makeup of the continent at the time in question. May I suggest Lieutenant McIntire and her geology department?"

"Agreed," Jack said as he looked over at Sarah. She was typing furiously on her electronic pad. "But as we discussed, no one outside of the complex is to be aware of what it is we are researching. Everything is on a need-to-know basis where inquiries are made to outside sources."

"Oh, yeah, need to know, that's always a good thing," Jenks said with a huff.

"Dr. Morales," Niles said, ignoring the pessimistic master chief as best he could, "we need that report on the Traveler in no less than three hours. Can you give it to us?"

"Europa, have you started collating the data from the file coded 'Traveler'?"

"Three thousand seven hundred and seventy-two historical references to the personages known as 'the Traveler.'"

"Thank you, Europa, complete cycle and we will be with you momentarily." He turned his attention back to Niles and those around him. "We'll give you what we can in one hour, anything later and we would be redundant as I suspect that Europa will have everything on this woman there is to know—if she's still alive, that is. Moira Mendelsohn will soon not have a secret to hide, if she has any."

The conference room went silent as most sets of eyes went to the large main monitor where a lone picture illuminated the room with her black-and-white shades. The Traveler.

5

THE CONTINENT OF ANTARCTICA, 227,000 B.C.E.

Carl Everett collapsed into the large ferns that lined the game trail. The large rabbit he had trapped was lifeless in his hand as he managed a quick peek onto the game trail he had just left. For the past seven days he ate what was left of his rations from the escape pod and had supplemented that with berries and fruits he wasn't quite sure would poison him or not. He was looking forward to the protein the rabbit would surely give him. His appetite had returned in a most ravenous way after the effects of the over-oxygenated air had subsided to the point that his body slowly became used to the pristine air of an earlier world.

"Come on, where are you?" he asked no one. He examined the game trail but failed to see the large animal he thought he heard a few moments before. He hadn't seen the beast but he knew it was large enough to send the smaller wildlife scurrying for cover in fright. He placed the rabbit at his feet and covered it with the soft moist earth in case the blood that was on its fur attracted whatever it was that was stalking him. He slowly laid aside the bow and arrows and then withdrew his nine-millimeter Glock from his shoulder holster. He slid the slide back an inch and saw the chambered round. He had four bullets left. He had gone through his entire arsenal in just the first five or six days of this marvelous adventure and he regretted every time he remembered the rookie mistakes in safeguarding his firepower. He had become very efficient with his knife, traps, and his bow and arrows, but soon came to realize just how much he missed his everyday conveniences such as MREs and automatic weapons.

The slow wavelike motion of the earth originated north of him where the skies were black and red. Carl grimaced as the rolling sensation struck and he actually lost his balance as the earthquake shook the area. Mount Erebus was raising her skirt for the third time that day. The great volcano was spewing forth a noxious cloud of methane that seemingly rolled down its slopes and into the dying jungle around the base. The volcano was over a thousand miles away but the effects made it seem just out of view. In the three weeks Carl had been marooned he had calculated that the earth movement occurred far more frequently since the day he had arrived. He knew instinctually that Erebus was close to blowing. The fires caused by the eruptions had burned millions of acres of jungle and were driving the wildlife out of the area.

The earth movement slowed and then dissipated in its snakelike motion toward the east. He lowered his head at the soothing relief he felt when the ground beneath his feet ceased its movement. He knew he felt like all humans did when the only thing you ever trusted in the universe was the earth under your feet. When that was compromised you would lose faith in your abilities to stay alive. He lifted his head just as some very strange ratlike creatures scurried past his feet in flight. He shook his head knowing his clawed adversary was near. He had soon learned that every species of animal alive at this time had either very large teeth or equally large claws—and they used them with great advantage. He was but a puppy in a savage world never meant for mankind.

He sniffed the air and that was when he caught the scent of the animal as it crept closer. He cocked the nine millimeter and waited.

Suddenly the green foliage parted with a crash not thirty yards to his front. His eyes widened when he saw a large flock of chickenlike rocs as they broke cover. The eleven-foot-tall birds were flightless but made up for that deficiency with their strong legs and fierce claws and beaks. The very large rooster at the head of the charge swerved to the left, quickly followed by five others. Then a hen broke cover just as a loud and fierce scream of an animal Carl had yet to see in action chased a smaller roc that exited the jungle just behind its mother. This one was followed by a second youngling. This was a red-hooded rooster that was close to full grown. It swept quickly to the right to avoid something that crashed through the jungle just behind it. The rocs as a whole started their high-pitched screams as the terror was seen for the first time. The small, useless wings of the rooster flared as four giant claws struck out just as the beast broke cover as the flock reached safety on the far side of the small clearing only fifteen yards from where Carl huddled with his forgotten lunch. The claws raked the roc on its left flank and the bird went down. Before the roc could react and recover, the giant black panther was upon it. The cat was no less than seven hundred pounds and was the first of this species Carl had seen in his three weeks here. The panther's green emerald eyes flared with the brightness of the night stars as it placed its foreclaws on the injured bird and then screamed in triumph at its fallen prey.

For many days to come Everett could not figure out why he did what he did that day. For a reason that was now unfathomable he grew angry and decided that enough was enough. He was no longer going to allow the animal life of this screwed-up time to scare him to death. He stood and slowly stepped into the open.

"Get off of him!" he called out as he raised the nine millimeter and advanced.

The panther was taken by surprise and turned and screamed. The cry was so loud it made Carl squint and then wince as the angered cry shook the jungle around him. The smaller roc was trying desperately to gain its feet but the massive claws of the cat held it firmly in place as it spit its anger at the small man walking toward it. Everett saw the desperation in the roc's actions as it struggled and that struggle struck a chord with him. He felt he was once more doing his job, and that job was to stop the bad guys from winning. Not for the love of the aggressive giant chickens, but because he just didn't like the panther.

The black coat was thick and it shone within the confines of the darkened jungle with a luminescence that was surreal. The coat shimmered as the enormous muscles of the animal flexed and braced for a jump that would quickly carry it to this small threat coming at it.

"Come on, you son of a bitch. I'll dance with ya."

The giant cat screamed as it used the smaller body of the roc as a springboard for launching itself at the man.

Carl saw the animal was far faster than he could ever have realized. It was airborne before he could bring the pistol into action. He actually felt the onrush of air as the beast launched. He tried to fire but quickly realized he would never get the weapon up fast enough. So much for being the new sheriff in town.

The injured roc used its long neck to twist with lightning speed just as the relief of weight was off of its feathered body. The large parrotlike beak shot forward and grabbed the cat's left hind leg just as it was free. The beast was halted in mid-jump and quickly twisted its large frame to turn and swipe at the downed roc. Everett saw the advantage that the young bird had given him. He raised the Glock and fired once, hitting the cat in the side of its head. Carl's eyes widened when he saw the panther flinch only momentarily as the round struck its skull and ricocheted off into the jungle. The cat didn't even scream. It just slowly turned its head to face Carl and hiss. It swiped one last time at the fallen roc, who relinquished its powerful beak after the claws slammed into its hard surface. The roc's head was slammed into the jungle floor where it went still. The cat shook free of the now limp roc and advanced on Everett.

Carl fired the second of his four rounds and the bullet struck the panther in the right front leg. This time the bullet lodged itself in the beefy part of the forearm but didn't slow the deliberate pace the panther kept to reach its antagonist. Its body went low to the ground in a stalking position. The rear legs bunched for a final jump. Carl fired again. This time the round hit the beast in the chest and the cat recoiled in pain but quickly recovered.

"Uh-oh," Carl said as he knew he was down to the last bullet in the world and was afraid this one would be just as ineffective as the first three.

He aimed just as the panther sprang. The bullet hit the beast in the nose. This time there was a great spray of blood but he knew that the last bullet would not stop the great cat from its mission to shred him to pieces. The panther's teeth were a few inches from his throat when its forward momentum came to a crashing and bone-crunching stop. Carl hit the ground and then rolled away as the full bulk of the cat came crashing down. His eyes widened when he saw the beak of the large roc had been sunk deep into the panther's back, snapping its spine like a piece of brittle driftwood. The young rooster twisted its head until it felt the satisfying crunch of more bone and this time the cat, paralyzed, couldn't even scream. The roc actually dragged the large panther backward until it was satisfied that the animal could no longer do it harm. The enormous clawed feet of the bird were perched triumphantly upon the shiny coat of the black panther as it raised its bloody beak to the sky and flapped its small wings as it screamed to the heavens, informing whoever was up there that the young rooster had triumphed over the great cat.

Carl finally managed to slow his heart rate as he watched the scene before him. The young roc lowered its head and nudged the now dead panther with its newly battle-scarred beak. The wound to its body was bleeding but Carl knew the giant bird would not feel it for a while. He could see the youngling was in a mood that would last until its adrenal glands emptied.

Everett took a deep breath and then rolled onto his back and looked up at the ash-laden skies above the central plain of Antarctica. That was when a giant beak flared overhead and he was suddenly looking into the yellow eyes of the large rooster that had been leading the headlong flight of the flock. The roc hissed as it opened its beak to bite Carl's face off.

He heard the scream of the smaller rooster, and then the face and beak of the larger bird was knocked from view. Carl rolled until he was safely in the bush once again. He finally braved a look up and the sight froze him. The roc he had saved was standing over its fallen alpha male. The larger roc tried to stand but the smaller rooster had found some of its sand and angrily hissed at the patriarch of the flock. The large bird scrambled to its clawed feet and then hissed back, but Carl noticed its superior enthusiasm had vanished. With a last look at Everett, the large rooster broke and ran.

The smaller roc watched the quieting jungle for a moment and then its yellow eyes traveled to Carl. It turned its large red-feathered head to the side and examined the creature that had saved it from a horrid death. It slowly raised its small wings and flapped them three times. It continued to watch the human as it flicked its eyes left and right in its examination. Everett could see the slow drip of blood and thought that the wound was survivable. The three deeply etched claw marks on the left side of its beak bespoke of the power of the giant panther's needlelike claws.

With one last look at Everett, the future alpha male of the flock jumped into the bush and quickly vanished, but not before it hurriedly snatched Carl's prized rabbit from the ground.

"Hey!"

All he heard was the crashing of the large redheaded rooster as it made off with his lunch.

UPPER EAST SIDE OF MANHATTAN, NEW YORK

The knock sounded lightly upon the ornate double doors.

"Madam, I have news from Jerusalem."

The clearing of her throat and then the eerie silence from the darkened room meant that his employer had indeed heard what he said. The man swallowed when the twin doors slowly opened. Before they swung completely open he saw the interior lights slowly fade as they were dimmed. He heard the motorized chair as it left the doorway. He stepped inside. He saw the still frame on the large-screen television of Clark Gable's backside as he left Atlanta for the last time in the film *Gone with the Wind*. He saw her as she motored around her desk, shutting down the film by remote control as she did. The desk lamp was off and he could only see the outline of darkness against the drawn shades. She was silent as he stepped into the large study and then turned and pulled the doors closed behind him. His employer was patient as she waited.

"I always stop the film at this spot anyway. I can never stand to hear Vivien Leigh say those damnable words, 'After all, tomorrow is another day!' Such a foolish girl saying something some hack wrote in a book. Not very realistic by literary or even Hollywood standards."

"Yes, Madam, very unrealistic," the man said, facing her as he stood in front of the large desk. He saw her elegant hand reach for the ornate box on her desk and then she pulled out a cigarette and lit it. The smoke clouded the man's view even further. "Our contact in Jerusalem reports that the Mossad may have leaked your file to an outside source."

There was silence as the woman in the darkness smoked and listened. He became uncomfortable during the drawn-out silence. Finally he could see her silhouette as she placed the cigarette in an ashtray.

"I thought we hadn't any more contacts in the government?"

"He reported out of loyalty, even though he has not been paid in over five years. He said he owed you for past services."

"A kind euphemism for past bribes. Well, if it eases his conscience, who am I to argue?" Again she retrieved her cigarette and smoked.

"We haven't the contacts to pursue any intelligence on who received the file. We won't know who has it until someone comes knocking on the door."

"The Mossad has little interest in me any longer. They couldn't get any information from me for seventy years, so perhaps they have contracted out for their intelligence gathering."

"You know the Mossad doesn't contract out to anyone. I have been informed by that same asset that is so loyal to you that a General Shamni, head of the Israeli intelligence service, has been sacked by the prime minister. The rumor is he allowed an intelligence asset important to the state to flee the country."

"Sounds like our little secret may have leaked out somehow. And all this time I thought they and others had forgotten about us." She placed the cigarette down into the ashtray once more and then switched on the lamp that sat on the desk's polished top.

The man saw her clearly in the light. The ornate motorized wheelchair moved and she came from around her desk. She stopped in front of the tall man. Her hair was gray and came to her shoulders and she wore a black mourning dress as she always did. The sleeves were long and her hands were as elegant as ever. He avoided looking at the crooked legs that angled to the right as she sat in her chair. Her face was lined but in the beautiful softness few ladies of her age ever possess. She reached out and took his large hand into hers.

"Alert all of our children and tell them to be aware of busybodies looking for a story." She patted his hand and looked into his brown eyes. He nodded as he knew they hadn't the funds to do anything outside of warning the family that they might have been discovered. They were helpless before the powers that had their information. He covered her petite hand with his own and then his eyes fell on the tattooed number on her white fleshy forearm where the sleeve failed to cover it. The tattoo had not faded with age: 674392. She smiled, removed her hand, and motored back to her desk and then smoked as she watched him. She slowly reached out and turned off the desk lamp. "I'm in the mood for a musical. All of this drama has drained me."

"Yes, Madam," he said as he started to turn away.

"Julien, tell the children not to be frightened by this. Remind them all they have been through worse."

"I will, Madam," he said as he opened the double doors and then left her study. He paused as he made sure the doors were closed as he heard the video player start once more. This time it sounded like Fred Astaire singing an opening number.

The man stepped away and then pulled up his coat's sleeve and saw his own numbered tattoo and sighed. He lowered the sleeve and then went to make 236 phone calls.

The children of the Traveler had to be alerted.

EVENT GROUP COMPLEX, NELLIS AIR FORCE BASE, NEVADA

Jack waited with Niles Compton inside the conference room. They were alone for the moment.

"When and if we find who we are looking for, that's when the expenditures of manpower and funding will be noticeable. I figure we'll need the full one-hundred-hour grace period the president promised. I figure we'll be stepping on the toes of more than just one agency here. We could possibly make enemies for the president without him even knowing we made them."

"At least for a hundred hours," Compton countered. "Look, Jack, if we get this one chance at getting Carl home I'm willing to alienate far more than just my best friend, I'm willing to put my career on the line."

"This is the wildest long shot we've ever taken, a Hail Mary without much hope the ball will ever come down. But it's the only shot we have. All other areas of investigation have run into a brick wall. Other than the alien technology we no longer have access to, we have nothing other than this Traveler story we have yet to even confirm."

Niles took a deep breath and then fixed Jack with his one-eyed gaze. "Anya seems convinced that the Mossad believed the tale. Enough so they detained her brother after the war for further interrogation, what they euphemistically call a debrief. If a hard-nosed organization like them believe her story, then we have to give it due credence." Niles shook his head and looked at the wall clock just as the conference room door opened and Xavier Morales and the rest of the team started to filter in. Niles slowly made his way over to the conference table.

Virginia sat and then nodded and pushed a sheaf of paperwork toward the director.

"Dr. Morales, we don't have much time. What have you come up with?" Compton asked.

"Actually, Moira Mendelsohn was quite easily traced. She was at one time listed in *Forbes* magazine as one of the top-ten richest women in the world. She hasn't been listed since 1972, but she *was* listed."

"Is she still alive?" Charlie asked.

"Very much so, at least as far as the latest New York City census."

"You mean she lives here?" Niles asked.

"Yes, sir, she immigrated to the United States in 1950 from Jerusalem where she lived right under the noses of Israeli intelligence. Her ten American companies at one time owned seventy-six electronic and light-emitting patents." Xavier looked at his electronic pad and then looked up. "As far as Europa can tell, Miss Mendelsohn spent no less than three fortunes on philanthropic endeavors."

"Such as?" Alice asked.

"Scholarships mostly. Grants to the poor and immigrants for educational opportunities. She's garnered so many accolades from the New York City establishment that she's highly thought of. But she has become reclusive in her later years."

"Excuse me," Master Chief Jenks interrupted. "You say she owned patents on light-emitting technology?"

Xavier spoke softly. "Europa, place the patents for Weisberg Industries on the main screen, please."

On the large monitor Europa placed the listing of all legal patents held by the company. Jenks looked at the list and then compared it to his notes on his own electronic pad.

"Lasers and lens grinding. Those stand out. Also the power distribution nodes." He thought a moment.

"Master Chief?" Niles said as Jenks was deep in thought.

He had read as much as he could on Einstein's theories about time displacement and saw that what was on the patents list would be required elements to any attempt at what these maniacs would expect for an experimentation at quantum displacement. He shook his head.

"A laser system and power production technology the likes of which we have never before seen would be needed in any attempt at what you are suggesting."

Everyone in the room got that same feeling of discovery when something uncovered made sense to their trains of investigation. They sensed they had a strong lead.

"Would this interest you, Chief?" Xavier said as Europa placed one more item on the list.

"That's Master Chief, boy."

"Yes, sorry, I have yet to get a feel for military etiquette."

Jenks grumbled but looked at the item listed on the monitor.

"Industrial-grade blue diamonds. They seemed to be a vital part of whatever they were doing, and then the supply dwindled to nothing and that was the end of their collecting blue diamonds."

Jenks looked at the new kid on the block and thought he might have something.

"That makes sense," Jenks said, surrendering to the enthusiasm of the combined Group. As he stood and made his way to the monitor, Virginia saw what the master chief was seeing only because it was her area of expertise. "Industrial blue diamonds have become very hard to come by these days. It makes sense that these people had to come up with an alternate light source—"

"Lasers," Virginia finished for him.

"That's right, Slim, lasers, and specially ground lenses for those lasers."

Niles cringed at the cavalier way Jenks spoke to his assistant director, but Virginia seemed like a schoolgirl when it came to the brutish little engineer. She was smiling as he looked at her.

"That coupled with the massive power they were obviously seeking, well, I have to admit you may have something for your ridiculous theories department." The master chief snorted and then placed the dead cigar in his mouth and went back to his seat. Virginia winked at him and he looked away embarrassed.

"Any major holdings as far as laboratory or manufacturing concerns?" Niles asked Xavier.

"Not really. Most have been sold off as the fortunes of the company plummeted in the late seventies."

"You mean with all of these patents the company failed?"

"Europa could find no clear-cut reasoning behind that failure except for poor management. The income the last few years has been royalty-based percentages. Still, our lady friend brings in no less than one hundred and ten million dollars a year on those royalties alone."

"So, no manufacturing at all since?" Niles asked, intriguing Xavier to finish his assessment. He was amazed at how quickly the young genius had assimilated into the style of investigation. He suspected that Europa might be teaching him as much as he was her.

"Nineteen seventy-two as far as we can see. However"—Xavier noted one variance as he ordered Europa to place a slide onto the screen—"we did find this."

On the screen an aerial view of a waterfront appeared. There were rows upon rows of warehouse-type buildings facing what looked like dry dock areas. The view was of an old system of buildings. Europa zoomed the satellite view until they were looking at a single building. It was long and made of redbrick. The facade was ancient and looked unkempt. On the photo they did see one curious thing. There was a guard shack just in front of the main entrance and they counted no less than five guards. That caught Jack's attention as he now knew what set of buildings they were looking at. But Master Chief Jenks beat him to it as he had spent a good portion of his naval career in and around that old facility.

"The Brooklyn Navy Yard," Jenks said as he examined the photo intel.

"Precisely, Chief . . . ur . . . uh, Master Chief," Xavier corrected himself before the brutish little man did the honors. "Building one-seventeen. The absolute only property holding outside of her East Side apartment building."

"For an old building they seem to have a lot of security," Farbeaux said as he studied the picture. "I have had dealings in the navy yard. At all points entering the property there are posted guards, so why does this particular building need the extra protection? My bad-guy senses are intrigued."

"I assume we can locate our Miss Mendelsohn?" Niles asked.

"She's lived in the same building since 1955," Xavier quickly answered.

Jack Collins stood up from his chair and nodded at the director. "Henri, you just named your own poison. Captain Mendenhall, you come with us. Commander Ryan, watch the shop since you tend to stand out in a crowd lately."

Ryan looked over at Mendenhall, who could see he was about to explode. But he just nodded instead.

"Master Chief, since you speak both English *and* egghead, we may need your opinion in case we do dig up something. I would rather have a firsthand opinion than wait for you to examine pictures."

"Lovely. I was hoping my second-language course would pay off someday."

"And where will we be off to?" the Frenchman asked as he, too, slowly stood.

"To meet the woman they call the Traveler."

Farbeaux slowly shook his head. "At the very least this will be interesting."

The Event Group had a very large lead indeed.

UPPER EAST SIDE OF MANHATTAN, NEW YORK

Mendenhall paid the cabdriver an hour after landing at LaGuardia Airport. He joined Jack, Farbeaux, and Jenks as they stood before the redbrick monolith that was the Grenada Building. When away from Virginia and free of the sterile Event Group complex Jenks was free to puff away on a cigar. He glanced upward and then looked away, tossing the stub of the cigar into the gutter, which elicited a sour look from a passing woman and her snotty little white dog.

"I don't know about you girl scouts, but my hackles have just risen."

"Yeah, they've been eyeing us since the cab pulled up." Jack looked at Henri.

"You get the feeling that someone may have been expecting company?"

"If they were, the only way it could have leaked that we were looking for the Traveler was through Anya. You don't think she would be on both sides of the playing field, do you?" Mendenhall asked, wishing Collins would have allowed them to bring firearms, but the colonel had insisted they leave them on the Air Force Lear Jet waiting back at LaGuardia.

"No, not with what she has been through with her own people. I've noticed the Israelis for the most part have been very unforgiving of late for mistrust, and I believe being caught with classified intelligence, no matter how old, can make you vanish very quickly in Tel Aviv. No, that's a woman in love."

Jack looked at Farbeaux as he walked past the three heading toward the covered awning of the front portico. "That your expert opinion, Colonel?"

Farbeaux smiled as he caught the reference to Sarah McIntire.

"On the Israeli attitude of the equation, yes, on the love side, believe me, I'm only guessing." He smiled with more enthusiasm when Jack paused and looked at him. "As we all are."

Collins, like Henri seconds before, caught the innuendo. He decided to let it go. He walked to the steps and went up to the glass and wood front doors.

Jenks stopped by Farbeaux's side.

"Someday I think you're going to press the wrong buttons on Patton there and something bad may ensue." Jenks eyed the Frenchman.

"Ah, you mean he has a breaking point for someone he loves? Like you and your"—he smiled even wider than before—"boat?"

"You son of a bitch, I am gonna—"

The doors opened, silencing Jenks as he watched Henri and then a curious Mendenhall take the steps. He angrily followed.

The man standing at the open door wore a black suit jacket and black turtleneck shirt underneath. His beard was closely kept and his brown eyes took in the men at the door. Jack saw his eyes wander to their waistlines and then examine them for any bulges that would mark them as armed. The man stood there, not saying a word of greeting.

"We have come to see Ms. Moira Mendelsohn," Jack said as he sized up the large man in the doorway. He was stout and would be a hard candidate to get through.

"Madam receives absolutely no visitors, I am sorry. Leave a name and note and if she wishes to get back to you, she will. Good day."

The door started to close but it was Henri who acted first and placed a hand on the old leaded glass of the door.

"She'll wish to see us," Farbeaux said as he eyed the man blocking their way.

"And this is so because?" the man asked, amused at the blond man who thought his hand could stop him from closing the door. He huffed as he took in Henri.

Collins lowered Farbeaux's hand from the door and looked at the well-dressed man who had a weapon's bulge near his shoulder.

"Inform Ms. Mendelsohn we wish to speak to her about her 'doorway.'"

The man held his blank expression well. He looked unaffected at Jack's comment but there was a noticeable difference. Three more men stepped out from behind the first. The large man turned and looked at the men who had joined him and then nodded that they could return to their duties. He stepped aside and allowed the four men to enter the foyer of the large first floor.

They saw that the entire floor, with the exception of a large desk in the middle, was completely empty. In a city like New York where living space was hard to come by, this place was a gold mine if renovated. Collins had the distinct feeling this Mendelsohn woman didn't care much about that.

"Madam has been expecting you, or someone like you."

The silence from the four men was stark as they waited for the man to finish.

"And why is that?" Mendenhall asked, anxious to discover why they were expected. He was also worried that the colonel might have made a mistake in not allowing them to be armed.

The man ignored Will's question. "Suffice it to say, gentlemen, if you are here for any ill purpose, rest assured you will not leave this residence breathing."

Henri looked at Jack, and Will had to place a hand on Master Chief Jenks's arm as he reacted to the threat. The man did not smile, he did not frown. Jack could see that his threat was just a fact of life.

"We have no ill will toward your employer," Collins said as he looked at the emptiness of the 150-year-old building.

"Follow me please, gentlemen." The large man turned and went toward the old-fashioned gated lift.

"No announcement?" Henri asked as he looked around the closed space of the elevator.

For the first time the man chuckled as he lifted an ancient handle on an even older annunciator and switched the handle to 16.

"Madam knows you are here, she was just curious as to what purpose." The lift started up with a small jolt.

"You know, elevator upgrades are a good thing in our modern world," Will said as he subconsciously grabbed the wooden railing as the lift shook and rattled.

"Madam likes things the way they are. She is quite content." He looked back at Mendenhall. "And our lift system is inspected every six months, so if something happens during your visit it will not be the ancient elevator that kills you."

Jenks had had a bellyful of the two threats made thus far. He stepped toward the front of the elevator car but Jack forced him back by placing a hand on the master chief's barrel chest.

"Virginia specifically told you to behave." He faced Jenks. "I'll tell her if you don't knock it off."

Jenks frowned and then backed away as the elevator came to a stop. The man smiled at Jenks and then stepped off the elevator. He mumbled, "I'm not afraid of her," but not too loudly.

The long hallway was of polished wood. The floors, the walls, and the ceiling were buffed and shined as if polished only this morning. The lone desk just outside the elevator was manned by a younger gentleman in a blue suit. He was writing on a clipboard as he saw the men step from the elevator. He had his jacket unbuttoned and they could all see the Smith & Wesson nine millimeter in a shoulder holster.

"Madam is expecting you," the guard said as he laid the clipboard down and then eyed Collins. "Gentlemen, are you armed?"

"Look, Peaches—" Jenks started to say but stopped when the double wooden doors at the end of the fifty-five-foot hallway opened, and that was when they saw the Traveler for the first time.

"If they wanted to kill me all they would have had to do is spike my weekly order of gin." She motored the wheelchair backward and then opened the doors wider for her guests. "Come in, gentlemen, you are cutting into my motion picture time."

Jack took a breath and followed the trail of birchwood flooring to the main penthouse apartment. The man followed the four to the door and stopped them from entering.

"Madam may take this lightly, but rest assured, gentlemen, we take her security very seriously. Also keep in mind Madam tires easily."

"We understand," Jack said as he turned from the serious-faced young man. "You need to get out more, Master Chief, people usually don't travel long distances to kill an old lady for the sheer fun of it. This isn't Los Angeles."

Jenks walked past with a hard brush, which made the security guard smile and shake his head as he stepped inside and closed the door.

The large entranceway was dark. There was small lines of light that danced with dust particles streaming through the closed curtains. Other than that the only source of light was from the ornate wall sconces that were made sometime in the late 1800s.

"I think this whole building ought to be in one of the director's artifact vaults," Will said as he examined the forty-foot-high ceiling. The absence of the things that made a home was the first thing he noticed. The walls were bare of family photos and art. The rich wood paneling had nothing at all upon their shiny surface. Jack followed the hallway toward the large study. He looked inside and saw the shiny silhouette of the old woman as she placed her wheelchair behind a large desk. The others joined Jack just inside the sliding double doorway.

Henri saw that this room was different from the outer areas. Here there were pictures, old black-and-white photos ensconced in old-fashioned bubble frames. Some were of family but most were of children, two of them in particular. Jack and the others recognized a young Moira Mendelsohn as she was standing next to a small boy with the same color hair and the same soft features of Moira. There were no less than six of these pictures with only the boy and the young woman in them. The rest were old-world European pictures of family that had long since departed this life, one way or the other, in Eastern European standards of the time—especially if you were Jewish or Gypsy or any other malcontent as seen in the eyes of Nazi Germany.

"You must have very strong contacts in the Israeli government to come up with my name, gentlemen." The old woman who looked surprisingly healthy for her eighty-seven years slowly lit a cigarette and then fixed Jack with a kind stare. She gestured to four ornate chairs that had been placed in front of the large desk."Please, I hate people looking down at me . . . have a seat."

"No, Madam Mendelsohn, we do not," Collins said as he took his chair. "What we did have was a frightened woman searching for a man who has been lost. A very good incentive for treason, at least for some."

"Love, while not always sane, is at most times a good reason. Gentlemen, tell me what it is you wish of me. If it's blackmail of some kind, I'm afraid those money years are far behind me, so, what can I do for you?"

"Can you tell us about Professor Lars Thomsen?" Collins asked.

Moira Mendelsohn became silent as she puffed on her cigarette and looked the four men over. Instead of answering she pushed a button on a small device.

"Angela, please bring in some refreshment for our guests."

Collins saw the woman study them as she smoked. She made no attempt to answer Jack's query as she waited.

It wasn't long before the doors were parted and a cart with many bottles on it was rolled in by a petite lady in a nice skirt and blouse.

"Gentlemen, what will you have?"

"Nothing for—" Jack started to say but Henri stopped him.

"I am a man of your own tastes, Madam, I will have a gin and tonic with a twist." He looked at Collins, hoping Jack would catch on that this woman wanted to sit and talk. Not having a drink was an old-fashioned way of saying just hurry up and spill your secrets. Henri knew how to question people to get what he wanted. "Mr. Collins here and the others will have the same."

The old woman nodded toward the woman and she started making ice-clinking noises. When she was done she left the cart, and the bodyguard closed the doors behind her.

"A true cold-blooded son of a bitch."

Jack almost choked on his drink as she said the startling words.

"Excuse me?" he asked when he gained control of his coughing. Then he realized she was just answering his earlier question.

"Thomsen was a sadistic bastard who would do anything to prove his theories correct. Anything." She took a drink of her gin and tonic and then crushed out her cigarette. "But then again you have my debrief file from the Mossad; you know what I said in 1946 about the man. It should come as no surprise that time has not healed all wounds, nor dare I say blurred the memory. It never will." She became still as the four men saw she was deep in thought of the memory of Thomsen and his brutal displacement theories.

"As brutal as this Kraut doc was, did he ever prove what it is he was out to prove?" Jenks asked as he quickly drained his gin and tonic, burped, and then looked at the old woman. She lit another cigarette as the master chief rose and poured his own drink; this time it was forty-year-old whiskey. He returned to his seat and awaited the answer to his question.

"You know he did, at least if you read my file. That is if you believe my tale; the Israeli government did not. They filed it away as insanity brought on by years of incarceration. So, according to the powers that be, I'm insane."

"Are you?" Henri asked, cutting directly to the point.

Moira Mendelsohn laughed out loud and placed the cigarette into a glass ashtray and then clapped her hands together. Even her bodyguard bent over to stifle a laugh.

"Absolutely, certifiably insane." She continued to laugh until finally she had to moisten her throat. She looked at Jenks, drained her own glass, and then held it out for a refill and the bodyguard moved to supply it. He also removed Jenks's glass and refilled it once again.

"We know it worked, Ms. Mendelsohn," Jack said as he placed his glass on the desk and then eased back in his seat. The laughter stopped.

"Blue diamonds, patents on light-emitting technology and power amplification. Yes, we do know you did it, there *and* here."

The old woman looked at Collins and then took a drag off her cigarette. She watched Jack for the longest time—long enough that he thought his abrupt declaration about her involvement had made her scared and thus she'd clam up. Jack decided to push it and nudged Henri's leg and nodded.

"Please, tell us what it is," Farbeaux asked as he took in the shaking fingers of the lady in the expensive wheelchair. "They wouldn't allow you to elaborate during both your British and Israeli debriefs. Once you mentioned what Nazi science was up to their attention span waned somewhat as the Allied mission at the time was solely concentrating on the criminality of Thomsen and his experiments. Am I correct in assuming this—Traveler?"

All of them, the large bodyguard included, stopped and watched the visibly shaken woman. She tried to light another cigarette but then noticed she already had one lit sitting in the ashtray. She closed the top of her decorative cigarette box and then looked away from the men. It took a full minute but she finally turned back.

"I haven't been called that in seventy-four years." Her eyes were downcast as she seemed to be going back to a place she did not care for at all. That was when Will nudged Jack and they all saw the numbered tattoo on her forearm. She made no attempt to hide it when she saw them looking. "Please do not refer to me as . . . well, as that name. It was their name for me, their little code-induced paranoia." She seemed to calm somewhat when she took a large swallow of her drink. The large man came to her side and leaned down close to her face. She whispered that she was all right and patted his thick arm. With a dirty look at the four visitors, the man made his way to the back of the study and waited in the shadows.

"Did his theory work?" Jenks persisted, suspecting that the truth of this historical farce would soon be disclosed by the very woman who began the rumors over seventy years before.

"Yes, six times."

The silence that greeted her comment seemed to go on forever. The only thing that happened was a frown from the large bodyguard as he suddenly turned and left the study, closing the doors behind him. "Gentlemen, please, what is it you want of me *and* the Wellsian Doorway?"

"Wellsian Doorway?" Jack asked.

"Yes, their euphemism for the one and only time machine ever constructed. And, yes, it worked. Personally I believe H. G. Wells would roll over in his grave to know the Nazis had crowned their scientific achievement by naming their machine after him. But the Nazis didn't care for much, as history tells you. As for me, I learned it firsthand."

"Six times you traveled?" Jenks asked, still not believing.

They all saw the hesitant action of Moira as she puffed her cigarette and looked upon her questioners. It was the question posed by Jenks that made her hesitant.

"Yes, six times I traveled two years into the past. Same space, differing times."

Jenks looked at Jack and rolled his eyes.

"Impossible," the master chief said, not caring what Collins or the others thought. He was an engineer and if someone told you about the impossible you had to go with what you knew.

"Yes, it was impossible, until it wasn't," she said as she again crushed out her cigarette. "The theory has always been sound, but having the equipment, and for that equipment to be placed at the right time is the key. Without two corresponding doorways, there is no displacement. The link between time and space has to meet and you need a doorway to do that. And the doorway can only be placed in the past, or otherwise just how are you going to build a doorway in a past that has already happened?"

"In other words you're saying that in order to time travel successfully you need to have built an identical doorway to the one you are using. Without that . . . ?"

She looked at Jack and smiled. "You would end up anywhere but where it is you wanted to be. Even another dimension. The possibilities are endless and unfathomable."

"You duplicated the experiments, didn't you?" Henri asked, pushing just a little more.

Again Moira became silent as she watched the men before her.

"I sense you are not bad men." She looked at Henri for a moment longer than the others. "Not all bad anyway," she finished as Henri smiled and winked at the old woman. "What do you want the Wellsian Doorway for? If it's a military application, I would just as soon blow my own brains out than to have that happen again."

"We lost someone," Jack said. "A friend."

Moira listened as Jack explained for a few moments. She turned her chair away from them as she thought about their lost friend.

"I'm sorry, gentlemen, but your friend will forever remain lost to you."

Before she explained both Jenks and Jack saw the flaw in what they were asking.

"We don't have a doorway in the past for us to lock on to," Collins rightly guessed at her answer just as his hopes deflated. Jenks was thinking another way but remained quiet.

"I am so sorry."

Henri wasn't in the least defeated.

"Can you tell us what it is you have hidden at the Brooklyn Navy Yard, building number one-seventeen, the one with the inordinate amount of protection?"

She smiled at Farbeaux, knowing she had pegged the man correctly. He was a cad and a bounder and she immediately liked the Frenchman.

"You *are* government, aren't you?"

"Yes, but we are *your* government. And if we ever have an opportunity to prove this displacement correct, it would be used once and destroyed, as per orders from our director."

She laughed heartily. She stopped and fixed Jack with a glaring look.

"Then your director must be a highly unusual man to throw away such power."

"He is," Jack and Will said at the same time.

"Such loyalty gives a man great power when his subordinates love him so much." She smiled again as she lit her fourth cigarette. "Much like another man in history—he had loyal followers, too."

"Madam, our director, how can I explain this? Well, he's no Adolf Hitler. He can sure as hell come down on you sometimes, but he is the best man outside of this room that I have ever known," Will said as the old woman looked at Jack, knowing the young black man was referencing not only their director, but the big man sitting right in front of her. She took up the old-fashioned phone receiver that looked as if it could be used as a lethal bludgeon and made a connection.

"Peter, yes, I will have four men stopping by this afternoon. Allow them total access to building one-seventeen, please. Full cooperation will be given. Thank you." She hung up and then fixed Jack with her stern look. "I know how it is to lose someone who is close to you and cannot get them back. I know, I have tried on more than those six occasions you mentioned. But since you cannot make any attempt for displacement without a second doorway, I see no harm in allowing you to see it."

"See what?" Mendenhall asked.

Moira Mendelsohn started the silent electric motor on her wheelchair and then made her way to the door, which magically opened as she gestured that their appointment time was up. She did turn and smile as she waited next to the guard. "To see what it is you came to see, gentlemen."

The four men stood as they knew they were being asked to leave.

"And that is?" the master chief asked gruffly as he placed a cold cigar into his mouth.

"Why, my own Wellsian Doorway, of course."

Jenks smiled as did the others with the exception of Collins. For Jack suspected that without a second doorway the mission was lost to them. But Jenks couldn't contain his enjoyment.

"Now this I have to see."

6

BROOKLYN NAVY YARD, BROOKLYN, NEW YORK (BUILDING 117)

They passed through the main gate of the old navy yard, a starting point for hundreds of thousands of American troops in two world wars and was the building site for some of the most famous warships this nation has ever produced. From heavy cruisers to battleships, the navy yard had seen it all, but in 1966 the Department of the Navy decommissioned the yard and she had fallen on hard times since. The yard was now in the middle of a preservation fight and was modernizing most of the old buildings where 70,000 workers once made the United States Navy the most powerful afloat.

"I have to admit this place is looking better than it did a few years ago. I almost built USS *Teacher* here but decided New Orleans was better suited to my style," Jenks said, and then looked over at the Frenchman and gave him a dirty look.

"Master Chief, I was never on your marvelously designed boat, but from what the colonel says, it was a real kicker." Henri smiled over at Jenks.

"All right, you two, we'll turn this car right around," Will said, turning in the front seat to face the two opposites.

"Where in the hell is this Julien fellow taking us?" Jack asked as he maneuvered the rental car around a series of old wharves and warehouses.

"Maybe the old woman decided not to be so cooperative," Will said, feeling somewhat better having weapons in the vehicle.

"No, you can see she's been a straight shooter all of her life." Jack looked over at Mendenhall. "Besides, I give anyone who went through what that woman and millions of others went through the benefit of the doubt."

"There it is," Jenks said from the backseat.

Jack saw building 117 through the rain that had just started to fall. Collins hit the pulse wipers and cleared the glass as he pulled in behind the Range Rover. They all watched as Moira's man Julien and two others stepped from the navy blue vehicle. They were met by a uniformed guard and together the four men went to the front of the building.

Jack stepped from the car and as he did he examined the exterior of building 117. It was lined by an old dry dock that might have been used for commercial ships because of its compact size. The building itself was unremarkable. Brick and mortar. The glass windows, about five thousand of them, were all painted over and secured with outside locks. The small arch covering a loading dock and main office entrance had seen far better days as both awnings hung limp and shredded. The building wasn't one of the oldest built in 1806 when the yard first opened, but it was in the same century range.

Collins stood in the lightly falling rain and then saw the old dry dock area next to the building. He saw the pile of bricks next to the water and walked the few feet over and then knelt down. Weeds had covered most of the fallen brick but Jack managed to tear some of this loose. Underneath he saw an old green-tarnished bronze plaque and he leaned closer. He removed a handkerchief from his coat pocket and brushed away years of grime that had covered the words.

ATTENTION

ON THIS DAY OF SEPTEMBER 21, 1864

COMMISSIONING CEREMONIES WERE CONDUCTED FOR

U.S.S. ARGO

MONITOR CLASS VESSEL

Jack pulled the kerchief away and then smiled and shook his head. He remembered the tale as told to him by Niles Compton and Garrison Lee over ten years before. He stood up and wiped his hands.

"What is it, Colonel?" Mendenhall asked as he stepped up to see what had interested Collins.

"Nothing, just a coincidence, a strange coincidence, but one nonetheless." With one last look at the old and forgotten plaque, Jack made a promise to have the dry dock marker removed back to the complex—it needed to go home.

As Collins turned away, Mendenhall saw what he had been studying. He raised a brow, confused, and then followed Jack to the front doors.

"Well, shall we see what there is to see?" Jack said as he moved to the steps that led upward toward the office.

The uniformed guard held the door open for the four men as they entered. The rain started falling harder and the guard quickly closed the door. All four turned as one when they heard the outside locks being engaged.

"The building is secured on the outside and inside at all times," Julien said as he stood before a large aluminum door.

"Yeah, and what does the New York City fire department have to say about locking folks inside a dilapidated building?"

"They say nothing, because we have paid millions in bribes to keep them from saying anything," Julien answered as he gave Jenks a curious look, as if bribery was an everyday occurrence.

"Oh," was all he said.

The large man was joined by his two companions and together they unlocked the aluminum door, and then one hit a large red button and the door began to go up. Jack and Henri both noticed that all three men stepped away from the darkness beyond the door as it rose. Julien in particular looked as uncomfortable as any man Jack had seen opening a door. He and Henri exchanged questioning looks.

Julien swallowed and then reached into the darkness and switched on a light. He quickly pulled his hand out and then faced the four men.

"Through the door and down the stairs, two flights." He handed Jack a set of two keys. "One opens the work areas, the other the main laboratory; you'll know which. The noise you'll hear are the pumps needed to keep the basement and subbasement clear of water from the river and dry dock area. You have thirty minutes."

"You and your men aren't accompanying us?"

Julien's try at a cocky smile failed on the large man. "No, uh, we are not allowed."

The four men watched as the large personal protector of Moira Mendelsohn and his men left for the front of the building.

Jack didn't have to comment on the strangeness of the three men—they just moved into the room and down the two flights of stairs.

Jack used the first key and unlocked the large steel door at the bottom of the stairs. The hallway was lined with other, larger doors for allowing heavy equipment to be moved in. There was even a large lift that rose the three flights. They all heard the continuous dripping of water as it seeped through from the rain outside and the river and its constant assault on the old navy yard.

Jack opened the door and the lights inside automatically flared to life.

The sight that greeted them nearly caught them all off guard. The brightness and cleanliness of the giant space amazed them. With the exception of the two inches of water they found themselves standing in, the home of the Wellsian Doorway looked as if it popped right out of a science fiction movie. They were in a circular room that sat elevated above an amphitheater-style laboratory. Circular row upon circular row of electronic panels and technician's stations sat empty as all stations looked down upon a round blank spot made of steel.

"The damn thing isn't here!" Jenks said as he angrily tossed his cigar into the water at his feet. "I should have known the old dame was nuttier than the Frenchman here."

Henri smiled over at the master chief.

Jack shook his head and then moved to the main monitoring station in the center of the first console. He saw the plastic cover that was marked simply "PIT." He took the second key and lifted the cover and inserted it. He twisted the key and suddenly the lights dimmed and an amazing sight met their astonished gaze.

The center of the floor started twisting in a corkscrew fashion and as it did the edges slid into the wall. Fluorescent and indirect lighting started to flare to life far below them. Jack smiled as the circular floor spiraled away to nothing. The difference was that the giant room below was as clean as if it had been built yesterday. There was no water anywhere in the spaces below. That was where most of the powerful pumps were stored.

"I'll be damned and buggered," the master chief exclaimed as he stepped toward the glass.

"Okay, I think I made a little pee pee here," Will said as all eyes fell on the machine that occupied the center of the room.

Spotlights came on and their adjusted beams sliced through the darkness and fell upon a gleaming chromed steel and glass sphere. It was open to the air but the glass enclosure was made to reflect something back into the large, sixty-five-foot object.

"Look, there are laser amplifiers and portals all aimed at the inside of the . . . the—"

"Wellsian Doorway I believe are the words you are looking for, Master Chief," Henri said as he too had to step forward to see the giant ball of glass and shiny steel.

"Yeah, I guess that's what you would call it," Jenks mumbled as he took it all in two stories below them.

"Look inside the sphere," Will said as he stood next to Collins.

"Oh, my," Henri said as they all saw the same thing.

"Are those?"

Jack had to chuckle.

"Seats. I count twenty of them."

The four men were actually shocked that what they had desired to see was actually there.

"I don't believe the old broad built the damn thing," Jenks grumbled.

Henri looked at Jack and they both thought the same thing at the same moment but it was Jack who faced the machine below and voiced it.

"Yes, Master Chief, she did build it." He faced the men in the control room. "The real question is, why did she build it?"

Jenks, Will, and Henri all looked at the amazing piece of equipment below and the question hung in the air like a guillotine. The four men were silent as they tried to take in the ramifications of what was represented below. Jenks popped a fresh cigar in his mouth and articulated the moment with vivid verb.

"A goddamned time machine."

PART TWO

THE TIME MACHINE

There are really four dimensions, three which we call the three planes of Space, and a fourth, Time.

—**H. G. Wells,** ***The Time Machine***

7

The old and shattered camp was the fifth one Everett had come across since he had found himself hundreds of thousands of years in the past. Military equipment that should not be here was strewn haphazardly around a small clearing. Vines and other vegetation had grown around and through the rusty and shattered tools of military conquest. This camp was far different from the four he had discovered in the days before. This was what he knew to be a Roman stockade. He had done his Annapolis dissertation on Roman tactics during that empire's reign throughout history. Everywhere there were rusty and broken swords. Spears with their shafts shattered. Helmets, rotted red cloaks, and the remains of many campfires. But strangest of all was the semi-modern Japanese equipment lying about, intermingled with ancient Roman gear.

"What the hell was this?" he asked himself as he examined the two very different sets of finds. He checked the more modern Japanese rifles and saw that none of them had ammunition, a sorrowful discovery that lessened his chances of living through this. He tossed a broken bolt-action rifle down and then looked around the eerie setting. No remains were evident as he scanned the area with his bow at the ready.

Suddenly a memory occurred to him that had skipped his train of thought. He now remembered Sarah's discovery during the search for the alien power plant that the Iranians had conducted experiments with the dimensional wormholes and had disrupted time to the point that they had succeeded in snatching Roman, Japanese, and even Chinese troops from their own planes of existence. These must be the remains of those lost souls. As he looked around the stockade he came to the conclusion that these differing warring entities came together for a common cause called survival. And from the looks of the stockade that mission failed and failed big time.

His boot kicked at a small bush that had entwined itself around an object that was solid. He reached down and cleared away the undergrowth and then his eyes widened in surprise. He lifted the heavy piece and examined it with a smile, knowing that the theory about the Iranian experiments were accurate. In his hands was that proof. The large golden eagle was ornate and tinged with mold but was otherwise intact. The shaft that once attached the eagle had long since vanished but the object was as familiar to Everett as his own flag. The Roman numeral for nine, IX, marked the eagle as the standard for the famous and very much ancient Ninth Legion of the Roman Empire. The very same legion that had mysteriously vanished during the occupation of Britain.

Carl allowed the eagle to slide from his hands as he felt the shudder of the earth beneath his feat. As he looked around at the growing darkness, the ashfall began in earnest.

The rumble of Mount Erebus proclaimed that if the animal life in Antarctica didn't get him, the volcano would.

Carl Everett knew that he and the last continent on earth that wasn't frozen over were now living on borrowed time.

Antarctica was beginning its death throes.

EVENT GROUP COMPLEX, NELLIS AIR FORCE BASE, NEVADA

Jason Ryan tugged at the loose-fitting desert BDUs he was issued. Colonel Collins had issued orders that any field teams would go in the guise of Army Corps of Engineers as their cover, thus the desert BDUs with their computer-designed camouflage. He saw his reflection in the white plastic wall of the curving hallway as he made his way to the cafeteria. As well as the blue and red tattoo that seemed to make people, women especially, step a wide path around him, the new military clothing line did not meet with his approval.

He was about to step into the large eating area when he saw something that made him stop at the entrance and watch. The three women moved as if they were in the midst of a prison break. He shook his head as he watched Alice Hamilton, Sarah McIntire, and Anya Korvesky turn a corner heading for the bank of air-cushioned elevators. He started to walk in for his lunch and then decided what he had seen didn't quite look right. He turned away and followed. At the corner he saw them enter the elevator and he watched from the rounded corner as the doors closed. He watched the elevator's annunciator as it traveled down only two levels to nine. He went to the second lift and followed.

The knock on the clean room door brought Xavier Morales's head up. He closed the electronic pad he was using and then looked at Charlie. He shrugged.

"If they don't have clearance they will go away," Ellenshaw said as he turned back to his own electronic pad and perused an old geology report on back-scanner results from the Antarctic.

Suddenly the door buzzed and it slid open.

"I guess whoever it is has the clearance," Morales said as he watched the doorway.

Alice Hamilton smiled as she, Anya, and Sarah walked into the clean room. They had the required antistatic clothing and hairnets, which made them look like nurses. Xavier had reinstituted clean room policy until he got the kinks worked out on the nervous breakdown, as he called it, of Europa.

"Mrs. Hamilton, ladies, what may I help you with?" Xavier asked politely, not liking the smile on the older woman's face.

"Uh, Niles would be hard-pressed to know why you're here," Charlie said timidly.

Alice only smiled and looked at Ellenshaw until he swallowed and turned away. Then Alice placed a hand on Charlie's shoulder and leaned in.

"How many field assignments did I okay with your name on them when you weren't cleared to go?"

Charlie looked at Xavier and half smiled.

"A few," Ellenshaw said.

Alice squeezed a little on his shoulder. "Charlie, how many?"

"Six . . . uh," he said as she squeezed again, the way Garrison taught her a million years before, "Ah, ah, okay, nine, nine."

Alice looked at the two women with her. "Charlie's adventures, I call them." She turned and looked at Xavier. "Hello," she said as she rolled a chair over and sat next to Morales's own wheelchair.

"Mrs. Hamilton, I can guess why you ladies are here. And I have caught up on not only these members and their personnel files, but yours also. 'Perused' may be a better word. But on the advice of Director Compton I spent an inordinate amount of time on *your* particular personnel file, Mrs. Hamilton."

Alice kept the smile on her face but inside she cursed Niles for his vision.

"What you have done for this agency and her charter is nothing short of amazing. You and former Director Lee, you could field volumes of adventure novels, but what you came for today cannot happen. I can guess, from listening to other Group members, and from your file that you are here to represent these ladies and argue that they should be listed on any field team action. That, I dare say, is out of my control."

"We have a large stake in this mission," Anya said, but then stopped when she saw Alice look her way and then imperceptibly shake her head. Anya got the hint. Sarah knew enough in her years at Group to let Alice handle the subversion tactics.

"You want Europa to insert your names into the mission profile if anything is found, right?" Charlie asked, and then looked away when Alice raised her beautiful eyebrow at him. He decided to allow Xavier to try to stop the unstoppable force of the Event Group.

"I believe both Anya and Sarah will complement any field team if and when they are a go," Alice said as she eyed the young Morales. "There was one reason I was onboard when your name came up as a replacement for Pete, and Niles and Jack both agreed."

"Because I'm handsome and the best computer man in the world?" Xavier asked with a wink and a smile.

"No, because you have a soul. You think outside of the box, as they say, as recently demonstrated by your unadvised foray into the world of worldwide drug cartels. You do what you think is right, no matter what the personal danger is to yourself."

Xavier felt the trap as it slowly closed.

"And these ladies have the same right as yourself. They want to be on this mission, but Jack won't allow it because, to tell you the truth, it's just far too hazardous. We feel you can work your way around that stipulation somewhat."

Xavier produced a list from his shirt pocket and then wheeled his chair around and handed the list to Anya. She looked it over and Alice and Sarah both saw the smile start to form on the young Gypsy's mouth.

"What is it?" Sarah asked.

"It's the mission roster that Europa recommended to Niles over an hour ago."

Alice again raised her brows and then accepted the list from Anya. She looked down at the bottom.

"Dr. Morales, Europa has a certain protocol in her system that is basically a countersign to warn someone if the order actually originated with the Cray system." She held out the list and pointed to the lower right-hand corner. "If the recommendation originated with Europa, there would be a series of numbers and code right here." She tapped the lower right-hand corner with an elegant red nail. She looked at Xavier and returned his wry wink.

"It seems I've been caught," Xavier said as he turned toward the glass and the visage of Europa beyond. "You could have said something about the code, Europa," he said, shaking his head.

Europa didn't respond. It sat silent with its billions of bubbles slowly rising and falling in their elongated acrylic tanks.

"What does that mean?" Anya asked as Charlie grimaced.

"It means that our new friend here manually entered the mission roster," Charlie said, knowing what Xavier had done. "If you're caught, Niles will forego the welcoming party for you and turn it into a necktie soiree. He will hang you, Doctor."

For once Alice agreed that Charlie had the right call. Her plan was to seduce the young whiz and then if caught do what she always had, pull rank and then take the responsibility. She handed the mission roster back to Xavier and smiled.

"I'll correct this immediately," was all he said.

"As of this minute, if asked, you will say you were coerced into issuing the roster by me . . . understand, young man?"

Xavier looked at Alice and then just nodded. Anya for her part was more of a romantic and leaned over and pecked the computer genius on the cheek. He smiled in embarrassment.

"Yeah, you'll fit in just fine with us Group of pirates," Sarah said as she, Anya, and Alice left the clean room.

"You may have gained the respect of Alice, Anya, and Sarah, but if Niles finds out you falsified a Europa recommendation, even for Alice, oh, mama!" Charlie hissed.

"In my short years of life on this messed-up planet I have come to one resolute conclusion: never, ever allow rules to get in the way of discovery and investigation. They deserve to go."

Charlie looked at Xavier and had to admit that he might be the answer to the absence of Pete Golding, after all. Pete would have done it without having to be asked by Alice, just as the kid had just done.

"Uh, you didn't falsify my spot on the mission roster, did you?" Ellenshaw asked.

"No, of course not. Dr. Compton specifically called for you to go."

Charlie smiled, feeling his worth.

"He may just be wanting to get rid of you." Ellenshaw lost the smile and then looked toward Europa, unnerved by the comment.

Morales smiled at his small joke.

The three women had stopped just outside of the clean room when they came face-to-face with the tattooed Ryan. He saw the guilty look on Sarah's and Anya's faces but only a wry smile from Alice.

"All right, what's going on?"

"Absolutely nothing, Mr. Ryan," Alice said as she stepped to the side and tried to pass, but Jason stepped to his right and blocked the escape, forcing Anya and Sarah to bump into her backside.

"You're kidding me, right?" he asked as he took a step back so he could see all three faces. "After all of these years you're going to claim that, to me?"

"Mr. Ryan, I assure you that—"

"Save it. Now, what are you doing? Does this have something to do with you three being left off the duty roster?"

"I can most assuredly say not," Alice said as she stared Ryan down.

"Liar, liar, culottes on fire."

"Okay, Mr. Ryan, I want these ladies to have a spot on that roster. They need to be there. Anya in case Carl is not found, Sarah because she knows it's in all probability that Jack won't be coming back. They can handle the danger."

"Alice," Jason said holding his ground. "I was recruited into the Group by men who I respect above all others. If they say to keep something to a minimum, like personnel on a mission, I do it. I found out the hard way that going against the colonel's recommended manpower structure tends to get my ass chewed on, so this is self-preservation."

"Jason—" Sarah started but then stopped when Ryan became angry.

"Listen, the mission will be hazardous enough, and no matter what coercion you just used on the new kid in there, it won't change anything. Dr. Compton will see right through it, and if for some far-out reason he doesn't, Jack will. The answer is no."

"Damn," Alice said as she turned to the two disappointed women.

"He's turned into a snitch for the director," Sarah said, aghast that Ryan, a usual conspirator in crime with the rest of them, had turned his back on the two women.

"It's not Jason, it's Jack." Alice looked at them and then waved them onward. "Come on, ladies, we'll be expected in the director's office at anytime for our royal ass chewing."

"Great," was all Sarah said, knowing Jack would be informed of her crimes against his orders.

BROOKLYN NAVY YARD

The three bodyguards had waited inside the outer office area. The visitors to the doorway had not taken the time to examine the equipment in the PIT, even though the gruff little man with the cigar had thrown a fit when his boss told him to wait on someone named Virginia. The large man, Julien, waited by the doors of the elevator as his cell phone chimed.

"Yes, ma'am," he said as his eyes watched the annunciator above the large elevator rise. "They what? Ma'am, I warned you, the world will find out if we allow this. I will try, Madam." He closed the cell phone and then looked at his two companions and with just a flick of his eyes they knew they had problems. "Madam is about to be taken into custody by federal authorities."

The two men immediately spread out just before the elevator doors opened. The large Julien pulled a nine-millimeter Smith & Wesson from his shoulder holster and waited in front of the doors. They opened just as he cocked the weapon.

It was empty.

He felt the brush of cooler air from behind as the pistol cocked. He felt the pressure of the weapon against the back of his head.

"Now what were you planning to do with this?" the voice said as a hand reached around and removed the nine millimeter from his beefy hand. Will Mendenhall tossed the weapon back to Collins as Henri Farbeaux finished disarming the other two bodyguards.

"We didn't have orders to harm you," Julien said as he was quickly frisked by Will and then pushed over with his two companions.

Jack looked at the weapon Will had tossed to him and ejected the ammunition clip from its handle, but remained silent.

"Madam does not deserve this," Julien said as he lowered his hands when he realized they weren't going to kill him. "She is one of the greatest women of all time, and you have her arrested?"

Jack and the others could see the passion these men had for their matriarch and he respected that. He still remained silent as he studied the three men. After all, this Julien fellow seemed very talkative.

"We were going to ensure the doorway did not fall into government hands. We cannot allow that."

At that moment Jenks stepped through the door that led to the stairwell that the others had used to sneak back up to the main floor when Jack's hackles had risen. He suspected a trap after he had informed Niles to take Moira Mendelsohn into protective custody.

"Oh, so your guesswork paid off. They were going to plant one in our heads."

"No, that is not true. Our orders were to dismantle the laser system, that's all."

Jenks snorted. "Son, it would take their people all of five minutes to design a replacement, a far better one than the original, so what did you hope to accomplish?"

Jack could see the man was caught off guard. Moira and her cohorts never expected the doorway to be discovered, thus their laziness in dismantling it. Now the question was why they were so determined to not only protect the doorway, but the extent they were willing to go to protect Moira Mendelsohn.

Black sedans and vans of every size and shape burst through the Brooklyn Navy Yard gates simultaneously. The guards at the main entrance off of Flushing Avenue caught the civilian guards completely unaware as their cars skidded to a sliding stop. The same happened at the gates fronting the Sands, Cumberland, Vanderbilt, Clinton, and Clymer streets. The entire Brooklyn Navy Yard was secured in less than three minutes. The buildings on the north side of the yard were evacuated and told by the FBI that a major drug raid was in progress.

The men heard the cars as they surrounded the building they were in. Jack looked at Mendenhall and then nodded. Will ejected the clips on the two weapons he had taken from the two other bodyguards and then handed the nine millimeters back to them. Jack did the same with Julien's weapon. His raised brows was the only indication of his confusion.

"Put those away and keep silent. We don't wish you or your employer any harm or legal entanglements. We work for the government, but are not *the* government."

Confusion masked the bearded man's worry.

The door opened and the civilian security guard was moved into the room ahead of three men in navy blue Windbreakers.

"Which one of you is Colonel Collins?" the first of the FBI agents asked, pushing by the guard.

"That would be me," Jack said, turning away from a startled Julien.

"Sir, Special-Agent-in-Charge Williamson is outside and needs a word."

Jack eyed Will and Henri and then made sure they understood that no one, especially the federal agents, would have access to the lower levels of the building. He moved to follow the agent.

"Colonel, how are you?" Special Agent Williamson asked as he stood in the rain with an umbrella over his head.

"Jim, long time," Jack said as he stepped to the nondescript sedan. "All secured?"

"For the moment, until some of these tenants start screaming bloody murder to the NYPD. I figure you have about an hour before lengthy explanations are in order."

Jack nodded and started to explain. "Allow tenants in every area of the yard to return to work, but everything north of Clinton Avenue belongs to us. How much trouble will you be in over this?"

"We had a tip on interstate meth exchange with a possible manufacturing point here in Brooklyn, all a false alarm. I figure you can have the northern area for about forty-eight hours before some serious people start frowning."

"That's all we'll need."

"Good, because the bureau would come down pretty hard if they knew who I was really working for."

Collins laughed. "It all depends on who you fear more, the President of the United States or Dr. Niles Compton?"

"Forty-eight hours, Jack."

"Got it."

Special-Agent-in-Charge James Williamson had been recruited by Jack personally ten years before upon his graduation from Quantico. The agent was just another of the cards Jack and Niles held up their sleeves that no one knew about, not even the president and his constitutionally guaranteed oversight.

The agent whistled and all fifteen of the securing agents left the area and secured the perimeter a mile around building 117.

The Wellsian Doorway was now secured and in the hands of Department 5656.

The countdown against the presidential edict had begun.

The Event Group now had one hundred hours of undisturbed oversight to complete the most amazing mission in world history before the rest of the American federal agencies became aware of some strange goings-on within the borders of the United States.

8

The bodyguard stepped away from the building when he saw the big man move off to confer with the FBI teams that were heavily deployed around not only the building but also the dock area. His eyes easily picked up this man's companions. They were conferring underneath an umbrella as they talked. The black man turned his way and then back. That was when he quickly brought out his cell phone and punched a number he thought he would never use. It was answered on the first ring.

"I think Madam's judgment is in question. Building one-seventeen is—"

"Yes, I have that information already. If I had relied solely on you I am afraid I would have been caught unawares."

"You said this would come about."

"I assume the FBI has fabricated some sort of cover story for the raid on Madam's property?"

"Yes, I heard drug manufacturing," Julien said worriedly.

"That would never hold up to scrutiny," the man said on the other side of the cell. "I understand they are preparing Madam for transport."

"Oh, God, where to? They wouldn't dare arrest her?"

"That, I would welcome. No, from our intelligence inside the house, our federal friends are taking her to Brooklyn."

"Have the rest been notified about Madam?" Julien asked, lowering his voice when he saw the black man look his way once more. He held the cell closer to his body to protect it from the increasingly violent rain.

"No, and they must not be. They are only students who don't understand the dangers of what could happen if the world learns the truth. No, they are not to be notified."

"But Madam? What is she and these men up to?"

"Tell me of these men who confronted you and Madam at the Grenada."

"I don't have a clear picture of who they are. Two, maybe three look military. The shorter, bear of a man was babbling on in scientific terms, so I can't really rule out any agency at this point."

"That is not what I was hoping to hear. If this is military we could lose the security of the doorway and many, many secrets would be spilled, which is unacceptable as more people other than myself have plenty to lose if this technology is compromised."

"Maybe Madam has reasons for sharing the information. Maybe they don't know what the doorway is."

The silence on the other end of the line sent a chill down Julien's spine. He knew this man and a few others like him did have plenty to lose if a spotlight were shined on them. Maybe even more to lose if Madam had knowledge of what they had been doing. The pay he received to inform on the household goings-on was not enough for this.

"Listen, stay close to Madam," the voice said.

"What are—"

"Shut up and listen. Stay close, I will have to deal with this myself with outside resources."

"I will not allow Madam to be harmed, we would defend her to the—"

A large hand reached out and gently removed the cell phone from Julien's hand. The black man was there and he immediately hit redial. He saw the number and noted it. He shut off the glass-faced phone and looked at the very much larger Julien.

"All information coming and going is to go through either the FBI or one of these fine gentlemen," he said, indicating Jenks, Henri, and Jack. "Clear?" Will Mendenhall said as he walked away toward the building and then tossed the confiscated cell phone to the man they referred to as the colonel.

Julien swallowed as he now feared what he might have unleashed in making that call. There were no limits as to how far certain men would go to protect their secrets, and Julien now feared he had unleashed a tornado and placed his beloved madam right in its path.

EVENT GROUP COMPLEX, NELLIS AIR FORCE BASE, NEVADA

Alice Hamilton stood next to her desk and watched the door to Niles's office and the conference room. She had her arms crossed over her chest and she tapped her heeled shoe on the carpet. She felt the eyes of the three assistants on her back as the two men and one woman looked on nervously, as they had never seen Alice Hamilton so worked up about anything.

The pneumatic elevator chimed softly and the doors parted. Alice raised a brow when she saw it was one of the kitchen stewards. He had a tray with a covered dish and coffee cup and carafe. As the steward walked in Alice went to him and quickly relieved him of the tray. She nodded for him to open the director's door and he did so after a warning look from the female assistant. Alice walked into the office and then instead of waiting for the steward to close the door she reached back with her shoe and closed it for him. With a frown and a worried look the steward left the outer office.

"Just sit the tray over there, Josh, thank you," Niles said as he studied an Antarctic field summary. He had a frown on his face at the incompleteness of the report issued through Charlie Ellenshaw's crypto department.

Alice turned and placed the tray on the credenza and then removed the cover from the plate containing the egg salad sandwich. She took it and placed it in front of Niles, who looked up when the dish landed a little hard.

"I know we're shorthanded, even in food services, but having the director's assistant delivering meals?" he asked as his smile stayed put, even though he had to swallow as he faced Alice.

"I've been delivering meals to directors around here for over sixty years, I imagine one more won't kill me," she said as she sat down in a chair facing his desk. "By the way, I believe your doctor's prescribed diet doesn't allow that sandwich. I believe there was a bowl of soup and a salad mysteriously canceled at the last minute."

"Nothing has ever gotten by you, has it?" Niles asked as he closed with tired resignation the file Charlie had sent him.

"No, I pretty much hear and know most everything."

Niles felt the twinge of his headache returning and he took a breath and waited for what he knew was once more coming his way.

"You just missed Mr. Ryan," Niles said as he ignored the headache as best as he could and reached for his sandwich. He started to take a bite and thought better and placed it back on the plate and looked at Alice. "With the report that Charlie just delivered, if and when we send a team in they are more than likely going to be confronted with wildlife that has been extinct for a minimum of ten thousand years."

Alice waited patiently as Niles had to think every comment out carefully before committing to an answer about anything. It would take the average man more than just a few minutes to coordinate this in his head, but for Niles it was milliseconds. She reached over and set the saucer that was covering Compton's coffee off to the side and she slid the China cup closer to the director. All the while her eyes never left his.

"In other words, Alice, we just don't know what will be waiting for them when, and if, they get there."

"These two Group members deserve to go, not only for their personal connection to the mission, but because they are qualified to go. You see, Niles, I've been conducting my own research and it clearly indicates the need for Sarah's expertise in geology. The world they will be traveling to is most likely on the verge of destroying itself due to what we know is an historical eruption of Mount Erebus. Sarah will be able to give a precise time frame of that event if she is there to witness the conditions. She is needed."

Niles stirred sugar into his black coffee and patiently listened to his conscience as she spoke. "And Anya? I don't know of any situation in Antarctica's past that would justify sending in an intelligence agent with the mission team. Do you?" he asked as he eyed Alice over the cup of coffee he sipped from.

"Nothing, other than the fact that she's good with a gun." Alice finally committed fully to her guilt-driven attack. "And for the deal you had me make with General Shamni and his Mossad offices."

Niles placed the cup of coffee down and shook his head, angry that this was going to be Alice's arguing point. She was feeling guilty for the secret pact between him and the head of the Mossad.

"What I offered was a deal to assist us in getting a very valuable member of this Group home again. I would have signed away my own mother to get that done. After all of these years in this facility and the deals that you and Garrison brokered to protect your people, you now have the gall to question what it is I'm willing to do?"

Alice lowered her head. She knew that the remark was too much and was hard on Niles. After all, it was true, she had done far worse to protect their people in the past. Maybe she was finally too damn old for the intrigue of today's "game."

"So we send her off on a mission that has a very low rate of probable success, just so she can possibly die with Carl. That's her reward? No, the mission roster is set." He sipped his coffee but kept his good eye on Alice. "I would warn you about sentiment, but then again that would make me out to be a liar, something I've never done. Sentiment is exactly why we are attempting to do the impossible. But that same factor can get my people killed and thus I can't allow it to interfere with Jack's mission plans. Sorry."

Alice nodded her head and stood.

"And tell Dr. Morales, nice try. But I've been doing this for years now, and I have learned a few things over those years and I learned from the best, Pete Golding."

"You knew we would ask before he even decided to help us, didn't you?"

"Yeah, Alice, because it's exactly what both Pete and I would have done."

Alice started to turn and leave, defeated for the first time since her arguments with Garrison Lee. Just as she closed on the double doors Niles stopped her. He was busy writing something and when finished held it out to Alice. She read it.

"I take it you heard from Jack?" she asked as her mind went into preparation mode immediately upon reading the action order.

"Yes, our one-hundred-hour window has been opened and we have to go through it very soon or we'll get it slammed down on us."

"I'll call it."

All thoughts of mission team members went out the window as Alice was now in full Event mode as she hurried from the office. Niles turned and watched the doors close and then he grimaced as if his coffee was bad. He shook his head and wondered if he was doing the right thing. He had traded Anya Korvesky for the mere chance of getting the file on this Traveler, and now he refused to even allow her a chance at seeing the man she loved one last time. He felt the guilt as it coursed like the bitter coffee down his throat.

He heard the tones that sounded loudly throughout the massive complex. His people were going to do what they did best—fight the impossible odds.

Alert tones sounded throughout the Event Group facility and sixteen departments, totaling 512 civilian men and women, with their military contingent of 212, went into action.

The Group had just declared an Event.

BROOKLYN NAVY YARD

Jack stood over a map spread out on a desk in the upstairs office area that once fronted as a furniture repair warehouse after the Department of the Navy had started selling off the property in 1966.

"Okay, when our people get here, we secure the inside of the building and the FBI the exterior and surrounding grounds." He looked at Mendenhall, who was taking notes on the electronic pad he had been issued for this particular op. "No one who isn't Group gets inside for the duration of our time on station."

"Yes, sir. I'll coordinate with Mr. Ryan when he arrives with Assistant Director Pollock and her nuclear sciences team."

"Good." He looked at the master chief, who turned somewhat pale when he heard that Virginia would soon be on station. "You okay, Master Chief?"

Instead of telling the truth, he grumbled and then stabbed his cigar end at the map.

"I don't know if you've noticed, Colonel, but do you see these power lines here and here?" The cigar stabbed at the two locations nearer the street.

"Yes," Jack confirmed.

"If we are able to somehow get this ass-backward contraption runnin', those lines won't carry any sort of load close to what we would need." He looked up and placed the cigar back into his mouth. "Not if the wattage we need is to carry the transformers I saw down in that pit. The old woman said she used bribes in the old days to get her power, but she didn't explain it well enough. I'm sure the Borough of Brooklyn won't be happy when we blow every electrical transformer from here to Bay Ridge."

Collins looked at the map again and the eight-hundred-foot space where the old dry dock used to be. It was sitting dry as the riverside gate was closed.

"Yes, I did notice and have informed Virginia about the power problems we could be facing. She said that she has a plan for that and she wanted me to inform you that she needs your naval expertise to work out a few minor problems. She said to gather everything"—Jack looked at his pad and the notes he had written—"on the power output for either the *Maitland*, or SSN-688. I assume you know what that first name refers to?"

Jenks removed the cigar once more and shook his head as if in wonder.

"Smart lady there. I didn't think of that," he mumbled. "Yeah, I know what she's referring to. Ballsy, I must say."

"Yeah, we've noticed that about Virginia," Jack said, wondering to what level Jenks's real fear of Virginia extended. "It must be all of those letters that follow her name and title, huh?" Jack smirked at the master chief. "Well, she said she's also studied the aerial photos from Boris and Natasha and suggests you may want to get a start on—"

"Hah! Filling the dry dock area," he said triumphantly. He looked from Mendenhall to Farbeaux. "See, I can think just as fast as her."

"Oh, yeah," Will said as he turned away and laughed.

"Okay, you get on that, Master Chief."

"And myself? Am I to run out for coffee and doughnuts?" Henri asked.

"No, we're going out in the rain and assisting Madam Mendelsohn inside for our meeting with Xavier, Niles, and Europa. It's time to see if we have a chance at using this"—he looked at Jenks—"half-assed-contraption."

"That's ass-backward contraption," Jenks mumbled as he corrected Jack with a disgusting smirk.

"And I'm included here because . . . ?" Henri asked as he straightened from the map of the navy yard.

Jack smiled as he put his coat on. "I like to have a man know just what it is he's volunteering for."

Colonel Henri Farbeaux lowered his eyes and wondered when and if his time in hell would ever be served. He watched Jack as he held the door open for him, intentionally not answering Henri's question but avoiding it with another mystery.

"Did you ever catch on that I really don't care for you, Colonel?" Henri walked past Collins and then out of the office.

"Really. But I thought we were actually getting to be friends."

Moira Mendelsohn sat in her chair and looked out from the glass-enclosed gallery at the doorway laboratory. She adjusted the quilt on her legs and then looked away.

"I didn't think I would ever lay eyes on that damnable thing again."

The doorway was sitting silent without any power in the semidarkness of the spotlights. Moira looked around the gallery.

"I remember looking up through a glass wall very much like this one. That is why I have always told my scholarship students not to lie to their children."

"Concerning?" Jack asked as he and Henri sat in the gallery seating section, flanking either side of the woman they knew as the Traveler.

She smiled and looked at the colonel.

"Why, that there really are monsters in the world." Her smile became a conspirator's smirk. "I know, I've seen them myself through glass walls just like these." She gestured to the seats and the gallery glass separating the viewers from the time machine that sat beneath them.

Jack remembered her file. He looked at Henri and knew he was thinking the same as him. Moira had really seen monsters in the flesh and most had red and black swastikas on the sleeves and death's-heads on their caps. The tale she related in remembering her concentration camp debrief told the bizarre story of Heinrich Himmler and his plan. Yes, she had seen monsters. Jack studied the tired face of the woman who sat before him.

"I trust you want to use the doorway for something of your own design?" She looked from Jack to the doorway below and the shiny instruments that gleamed in the sparse lighting.

"Is it still possible?"

Moira Mendelsohn snorted and chuckled, worrying both Collins and Farbeaux, but Henri far more since this was a machine owned and possibly once operated by her, so he hoped her insanity was a recent development.

"Oh, yes, I imagine it is." She used the chair's toggle to turn her chair to face Jack full on. "But why would you wish to go there?"

"Go where, ma'am?"

"Germany in 1943, of course."

"We wouldn't wish to if at all avoidable," Henri said chiming in.

"Then I suspect you have a Wellsian Doorway at the selected location?"

"Not following," Jack said, feeling his heart skip a beat.

"My dear, you have to have two doorways for the system to work. Didn't you read my dossier and specs thoroughly?" She managed to actually look sad at the way Jack's face dropped. "The only other doorway is in the Germany of the past, 1943. There is no other."

Collins stood and faced away from Moira. He saw the look from Henri. While not at all sad about hearing the news, he did feel for these people, for when the news broke that what they wanted to happen was now an impossibility, their hope would be dashed. The Frenchman had read the entire dossier and understood far better just how devastating this new information was.

Jack opened the door. "Master Chief, come in here, please." He then turned to the monitor that had been installed by Mendenhall. "Dr. Morales, are you with us?" he asked as Jenks entered the gallery and saw the long faces and then sat down. He removed his ever-present cigar and then nodded a greeting at Moira.

After a few seconds the young face of Morales filled the screen. Jack knew he would have to eventually get used to the new kid running the most intricate computing and AI system ever designed. He just hoped the young man was up to the task. They would soon see if the moniker that had been bestowed upon him was accurate . . . that of genius.

"We are here, Colonel, and we do have some information. Professor Ellenshaw—"

"Doctor, we may have a problem that will take priority over everything else. And note, Doctor, we are not secured on this end, we have a guest. May I introduce Ms. Moira Mendelsohn."

The old woman smiled when she saw the youth of the man on the monitor. She nodded.

"Ma'am, it's truly an honor," Morales said with something close to awe.

"He's so young," she said through the side of her mouth, and then nodded and smiled again at the young man blushing on the screen.

"Doctor, listen to what Ms. Mendelsohn has to tell you. Then I want you to use some of that brain stuff we rescued you for. Find an answer. Master Chief, help fill him in."

"Europa is just now getting her act together, so I'll do my best."

Jack excused himself and gestured for Henri to follow. They stepped out through the gallery and then took the elevator up to the old office area. Will was there figuring out a duty roster for his men when they arrived from Nellis.

Jack opened the door with Will and the Frenchman in tow and they stepped out underneath the old and tattered awning that covered the front stoop.

"My God, how can we pull this one off?" he asked.

Will was filled in by Henri and could see that the colonel was feeling physically ill being defeated at such an early point in the Event call.

"What now?" Will asked.

Jack just shook his head and then stepped out from under the awning and walked down the steps. He raised his face to the sky and allowed the rain to cool his face.

Will and Henri watched a man realizing defeat and it was something they could both see didn't sit too well with the former Green Beret.

The ruse had taken two and a half hours to formulate and execute. The van was actually stolen from the federal building parking lot in Brooklyn near the courthouse area and now sat idling at a closed and deserted gas station on Flushing Avenue. The driver of the van eased himself from behind the wheel and then joined the three men watching the main front gate of the navy yard.

"That is one drive I don't want to make again. I must have passed a dozen cops on the way here," the man said in Russian. "I didn't know if any of their radio signals would set that shit off. It would have blown half of the neighborhood straight to hell, not that it would be missed."

The smaller of the three men turned and faced the driver. "The explosives are detonated on a sealed circuit, you idiot, I have told you that. Radio signals cannot set them off."

"If you have to explain to your men their duties more than once, I wonder how well mine and my colleagues' money was spent. Perhaps we chose the wrong organization to handle our problem?"

The small man turned and faced his contracted employer. "Have we yet to fail you and your . . . colleagues in any capacity?" He snorted with a chuckle at the euphemism this dark-haired man insisted on using.

"I fear there is always a first time," the man said as he pulled his expensive coat closer to his throat. He hated dealing with these Eastern Bloc idiots. But they were the only people brave, or foolish, enough to take on the hard jobs called for to help him and his associates from time to time. These brutes had their own business concerns, but did this kind of work on a contractual basis and the Russians and the services they provided were not known to come cheap.

"If there is failure the first time, there will be a second, a third, even a fourth attempt until you are satisfied our contract has been fulfilled."

"As long as you are aware of the situation and the people you're putting into harm's way. That's the FBI over there. You may get through the civilian guards at the gate with your falsified van, but not them."

"Obstacles to be swiped aside like dirt." The small man laughed. "The FBI has been trying to shut us down for many years, my friend, yet here we are."

"Have your people compensated for the design of the building and the fact that your target is in the subbasement?"

"How did you get into the position you are in by worrying about such small details, my friend? You should know that with enough explosive you can do anything." The man turned and watched as the civilian guards started their shift change. He faced the driver. "Once through the gate you will get out at the first blind corner; my men will take it from there. Just be sure to turn on the remote device before you leave the van."

The driver nodded in understanding. He turned and went to the van and carefully eased out of the deserted gas station and crossed over Flushing Avenue and into the navy yard without a second look from the harried guards at the gate. With a flash of the FBI magnetic lettering on the doors and the government-issued license plate, the dark-haired man watched the most powerful explosive ever to be used in the borough of Brooklyn on its way to kill the Traveler and any evidence of their past crimes.

He placed a hand on the Russian's shoulder. The sleeve of his expensive coat was pulled back and the contracted killer looked down at the man's exposed arm.

"Let's hope we don't have to try this again."

The Russian watched the dark-haired man of forty lower his hand and turn toward his chauffeured car, which waited in the back of the station.

The Russian was left wondering about the strange numerical tattoo on the man's forearm as he stepped into the old station's store area that had not seen a customer or worker in over eighteen months. His men were there and as he looked at the bespectacled Russian sitting at the small desk, the contract killer could see by the red flashing light on the boxlike detonator that the remote system was indeed operational.

The driver slowed his beating heart as he passed through the main gate with nothing more than a cursory wave from the oncoming shift of civilian security guards. He drove slowly, obeying the posted limit of five miles per hour as he watched the deserted and rain-swept road near the back of the navy yard. The pulsing of the windshield wipers lulled him as he pulled around the blind corner. He immediately saw the bright lights that had been installed around building 117. He looked around as he placed the van in park and then allowed the van to idle. He didn't wonder how the men who had hired him rigged the van, he just wanted out of it. He reached for the door handle and then he remembered to set the remote system on the dashboard. He took a breath and then flipped the small toggle switch. A small red light illuminated, indicating the arming of the system. Little did he know that it had also armed far more than the remote control. He pulled on the door handle—nothing.

"What?" he said as he felt the first stirring of fear down in the pit of his stomach.

He pulled on the handle again and the door still didn't open. He put his shoulder to it and still the door remained locked and closed. Suddenly he heard the gearshift move from park to drive and his eyes widened. He hurriedly reached out and hit the toggle switch again. The light remained brightly lit. He repeated the same action with the same result. He yelled an obscenity and then slapped at the small radar-looking device, sending it crashing to the floor. Still the van moved forward toward the first taped-off line where two agents of the FBI waited in the rain. He hurriedly tried to shut the key off. It turned but the engine didn't stop. He tried desperately to slam the gear lever into park but the van was moving so fast now that the transmission just clicked loudly as he sped onward.

The accelerator pedal magically went to the floor and the unsuspecting patsy was thrown back in the driver's seat as he realized the ruthless Russian mob had murdered him for their own ends.

The FBI van hurtled toward building 117 with over a thousand pounds of the hybrid mix that crystallizes conventional plastique to HMX, the most powerful military explosive in the world.

In a combat situation, Colonel Jack Collins was an unparalleled warrior as far as instinctual awareness was concerned—unparalleled with the exception of a man who not only was trained the same as Collins, but one who also had the instincts of a developed criminal mind—Colonel Henri Farbeaux.

Before the two FBI field agents jumped free of the path of the rampaging navy blue van, which the newly installed Krieg lighting illuminated clearly, Henri had his nine millimeter free of its shoulder holster and had fired six times before Jack had even reached for his weapon. Soon he added his and Mendenhall's firepower at the onrushing target.

The van careened wildly as if the driver had no control. The two agents had barely avoided being crushed as the van sped past their checkpoint and the wooden barriers that the FBI had installed. The wood shattered and the two men rolled free. Bullets slammed into the windshield as the van cleared the security checkpoint a hundred yards from the building. Henri had already expended a clip and had placed a new one into the Glock and continued his rapid fire at the oncoming threat.

Collins lowered his weapon to reload but before he did he could see the dark shape of the driver as he fought the wheel of the van. The man was wide-eyed and terrified as the van hurtled beyond the running FBI agents as they piled from their field vans and into the rain.

"Wheels!" Jack yelled and immediately Henri and Will adjusted their fire. They were satisfied to see the bullets striking the old and broken asphalt that lined the waterway. Rubber was starting to shred from the front right tire and sent the van careening to the right. It bounced off an old pier piling and then rebounded back into the roadway. The van rode on two wheels as the force of the turn threw the screaming driver to the floor of the van.

Finally the right front wheel sheared off the front axle and the van screamed past the three men after hitting the crumbling facade of building 117. Jack jumped free as Will and Henri kept firing into the glass and engine compartment of the FBI van just as it zoomed by. The engine compartment exploded in a gouge of flame as the van careened back away from the building. The van then hit a pier piling and jumped into the rainy night air. The van struck the water and immediately started to founder. The spew of water into the broken windows sent geysers into the air.

As FBI field agents started running forward as Jack was just standing after throwing himself onto the ground, when he was once again knocked off his feet and flipped over until he slammed into the redbrick of building 117. The detonation was so powerful that Farbeaux and Mendenhall were tossed from the stoop of the old building until they too were slammed into the old facade. The wall of water inundated the building, pier, and dry dock area of building 117. The wave hit Jack and he was washed away like he had been caught in a flash flood. The two FBI operation vans were caught in the artificial tsunami and slammed into the vacant building 115 where they were crushed underneath tons of water from the river. The running field agents were caught just as the wall of water slammed into the protective river-wall that lined the roadway. Parts of the old building started crumbling into the white water as the river started to calm.

The geyser that erupted from the water traveled seven hundred feet in height before the wall of water had started to expand, freeing itself from the cold waters of the East River. Collins was washed backward toward the still roiling river and when he thought he was being whisked into the water, hands grabbed him and pulled him to safety. Jack spat foul-tasting water from his mouth and then looked up and saw Will Mendenhall with a serious gash on his head, and the arm he had broken in Antarctica was hanging limp at his side. Henri was spitting blood as he made sure Jack was breathing and then he ran to help some of the field agents as they struggled to stand. The rain masked the sounds of men moaning in pain from the underwater concussion that had rent the air around the oldest section of the navy yard.

Will pulled Jack to his feet and he shook out some of the cobwebs.

"That was one hell of a punch," Will said as he pulled Jack to higher ground as the waters receded back into the East River. His bad arm was now working again as the injury was only temporary in numbing his extremity. He rotated to make sure he didn't break it.

"What in the hell was packed into that damn thing?" Collins asked as he felt for the nine millimeter that was no longer there. He angrily pulled his sport coat free and tossed it onto the top step of the stoop. Then he heard the sirens. He took Will's arm and pushed him toward the door. "See if Jenks and the Traveler are okay. Then lock up and allow no one inside. We'll get the fire and police departments looking in the wrong place for now, but they're not stupid, they may believe that building was the intended target."

"Right." Will quickly entered the broken building.

Henri and the FBI agent-in-charge, Williamson, the Event Group operative, quickly formulated a plan just as the navy yard fire brigade showed up and were quickly followed by both the FDNY and NYPD. The place was starting to look like ground zero and that was attention Jack and his team had to avoid at all costs. They just didn't have the time for lengthy national security debates. Jack allowed the FBI to taint the trail and explain that a van filled with methamphetamine liquid exploded after trying to get by the FBI investigative team. The hard part would be getting Williamson's own field team to go along. Thus far the Event Group plan was in shambles. No second signal for the original doorway to lock on to, and now there was someone who wanted the Wellsian Doorway kept on a more private basis and was willing to kill fifty federal agents to do it.

Jack ran to the river and looked at the settling water and saw the bodyguard Julien as he stood wide-eyed in the rain where he thought he was unobserved. The other two were busily speaking beside him. They were animated as the larger man stared out at the spot the van had exploded. Then he saw Jack looking at him and before the colonel could move, Julien and his two companions turned away and vanished into the night. Jack turned and then headed for the heavily damaged building 117.

Jack found Will tending to a gash on Jenks's head as he avoided the smashed and shattered glass from the viewing gallery. Mendenhall nodded toward the Traveler, who was looking through the broken window frame at the water that had cascaded into the PIT from the river. The explosion had ripped a hole in the seawall that protected the navy yard from the raising and the lowering of tides. The base of the building had survived two hundred years of rot and decay only to be smashed by what amounted to an underwater depth charge that smashed the ancient wood and concrete pilings. Collins could see that Moira Mendelsohn was in shock as the water bubbled and rolled over the equipment it had taken her a lifetime to design and build.

Sparks momentarily flew from a bank of old computer panels and several of the old spools of magnetic tape blew free from their cabinets and splashed into the rising waters.

"I am sorry."

Jack heard the words and he felt the woman maybe wasn't sorry for the loss of the doorway, but for the lost chance at helping them get their man back from the past. Even though she had informed them that the doorway needed that second signal to lock on to, she had not given up on the vast possibilities. She took a deep breath and it came out as a sigh.

"Ma'am, are you hurt?" the colonel asked as he leaned over for a look. He reached down and retrieved her blanket and spread it over her exposed legs. Jack's eyes locked on the numerical tattoo that had been brutally applied in greenish-blue ink. She saw him looking and she slowly pulled the shawl closer to her body. She nodded, indicating that she was all right. Her eyes went back to the rising waters covering her life's work. "You need to tell me who your enemies are." Jack saw the stunned look on Jenks's face as he removed the cigar from his mouth and stopped Will from tending his cut as he strained to hear what the woman had to say.

"I have no more enemies, Colonel Collins. A woman my age actually becomes more secure the older she gets simply through the assault of time. Old age makes for an exceptional ally in avoiding enemies from the past."

"How about out of time?"

She smiled. "I am not following you, Colonel."

"Who doesn't want this machine falling into hands other than yours?"

Moira turned her chair and then faced Jack. She watched his eyes for a moment and then shook her head. "Perhaps you should check your end of that equation, Colonel, not mine."

"Your bodyguards mysteriously vanished after the attack—why?"

"Julien and the others have left me?" she asked, a momentary look of panic filling her expression.

Jack remained silent as she thought and he realized that the information had truly stunned her. She looked away and Collins saw the tough old woman's lips tremble. He placed a hand on her shoulder and then moved off to Will and Jenks.

"Look, can you duplicate that design if you had all of the specs?" he asked Jenks in a low tone as he watched Madam Mendelsohn move back to the broken viewing glass and stare down at her submerged doorway.

Jenks also watched the Traveler and then placed the cigar back into his mouth as he allowed Will to apply a gauze pad and tape to his cut.

"Yeah, if I had ten years and about three billion dollars, you bet," he growled, and then tossed the cigar stub away. He stood and went to the viewing window and looked out. "No, our only shot was right there," he said, pointing to the rising waters. "So I suggest you get some pumps in here and some engineers and get that leak sealed up tight. Me and Ginny will figure something out after we dry everything off."

"Ginny and you will figure what out, Harold?" The voice made Jenks turn. He smiled and then quickly caught himself and spat onto the wet carpet. "Classy as always," she said as she saw Jack and Will and nodded. Then her eyes fell on the Traveler and she quickly made her way to the electric wheelchair.

"That we maybe can salvage . . ."

Jenks's words trailed off as Virginia Pollock kneeled down on the wet floor and faced Moira.

"Dr. Mendelsohn?"

Moira looked up and her smile grew as this was the first time in her life that someone from the outside world had addressed her as "Doctor."

"Yes," she answered as Virginia took her old and silken hand into her own.

"I have read your thesis on the alternating poles of influence in regards to ion particle research—an amazing piece that I use quite often in my courses on light-emitting and amplification lenses."

"I didn't think anyone had access to my old work."

Virginia looked up at Jack with a questioning look. "She hasn't met Xavier and Europa as yet?"

Collins shook his head. "Just Dr. Morales, not Europa."

"Well, suffice it to say I can't wait to get into your head about certain things regarding your research and the practical application of your work. I need to know so much. The mission into the past, I would love to see the records on those."

The smile vanished from Moira as she eased her hands free of Virginia's. The move was caught by all. Jack suspected Moira was hiding something huge but for now his only concern was the repair of the doorway and its application in assisting them getting Everett back home. And in the middle of all of that they now had a mystery concerning who would be willing to kill federal agents to stop the doorway from being compromised.

"All of my notes have been lost over the years. I'm afraid the only record of mission parameters is in here," she said, pointing an old finger to her temple.

"Master Chief, get the assistant director up-to-date. Moira, you and I need to speak after we get this thing moving. Right now I have to see how much of our cover story has bitten the dust."

"Do you mean the problems outside?" Virginia asked as she straightened up and looked around at the devastation caused by the suicide attack.

"Yes," Jack answered.

"Well, it looks like the FBI is under attack by the civil authorities representing the Borough of Brooklyn. Agent Williamson said to tell you they are being pulled off the detail and turning the investigation over to the NYPD vice squad, ATF, and the DEA."

"Damn, I have to speak with Niles. We're going to need some special interference ran for us."

"You mean we're going to add another criminal charge to our growing list?" Virginia asked.

"Something like that, yeah. Now, we need your teams to get in here and start cleaning this mess up so we can see just how screwed we really are. Then the priority is to get the linkup with Morales and Europa up and running on a dependable basis. We need her computing prowess here ASAP. Will, get Ryan to grab us six field security teams out here from Nevada, I want our own people managing security from here on out." Collins looked at his watch. "We have ninety hours left before the president will have to explain to a lot of angry agencies and cities why he is acting so slowly on this. And it's now a lot larger problem than it was just an hour ago."

Jack turned and left the gallery and caught the lift to the top floor. All the while he felt a helplessness he hadn't felt since he saw Everett push him away and then vanish into a wormhole.

The Event Group was losing its race with time and technology.

9

BERNSTEIN, FRISCH, JODLE, AND WACHOWSKI INVESTMENT GROUP, NEW YORK CITY

The Russian didn't exactly feel out of place in the financial district as he rode the plastic-lined elevator on his way to the thirty-fifth floor of the Halas building, as money never, ever, frightened him, nor did the men and women who had it in droves. The fortress of glass, white marble, and steel ugliness set itself apart from the gleaming spires that replaced the old World Trade Center, which had come to an abrupt end on September 11, 2001. He looked at the three Wall Street types next to him as they stepped off on the floor below his destination. He knew very few people ever rode the elevator to the topmost floor. He smiled as the doors closed at the haughty mannerisms the departed men had about them, which he found distinctly funny. *After all,* he mused, *we are practically in the same business*—the procurement of money and the acquisition of power. He punched in the private code on the keypad and the elevator continued upward one more flight.

The doors opened and the small Russian stepped free of the richly paneled car and saw the two security guards flanking either side of the double glass doors. The first rose from his small desk and confronted the visitor. He held out his hand and the Russian smiled and held open his black coat and sport jacket to show the guards that he carried no firearms. He smirked at the naiveté of the investment firm. He lowered his hands and the second guard issued him a visitor's pass. The small plastic card was computer coded and it allowed him access to the thirty-fifth floor of one of the most advanced and profitable investment firms in the financial world.

"Mr. Frisch is expecting you. His assistant will escort you. Sir, your visiting privileges extend only to the boardroom."

The Russian smiled at the seriousness of the two guards. He had seen no less than three alternate ways of entering this so-called secure haven in less than the two minutes it took to ride the elevator to his richly appointed destination. But that was information he would file away for another day.

"Mr. Jones, please come with me," said a matronly woman in a gray suit. He smiled at her overstated manliness and at the tie she wore. American women in their struggles to be competitive drove them to extremes, in his humble opinion.

The Russian saw the boardroom he had been in many times. He was the only person inside the vast organization to actually see and have an audience with the men behind the curtain, the wizards, as he liked to refer to them. He stepped inside and saw the lone figure of a man sitting at the head of one of the longer boardroom tables the immigrant Russian had ever seen. The gray-haired man looked up from the newspaper and nodded that the visitor should sit.

"Ask Mr. Jodle to join us please, Mrs. Abernathy."

"He has been notified, sir." The woman closed both doors as she backed out with a hard look at the man visiting her boss. She obviously knew of his special talents.

The older man, in his late fifties, looked up and then slapped the morning edition of *The New York Times.*

"Care to explain this failure?" the man asked as he stood and went to the sidebar and poured himself a cup of coffee. The Russian noticed the coffee service was probably worth all of the meager salary he ever made inside the Moscow Police Department. He also noticed coffee was not offered to him. The Russian sat down with a smirk. The chairman of the board noticed but chose not to say anything as he returned to his expensive high-backed chair that appeared to have been custom designed to look down at the other eighteen chairs around the table.

The door opened and a well-dressed man in an expensive three-piece suit strode in and without a greeting to the visitor sat down next to the chairman of the board. He folded his hands in front of him and then glared toward the small man at the end of the long table. Another sniff of humor from the small man as he noticed how much the well-appointed man acted like a schoolboy in front of the gray-haired chairman.

"Failure?" he asked, hinting at confusion.

"The police have already cleared the navy yard and proclaimed a major victory in the war on drugs inside the city. And yet, the building still stands. Madam is still breathing."

The Russian stood and made his way to the coffee service and poured himself some coffee without invitation. The younger partner was about to say something but the older man placed a hand on his and stilled him from the complaint. The Russian went back to the far end of the expansive table after pouring an inordinate amount of sugar into the china cup.

The visitor sipped his coffee and then placed the cup down on the polished surface. He reached into his coat pocket and produced something he placed on a water tray after removing the empty carafe, and then slid the items and the tray down the long table where it came to rest in front of the two men.

"It seems I was not told the exact situation by your young colleague."

The older man picked up the photos from the tray. His eyes went from the Russian to the photos. They were in night-vision format and the man could see that the photographer had used a long-range camera to take the shots. They showed three men in civilian dress as they fired upon the van as it hurtled toward building 117. The other men and women in the photo all wore the distinctive FBI Windbreakers that were so recognizable to the world.

"You were told enough to complete the contract you agreed to. Now, what is so amazing about these photos?" The older man passed them to his younger partner, who had been at the attack at its outset.

"Who are those men?" he asked as he lifted the china cup to his lips and blew lightly to cool the liquid. He sipped and waited.

"FBI? How in the hell are we to know?" the younger man named Jodle said with indignity as he tossed the photos back onto the silver tray.

The Russian laughed as he set the cup back onto the table. "No, I'm afraid all of the local field agents within the five boroughs have been tagged by my people. These men are not agents of that particular law enforcement group."

"Local police, possibly agents from Washington, who in the hell cares? Your job was to permanently shut that building down and to eliminate any possible contact between Madam and the federal authorities."

The Russian was growing weary of the answers he was receiving. "Your man inside Miss Mendelsohn's sphere of influence, this Julien, says that these strangers are military."

"So, what does that have to do with this?" the older man asked as he leaned back to hear the answer. "And where is Julien? We wish to speak to him at the soonest opportunity."

"He was rather shocked at the extreme measures for which I was contracted." He sipped coffee and then smiled. "He's what you would call 'disillusioned' at your harsh tactics. He and his men are currently under my care."

"Bring him and the others to us. We would like to question them ourselves," Jodle said as he tried to look intimidating but failed miserably.

Silence.

The two investments men exchanged worried looks when the Russian said nothing. But his grin said everything.

"Secrets, secrets, secrets. Some are good at keeping them, others good at learning them."

Both men got the same gut-wrenching feeling in their stomachs at the exact same moment. The visitor pushed the coffee cup aside and then leaned forward in his chair. He fixed the two men with a knowing look.

"I guess it was divine providence that these men you so casually shrug off as FBI field agents shot the tires out of that van, otherwise we might have destroyed one of the most valuable pieces of equipment in the history of the world, and the person responsible for its construction in the same process. Leaving us poor working peasants wondering just why you gentlemen wanted to permanently stop the advancement of science. Could it be for other than humanitarian purposes? Shame on you."

"You have been contracted to complete a job, this was not done," the older man Frisch said with as much indignity as he could foster.

"The conditions settled upon in our previous agreement will have to be reworded, I'm afraid."

The statement was met with shocked silence.

"My organization has decided to wait and see just what is planned for that old building." He stood from his chair and then buttoned his thick coat over the sport jacket. He smiled at the two men who sat looking white-faced. "Oh, and we have decided that it would be far more beneficial to speak with Madam Mendelsohn ourselves to understand better just what an amazing piece of equipment she has in her control."

"Look, we can work out a much better and safer conclusion to this small problem."

The small Russian fixed Jodle and Frisch with a look that now lacked the good humor of his smile.

"Safer for whom?" The look was one filled with disgust at the two very rich men. "Betrayal of one's savior, it seemed worth far more than forty pieces of silver for some."

The two men watched the Russian mobster leave the boardroom. The older man closed his eyes as he was seeing the secrets that drove his world come crashing back into his life. He turned to the younger man.

"You brought this man to our attention, and now he threatens blackmail at the very least, and what is far more terrifying is that now, thanks to that fool Julien, he has knowledge of the one thing that cannot ever be brought to the attention of the authorities."

The younger man felt his prestige within this firm being driven from him.

"I will—"

"Fix this, Jodle, fix it or we all go down, and we cannot allow that."

The young partner watched the chairman angrily rise and leave him sitting there. He looked up as the senior partner turned and faced him.

"There is no telling what that Russian is thinking. Blackmail may be the least. He may try for something that may be far more profitable than that."

Joshua Jodle felt his heart fall to his gut as he turned for the double doors of the boardroom as the old man angrily called after him.

"He's going after the doorway."

BROOKLYN NAVY YARD

Jack saw the last of the FBI close up shop and leave. Special Agent-in-Charge Williamson apologized to Collins, but there was nothing he could do since the locals claimed jurisdiction when it was proven that drug manufacturing was not the reason behind the FBI involvement. The remains of the van, very little to speak of, were raised by the NYPD and FDNY just as dawn broke over the city. Jack watched it all from the privacy of the office windows. The last of the police also finally finished after a brief inspection of the surrounding buildings. The PIT inside building 117 was closed and the fire department skimmed right over it in their perusal of the building. A sigh of relief could be had by all.

An hour after the overcast skies allowed enough light in to see, Collins saw the long line of vans as it progressed through the spot where the stolen van had crashed through the FBI barricade the night before. Jack walked down the steps and waited.

Niles Compton was assisted from the lead van and Jack moved to meet him.

"Quite a night in old Brooklyn, I understand?" he asked as he settled the crutch under his arm. Collins took him by the elbow for added support.

"More than we ever bargained for."

"How bad is it?" Niles asked briefly, stopping as the other white vans pulled in behind the first.

"The explosive, an exotic one at that, took out the electrical lines under the river. No power to six of the seven buildings, including ours. But that's the better part of the news," Jack said as he shook his head at the devastation of learning what he had in the hours leading to Niles and the Event Group technical team's arrival. "The attack also took out the base foundation of the building, flooding the PIT where the doorway was secured. Virginia said it looks hopeless, at least until she can get her full nuclear forensics and Jenks's engineering teams in there."

"Well, maybe I can help with that part at least."

Jack saw the technicians as they started unloading material and boxes from the inside. That was when he saw Sarah and Anya. His eyes went wider when he saw Alice Hamilton giving instructions to the more than seventy engineers. He looked questioningly at Compton, who smiled and shook his head. Jack knew Niles would be inundated with the requests of at least two people who wanted to be included on the field teams and he knew they had forwarded those requests through the office of one Alice Hamilton. Jack knew without being told that Niles had held his ground but caved in at least allowing the two women on site during the mission.

"I knew you were afraid of Alice. You traded her their mission status to be on the home team in Brooklyn, didn't you?" Jack said as Niles turned and started for the door.

"Yep."

An old meeting room originally intended for naval engineers in the previous century had been cleaned and a dozen large monitors installed. Three of these monitors had a view of the PIT, which had been opened since the all-clear was given by the FDNY. The silent men and women sat around the elongated and very chipped-up Formica table and stared at the water-damaged devastation below their feet. Men and women technicians had pumped the remaining water from the PIT but most could see that the doorway would never function again in the shape it was in.

"First order of business," Niles said as he rapped his knuckles on the table to get everyone's attention. "Securing this site, Jack?"

"I assigned Colonel Farbeaux to that task." Jack looked across the table at the Frenchman, who had conveniently arranged his seating assignment to sit between Anya and Sarah. He smiled at Jack for only a brief moment. He pulled up his notes on the electronic pad. "Henri?" Collins looked questioningly at Sarah, who shrugged her shoulders and then winked at Jack, which got her a return frown.

"With the assistance of Dr. Morales, I have learned that we may have a break in who was responsible." Henri tapped another button on his pad and a monitor came to life. "This is a Russian immigrant whose real name is a mystery, but the NYPD has dubbed him the 'Bolshevik.' Goes by the name of Jones. Not very original, but most Russian mob types aren't known for their originality in any areas except murder. That is this man's specialty."

The picture on the monitor was of a man with a black beard and one who seemed very jovial in the surveillance clip stolen by Europa from the NYPD.

"What led you to him?" Niles asked the Frenchman.

"Probability. Nothing happens in Brooklyn without this man knowing or being responsible for it. He is a former police captain with the Moscow Metropolitan Police. Very skilled. I once read a dossier on him back in the good old days when intelligence services could track him. As corrupt a lawman as there ever was. The man is a killer and is known to use nothing but military-grade weaponry and explosives."

"But you're not a hundred percent sure that he's responsible?" Compton persisted.

"I know you people would like absolutes, but you'll have to trust my instinct on this. This was well planned and very nearly flawlessly executed. Yes, I'm sure he at least knows about it and who did it."

"I concur with the colonel," Jack said as he studied the face on the monitor.

"Why?" Virginia asked out of curiosity.

"Let's just say I believe he has insight to men like this, at least from Henri's unique perspective."

Chuckles sounded from around the table.

"Okay, get our friend here a link with Europa and get this man found and out of our way. I don't give a damn about his reasoning for now. I just need this project secured. Needless to say the president was briefed this morning on what happened here last night and knows we are involved. He is still allowing us his new leeway time for oversight, so let's not waste it. The directors of the FBI and CIA will soon start adding the two plus two here and begin asking questions the president could never begin to answer."

Henri nodded and then shut off the program from his electronic pad.

At that moment the door opened and a Marine allowed Moira Mendelsohn into the room. The motorized chair stopped just inside the door. Niles, with difficulty, limped over and stood in front of her and introduced himself. Jack and the others were clearly seeing the respect Niles had for the Traveler. When Niles moved back to allow the Traveler inside several others, including Anya, stood to greet the great mind in the room. Moira's inquisitive brown eyes went to Jason Ryan and she had to hang on to his hand a moment longer to examine his tattoo better. He half smiled and then pulled his hand away and sat next to Mendenhall, who held back a snicker at Jason's facial design.

"What do you have, Virginia?" Niles asked as he watched Moira move in next to Jack and Charlie Ellenshaw.

"Professor Mendelsohn inspected what's left and even with Europa's help, as it was explained by our host, it would take at least seven months for her to reprogram the system and repair the water damage."

"Not knowing just what this Europa is and its limitations, I would have to stick to my estimate," Moira said as she took in the people around the table.

Virginia lowered her head and Jenks patted her leg, which elicited a kind look. The room was silent. Jenks slid his estimate for the loss of power lines and other damage to the local grid supplying power to the building as also a cause for concern, but now it seemed a moot point so he remained silent.

"Even if the doorway were operational and the power supply problem sorted out, we have no connecting doorway for our signal to lock on to," Virginia said with a nod toward the Traveler.

"If I may ask a question that I am sure is readily known by most in this room," Moira said as she faced the Group, "but if you had a repaired doorway, or maybe even a duplicate, second doorway, how far back, dimensionally speaking, are we talking about?"

Looks were exchanged and the room became just as silent as before. Niles cleared his throat and then nodded for Virginia to answer the question.

"Approximately two hundred and sixty-five thousand years. Exact location, unknown, the location we have—Antarctica."

Moira was silent as the outrageous answer stunned her. She did notice the young dark-haired woman lower her head and then the smaller woman saying something to her softly, both expressing the bad news on their faces.

"Considerably further back than I have traveled, my dear. The astronomy calculations alone would take a supercomputer a full three years to even get a bearing on a location that far back." She shook her head and then used her wheelchair's toggle to turn away from the group of curious eyes as she thought about the difficulties involved in a dimensional transfer that far back.

As for the group, none wanted to say they had the most powerful supercomputer ever devised at their disposal, but what would that serve? What the Traveler was trying to explain went over the heads of most everyone in the room. "I hope someday you will allow me to know how the subject of this far-flung dimensional jump managed to achieve this."

"It happened during the recent war."

She turned in her chair and looked at Compton with excitement on her face.

"The wormholes?" she asked.

"Yes."

"I knew that would be the only way they could get here from such a distance. They actually time-warped here?"

"Yes," Niles said. "Is that helpful to you?"

They all saw the sadness in the Traveler's face. She shook her head. She looked at the fallen face of the woman with jet-black hair as she swallowed hard and then held the smaller woman's hand tighter. Moira wanted to reach out to the young woman but held back as she knew she had not delivered the news that was so badly needed to be heard.

"We did uncover something concerning our Traveler friend here," Master Chief Jenks said, shrugging off the warning elbow poke he received from Virginia.

"What is that?" Niles asked, not wanting any more bad news at the moment.

Jenks tossed a small device onto the table with a clang. The wires leading from it looked like it was attached to a bomb, but then most saw the old clock face and digital readout were blank. Jenks quickly connected the wires to an adapter and then plugged the device in and the clock face flared to red and blue brightness. Moira was the only person in the room besides Jenks and Virginia to know what it was.

"The time stamp," Moira said as she eased in closer to the table as Jenks picked up the small timepiece.

"Time stamp?" Niles asked.

"Yes," answered the Traveler. "It records the date and time of the displacement jump."

"Do you remember the very last date of your final dimensional shift?" Virginia asked, now curious to hear her explanation.

"Of course, September 25, 1973. The time should be frozen at zero three forty-five hundred hours and fifty-one seconds on that date."

Jenks held the recorder up so all could see: 05/17/1987 0120 hours and 22 seconds.

All eyes went to the Traveler, who was in deep thought as she read and then reread the numerical display.

"That cannot be correct. Maybe the water damage?"

"It's a sealed unit, ma'am, you know that," Jenks said as he sat back in his chair, not feeling too good about confronting the Traveler with a false statement on her last use of the Wellsian Doorway.

"I have no explanation for that."

They could all see the consternation that Jenks and Virginia's revelation had caused the old woman. She lowered her head in thought.

Niles was about to speak when the main monitor that had been installed flared to life. On the screen was Xavier Morales as he sat in the clean room in Nevada.

"What have you got, Doctor?" Compton asked, knowing nothing could assuage the news they had already received.

"Europa may have something, a little out of the ordinary, but you may wish to investigate on your end."

Moira looked up into the young face of the man she had met earlier.

"We were poring over the original blueprints for the Brooklyn Navy Yard buildings. It took Europa to uncover the original specs for the renovations made during the sixties and seventies. It seems in late 1985 building number one-fourteen was purchased. No design specs were ever turned in by the contractor other than a sprucing up of the building. Janitorial reports mostly and some asbestos removal, nothing major."

"What has that to do with this building?" Jack asked.

Xavier looked sad for a moment as he looked at the people gathered in Brooklyn. "It seems the building was purchased by Grenada Holdings."

Everyone looked over at a stunned Moira Mendelsohn.

"Ms. Mendelsohn's own corporation," Morales finished.

"I don't have a second property here," she said in her defense.

"Signed by your corporate board, a Mr. Joaquim Wachowski. Europa says he is a former associate of yours, ma'am," Xavier added, still not feeling good about placing the old woman in a corner.

Moira Mendelsohn felt physically ill.

"My God, they constructed a second doorway."

"Who?" Niles asked as he was sorely tempted to stand and shout the question.

"Some very unscrupulous men with whom I once trusted with far too many secrets"—she looked away—"and lives."

Questions stirred and hopes were raised, for how long this saving grace would exist, none of the Event Group knew.

"May I suggest you get someone over to building one-fourteen?" Morales said as he watched the stunned inactivity on his own monitor from Nellis.

Before anyone could issue orders, Jack had assisted Henri from his chair and along with Will and Jason, hurriedly left the room.

"Now, perhaps we better go into a little more depth on your past financial partners." Niles was watching her as Jack and his men exited the makeshift conference room.

An angry look crossed the Traveler's countenance. "Yes, let's do that."

10

Collins checked with his outside security and found that the last team of news vans and reporters had left the navy yard twenty minutes before. Jack, Will, Jason, and Henri all stood underneath the pewter skies as they examined building 114 from a distance. The 150-year-old redbrick building had its facade renovated in the eighties to make it aesthetically in line with its occupied neighbors. The owners of the property spent money on the outside to keep the navy yard development people in check, but according to Europa and Morales, refused to refurbish the inside. Europa unscrupulously uncovered the plans from the city building inspector and saw that no refurbishment of the interior was ever ordered, or at least reported. It was purely a real estate investment for the Grenada Holding Corporation and their extensive real estate portfolio.

"You say the last reporters left some time ago?" Jack asked as he took a step toward building 114 situated across from the newly flooded dry dock that separated building 114 from its sister, 117.

"According to Lance Corporal Ramirez, yes, sir," Will answered.

Collins glanced at the rain clouds above them and acted as casual as he could.

"Well, someone with a camera seems to be lost," he said as he walked toward the building and then stopped. The others stopped with him. Only Henri knew why. "Mr. Ryan, eleven o'clock, building one-eleven, rooftop, two men, one with a camera and one observing," he said without turning to look at the abandoned ghost of building 111.

"Correction, three men total, two of them are armed with more than a camera," Henri said as he reached down and acted as though he was looking at something.

"Jesus, how in the hell can you two see that far?" Will asked as he was always amazed at Jack's prowess in spotting danger. Needless to say Henri's ability came as no surprise at all.

"Be careful you two," Jack said as he finally saw the third man that the Frenchman had seen. "I need answers, not dead men—well, if they're reporters, that's a judgment call," Jack said with his wry humor due to his experiences with reporters.

"Right," Jason said as he and Will left Henri and Jack and made their way to the back of the old buildings and then quickly vanished.

"Shall we?" Jack said as they made their way to building 114. Henri gestured graciously for the colonel to lead the way.

Collins felt the weight of the nine-millimeter weapon in his shoulder holster but knew as long as they were being observed he wanted no obvious intelligence for those watching. They would have to guess at their armed or unarmed status.

As they approached they saw that the building was actually in far worse shape than its neighbors. The bottom row of windows were completely lined with broken safety glass and the brick had not been sandblasted since 1984. Large and flowing rust stains scarred the facade and weeds grew between her brick-and-mortar foundation and entwined the wooden structure above. Henri didn't feel it, but Jack took an exasperated breath when he realized they were probably barking up the wrong tree. He made his way up the crumbling concrete steps leading to the front offices that had once witnessed the launch of the USS *Arizona* from the very same dry dock facility fronting the five buildings on this end of the yard.

"I do not believe this is much of a going concern," Henri said as he walked through the shattered front door with Jack in the lead. Once out of sight of any onlookers on rooftops, Jack pulled out his pistol and Henri, with raised brows, followed suit.

Collins eased over a fallen file cabinet and saw papers and old files scattered across the floor. In the far corner Farbeaux was startled by a large wharf rat that scurried across the debris on the old green-tiled floor. Jack saw a place where a secretary and several others worked that looked as if it hadn't seen a live person since the 1960s. Jack lowered his weapon and then looked at Henri with concern as he holstered the Glock.

"Seeing as how the design of the two buildings in question are so similar, it would stand to reason they would secure anything they were trying to hide just as they did in building one-seventeen."

"Covertly speaking, is that what you would do, Colonel?" Jack asked, knowing how Henri's criminal mind worked.

Farbeuax also holstered his weapon and then smiled. "No, if I were to build a second doorway that I wished kept secret from my benefactor, I would have built it in Wyoming."

"I guess they are not quite as accomplished as you," Jack said, and then made his way over the trash of the front offices and walked out through the door marked MANUFACTURING DEPARTMENT in chipping red paint.

"No one is as accomplished as myself, my dear colonel."

The hope Jack had been feeling a few minutes before was quickly dashed when he saw the empty space where you could fit an old World War II battle cruiser. Rats scurried hurriedly from one place to another as the weak light filtered through the dirty and painted-over broken windows.

"Colonel?" Henri said as he nodded to the darkened far corner. Jack saw the heavy elevator lift with several old wooden filing cabinets overturned and resting in front of the old gates. "It only makes sense that if one doorway is closed, go to another, in the exact same place the first one was hidden."

Jack nodded and they both started moving the detritus from the floor in front of the lift. Henri reached out and flipped the light switch two times with no result.

"Afraid of the dark?" Jack quipped as he slid the old-fashioned wooden gate up and then the steel screen aside as he stepped into the lift.

"No, I'm afraid of what's hiding in that darkness, Colonel. That is how I've managed to stay alive for so long in a business that does not encourage active and peaceful retirement."

Jack pulled out his gun again and waited for Henri. "I see your point."

"Well, no power, let's hope this thing still has gravity brakes."

Jack reached out and lowered the wooden gate and then slid the steel doors closed. He found the elevator's annunciator handle and then pushed it forward. Henri ducked when a loud clanking sound was heard and then the sound of a hundred pigeons below alighting as the noise drove them to flight somewhere in the abyss below. The lift started to gravity-descend to the basement area. Both men flinched when the elevator became bathed in white, clean light from the fluorescent tubes lining the elevator shaft. Collins was suddenly feeling better about their odds.

"The building has its own power source. This one should be as dark as building one-seventeen," Henri said as he eyed the passing concrete of the reinforced shaft. "The explosion from the attack severed all of the conduit lines coming in under the river."

"This is considerably deeper than the first," Collins said as he watched the hundreds of feet of reinforced concrete slide by as they continued down.

Finally the huge car started to slow. Jack knew that the lift was governed by something other than gravity as the car sensed it was close to the bottom of the long shaft. Henri looked at Jack and he nodded at the Frenchman as he pulled open the gate and then slid the wooden doors up. He scanned the area in front of them and saw an exact duplicate of the viewing gallery that now lay smashed in building 117. The only difference between the two was the plush design and creature comforts. Two wet bars sat at each end of the gallery and would serve the twenty seats that sat arrayed over the gallery's clamshell floor below them. Henri smiled and then looked at Jack and holstered his own Glock.

Collins examined the gallery that looked as if it came out of a gothic novel where doctors sat observing a world-famous surgeon strut his knowledge below them upon the surgical stage. But who was it that occupied those chairs to watch the world of the impossible as it unfolded in front of them? Jack saw the plastic cover on one of the observation seats, which was different from the first in building 117. This button was situated on the arm of an ornate chair as if whoever sat there was in total control and wanted the others in the gallery to know it. Jack sensed power there. Whoever they were dealing with was smart and resourceful. As he approached the gallery the dim mood lighting came on and the soft hum of power generation was somewhere below their feet. Jack stopped and looked at Henri, who pointed at the walls and the glass-enclosed sensors there.

"You tripped the motion detectors." The Frenchman raised a brow as he studied the sensors after standing on a chair. "Not only did we switch on the power"—he tore the darkened glass fixture from the wall and tossed it to Collins—"we have alerted whoever is responsible for this. It's also a silent alarm."

Jack shook his head and then placed the sensor in the chair. He quickly raised the plastic cover on the arm of the chair and with one last concerned breath he hit the switch.

The lights dimmed and the silent world around them was shattered by an alarm that blared like a diving submarine. They both cringed at the loudness of the machinery hidden somewhere in the depths of the building. It was obvious someone had lied to the building planners, inspectors, and navy yard development corporation—this was most definitely renovated far beyond anything in the ancient shipyard.

"Please stand away from section twenty-three," a mechanical voice sounded from the speakers overhead. The announcement made both Henri and Jack momentarily

believe they had been joined by the very men who had built the facility. *"Please stand away from section twenty-three."*

Suddenly the floor below them started turning like a record on a player. Jack smiled as he knew exactly what he was seeing. The floor turned and they heard another motor kick in somewhere and then the floor started to separate and begin to corkscrew into the depths of building 114.

"All technical staff please initiate shielding procedures. Set condition Blue, nuclear safeguards are now in effect."

"Oh," Henri said as he and Jack exchanged worried looks. Jack stood at the glass and saw the spotlights as they illuminated the descending floor below the thick viewing window. As they became exposed, the walls were lined in white plastic much like the Event Group complex interior. Collins knew that plastic was the best electrical grounding you could get out of most building materials. The walls were also lined in blue-colored fluorescents, which illuminated as they became exposed. What worried him were the nuclear triangular warning symbols that lined the shaft as it went lower into the bowels of Brooklyn.

"My God," Henri exclaimed when he saw what was buried underneath building 114.

Jack smiled for the first time in what seemed like days as he took in the scene. He removed the secured cell from his jacket and then punched in only one number.

"Boss, it looks like we may be in business. Start Dr. Morales and Europa on finding that second signal we can lock on to." Jack shut the phone down and then looked at Henri.

Farbeaux watched as the world of tomorrow's science came into its full glory. Glass, steel, and white ceramic glass gleamed in the controlled atmosphere of the laboratory. Row upon row of consoles sat silently waiting for orders that would send a traveler through to a past that had long vanished.

Then Collins and Farbeaux lost their approving smiles almost as quickly as they had appeared.

"Shit," Jack mumbled as the lights came to full illumination below.

"May I suggest you inform Commander Ryan and Captain Mendenhall the situation has become much more serious?"

Collins reached for his cell phone as his eyes scanned the console stations below. Each station had a white lab–coated technician sitting at it. For his part Henri looked around and his weapon was no longer held without killing intent.

The gleaming white skeletons stared at consoles that had been the last thing any of the twenty-six technicians would ever see again.

Only the gleaming surfaces of the duplicate Wellsian Doorway that sat before them in all of its gleaming glory had been witness to their sudden and brutal execution.

BROOKLYN, NEW YORK

Julien felt his bladder release in a flood of wetness that he could not hide. Thus far the five men had not laid a hand on him, but their mere presence made him wish he were safely in the company of Madam Mendelsohn. He twisted the plastic tie that bound his hands behind him and felt the slicing pain as the sharp edges cut into his wrists. The five brutes watching him had nothing to say to his protests over his treatment. He knew he should never have trusted the men Madam Mendelsohn had expunged from her business and her life.

He heard a door open behind him and the five men stepped away from the man in the wooden chair. He looked around but his view was limited. He saw beer kegs and other items associated with a drinking establishment. He twisted but could not see who entered the room. He heard a chair as it was moved behind him and wondered if he was about to receive a blind-sided blow he wouldn't soon recover from. He was far more worried when he saw who had the chair.

The man known as Mr. Jones, or more precisely, the man Julien knew as Alexi Doshnikov, turned the old wooden chair backward and then sat down. He smiled as he looked at the frightened Julien and then placed his crossed arms over the back of the chair and smiled. The Russian reached out and patted his right leg as he calmly and slowly lit a large cigar.

"Why am I here? I told you everything you wanted to know."

The small Russian kept his smile and then removed the cigar. He slowly blew smoke into the frightened man's face. His smile grew and then he looked up and gestured for one of his henchmen and he was handed a bottle of spring water.

"You must try this water, it's from the Ukraine. Artisan." He clenched the cigar in his teeth and then uncapped the green bottle and held it to Julien's lips and he drank. "Yes, that's good stuff, isn't it?" He pulled the bottle away, spilling a little on Julien's shirt. "Oh, I'm sorry," he said as he handed the bottle back to the bodyguard. He used a silk handkerchief to wipe the water from the shirt. "I do have one more inquiry for you, my friend," he said as he removed the kerchief and then tossed the just-lit cigar away. Doshnikov leaned over and pulled up the man's left shirt sleeve. He saw the numbers on the forearm and smiled. He lowered the shirt sleeve and then fixed the former bodyguard with his most disarming smile.

"I don't know anything else," Julien said as he watched the Russian start to place the handkerchief back into his coat and then thought better of it and threw it on the floor in mock disgust.

"I can see by your numerical artwork on your arm that you have been through some hard times. I do not wish to add to those . . . distant memories." He held a hand out and then one of his men placed a photo into it. The Russian held the picture up so Julien could see. "Which one of these five men can operate the machine you have dubbed the Wellsian Doorway?"

Julien looked at the picture and then at the Russian. "The chairman placed the responsibility for the doorway into the hands of that man." He nodded at the photo, making the Russian lose patience.

"There are four men, which one?"

"The younger man, Jodle."

"Aw, this makes sense. I find that man most disagreeable, but one who would protect a valuable asset with fevered purpose. I know the type. I have been surrounded by them my entire professional career."

"Most do find him dissagreable," Julien said with a faltering smile, hoping the comment would assuage the Russian. He felt better when the forced smile was returned, he just hoped it was more genuine than his own.

"Yes, you understand completely." He turned to the five other men lining the basement of the Russian's nightclub and handed the picture back. "You see, I told you these people are far more cooperative than any of you would believe." He patted Julien's leg once more and then stood up and twirled the chair around and moved it aside. He buttoned his sport coat and smiled down at Julien. "And you have actually witnessed this machine in working order?"

"Yes, it is an exact model of the first doorway. It works, I know."

The Russian smiled wider as he rubbed at his gleaming black beard. He knew the large man was telling the truth because he had seen something few ever saw— he saw the tattoo. This time he patted the man on his shoulder as he made eye contact with one of his men.

"I admire you, my friend, to overcome so much and to be so forthcoming in regard to my inquiries. I salute your past, and I have planned for you a brighter and far less frightening future." With one last smile the man known as Mr. Jones, aka Alexi Doshnikov, left the basement as he whistled an old Russian folk song.

Julien watched him go and was expecting his bonds to be cut. That was why he wasn't expecting the send-off that he did finally receive. The plastic bag fell over his head and face and was pulled tight.

The last thing Julien ever saw was the light dimming as the world slipped away in the distorted and obscured view of the plastic bag.

At thirty-one years of age, one of the youngest survivors of a cursed event that claimed the lives of over six million members of his race, had finally succumbed to time and the new brutality of the modern world.

BROOKLYN NAVY YARD

Will eased the picked lock from the back of the old building and pushed the door open. He stopped and listened for movement and heard none. His eyes went to the front and he saw Jason Ryan as he advanced into the darkened warehouse. In the diffused light entering the renovated building from the outside, both could see the hundreds of pallets of plastic-covered, newly made boxes. They were flat and the area must have housed over a million of them.

Jason used the muzzle of the Glock to indicate a stairwell. Will saw one also on his end. Both men made their way to the stairs opposite each other and eased themselves into the darkness. Mendenhall reached the top and saw the trapdoor. The broken lock was a clear indication that the men on the roof more than likely didn't lease or own the property. Will used his elbow to ease the trapdoor up, hoping a loud squeak didn't follow its opening. His eyes quickly fell upon the two men standing at the false facade of the building and they were not even attempting to hide their presence. The colonel and Farbeaux must have disappeared into building 114 and that was the reason they were so casual and indifferent.

Before Mendenhall could react, the door was pulled from his hand and the muzzle of a small automatic weapon was pressed against the top of his head.

"Tell me, little groundhog, do you see your shadow?" the voice said with a thick Russian accent.

"God, I hate smug assholes with witty little sayings," Will mumbled as he was roughly pulled out of the trapdoor space by the collar. He straightened and saw the stockless version of the world-renowned AK-47 leveled at his chest with two unnaturally large and bearded men smiling at him.

"Oh, look, little groundhog has a roommate," said the second man as he nodded toward the far end of the green-painted roof. Will frowned as he saw Ryan, who was also being pushed out of that side. He was then poked in the liver and pushed toward the two men taking pictures with a telephoto lens. "You may stop that, Victor, we may have another source of information—well, two actually," the man said as he nodded at the weapon-wielding man and Will was pushed toward the skylight where he met Ryan. "These two don't seem to be very good at their jobs," the man finished and the other seven men who had appeared on the roof laughed. The man examined the intruders' two Glocks, and eyed closely the strange cell phones. He pocketed the phones and handed another man the weapons.

"This is embarrassing," Jason said as he counted his way to the conclusion that they stood no chance at fighting their way out of this one. He looked down and over the side of the building and saw that there were no witnesses on this side of the navy yard. He felt his hope dwindle further when he saw Flushing Avenue on the other side. No, the only way was to jump over the side and fall into the busy street, dodging a fifteen-foot-high fence in the process, only to die in the street below instead of on the roof.

"Well, you'll have to excuse us, we've had a hard few months," Mendenhall said as his eyes fell on the fifteen-foot elongated skylight. His eyes went from there to Jason, who also spied the escape route. He closed his eyes and shook his head as he tried to remember just where the warehoused pallets had been stacked.

"Call down and have the van brought around." The man in charge gestured to

Will and Jason. "We have some questions to ask. You don't mind coming with us, do you?"

"Actually, we'd rather not," Will said with his hands raised as he stepped forward at the same moment Jason did, and then they both high-stepped into midair and gravity did the rest.

The eight Russians were so stunned they actually laughed for a moment at the stupidity of the two Americans. They briefly exchanged looks and then stepped to the broken glass and looked down in time to see Ryan and Mendenhall scrambling from the palletized boxes far below, hopping from one stack to the next lowest. The small man with the horrid face tattoo stopped, looked up, and shot the men the finger. With a wide smile he saluted and jumped to follow the black man, but not before finding out that he had hurt his backside when he jumped. He cursed and limped after the black man yelling and asking a running Mendenhall, "How come you never hurt yourself?" The Russians broke for the trapdoors on both ends.

Before, the Russian leader, who was still standing and watching his men scramble after the two escapees, didn't realize anything amiss. The cell phones they had taken from the two Americans that he had placed in his coat pocket became a reason for major concern as both cell phones simultaneously, and on orders from Europa 1,700 miles away, issued a destruct order to the phones after she had received alternate DNA prints on the Event Group–issued cell phone marvels. The internal charge was not enough to cause an explosion, but plenty large enough to burn through the memory card and the processor. Both phones immediately started to melt inside the man's pocket. He hurriedly ripped the two phones free and tossed them onto the roof of the building. He hissed as melted plastic stuck to his hand. The brute in charge of the surveillance detail angrily looked at the man who had the camera around his neck.

"Get that to Mr. Jones," he said in angered Russian. Then he jabbed a finger into the chest of one of the larger killers. "Get the ground team and bring them back!" the leader called out.

The cell phones had melted to an unrecognizable glob of black plastic and the man angrily kicked at their smoldering remains.

Will smashed through the front doors with a limping Jason close behind. They both felt naked without their pistols as they frantically looked around for an easy escape route back to the main drive of the shipyard.

"Look, that van!" Jason said as he and Will broke for the white-panel van sitting in the small drive beside building 111.

They were fifteen feet from the van when its sliding door opened and three more men spilled out of the interior and each had a large handgun.

"Jesus, what is this, the Kremlin parking lot?" Will said as he skidded to a stop.

"Through the fence," Ryan yelled when his eyes fell on a break in the chain-link. He pushed Will forward toward the bushes that covered most of the fence. Both men vanished just as four of the eight Russians broke through the front and back doors of the building and gave chase.

Jason was almost struck by a passing car that honked and swerved out of the way at the last second as they crashed through the fence and bushes. Will let go of Jason's collar and they both saw that backtracking to the safety of where their people were was impossible from this side of the fence.

"In there, we have to get to a phone," Jason yelled as he started running, favoring his bruised ass. Will saw the sign above the doorway of the small and nondescript building.

"Brooklyn Social Club," Will read as he ran after Jason.

The three men and the bearded brute from the roof broke through the bushes and the fence in time to see the two men scramble into the small establishment on a smaller side street off of Flushing Avenue. The four men split up with two going to the front and the other two to the back of the small, nondescript white building.

Jason and Will had trouble adjusting their eyes to the darkness of the room. They saw several round tables with older men sitting at them. Some were playing cards, others just sitting and speaking in low tones. Jason, out of breath, turned and saw the bartender standing and staring at the two harried men. The bartender concentrated his glare on the smaller man with the sickening tattoo on the right side of his face.

"This is a private club, *gentlemen*." The emphasis had been placed on the last word.

"We need your phone."

The eyes went to the larger black man. "You don't hear so good?" the bartender asked in his Brooklyn accent.

Several men at a nearby table were younger than the older ones they had first seen inside. The older men in the darkness in the back of the room continued to play cards without much notice to the visitors. The younger men in running suits and others in nice sport coats took another view entirely of the interruption to their day.

Will swallowed when he realized just what sort of club they had stepped into.

"Boy, you just have a sixth sense for getting us into this stuff, don't you?" he said to Jason out of the side of his mouth just as the front and rear doors opened and their pursuers joined them.

The younger men at the farthest tables tensed but remained seated when the four dark-haired men came in. Some of these young Turks looked to the back and the others at the front of the club. All eyes watched the confrontation without comment, with the exception of the burly little bartender.

"As I told these two, this is a private club."

The man leading the well-dressed charge into the club turned at the front door and smiled at the bartender. He was also out of breath.

"We have no wish to intrude," he said as he dismissed the bartender and approached Mendenhall and Ryan, who stood their ground defiantly. "We just came in to help you with your vermin situation. We shall remove them and be on our way."

All the men, twenty plus of them, with the exception of the nine old men who continued to smoke cigars and play cards, along with another two who sat in the far corner playing checkers, exchanged looks at the funny accent of the bearded man in the black silk suit and shiny shirt. The gold chains around his neck were fully exposed to show off their glory.

"You do that outside," the bartender said as his right hand vanished beneath the counter.

"Gentlemen, I am Captain William Mendenhall, United States Army; this is Commander Jason Ryan, U.S. Navy. We really need to use that phone," Mendenhall said as he looked from the men sitting at the tables and then back to the bartender.

"Now, now, does this man look as if he's in the U.S. Navy? Has the navy's standards fallen so low as to recruit men such as this?" the Russian said in perfect English as he slowly advanced on the two men in the middle of the room. The men at the tables remained silent as they took in the situation. "We will not bother you further," the man said, slightly turning his head toward the beefy bartender as he gestured for his three men to take the two outside. "Come, we have much to discuss." He tried to take Mendenhall's arm and the captain pulled away.

"Don't touch me, Russian."

This caught the attention of the men in the room. Even the older men stopped playing cards and looked up at what was happening. Several of their eyes went to the older men playing checkers. Even they had stopped and were watching the scene unfold.

"Come, come, let's not make a scene. We have a few questions and then you can return to your commander, whoever he is."

"Thought you said these men wasn't in the army or the navy?" the bartender asked.

"Friend, please mind your own affairs, before something bad happens to you," the Russian said as his three men encircled Ryan and Mendenhall.

"Something bad?" the bartender asked with a wry smile etching his face.

"Do you have a hard time understanding English, my friend, or do you only understand that lost tongue of Mama Mia Italiano?" The man laughed and looked at his men as they joined him.

Before the Russians knew what was happening every younger man had risen and had produced handguns before the Eastern Bloc mob could even blink and drop their silly grins. The bartender charged the sawed-off twelve-gauge pump shotgun and leveled it at the bearded leader. The bartender looked to his right at the table where the old men sat playing cards, and then finally to the two gentle-men who sat and watched from their interrupted checker playing. All sets of eyes were on the Russians, who had suddenly started to deflate. An old man in a green sweater and old fedora placed his checkers down on the board and then slowly nod-ded at the bartender.

"As you can see, Russian, we speak both languages rather well. And while we have no love for some of our more aggressive federal authorities, never think that relates to boys in uniform, ever." The bartender pointed the barrel of the shotgun directly at the Russian's head. Will and Jason had to admire the fact that the bearded man never blinked; instead he looked bemused. "You two better make for the door before these boys and us have a serious disagreement." The bartender nodded toward the front of the building.

"You don't know what you're involving yourselves in," the leader said as his men wondered if they stood a chance if they resisted the Italian's orders.

"We know exactly what it is we're involved in, Russian," the bartender said as if the word was a bad-tasting cheese. "For years we've noticed. You boys go about things in a not very professional manner." The shotgun became the main focus of the Russian's attention. "Now you two get to runnin', these boys are going to sit and have a drink while we explain a few rules we have in this particular area of town."

Will and Jason exchanged looks and with a nod at the men in running suits and sport coats, they ran through the front door and vanished.

"Now, what will you gentlemen have—vodka?" he asked as the young bucks of the Gambino crime family gathered the handguns of the arrogant new kids on the block, who were finding out that old grudges never really vanished with certain families.

The bearded man looked at the men disarming them and smiled—if only briefly.

"Yes, vodka will do." He gestured for his men to sit.

The bartender's eyes flicked to the old men at the table who had resumed play-ing cards. One of then looked up and raised his gray-colored brows. The man took a dusty bottle from the bar and came around with glasses and approached the angered Russians. He placed the glasses down with the bottle of vodka.

"On the house."

The bearded man looked up as a small shot glass of clear liquid was placed in front of him. He raised his glass in toast and turned to the old men at the card table and then finally at the two men playing checkers in the far corner. The oldest man was recognizable as Paul Gazza, the head of the Gambino crime family. The man posed no threat to the power of the Russians, at least according to Russian sources.

"To old times," he said with a sad smile, and then drank and slammed the glass down.

The men looked up and their silence made the Russians feel uncomfortable. The old man in the hat nodded his head as if in agreement as he smiled at his friend across the table and jumped several red checkers over black ones.

"Ah, checkmate!" he said with a laugh.

"You're playing checkers, old man, not chess. There is no checkmate in checkers," the Russian said with a bemused smile.

The old man in the moth-eaten fedora looked up and his smile vanished as his eyes narrowed. "There is always a checkmate, no matter what game you play."

The Russian mobsters never knew what hit them as several silenced weapons thudded in the darkness of the social club on a small side street just off of Flushing Avenue.

The card game, among other more dangerous games in New York, continued within the Brooklyn underworld as if nothing extraordinary had just happened.

11

BROOKLYN NAVY YARD

As Virginia's nuclear sciences team and Jenks's newly aquired engineering department examined the doorway like ants crawling on a hill, Anya sat next to the Traveler, Moira Mendelsohn. The old woman looked at the sad countenance of the young raven-haired woman. Her eyes would wander back to the activity below in the newly discovered PIT where a machine she never knew existed sat in its sparkling glory as the Group went over it with all the advanced science at their disposal—equipment Moira had never seen before. Soon the old woman's eyes were back on Anya, who felt her gaze. She faced the smiling Traveler.

"You keep looking at me as if you have something to say," Anya said not unkindly.

Moira smiled wider and then fixed her with her brown eyes.

"You were the young lady who stole my debrief file from the Mossad?" she asked.

"Yes."

"Dangerous games. Very dangerous."

"Yes, I hurt someone very close to me to get that file." Anya smiled as she looked away and watched the technicians below. She felt Moira studying her once again. "For a deed that I will eventually pay heavily for." She gave the Traveler the briefest of sad smiles. "Deals with the devil and so forth."

"But then again you would still go about hurting anyone to get back what was lost, yes?"

Anya looked at the Traveler and she could see the woman was speaking from a past fraught with the same sort of decisions.

"Yes, a million times over." Anya turned away and looked at her watch. "If you'll excuse me I have a meeting I'm late for." She started to rise as Moira placed a hand on her wrist.

"You are a Gypsy?"

Anya stopped and looked down at the withered but elegant hand and then into the Traveler's eyes. "Yes."

"I knew many Gypsies in the old days," she said as she looked away momentarily, and that was when Anya saw the tattooed number on her forearm as she absentmindedly adjusted the blanket around her legs. Moira looked back at Anya as she released her wrist. "I hope your quest turns out far better than my own." Moira used the wheelchair's motor and turned away to concentrate on answering Dr. Pollock's technical concerns.

Anya watched her a moment and wondered what quest the Traveler had referred to. She thought a moment and asked herself just what secrets did this brilliant woman possess that she wasn't mentioning.

Anya Korvesky knew she had to dig a little bit more into the Traveler's past before men and women risked their lives for her and Carl.

EVENT GROUP COMPLEX, NELLIS AIR FORCE BASE, NEVADA

Xavier took a long swallow of Mountain Dew and then looked at the sandwich the mess steward had delivered to the computer center where he and his newly acquired staff were looking for any avenue that would allow the Wellsian Doorway to lock onto the correct time frame. Thus far there was nothing that could duplicate the signal from the second doorway. They had hit a definite dead end. He pushed the plate with the sandwich on it away from him in frustration. He placed the plastic bottle of soft drink down and then spun his chair to look down onto the floor where most of his techs were working with Europa to find a solution. They looked almost as frustrated as himself. His eyes scanned the monitors below and his sight caught something that made him think.

"Uh, Mr. Styles, is it?" he said into his microphone at his personal station, which overlooked the extensive computing floor below.

The tech was leaning over a station where another worked. The tall, thin technician looked up and back at his new boss. "Uh, yes, sir," he said.

"What is that on your monitor?"

The technician looked up and saw what the youngest and newest department head in Department 5656 history was seeing.

"Oh, we were just going over the supply situation Mr. Everett would have had in the escape pod. We have come to the conclusion that he would have run out of supplies a month after crashing. If that long. His ammunition supply was—"

On the monitor below there was a schematic that showed the small escape pod that was used on the battleship HMS *Garrison Lee*.

For no apparent reason Xavier smiled and then slapped his hand down hard on his leg, not feeling the impact due to his paralysis.

"Transfer those specs to my station immediately, please. Join me up here, we have some work to do. Europa, I need everything that you have on escape pod design number 22167."

Energy started to fill the computer center as an avenue for science had just been opened and they now had a chance at answering the question for how they would lock on to the correct time frame for Everett's rescue. The Event Group came alive with a small thread of hope.

BROOKLYN NAVY YARD

Collins, Mendenhall, and Ryan were the last to be seated in the overcrowded upstairs office. The space had been cleared of the window-dressing mess that had camouflaged the true intent of building 114. The main addition to the room was the large eighty-eight-inch monitor against the far wall. Xavier Morales was on the screen and all but Mendelsohn knew Europa was there also.

Niles Compton sat at the table's head and Alice Hamilton was on his right as was customary with Virginia next to Alice. Jack was directly across from Sarah, Charlie Ellenshaw, and Anya. The rest of the various departments that had something to add to the meeting were present. Jenks was in a hurry to get back to the newly discovered PIT to reverse-engineer as much as he could as he still wasn't that trusting of Madam Mendelsohn. Jack looked at Sarah and let her know with his eyes that he didn't like the fact that she and Anya, with Alice Hamilton's help, had tried to sidestep his mission parameters and insert themselves into the field team. Sarah knew Jack wasn't happy.

"Okay, Colonel, are our two adventurers unharmed?" Niles asked as he looked over the wire-rimmed glasses that covered not only his good, but also his patched eye.

"Aside from needing a refresher course on covert egress of an enclosed facility, they're fine. Although two DNA-coded cell phones will be coming out of their pay," Collins joked without a smile at Ryan and Mendenhall.

They would both thank Collins later for the public shout-out.

"Commander, you reported that the men who accosted you and Captain Mendenhall were Russian speaking?" Niles asked as he continued to look at the two men at the end of the table. His good eye kept wandering to Ryan's facial anomaly that was unavoidable, thus it was hard not to smile at the young naval officer's discomfort.

"Well, I wouldn't say we were accosted exactly," Jason started to protest.

Niles waited patiently even though time was short—but even the director couldn't waste an opportunity jabbing a teasing blow at Jason and Will.

"Yes, sir, definitely Russian. From the sounds of it, maybe organized crime, not sure."

"Yes, sir, it seemed the Italian gentlemen who assisted us"—he looked at Collins—"in our egress from that particular enclosed facility"—he then looked back at the director—"didn't seem too fond of them. It seemed those gentlemen might have been organized types also." Ryan shot Collins a look.

Jack smiled, knowing he had angered both of his men and knew they deserved the return strike. He shook his head and then looked at Henri.

"Okay, we don't have the luxury of time to go out and hit these bastards first, and we've used our monthly quota of FBI assistance to find out exactly what they want and how they fit in here. You turn this thing over to our organized crime fighters, Will and Jason." He faced both Mendenhall and Ryan. "Get a Europa link and get as much as you can on this Russian outfit."

Will and Jason knew Jack was forgiving their small failure by not berating them further.

"And me?" Henri asked as he wondered how long his term of servitude would be—if he survived, that is.

"We stick as close to that machine as humanly possible. It seems Madam Mendelsohn's little invention has suddenly become very popular at the oddest of moments."

"'Oddest' being the operative word, I assume?" Farbeaux sniped.

"Par for the course around here," Jack replied with a wink.

"Okay." Niles nodded for the navy communications man to allow Moira into the room. He hadn't wanted to be briefed by Ryan until he knew who they may have been dealing with. The Traveler still caused many a person at this table major concern for not knowing her greatest achievement had been compromised, stolen, and then duplicated. She wheeled in and nodded to all those around the table with her eyes settling on Anya for only a brief moment. "Virginia?" Niles finished as the room quieted.

"In consultation with Dr. Mendelsohn, we have come to the conclusion that the Wellsian Doorway looks intact and fully functional. But that has not been confirmed as yet by our teams. The damage to the power lines coming into these buildings has not allowed us to bring the doorway online nor even her peripheral

systems. The building has a small supply of power coming through its own generating system, which we have fully refueled, but not anywhere near the power we
would need to get the doorway operational."

"Are we working on an alternate power source?" Niles asked Jenks.

"Not yet, we need—"

"Yes, we are covering that," Virginia said as she cut off the startled master
chief, who looked as if he had no idea what she was talking about.

"We have?" he asked with a grumbled look.

"Yes, *I* have," she said, looking at his confused face.

"Okay, what should the priority be?" Compton asked only for the benefit of
others around the table.

Virginia turned to Xavier, who nodded his head at the camera view supplied
by the supercomputer.

"Thus far I have nothing on how to gain signal acquisition without the second
receiving doorway being in place. The science just isn't there. An attempt made
without a corresponding doorway, as I am sure Madam Mendelsohn will tell you,
is quite impossible. At least according to theory."

"According to my engineering specs, Einstein may have come up with this
theory, but I don't see how this thing actually works, and sending people through
that damn thing without knowing the exact science behind it is damn well stupid."

Compton ignored Jenks's outburst and turned back to the large viewing screen.
"I sense a 'but' in there, Doctor," Compton said, watching the young man and how
he handled the pressure of research on an emergency level.

"That there is, Director Compton. In my briefing by Europa and reading the
final after-action reports by Colonel Collins, I may have a lead on something that
may help. It's a long shot but I do think it's worth looking into. I just need some
information from the master chief."

"Master Chief?" Niles asked looking to his left.

"Go for it, young Xbox jockey."

Compton frowned at Jenks.

Morales smiled at the intended slight of being called an Xbox jockey. "I understand this entire operation was started when Admiral Everett vanished in an
escape pod from HMS *Garrison Lee*, and then into the unnaturally generated
dimensional wormhole, is this correct?"

"Yes," Niles answered quickly just to keep Jenks from doing so.

"And the government of Great Britain recovered that same escape pod two
hundred thousand years, give or take fifty thousand years, after it crashed into the
historically and speculated inland sea on the continent of Antarctica. Is this also
correct?"

Silence as the room waited patiently, knowing the new man knew nothing of
how Niles ran his meetings.

"Master Chief, you designed those very same escape pods, am I correct?"

"That's right, the escape pods and the assault craft used in the operation."

"Brilliant designs, I might add," Morales said. "But I digress. Master Chief, I need the escape pod design specs. Europa may have come up with a solution. As I said it's a long shot, but it's better than what the alternative would be."

"What is it?" Jenks asked as he looked from Virginia to the screen.

"The pod was designed with a global positioning locater, correct?"

"Yes, it acts as a homing beacon upon ejection for search and rescue. All of the pods had them."

"Completely waterproof?" Xavier continued.

"Yeah, it's a sealed unit," Jenks grumbled as he wondered if the kid was questioning his design.

"This is important, Master Chief: What is the life span of the locator beacon?"

"Six months, maybe seven."

Morales looked away for a moment and his face was lost in the large monitor. He reappeared.

"Europa may have found a way to bypass a second doorway signal. She may be able to lock on to Admiral Everett's search-and-rescue marker if you can get this doorway open to allow her signal to get through to search for the correct frequency."

Anya felt her heart skip a beat. All others looked into the monitor absolutely blown away by the young Morales and his obvious and immediate connection with the supercomputer, Europa.

"Dr. Mendelsohn?" Compton said, looking toward the woman.

"I would need to know the frequency of the rescue beacon for the initiating doorway to lock on to, but this may be promising if the beacon is still active."

All eyes shot back to Niles.

"Virginia, you and Master Chief Jenks are excused. Get with Dr. Morales and see if we have something here.

"Professor Ellenshaw, I need the report by you and the anthropology department on the primordial situation we could be walking into on the continent of Antarctica two hundred twenty thousand years ago, give or take two thousand years. Lieutenant McIntire, the same goes on the geologic front. I need answers, people, on what sort of environment we will be walking into there. I also need the zoological department along with anthropology to get us a read on possible animal and humanoid life, and I need all of this yesterday. Alice will coordinate."

Niles conferred long distance with the other department heads sitting in the conference room in Nevada as Sarah and Alice both watched Anya eyeing Moira suspiciously. Both women knew Anya had discovered something about the Traveler that had disturbed her. As Moira explained some technical detail or other to Virginia and an attentive Jenks, Anya finally made eye contact with Sarah and nodded toward the door. Sarah looked at Alice and excused herself. Jack eyed the two suspiciously for getting up without comment. He looked at Henri and his head tilted ever so slightly in question.

As she stepped out of the office door, Sarah saw Anya looking out of a filthy window at the overcast and defused light outside.

"Alice and I wondered when you were going to let us in on what was bothering you," Sarah said as she laid her electronic pad on the table lining a stained wall and then sat on its edge, waiting as Anya slowly turned to face her and the inquiry.

"She is hiding something," Anya said, biting her lip.

"We all hide things, Moira probably more than most," Sarah countered.

"My brother," the voice said from the doorway.

Anya and Sarah turned and that was when they saw the Traveler sitting in her chair with her hand still on the old brass doorknob. She had been sitting there silently.

"Moira, I—"

The wheelchair slowly moved into the room and Moira examined the two women.

"I was searching for my brother. Sixteen times I made the transition through the doorway, and sixteen times I failed to find him." The old woman advanced into the old outer office where shipyard accountants and naval engineers used to sit huddled doing their jobs of long ago. The wheelchair was silent as she moved it across the floor. She stopped next to Anya and she too looked out at the dreary day over Brooklyn.

"The brother who was used as a hostage while you traveled?" Sarah asked, remembering her file.

"Yes. Joseph." She smiled at the mention of the name as she recalled his precious face to mind. She turned and took in both women as if she wanted them to understand. "I called him Flea, he was so small."

"You had to have known the doorway was destroyed behind you. You said it yourself in your postwar debrief to the allies and then again to Israeli intelligence. So why would you make an attempt at something that was now clearly impossible?"

Sarah saw the answer first as her training dictated she would. "The first Wellsian Doorway from the previous year, the first built in Germany," Sarah said as she watched Moira for the truth of her educated guess.

"Yes, the first doorway, built and unused for anything except for me and the initial experiments, the Nazi's own Traveler." She looked at the two women and smiled, a sad attempt. "The experiment was a closed one. That meant that when the bunker was evacuated after the construction of the doorway in 1942, it was left unguarded and in pristine condition for their test rat to emerge from that very first, abandoned machine. I would eventually use that first doorway and I and my team would attempt to bring my brother out of 1942 Nazi Germany. An impossible task, which was hard learned. We would go in two-week increments and search for him. First in Dortmund, and then at Bergen-Belsen, where we were all kept before the experiments had begun in 1942. We found nothing."

Sarah was more interested in Anya's reaction to Moira's explanation than the Traveler's words. Anya raised the black brow over her alternating blue-green right eye.

The door opened and Charlie stuck his crazed white head of hair inside and found Moira.

"Dr. Mendelsohn, Director Compton is ready for you." He looked at the serious expressions in the room and immediately ducked away. After all, Charlie had been receiving dirty looks most of the day from Ryan and Collins every time they saw him. The door quickly closed. He was beginning to think that the music fiasco would kill his chances at coming along with the mission group.

Moira looked at Anya and then Sarah before she turned the wheelchair for the door where Sarah held it open for her. Without a look back or another word, Moira went back into the meeting.

"Well, you're the Gypsy—is she lying? I thought she spoke the truth. Of course my instincts are based on nothing in particular . . . what does the spy in you say?" Sarah asked as she walked away from the door and faced Anya.

"No, she's not lying, Sarah." The former Israeli intelligence agent bit her lip once more and then looked at the door and the meeting beyond. "But she's not being straightforward either. She's not letting us completely inside yet."

"Dr. Morales said that when Moira covered her tracks in the sixties and seventies she did it better than anyone he had ever seen outside of black operations people. He said it will take him and Europa months to uncover her true past. He said he will eventually dig it out, but she was that good at covering and hiding her intentions to the world in general."

"Look, I know Jack and the security department have their hands full at the moment with this Russian mob aspect, but can you shift your duties to your assistant in geology? I think we girls need a trip into Westchester."

Sarah looked surprised.

"What's up in Westchester?" she asked as Anya faced her at the door.

"That is where the private home is located that our Miss Mendelsohn used as an orphanage. It's closed down after all of these years but it's still there. We need to see about these two hundred and thirty-seven orphans she supported. Let's see if we can track someone down who can tell us just why Miss Mendelsohn was so generous of not only her money, but her time."

"I'm not getting an evil, or even a bad vibe from Moira, and I usually get them from people with less-than-honorable intent."

"Yes, but as you so brashly pointed out, Sarah, I'm a Gypsy and a spy."

Sarah raised her brows and smiled as Anya opened the door to return to the meeting.

"Well, Jack's already pissed at me, so, what the hell, I guess we'll take a drive to Westchester County."

UPPER EAST SIDE OF MANHATTAN, NEW YORK CITY

The younger man watched the CEO place the silk scarf around his neck and then pull on the slightly heavier coat over his two-thousand-dollar British-made suit. Joshua Jodle watched the old man with ever increasing contempt. After being assisted with his coat the CEO faced the younger man. The ever-present smile was in place where it always has been. He handed him his expensive briefcase as they stood before the private elevator.

"Look, Jodle, I want you up at Lake Champlain no later than eight o'clock tonight. We have to get this ugly business sorted out soon before everyone from the FBI to the Securities and Exchange Commission starts a witch hunt." The dark eyes warned Jodle that if he wasn't part of the solution he could easily be made part of their problem-solving efforts in the next few days.

"Yes, sir, the helicopter will return for me as soon as I find out the disposition of our eastern friends."

"You do that. Now, the other members of the board are already onboard." The elevator doors opened and the CEO allowed Jodle in first simply because the chairman was just too important to push the button for the roof. Jodle did and then watched as the older man stepped inside. The doors closed and the elevator climbed to the fiftieth floor in silence.

The wind had picked up and the night had some bite to it as the elevator doors opened onto the roof of the expensive apartment building—one of the most exclusive in the city. The helicopter's rotor started to turn as the executive Sikorsky made ready for its run to the Lake Champlain meeting house where the entire board of directors would decide on how to handle the Moira Mendelsohn problem that seemed to be getting larger the longer they waited.

"Find out what that fool Russian is playing at. We need the details so we may respond appropriately."

"Yes, sir," Jodle said as the old man turned and walked briskly to the idling helicopter where the other six men of the board of directors waited inside the plush helicopter. Jodle even managed to wave his hand at the pilot, who nodded as the door closed. The idling engine went to full power for its liftoff from Manhattan. The gleaming Sikorsky lifted free of the helipad and slowly started to climb. It peeled off as soon as it cleared the roof and rose even higher over the East River. Jodle watched as his left hand held the elevator doors and his grip was pure white as he waited.

The explosion was bright and reflected off the heavy rain clouds covering the skyscrapers. The Sikorsky disintegrated and the pieces floated easily toward the water far below. The last to strike was the twirling rotor blades that hit with a spectacular wash of spray that shot high into the sky. Jodle closed his eyes when he knew he wasn't alone.

"There, that was a simple solution to a sticky problem, wasn't it? Now look who gets to take over the firm in the number one slot." There was laughter. "You can thank me later."

Jodle turned and saw the hand on his shoulder as the Russian stepped free of the shadows. Three of his bodyguards were with him.

"It was a risk to take them out before we are assured of Madam Mendelsohn's full cooperation."

"That's why we have you, my young friend. You were the last one of her orphans through the doorway, we just need you to turn it on for us." Mr. Jones, as he was called at all times, smiled and slapped the younger man hard on the back. "Besides, with the stolen list of your madam's children, the task of gaining her cooperation is made that much easier." The Wall Street trader grimaced as the blow to the back the Russian had administered a moment before almost made him lose the air in his lungs.

"It's a bit more complicated than that," Jodle said, hoping to dampen the high spirits of the cold-blooded killer.

He faced Jodle and the smile was gone.

"Let's hope it is not, for your sake." The Russian turned and started for the closed elevator doors and then waited on the younger man to catch up with him.

"And what do we do about those people at the navy yard?" The tall man waited for the Russian to acknowledge his concern. The bell chimed and the elevator doors slid open to reveal three of the mobster's men waiting inside. He hesitated before climbing into the car. He turned with his black-gloved hand on the doors, halting their closing cycle.

"As of now I have four missing men who were conducting surveillance on these strangers. It seems whoever these people are"—he looked up into the trader's face— "are very resourceful. That scratches most of the NYPD and federal authorities off the list. Especially since most of this borough's uniformed men work for me in one capacity or another." He stepped into the car and raised his dark brows until Jodle joined the four men inside.

"Regardless of who they are, they will nevertheless dismantle the doorway and remove it. And I assure you, Mr. Jones, the process cannot be duplicated. Times have changed and getting the necessary technology for duplication is highly illegal and, I might add in most cases, impossible to acquire. So if I may ask, how do you intend on getting the only working doorway out of the hands of these people?"

That irritating, knowing smile etched the Russian's face as the elevator doors started to close.

"We do what any civilized gentlemen would do: we ask politely."

The doors closed on the shocked face of the stockbroker.

FISHKILL, NEW YORK

The families were gathered to celebrate the birth of their first granddaughter. The proud parents held the newborn as the grandparents beamed while taking photos. The young woman was the only child of the couple who came to be parents a little later in life than usual, even for New York yuppies.

The grandfather had recently retired from a construction firm where he had served as an engineer for forty years. He and his wife considered themselves young and vital and prepared for the challenges of the second half of their lives. They felt it was all well deserved for the horrid first few years they had suffered. Benjamin and Natalie Koblenz were now complete and had guaranteed themselves that their strange legacy was going to continue in the grinning face of the newborn baby they now watched in their daughter's arms.

The house was quiet as the grandmother and daughter began to place dishes on the table for a late supper after the long day checking out of the hospital.

The light knock on the back door caught the two women unawares as they exchanged curious looks.

"The back door?" the daughter asked.

Just as the grandmother turned, the door opened and three men stepped inside. Her eyes widened when she saw the guns in the men's hands. The young woman gasped and before the strangers could react ran into the living room. She came to a sliding stop when she saw the second set of three men in the hallway holding the same menacing weapons as the ones at the rear door. Her eyes frantically went to the living room where she saw her husband standing with their newborn and her father staring wide-eyed at the intruders.

"Benjamin Koblenz?" the only black-clad man without a handgun asked politely.

"Yes," answered the silver-haired man, who took a step backward to shield his son-in-law and new granddaughter. He turned when he saw his daughter standing in shock and then suddenly run to be with her husband and daughter. His wife was moved from the kitchen to the living room with a gun politely sticking in her back.

"And this must be Mrs. Koblenz, the former Natalie Freiburg."

The husband remained silent as his wife came to his side. She was shaking and this infuriated the older man.

The talker placed a piece of paper into his coat pocket and then nodded to one of his men.

"My associate will assist you in gathering anything you may need for your child. Dress her warmly, we have a bit of a drive ahead of us."

Panic spread rapidly across the daughter's face like a wild flowing river as she removed her daughter from her husband's hold and sat hard on the couch, holding her child tightly to her heaving chest. "You can't take my baby," she cried as her frightened husband tried his best to shield them as he too sat.

The man shook his head. "We are not in the habit of killing children," the man lied as he had done just that a few months before with a freeloader and his family in Staten Island. "We need twenty-four hours of cooperation and then we will return you and your family to your home." He smiled. "Completely intact and unharmed."

"Who are you and why do you need us to go with you?" the grandfather asked as a diaper bag was tossed to him by one of the intruders.

"I will let Miss Mendelsohn explain that to you."

Both Benjamin and Natalie Koblenz exchanged worried looks.

"Who is that?" the daughter asked as she and her young husband were brought to their feet.

The silence that greeted the question was unnerving as the six men went about preparing to abduct the entire family.

A small portion of the Traveler's secret and extended family was being rounded up.

KATONAH, WESTCHESTER COUNTY, NEW YORK

The darkness had eaten most of Sarah's enthusiasm as she thought about how Jack and Niles were going to fly off the proverbial handle when they learned that she and Anya were in the process of going rogue on them. All of this after the director had allowed them all back in after being caught trying to manipulate the young Morales. No, this was not going to sit well at all.

"There it is," Anya said as she saw the address and the name on the black gate and the surrounding brick masonry that guarded the monstrous Gothic building.

Sarah slowed the car down and stopped at the chained gate and looked at the large mansion beyond. The darkness was complete. "Well, it sure as hell looks abandoned," Sarah said and then nearly screamed when a knock sounded on her window. Embarrassed, she turned her head and saw the uniformed security guard standing just outside of the car. He had tapped on the glass with a flashlight. The man stood straight when the car's dome light came on when Anya stepped outside and walked to the side of the car where the old man waited.

"You young ladies know this is private property?" he asked as he watched the gorgeous woman with jet-black hair approach. He was appreciative of her figure as his locked and loaded eyes made obvious.

"We just need some information," Anya said as she stepped closer to the older security guard, whose frame looked as if it hadn't missed any meals of late. "How long has the"—she looked at the brass name on the gate—"Briarson Home for Children been closed?"

"Oh, gosh, even before I got out of grade school. The town was sad to see it go, I do know that. The firm that supported the school and home was very generous to the local community. Let's see, 1983, maybe '84."

"Wow, that has been awhile," Anya said with a quick look into the driver's side window at Sarah. Then the plastic Taser came up and into the man's large belly. His eyes went wide and he became rigid as the electrical charge coursed through his body. "Sorry," Anya said as she tried in vain to ease the unconscious guard to the ground but cursed when he crashed anyway due to his unexpected weight. She quickly rummaged in the man's pockets and then stood and looked at a shocked Sarah McIntire. "We don't have a lot of time here for Q and A," she said as she turned and ran for the locked gate. She quickly had the chain removed as Sarah jumped out and started dragging the moaning security guard through the now open barrier.

"I think Carl and Jack are a bad influence on you," Sarah said as she used the officer's handcuffs to secure him to the inside bars of the ornate gate as the semi-conscious man kept mumbling incoherently. Sarah reached down and removed the guard's radio and threw it five feet away into a stand of overgrown bushes lining the gate. Both women went back to the car in silence and then drove through and closed the gate to keep outside curiosity to a manageable level.

The mansion was large and only a few lights burned purely for fire department safety. Moira, through her management firm, had kept the grounds immaculate and they hoped the same could be said for the interior. They parked the car in the front and used the large set of keys stolen from the guard to open the double front doors. The dreams of finding the inside as glorious as the outside were quickly and distinctly quashed.

"Boy, the housekeeping staff must have been the first employees let go when this place closed," Sarah said as she ran a hand through thirty years of dust on a sideboard table near the front door. Sarah started to reach for the light switch and Anya stayed her hand. She just shook her head. She clicked on a flashlight and gave it to Sarah.

"The guard may have a few friends."

Sarah nodded and they started looking—for what, they didn't know.

BROOKLYN NAVY YARD

The machine up close was gorgeous in its design if not daunting in its construction. Virginia, Jenks, and the entire nuclear sciences and engineering departments were crawling all over the doorway and its support systems. With the assistance of Europa they had devised that the time machine was in complete working order even though Europa was having a hard time saying the apparatus would or could actually work. The science was just too impossible, even for the Cray system as she was also having trouble without the right programs on quantum physics.

The daunting problems remaining were not in the control of Jenks or Virginia, but mostly fell to the responsibility of Morales and Europa in finding a corresponding signal from what might be as far back as 250,000 years, that coupled with the fact that they could not even power up the Wellsian Doorway without blacking out the entire eastern seaboard. Moira had explained that exact same thing had happened causing the famous 1969 New York blackout. She had even smiled when recalling the debacle she had spent millions upon millions of dollars to cover up.

The Event Group's duplicate, reverse-engineered, and far more portable Wellsian Doorway was now under construction next to the existing one. It would be able to be broken into components for transport to Antarctica to be reassembled there for the team's dimensional return—if there was one.

"Yeah, well I can't see anything working until we get some electricity in here that has enough umph to fire this damn thing up," Jenks said as he removed the stub of his cigar and nearly spit the foul taste from his mouth until he saw Virginia waiting to pounce on him for doing so. He swallowed instead. "Well, are you going to let me in on your little secret on how you plan to accomplish that particular electrical miracle since the portable power unit we have at the complex has to go with the field team into the past"—he smirked at Virginia—"if that's even possible."

The look down at Moira by an unbelieving Jenks was unmistakable as she sat and smiled at the master chief and his continuing doubts about the sciences involved. Moira knew engineers had very small imaginations.

"Look, there is only one portable power unit in existence capable of generating the output of the hundred and fifty megawatts we need. Bringing in the power lines from the city will cause a lot of eyes to look our way and even then we would probably blow every circuit from here to Montreal in doing so. So, maybe you should let old Jenksy in on your solution, huh, Slim?"

Virginia shook her head while she used a nonconductive acrylic wrench to twist a bolt on the old doorway as they were now in the process of adding their own features to the technology. "I'm working on that, Harold."

"What did I tell you about calling me—"

"Virginia, you're needed outside, the harbormaster is waiting on you."

Both Virginia and Jenks stopped bickering and turned to see Niles Compton and Jack Collins standing by the wheelchair of Moira Mendelsohn, who was looking up at them.

Virginia looked at Jenks and gave him a smug smile and then stepped down from the top of the doorway where she had been analyzing the lens cuts on the eighteen laser apertures in the rounded circle of the door's opening.

"Unlike engineers, my people know how the world really works," Virginia said as she hopped down the last few steps of the erected scaffolding.

"Smart-ass," Jenks grumbled as he snapped the last laser lens into place.

Niles watched the assistant director exit the platform area and then waited as

Jenks climbed from the erected scaffolding and confronted Moira for further instructions on how the doorway operated. Niles then pulled Jack aside.

"I had to bring the president in on this request from Virginia and I'm guessing the Department of the Navy and General Dynamics are going to start asking some serious questions soon."

"We knew it wouldn't last as long as we needed. Do we still have the eighty-eight-hour window the president promised?"

Niles pursed his lips and then limped to a chair and sat, staring up at the Wellsian Doorway and its newly born and much smaller reverse-engineered sister rising next to her.

"Yes, and those remaining hours are ticking away fast," Compton said as his eyes roamed over the most amazing machine he had ever seen outside of the magical *Leviathan*, the futuristic submarine they encountered during a harrowing field mission a few years back that was so appreciated by the members of the Event Group.

"Has Morales and Europa had any luck with the escape pod signal?"

"He seems convinced if we can get the doorway up and running he and Europa can find a corresponding signal from Mr. Everett's escape pod. Pete Golding Junior says that according to Professor Mendelsohn's figures, Europa should be able to shoot signals into every dimensional plain, no matter how many that may be." Niles smirked. "Hell, I don't know if the kid knows what he's talking about. I'm like Jenks there, this is so far beyond me that it hurts my head thinking about it." Niles smiled and looked up at Jack. "Europa was right in her choice of her new boss, our Dr. Morales seems more than capable despite his youth. Pete was right to want him on his team."

Jack knew discussing the replacement for Pete Golding always put the director in a funk. Pete was not only close to Charlie Ellenshaw, he had also learned most everything from the man sitting next to him—Niles Compton. Collins placed a hand on Niles's shoulder and then looked around the PIT and the hundred technicians who sat at consoles and had wrenches and welders in their hands.

"Have you seen Sarah and Anya?"

12

KATONAH, WESTCHESTER COUNTY, NEW YORK

The many upstairs rooms were divided into boys' and girls' dormitories that were appointed in richly woven carpet and had the finest built-in woodwork. Sarah and Anya could see that this was not your ordinary home for abandoned or orphaned children. The house was empty and as lonely a place as either woman could ever remember seeing before. The once childish laughter of its residents echoed in empty corridors and rooms. Not one stick of furniture was left behind and the office areas had been cleaned out of all paperwork and sent to the state offices of child welfare when the house closed its doors in 1982. With the last place they had to check being the basement, they were fast losing hope as to just what the Traveler had hidden from the Group, and for that matter, the world.

The stairs were steep and treacherous and by the looks of the gathered dust and mouse droppings, it had not had a cleaning visit in many years. The dampness was cloying in smell and in feel. Anya reached the bottom and Sarah joined her, adding both lights to the cluttered scene. There were a few boxes but it was mostly made up of stacked mattresses and old bedding that was piled everywhere.

"Boy," Sarah said as her light picked out the shambles of the cavernous basement.

"I don't know what I was thinking. If Moira is as smart as we all believe, she would never have left anything behind she didn't want found."

Anya slowly moved back to the stairs and Sarah was about to follow suit when her light briefly caught a water-worn box that had collapsed, spilling its contents. Sarah walked the few steps over and then lightly kicked at the spilled contents that were near ruin after years of water damage. She kneeled down and saw the names on the old assignment papers. She read names like Phizinberger, Rabinowitz, and Wachowski. There were more names as she scanned the old math pages. She looked up and that was when she saw the long dead incinerator. She stood and walked toward its open doors. Her light had spied something white inside.

"What is it?" Anya asked halfway up the stairs.

"Incinerator," Sarah said as she pulled the right-side door all the way open, allowing the smell of old trash and smoke to fill her nostrils. She waved her hand in front of her face to clear the air as she leaned in.

"Hope you don't find any bodies in there. I don't think I could handle that in the dark."

Sarah reached in and pulled out several pieces of half-burned paper. She shined the flashlight's beam on the first and she almost dropped the small, half-ashen bundle to the damp floor. Sarah swallowed and then looked at the graphic charcoal art. The disturbing work had possibly been done by a young, although talented artist. Her face screwed up into a mask of horror as she studied the drawings on page after page of heavy paper. Sarah reached into the gaping maw of the long-dead furnace and brought out even more of the heavy art paper.

"What is it?"

Sarah stepped away with her light's beam shakily illuminating the blackest, most disturbing artwork she had ever seen. She had heard the descriptions but had never imagined seeing anything like these in person. She looked from the names on the old math pages and then at the horrid bundle of half-burned artistry.

"No, no body, but definitely some old skeletons."

BROOKLYN, NAVY YARD

The dark and overcast skies had given way to fog, which suited Virginia and her team just fine. Mendenhall and Ryan had very nearly emptied out the security department with the exception of a bare minimum team at the complex and they were dangerously short on security requirements until they heavily recruited from the military, which is a very time-intensive process security-wise. The result was that they had shortcomings at both ends and Ryan took it upon himself to take both security gates at the complex off line until it was prudent to open them again. He didn't know if the colonel was going to gig him for that mission choice, but it was his decision to make. The word had gone out about their afternoon visitors and now the twenty-seven security men and women had M-4s, the very much smaller version of the venerable M-16, to accompany their sidearms.

Virginia stood with the general manager of the Navy Yard Development Corporation as he complained about the closing of the waterway, which was slowing water traffic. Ships were waiting to enter the river. The man was about to voice his second argument of inconvenience when Mendenhall approached with two plain-clothed security men, who carried their weapons at port arms. Will didn't have to say a word. He wanted this man out of the way before Virginia's surprise for Jenks arrived on station. The navy yard manager saw the weapons and then with narrowed eyes he turned and stormed back to his Mercedes and left.

"Signal the harbormaster that the dock has been cleared," Virginia said to one of her assistants. "Will, you can inform those boys from Groton their prized possession has arrived."

Mendenhall nodded and then used his radio to inform the men that stood just outside of the entrance to building 114. Six men in overalls and rain gear came into view as they lined the dock, which had been drained, cleaned, and then refilled with water. They waited.

Virginia greeted Niles and Jack as they escorted a grumbling Jenks to the quay lining the expansive dry dock area.

"Okay, we're here. I see Slim and a bunch of idiots standing in the fog. I've got simulations I need to run. In case you haven't noticed I still don't have any damn power. And thus far in simulations we have killed everyone on the team sixteen times before they even step through the gate. Those damn lasers will cut people to shreds if this thing doesn't work to everyone's expectations. Remember, Slim, these are Argon light-emitting lasers, the most dangerous light outside of the sun."

Niles smiled and then shook his head as if he were listening to a complaining school child. *Engineers,* he thought.

"Harold, will you shut up while we take care of that power problem you keep going on about?" Virginia said as she stepped closer to the river side of the dock and looked as if she was waiting for something. She raised a radio to her lips and the elegant woman half turned and saw Jenks looking on curiously. She smiled.

"Harold, what were you before you became our worst nightmare and an engineer?" She spoke softly into the radio to someone, and then turned and faced the three men on the dock. She saw Henri join the group with a questioning look on his face. Jack nodded toward the confrontation between Jenks and Virginia—a confrontation Dr. Pollock was about to conclude rather dramatically.

"You know damn good and well what I was," Jenks said as he chewed on the cigar and stared down the smiling nuclear scientist.

"Oh, yes, that's right, something about a career navy man, wasn't it?"

A sour look from the master chief answered for him.

"Then I hasten to question, sir, why in the hell did I have to think of this for your power solution?"

"What solution?" Jenks asked, spitting the cigar out and walking forward to join Virginia. Niles, Jack, and Henri followed. Will Mendenhall hung back grinning, knowing the master chief had finally met his match, of which said information would be spread throughout the Group in a matter of minutes.

Virginia touched his whiskered cheek and then took hold of his chin and forcefully turned his head toward the fog-enshrouded East River and the entrance to the navy yard.

"This is why the president is now murderously curious and worried beyond measure that our little mission is spreading out rather wide. The Department of the Navy is going to start throwing a fit when they find out what it is we have stolen," Niles said as he leaned on his crutch. "A lot of strings were pulled. I only hope it's not enough string to hang us all."

Suddenly Jenks saw the waves of rolling fog pushed aside as a hulking black form slowly emerged from the white undulating veil. Jenks heard commands being given as the giant sail and conning tower eased slowly out of the river proper. The giant moved as gracefully as she ever had. The maneuver was dangerous in the darkness and fog without a large naval docking team. However, Virginia, who had been employed by the General Dynamics Electric Boat Division in the early eighties, knew the skipper well and knew him to be the best retired boat captain in the U.S. Navy.

"I'll be damned and go to hell," Jenks said as he slapped Virginia on her backside, making her jump and yelp.

"You people never cease to amaze the unenlightened," Farbeaux said as he showed his shock at what was slowly approaching like a monster from deep-sea lore. He looked at a worn and tired Niles Compton. "Kudos, Mr. Director, I'm sure you made one or two enemies with this little party favor."

"Colonel, you have no idea."

Out of the fog came the black silhouette of one of the most famous vessels in the history of the U.S. Navy. Jenks smiled at the white numbers on her enormous sail tower. Her rounded bow moved the dark water out of her path with ease and efficiency. This was the class of boat that had scared the old Soviet Union to disastrous decision making in the seventies and eighties, and this was the lead boat in that particular class. Jenks smiled as the USS *Los Angeles*, the matron of her submarine class, eased into the softly moving waters of the docking area as the men on shore grabbed lines tossed to them by the civilian crew of the fast attack submarine. The numbers on her towering sail claimed that SSN-688 had arrived at her temporary berthing station.

"The old girl looks good, don't she?" Jenks said, and then slapped Virginia on her ass once more as he paced forward to watch the old lady tie up. He was joined by the others.

Gone were the massive sail planes that once shaded her deck from the enormous conning tower. The finlike diving planes had been replaced to make the boat more streamlined, but other than that the 688 lead boat had not changed in outward appearance since her deactivation in 2010, until she was finally decommissioned on February 4, 2011.

"Why is she out of her retirement barn?" Jenks asked.

"She was turned back over to General Dynamics for use as a test platform." Virginia turned and faced Jenks. "As a naval engineer I thought you would have been in the know." She smiled and then turned to watch the crew tie up the 362 feet of rolled steel. "But I guess some things slip by the old master chief, huh?"

Niles looked down to keep Jenks from knowing that Virginia had set him up from the beginning. His doubting her engineering prowess was starting to get on his assistant director's nerves.

"Okay, give," Jenks said as he looked from the men who seemed to be in on this little joke to Virginia.

"That, Master Chief, is your portable power source." She turned to walk away but stopped and faced Jenks once more. "Since her retirement she has been fitted with a new General Electric S6G reactor, capable of generating 242 kilowatts of power in an experimental power source scenario for disaster relief. She is now back in the hands of the men and women who had built her and is privately owned, and no one from the city power grid"—she looked at Niles—"or the president's other curious agencies will ever be the wiser. At least until General Dynamics reports her missing and overdue."

"Son of a bitch," Jenks mumbled as electrical cable started to be strung from building 114 to the submarine's engineering spaces. Others of Jenks's staff had been ordered to start spreading camouflage netting over the giant boat. He was too taken aback to face Virginia.

Each man turned from the boat and then Niles walked past the master chief first. "Yes, sir, that is one brilliant lady."

Then Jack walked by. "I knew I liked Virginia from the start."

It was Henri's turn. "What she sees in you, my salty old friend, I know not."

Will just stopped and looked at Jenks, who stood waiting.

"Now you see what us everyday mortals face around here." He laughed and then walked away.

Jenks lit another cigar as he saw Charlie Ellenshaw walk up and stare at the large submarine and the crew scrambling over her blackened deck like ants. He smiled.

"Great idea, Master Chief."

"Is that what you think, Nerdly?" he grumbled at a shocked Charlie and then turned and left. No one saw the gratified smile on his face as he thought about the woman he called "Slim."

The meeting started without Virginia Pollock, Anya Korvesky, or Sarah Mc-Intire. While the master chief explained that Virginia was with Madam Mendelsohn working on the new power grid, the whereabouts of Sarah and Anya were yet unexplained. Will Mendenhall had reported that even though the two had not answered their cell phones, Europa narrowed down their geopositioning markers as somewhere between Brooklyn and Upstate New York heading south. Will could see by the looks on the faces of Niles and Collins that the two men were not amused in the least that two members of the planning staff were not present for the final Antarctica brief before powering up the doorway.

"Okay, I was expecting the geology report from Lieutenant McIntire, but it seems that she and our new head of foreign intelligence decided to head north of here for some unknown reason," Compton said as he looked at Alice, knowing she knew something about the disappearance but was being mum on the subject.

Charlie Ellenssaw spoke up from his spot at the far end of the table. "I have been in contact with the geology department at Sarah's request and have combined the zoology report and the geological reports. If I may?"

Everyone saw the scar rise above the eye patch covering the damaged right eye of Compton. He took a deep breath and then nodded at Ellenshaw.

"I will start with what we know zoologically. For that it would be best to hand it over to Dr. Morales and Europa."

"Doctor?" Niles said, looking over at the large monitor where Xavier Morales sat waiting to divulge everything they had come up with. The technical genius had finally moved permanently from the clean room and privacy and into the far more expansive computer center to be with his tech people. He could see the young Morales was starting to feel at home.

"Yes. With direction from the natural history museums in Denver, Oslo, Denmark, and several more in the United Kingdom, we can honestly say with any certainty that we know absolutely nothing about the animal life at that time on that particular continent. It's hard to survey prehistoric remains when most are situated under two miles of solid ice. We can assume that at the time of the separation of the supercontinent eighty million years ago, that a mass abundance of animal life went with Antarctica when she decided to head south. From the time frame we can almost guarantee"—he almost looked sad upon delivering the news—"that if Mr. Everett survived the wormhole transit he would be faced with unknown and terrifying animal life of that time."

"Humanoid factors?" asked Dr. Dwayne Anderson of the anthropology department.

"Unknown. Europa has not come across any evidence on the current fossil record from the region. Again, two miles of ice is a deterrent to discovery. Europa has made an 'educated guess' as to the migratory pattern of early man and the odds are that Mr. Everett will more than likely run into humanoid life. What kind? We can't say."

"You have Europa making guesses?" Jack asked as he tried to keep his worrying mind from thinking about what Sarah was up to.

"Her educated guesses are like those of Mr. Spock, she's usually never wrong."

"Doctor, go ahead and give them the good geological news," Ellenshaw said as he pushed his own written reports aside.

Everyone in the room watched Charlie for a brief moment. He had been acting strange since the loss of Pete Golding. It was as if the good humor had gone from the man and he was no longer the easygoing and friendly crazy Charles Hindershot Ellenshaw III.

"The use of the words 'good geological news' was obviously an attempt by Professor Ellenshaw to lessen the dangers to anyone on that continent at that particular time," Morales said as he sat in his old-fashioned wheelchair in Nevada.

"I appreciate the attempt to soften anything you have to report, but we are precariously short of time, gentlemen," Compton said as he rubbed the bridge of his nose.

"Yes, of course. It seems Mr. Everett may have far more trouble than originally thought, if that's possible," Morales said. "Europa, report number 45454, please."

On the second largest of the newly installed monitors a map showed the current status of Antarctica. Europa then focused more specifically on the southern region of the frozen continent.

"Ross Island, its current state. Home of Mount Erebus, an active volcano."

"Yes, it's been active continuously throughout recorded history," Niles said.

"Yes, it has, but very active since 1972. The problem here is"—he looked away momentarily—"Europa, next slide please." The picture changed to show Ross Island without the ice covering. All eyes saw immediately that Mount Erebus had been joined by three other volcanoes.

"Four volcanoes in the same area?" Mendenhall asked from his chair next to Jason Ryan.

"Yes, and through deep ice core drilling and back-scanner ice intrusions we are more than sure these four volcanoes were extremely active during the time frame we may be looking at. So much so that three of the volcanoes, Mounts Terror, Bird, and Terra Nova, vented so heavily they became extinct. Mount Erebus is the only one to survive and live on."

"What are you saying, Doctor?" Niles asked, becoming increasingly angry at his head of the geology department for not reporting this herself. Yes, he was angry with Sarah just as much as Collins.

"Europa estimates that all four volcanoes were in eruption in the same time frame as Mr. Everett's disappearance."

"How does this affect the survival possibilities for a man?" Jack asked.

"Not very good," Morales said, and they could all see he was a patient and knowing teacher who answered in a way that the simplest mind could understand. The Event Group would have to be patient with the new man. "Europa does not agree with the proposed speculation of other noted geologists. She believes this eruption of four volcanoes simultaneously brought on a massive ice age the world over. The world as we know was mostly a barren landscape of ice and snow. What Mount Erebus did was deliver the coup de gras to not only the more exposed northern land masses, but effectively killed the entire continent of Antarctica. This killer eruption was the death sentence for the continent and its overabundance of animal life, which conservative estimates place at ten thousand times the amount of life in Africa at its height."

"Jesus," Jenks said, whistling.

"The air will become poisonous and the world will turn freezing if it hadn't already by the time of Admiral Everett's arrival there. We just don't have enough information to go on."

"So, if Carl survived the exit through the wormhole, and also the reentry of the escape pod, his chances of surviving the animal life and the eruption of these four monstrous volcanoes are not very good."

Morales nodded sadly into the television monitor at Compton. "Europa estimates the odds of survival at"—Morales changed tack when he saw the expectant and knowing faces around the table—"well, you said it yourself, Director Compton: not very good."

The room was quiet enough that most could hear Alice Hamilton as she tapped her notes on her electronic pad.

"Colonel," Niles said, trying to get the room back to some form of activity to keep them from thinking about the possible horrible fate of their friend, "how are you and Colonel Farbeaux coming with your team?"

"They're assembling now," he said with his eyes carefully avoiding Jason and Will, who exchanged concerned looks. Was the colonel really considering leaving the two men behind on this one?

"Master Chief, are the components ready for the portable doorway?" Compton asked, knowing Collins had some explaining to do to his security department over the choices for the doorway mission team.

"Two complete sets. I have to admit that Slim's, er, uh, I mean, Dr. Pollock . . . her division has been pretty damned impressive as far as reverse-engineering that damn time machine. Of course, it was my newly acquired engineering staff that pieced the portable doorway together in record time. But that is not my concern." The master chief pulled the unlit cigar from his mouth and looked at the director. "I'll say this, though, if anything happens to our only portable power unit, we've all had it. We'd end up dining with the cavemen if that power generator is lost"— he looked over at the monitor and Dr. Morales—"and I guess choking on volcano farts also."

"Well-worded, Master Chief," Morales said with a smile.

"That cannot be helped. The only other portable power generator is owned by the Russians and I don't think they have a current superpower loan department," Compton said, losing patience with the same arguments from the master chief.

Jenks was about to say something when he saw Collins lightly shake his head, telling Jenks that he had said enough for the time being.

"Niles," came the voice, and the image of Virginia appeared on the monitor next to Morales. "We're as ready as we'll ever be for the power-up and test. Europa has reworked the old programming and brought it into this century. We are now completely digital. Power source is hooked up and the *Los Angeles* is capable of giving us one hundred and fifteen percent of her reactor power."

"Very good."

Niles stood with difficulty and then placed his hand on Jack's shoulder and with a final look at Mendenhall and Ryan, nodded his good luck.

"Let's adjourn and see if we have a mission or not, shall we?"

As the group filed out to witness history, again, Jack waited on Will and Jason as he gathered his notes.

"No," was all he said when they approached him. He finally looked up and into the angry faces. "The team has been set and you two are sitting this one out."

"Look, we—"

"Sitting it out," Collins said with a stern look at Ryan.

"No disrespect, Colonel, but we have a right to go," Will said.

Jack placed his case down and then fixed the men with the look that said, "The order has been given, and that's that."

"If no disrespect is intended, why are you doing it? You have your orders, both of you. You will secure the building and the grounds. If that's too much then I'll assign Sergeant Rodriguez to the job and then send you two back to Nellis."

"Sir," Mendenhall said when he saw Ryan was too angry to say anything.

"Look, the odds are not that good for a return trip on this one. You two are not essential to the team and will therefore stay behind. We'll only be risking personnel that we feel can be lost without it devastating the Group."

"And just who in the hell would that be?" Ryan asked not too politely.

"Dismissed, gentlemen."

"Jack—" Ryan said, but stopped when Collins turned back to face them.

"We've already lost too much. You two are far more than just men in my department, you're my friends, and Carl would never allow that friendship to be placed in jeopardy to get him home. This is my job and yours, gentlemen, is to make sure everything you have learned from the both of us is carried on at Group. We've come too damn far to lose what we've learned over our years together. I'm sorry. And, Jason, you were right the other day, you did exactly as I would have done in Mexico."

They watched Collins walk from the room, leaving them standing and looking like schoolboys who had just received corporal punishment.

The same question came to each man simultaneously. Just who did the colonel think was expendable?

13

As the nonessential personnel gathered inside the observation room, Virginia went from one of her nuclear science technicians to the other, making sure their safeguards were in place. In case of any power fluctuation, especially when high-powered lasers were concerned, she wanted the ability for each team member to have the wherewithal to shut the test run down. The last item on her list were the power couplings that snaked in through the exterior conduit through the basement. The four-inch thick cables were strong enough to carry the current that would illuminate all of Chicago. The three power lines hummed with power from the nuclear plant generated by the USS *Los Angeles*.

Master Chief Jenks sat at the main control console with Moira Mendelsohn. The old woman was excited and near giddiness to see her doorway once again becoming ready for operations. She received the old butterfly feeling as she thought about her own heady and far-too-adventurous transports back into a world that no longer existed. With eyes smiling the old woman lifted a cigarette to her mouth and lit it. Just as one of his staff was going to inform Madam that there was no smoking, Niles shook his head. He was not about to tell one of the most brilliant people in world history that she couldn't smoke a cigarette—it was time to stop being ridiculous.

"It amazes me that anyone would have trusted this thing enough to go through it," the master chief mumbled.

Moira, with the cigarette dangling from her red lips, reached out and brought down the intensity of the floodlights that illuminated the large doorway. The ceramic composite material used in this second doorway was an advancement that Moira was unfamiliar with but she immediately saw the benefits of the material. Whoever the traitorous element in her company consisted of they had done a remarkable job duplicating her original doorway. She could not fathom how they reengineered the Welsian Doorway in the first place, but she did have suspicions that she kept to herself for the time being.

"This new material will have a far better effect at conducting the electrical charge suffered by the Traveler through their system without the pain associated with entering the field. Marvelous engineering."

"Painful, was it?" Jenks asked as he watched the Traveler sitting as calm as if she were at the opera. "The early experiments, I mean?"

She smiled and turned the rheostat for the lowest lighting mark. She turned to Jenks. "It was as if someone were drilling into your bones with a red-hot poker. And you asked why would someone go through an untested apparatus such as the doorway. Some of us had very little choice in that decision."

"Nazis, huh?" Jenks asked with an admiration he had yet to show for the woman.

"Yes, Nazis."

"Now those are some fellas I would have liked to meet up with."

"No, Master Chief Jenks"—Moira turned away—"you would not." She stubbed out her cigarette and then faced the doorway once more.

Jenks was about to say something when Virginia nudged him aside as she slid into her chair.

"Excuse the hell out of me," he said.

"Is he bothering you?" she asked Moira.

"No, just answering some of the master chief's naiveté."

"God, we'll be here all night," Virginia said as she hurriedly spoke into her walkie-talkie before Jenks could retort with something idiotic.

"*Los Angeles*, let's start off with only fifty percent power profile. We'll start here at twenty-five percent."

"*Reactor is at redline—fifty minus.*"

"Thank you *Los Angeles*. Emergency shutdown on my command."

"*Roger, control has the scram call.*"

"This is so far beyond my basic understanding of the universe and how it works," Ellenshaw said as he watched the glimmering square with the ceramic doorway in its circular form in the middle. The doorway was capable of fitting six men side by side and large enough for a tracked vehicle to traverse.

"Don't feel alone, Professor," Compton agreed.

"In essence the lasers engage a form of disintegration on the subject matter?" Charlie asked.

"It's a form of light transfer of solid material. The subject is basically sectioned by Europa. Back in 1942 it was a program that guessed at the reconstruction of the Traveler upon arriving in the chosen dimension and then reformed the subject, or the Traveler. The applications for this technology are far more than just dimensional shifting," Niles said as he watched below as a technician adjusted the focus of the sixty-five laser apertures lining the doorway.

"Are you talking about transport?" Jack asked as he watched Jason and Will walk in and set down at the far end of the room. They had just checked on security but he knew they were far from happy with him and his decision making of late. When the door opened he had hoped it would have been Sarah and Anya.

"Yes, real *Star Trek* stuff, I know, but there you have it."

"Doctor, we have discussed this before in our 'what if' sessions. This technology cannot be allowed to—"

Niles held up a hand, staying Jack's argument before it could be voiced, only because it was his *own* argument to begin with.

The lights dimmed and then flashed on and off as the *Los Angeles* sent the small percentage of power coursing through the building's old wiring system. The test was starting.

The protective glass shield below that fronted the technician's consoles that fed telemetry to the doorway's geopositioning system, a program hurriedly designed by Virginia and Jenks with the assistance of Europa, slid up from the rubber-lined flooring. The specialized glass was treated with gold shavings that assisted the electrical charge to disburse more evenly to protect the control personnel. As Moira watched on she saw many of the same design characteristics of her own doorway in building 117. But whoever built this had spared no expense, which gave her pause as she thought of possible suspects in the copying of her technology. The prohibitive cost alone eliminated most everybody in her sphere of influence—almost.

Moira looked over at Virginia, who stood leaning on the console as she looked at the Wellsian Doorway. She shook her head. "Incomplete science," she mumbled under her breath.

"I heard that," Jenks said as he reached for the ever-present cigar stub but forgot about the clean room protocols—with the exception of the Traveler, evidently. He looked at Virginia. "If you have doubts about this hunk of science fiction, you damn well better say so now," Jenks said as his eyes went to a smiling Moira Mendelsohn.

Virginia Pollock looked down at the master chief and allowed her thumb to lightly play at his hand and then she smiled.

"Sometimes, when you're desperate to help a friend"—she glanced at Moira—"you do it not just because you can, but because you have already lost far too many friends. Sometimes, Harold, you take risks."

"You said it yourself, it's an incomplete science. We don't know enough about this. What long-term effects will there be on the Traveler?"

"I daresay, Master Chief, that I will outlive you by a goodly margin," Moira said as she turned and looked at the copy of her creation. She thought inwardly, *Thomsen's creation is more accurate.*

Jenks took in a deep breath in anticipation of countering Virginia when she cut short the debate on the morality and safety issues.

"Initiate power sequencing."

Jenks was caught off guard as he saw the glass wall that had appeared in front of the station turn a darker shade as it reacted to the electrical charge coursing through it. This was another engineering feat coordinated by the Group. The brightness of the doorway's discharge could blind those watching from their tech stations.

All the technicians felt the flow of power as the energy supplied by the S6G power plant of the *Los Angeles* announced its arrival at the doorway. The LED lighting lining the rectangular outer frame flared to life, informing them they had acceptance of the electrical flow from the *Los Angeles* to the doorway.

"Initiate surge protection for *Los Angeles*," Virginia said into the extended and flexible microphone. "Okay, let's bring lasers one through seventy-eight online."

The room was illuminated as not quite half of the powerful lasing system became active. The straight lines of bluish-green light slammed into the lead-lined wall at the back of the test area. The soft metal started to melt as the light beams began to heat up.

"Master Chief, how is the propellant element in the collider?"

Jenks leaned over his console and studied the interior-mounted camera and spied the most precious part of the collider—the basic element in the universe— electrons.

Jenks leaned back. "Europa says the collider is online." His eyes went to Virginia and it told her that the master chief was still not comfortable. He understood the design and the theory behind it, but for some reason Jenks was terrified of this machine. Virginia knew he had good reason to fear not only the technology, but the philosophic ramifications.

"Coolant charge?" Moira asked, trying to get Virginia's attention away from the doubting Jenks. Moira was watching the glass above them and the people in the observation room. She locked eyes with Colonel Collins, who was watching her closely, enough so Moira felt pressed. Since the disappearance of young Ms. McIntire and the Israeli woman Anya she had felt the pressure to assist while she still had the credibility to do so.

"We changed out the coolant lines inside the collider. We installed the much more efficient heavy metal coolant. The collider should never reach beyond critical mass as long as the metal cools the system. Nothing to leak."

Moira was amazed at how efficient this group was in understanding a science it had taken her thirty years to comprehend. These people took the technology in stride without missing a beat. If she had had people such as these she would have succeeded with her true goal years ago. The Traveler shook her head in amazement.

Virginia took a deep breath. "Europa, are we ready to initiate revolutions?"

"Power at thirty-four percent. Test initiated at zero one twenty-six hours and thirty seconds. Ready to begin, Doctor," said the sexy voice, who seemed to be back to her old self thanks to Morales.

"Thank you." Virginia turned and looked up at the observation suite and the face of Niles Compton, who nodded that she had the go-ahead. Her gaze lingered for longer than necessary as she wondered for the thousandth time if what they were doing was morally right—they already knew it was highly illegal. She nodded and then turned her attention back to the console in front of her. She looked at the plastic cover over the start button and she reached out and lifted the clear protector. Without ceremony or another cautious thought, Virginia slammed her hand down on the switch.

"Initiating revolutions. Europa, power to remaining lasers, please."

"Power initiated, Doctor," Europa said, and then went silent.

The air was immediately sucked from the room and for just the briefest of moments it was as if the staff on the main floor felt the vacuum of space erupt inside. It passed after only a moment and then the world of building 114 exploded with bright blue and green light. The spinning doorway started revolving at tremendous speed as one magnet sent power to the next, creating a speed that only Europa could keep up with. The cylindrical light formed into a solid tunnel of blue and green and the doorway's opening slammed into the lead-lined wall in the back and then an incredible thing happened. It was like a wave of water breaking upon a surf wall. The light actually bent, straightened, and then settled. The magnets inside the cylindrical collider screamed as the air inside was pushed aside at light speed. Finally the mercury coolant was sent into the collider and the loud scream was silenced.

Every hair on every head and arm shot straight up before settling.

The Wellsian Doorway was now open, to what dimension was anyone's guess.

Eyes went wide and just as Henri Farbeaux entered the room the very air beyond the window came alive with energy. The effect was so powerful that Farbeaux felt the tug as the magnetic field momentarily gave all men and women in range a fit of anxiety the likes of which had never been experienced.

The flickering light beyond the glass had a surreal quality to it as Jack and Niles stepped closer to the glass. They heard Virginia call for an increase in electromagnetic flow to the collider as it started to spin faster and faster as the magnets started firing, forcing the tungsten steel that made up the walls of the collider to send the spinning doorway from one magnet to the next, firing at incredible speed so fragile that the timing had to be controlled through Europa for the instantaneous calculations that had to be made in microseconds. The laser system created a funnel that hit the lead-lined wall, but due to the low flow of power at only fifty percent, reaching arms of the doorway were held captive inside the confines of this dimension. The effect was spectacular and one of the more frightening either Jack or Niles had ever seen. The lasers created a tunnel-like effect that painted a bright picture of spinning fluorescent lighting. The tunnel would pulse every ten seconds and a bubblelike sphere would slam into the reinforced wall as it sought to break free of the power restraints forced upon it by Europa. This was a caged animal that did not like being controlled.

"We have a power loss on magnet's fifty-six and seventy-one. Europa is compensating with power to magnets fifty-seven and seventy-two," Jenks called out as the effect of the open doorway started to change the very air around them. Papers rustled and the flooring shook and then stabilized as the collider brought itself back into balance with the assistance of Europa.

"You must explain to me about this Europa someday," Moira said as she listened to the Marilyn Monroe voice synthesizer.

The rattling of equipment stopped as the doorway settled into a steady hum and the artificial wind calmed to a light breeze as if the air conditioners were on.

"What is the main core temp?" Virginia asked.

"Collider housing is at three hundred and forty-five degrees and holding, far below minimum safe."

Jenks heard the technician say "safe" and he huffed. "That's a hopeful euphemism."

"Knock it off, Harold," Virginia said as she tried to concentrate on the doorway and the effect it was having on the immediate environment. She did not care for the instability of the air near the spinning doorway. It wasn't just the effect of the powerful collider spinning in the opposite direction of the particle accelerator creating the false wind they were feeling, it was the smell. It was like they were breathing old, very damp, stale air from some place other than their immediate atmosphere.

"Status by station," Virginia said into the microphone as she slowly lowered herself into her chair.

"*Los Angeles*, engineering, reactor is optimal and power cables are holding, Doctor," came the calm voice of the civilian propulsion specialist onboard inside the old submarine's engineering spaces. "Power output at forty percent and holding."

"Electromagnetic halo is holding, two units down, and the compensation is holding," called out one of her nuclear specialists monitoring the power flow through the hundreds of magnets lining the collider.

"Damn right it is," Jenks said, as the new design was his contribution to what he now knew was madness.

"Go or no go is an acceptable turn of phrase, I believe," Virginia said without looking at Jenks. His being unnerved by a scientific experiment was starting to get to Virginia's psyche. It was the master chief's natural engineering skills and his inability to respect a very dangerous science that made her apprehensive.

"Collider is functioning at expected parameters," called out a nervous female technician as she monitored the X ray–like view of the spinning particle accelerator that enhanced the magnification inside the round collider by ten thousand power. The view was controlled through Europa and her electron microscope underneath Nellis Air Force Base in Nevada.

"Dr. Morales, are you ready to initiate signal search?" Virginia asked.

"As ready as we'll ever be," Morales said from his monitor.

Virginia Pollock tried to swallow her fear as Moira saw her face as she studied the spinning blue and green lasers as they created and animated a circle of spectacular light against the lead-lined wall. She closed her eyes and spoke. "Initiate power upgrade to sixty-five percent, please. Okay, let's target our initiated point for dimensional signal disbursement."

"What is that?" Jack asked Niles as they watched from above.

"In order to disburse the signal into as many directions and dimensions as possible, Europa will bounce the signal off the surface of the moon and have it bounce back to Earth; after all, we can narrow one parameter down as to where Mr. Everett is: Earth. Once the signal is brought home, so to speak, it will again disburse into all dimensions and start its search for the corresponding return signal from the escape pod."

"Right, I should have figured that out myself." Jack smiled and looked at Niles, who only nodded in appreciation of Jack's limited imagination when it came to quantum physics.

Inside the engineering spaces of the USS *Los Angeles* the propulsion engineer from General Dynamics, although he didn't know what was going on inside the building, frowned as he eased the power setting forward on the reactor core.

"Sixty-five percent power flow."

"Thank you, *Los Angeles*." Virginia, for one last time, turned and looked at Niles Compton. He looked at Master Chief Jenks and saw his frown. "Permission to open the doorway for signal acquisition search?" Niles nodded. "Make sure your target settings are at zero. Contact satellite transfer and get them our signal net. Let's slam this baby into the moon and see if this dog will bark."

"Doorway signal has satellite acquisition. The transfer is in motion, dimensional shift is bouncing off the surface of the moon at its equator. We now have a return from the moon, it is now in active search mode according to Europa."

The specified tone, an exact match to the rescue beacon's frequency that came in one-second intervals from the sealed unit inside the escape pod, shot free of its invisible cage and shot up into the sky, where it connected with the Group's own KH-11 satellites, *Boris* and *Natasha*. From there Europa sent it slamming into the moon for its return trip, almost like a radar wave. Europa had stolen the frequencies of no less than sixty-one communication and broadcast satellites around the globe. Europa had picked these orbiting relay stations to cover the entire surface of the planet with the signal as it searched for its mate through time and space. The real secret of the Wellsian Doorway was its power to send and receive signals that cannot be contained. Like water overflowing a glass, the wave of energy would cover the world and then start expanding outward as the Wellsian Doorway opened up to the many dimensional walls it breached. At the same moment the doorway came online, millions of television viewers the world over watched their screens go dark and then suddenly pop back on. The signal went out on a wave riding the coattails of the regularly scheduled programming and those late-night viewers never realized that their favorite shows had just burst through the time and dimensional barriers that only existed in the mind of a brilliant man named Albert Einstein.

The room once more exploded into light as the lasers rose to over half of their efficiency. The lasers slammed into the wall and then bounced back toward the glass wall protecting the technicians. It hit like a wave, the laser light actually bent as the particle accelerator created a dimensional shift that snatched the straight line of spinning light to rebound, and then it happened—the vortex started to take shape as the tunnel formed once more, only this time it was almost a solid field of light.

Jack and the other veterans of the space battle over Antarctica recognized the dimensional wormhole, which evidently was a form of nature that did not change from one application to the next . . . nature's own design of power and differing dimensions. The multicolored spin of the tunnel was creating its own weather system inside the building. The vortex of spinning laser light widened and then settled into a round spinning wall of waterlike illumination that approached the speed of sound and vanished after only a few feet, ending in a sparkler-type fountain that flew to nothingness. The doorway to other dimensions was now open. All they had to do was find the right corresponding doorway to catch the broadcast of Everett's escape pod geopositioning system and transponder beacon.

The room settled and the doorway became a steady hum of light and power. The artificial winds had calmed. Virginia took a deep breath. "The doorway is open, Dr. Morales. You and Europa can start your search."

In Nevada, Xavier Morales patted the console in front of him and then smiled at his new department personnel and up at Europa's enormous main monitor sitting in the middle of the main wall.

"Okay, Europa, old girl, let's start making some calls and see if anyone answers."

Xavier's new computer department watched as he gave Europa the order and they all heard the search-and-rescue tone burst from the speakers. Morales smiled as his searching signal went out into the newly expanded multi-universe.

"All right, Admiral Everett, I hope you didn't leave your phone off the hook."

14

BROOKLYN, NEW YORK

The New York City police captain wore civilian clothing as he always did when meeting with his financial partners. The large man was sitting in the back room of Kellum's bakery, a shop that used to be owned by his family in what seemed like a million lifetimes ago. Now it belonged to the man he was there to meet. The precinct captain was in serious debt to the man known around legitimate police officers as the "Bolshevik." Alexi Doshnikov had originally agreed to finance a failing bakery in a run-down section of Brooklyn—a bakery whose livelihood was threatened not by economic downturn, but by its resurgence. The fashion was now to buy, renovate, and then sell to the highest bidder for homes and businesses that once made Brooklyn work. It had taken an unsavory alliance for Captain Kellum's family to keep their business. An alliance with the Butcher, and the bill was coming due big time. The captain had managed to save his family from being run out of their home and business, but the cost of that was his soul.

He poured himself a glass of cold milk and then sat and waited by the stainless-steel table. As he did he removed the thirty-eight snub-nosed revolver from his ankle holster and then placed it on the shiny tabletop. He sipped his milk and waited.

He heard the back door open and the footsteps approach from behind him. He was tempted to finger the loaded weapon on the gleaming tabletop but instead took another swallow of cold milk and waited.

"It seems you caused my brothers in blue in Manhattan to work a little over-time tonight in the East River," Kellum said as he placed the glass down. He heard the refrigerator open and then close. The man known as Mr. Jones sat next to the captain and poured himself a glass of milk. He held the glass up in a toast and then drank deeply. The Russian smiled and smacked his lips.

"There were times a few years back something as simple as a cold glass of milk was nearly impossible for my family to grasp. Everything our region had in dairy was sent straight to Moscow and the rich bastards that ran things back then. We were lucky if we were allowed to keep the cow manure from the very dairy herds we tended to night and day." He drank again and watched the police captain. He set the glass down.

"We all have our hard-luck tales. It was no picnic growing up here either. Our stories aren't that much different."

The Russian eyed Kellum and then smiled. "Someday I will explain to you the difference, my friend."

Kellum didn't care for the smile.

"Now, as to the aerial mishap you mentioned with that business helicopter, tragic."

Kellum watched the man closely, knowing he had ordered the assassinations of the entire board of directors for Mendelsohn's company. However, he didn't want the mobster to know just how much of this he really knew or was guessing at—it wasn't healthy. He decided he would leave it alone.

The captain reached into his breast pocket and brought out a small notebook and opened it. "Your four missing men? Well, we just found two of them. They were fished out of the water near Coney Island two hours ago. Single tap to the head for each. I suspect we will find the other two in the same mint condition."

Doshnikov capped the bottle of milk and then looked Kellum over. He shrugged his shoulders. "No loss. If they were foolish enough to get taken out by the federal authorities, they're not meant to be in my employ."

"Well, there is a funny little wrinkle there on two fronts, Mr. Jones," Kellum said as he thumbed through a few pages from his notes. "It seems whoever is occupying those buildings in the navy yard are not the federal authorities. I can't get one single thread on who and why they are there. But I have been told by my superiors that it is none of my concern. The second matter is that you may have a sort of resurgence on your hands."

"And what is that supposed to mean?" the Russian asked, bemused.

"One of my C.I.'s in the neighborhood says the buzz on the streets is that your men were taken out not by these strangers in the navy yard, but by the Gambinos. And that, my friend, means you have a growing problem if they moved on your men, for whatever reason. I would say they showed very little respect." The police captain closed his small notepad and raised the glass of milk to his lips and made a silent, but mockingly irritating return toast.

"Gambinos." The Russian mobster smirked, his disdain for the Italians showing clearly on his face. "Your confidential informant should have told you that the Gambinos and all of those old men that call themselves the mob are nothing but ghosts from the past. Tales to scare little children at night." He eyed the captain as he finished his glass of milk. His look was one of fury for the briefest of moments, and then the facial features relaxed once more and he smirked. "Please, you know as well as I do that all the New York families are dying off one old man at a time and the men who will replace them are morons." He smiled and slapped the captain on the shoulder. "Besides, with what I have been working on the Gambinos can have Brooklyn after tonight. I'll be moving on to far greener pastures, as the Cossacks used to say."

Kellum just raised his brows. "And just how many people will be killed to get you to those greener pastures, comrade?"

The Russian laughed at the captain's little barb. "Possibly just a few of those people your police force cannot identify now occupying those buildings at the navy yard, maybe a few others, but then again the latter of those have died before, or at least should have . . . so no great loss."

Kellum saw that the man was wild-eyed with some scheme that seemed to make him oblivious to the dangerous situation he had entered into with the Gambino family and whoever those people were that had taken over the Brooklyn Navy Yard.

"Now about this request of yours, I don't—"

"It was not a request."

The smile was gone and the black eyes told Captain Kellum that the man was truly on the edge of sanity.

"Your order for me and my men to seal off that end of the navy yard from all observers, well, it will all depend on—"

"You. It's that simple. At two a.m. not one person is to be allowed into the navy yard. Interference for three uninterrupted hours. No one in, or out."

"Look, I can't control the damn fire department, the federal authorities, or whoever those people are who have credentials that would scare Comrade Stalin."

"Three hours and the building and the business you are now sitting in is yours for your family to do with as they please. Your obligation to my organization will be complete as will your loan debt. All cleared for a mere three hours of work. Not even Comrade Stalin could be so generous."

Kellum heard what he said but could not believe it. Russians never allowed any agreement to lapse. That was the difference with the Russians over the American mob—there was truly no getting out from under their dirty thumbs.

"Three hours. I can give you that."

"Then I can give you your family's livelihood back with a significant real estate investment to boot."

Kellum stood and buttoned his sport coat and retrieved the pistol from where it had been prominently displayed. "Just what in the hell is so important about three hours?" he asked as he turned to face the smaller man.

The Russian smiled again and then stopped at the back door. Amid the smell of baked bread and muffins, he said, "That's the time it will take for me to become the richest man in the world—legitimately. Imagine, me, legitimate." He laughed and then left.

Kellum had a bad taste in his mouth as he took a deep breath and then suddenly flung his empty milk glass against the door as it closed. It was then that the police captain swore that if he could he would find some way to go back in time and change how he saved his family business.

But he knew there was no such thing as a time machine, much to his regret.

BROOKLYN NAVY YARD

As Jason Ryan and Will Mendenhall secured the electric rolling supply trailer that would accompany the team into the doorway, Ryan turned and looked at Mendenhall. He sat heavily on a large plastic crate that contained a lasing system invented to protect a perimeter in the field.

"I'm sorry, I guess I screwed not only me, but you in the process."

Mendenhall placed a rolled tent onto the small trailer and then sighed. Mendenhall sat down heavily next to Ryan.

"Look, you did nothing that Jack or Carl wouldn't have done. How many times would the authorities have thrown both of those nut jobs into jail for the things they've pulled off?" Mendenhall slapped Ryan on the back. "No, you got the job done and that's just what the colonel looks for."

"Then why would—"

"Because I need you two here. The odds against us pulling this H. G. Wells crap off is just about a billion to one and I don't care what Albert Einstein Mendelsohn in there says."

Both men turned and saw Collins as he stood in the shadows watching them. He finally stepped into the light with a small case and placed it on the trailer. Ryan stood and faced his commander. Mendenhall pursed his lips and waited.

"Then why are you even attempting it?" Ryan asked, braving another confrontation.

"Why did you allow Charlie in on Morales's prison extraction?" Jack leaned against the trailer and looked up into the foggy night. "Why did you go back after Will in Chato's Crawl when you knew the Destroyer was in those tunnels? Hell, for that matter, why didn't you return to naval aviation after the board of inquiry cleared you in the incident over the Pacific?"

"Because Will and Charlie are friends; I know what they can do. As for naval aviation, I found out I care for the people at Group and didn't want to leave."

Jack smiled and looked at Ryan and Mendenhall. "That is why I'm going. I have a friend out there somewhere who's lost and I intend to try to bring him home. No matter how crappy the odds."

"Then why are you pissed at me?" Ryan asked, wanting the truth.

"Your performance during the prison break was outstanding. You took the people you trusted, and as things do with good people, it worked out. I wasn't mad at you, I was mad at me because I saw myself in you and our shortcomings. We truly respect, admire, and trust the friends we have around us and that is why I am going after Carl. I sat back and allowed others to seal his fate. The fate he encountered doing what he did when any one of a thousand men could have done the same. When you take this department over, and someday you will because I saw what you are capable of, you'll know what you have to do at the most horrific of times—

protect the people under you. I don't intend to lose one more person on my watch if I can at all help it. So, you stay, I go."

"But you just said that friendship—"

"You stay, I go. Someday you'll understand, Jason, believe me." He smiled and then slapped Mendenhall on the back on his way by. "I figure if the worst happens, I could be leaving the department in far less capable hands than yours and Will's."

The two watched Jack vanish into the fog. "I absolutely hate his object lessons."

Will Mendenhall had to agree.

On the large monitor situated above the dimensional collider, as Jenks liked calling the doorway, was a strange graphic supplied by Europa and Morales. It was a multiplaned series of levels. They undulated, changed positions, and then reformed. In between these colored planes a single line of light emerged, vanished, and then appeared on another multicolored level. Morales had explained that each line represented what Europa was reading as dimensional planes. She was able to track the light source as it split among different forms of atoms that made up the universe. Differing atomic structure that could only be seen by Europa and her wide sweeping band of sound waves. The signal reached out, penetrated, and then wormed into another level searching for its sister signal on the escape pod. The doorway had been searching and listening for the better part of two hours with no return bounce of the pulsating rescue beacon.

"Hell, I don't know," Jenks said louder than he wanted to. The noise of the open doorway made communication without headsets impossible. He found it hard to communicate with Virginia sitting right next to him. "Morales and that damnable computer are speaking a language never taught at MIT or the navy. Give a call out to Stephen Hawking or Einstein, maybe they can explain this differing planes of existence crap. I sure as hell can't. I see a bunch of lines and then another bunch of lines and I only have Europa's calculations that it's even feasible for us to locate that beacon."

"My God, how many different planes of existence can there be?" Virginia asked, mostly to herself as she studied the animation on the screen. It looked like a sewing needle as it thread from one line to the next, sometimes up and then down.

"Just think of it as a universe that has expanded beyond the control of its creator. With no more universe, it has to expand in some direction. Same space, multilevels of that space. It's trapped in a way. Without the dimensional planes our universe would die."

Both Virginia and Jenks turned to see Moira Mendelsohn sitting in her chair, watching the undulating lines on the monitor. He adjusted the small mic on her headset. "If only I had had access to this marvelous machine you call Europa, oh, what I could have done."

They saw the wonder in the old scientist's face as she studied the graph on the monitor.

"And just what would you have done?" Jenks asked as he removed the cold cigar and looked from the Traveler to Virginia with worry.

A faraway look came into the gray eyes of Moira. "I could have maybe—"

"We have a bounce back!" A technician said excitedly into his mic.

"Yes, confirmed at zero two ten hundred hours and forty-six seconds we have a return signal. Muted, but sustained. A little weak, but it's there," called out a female voice on all receivers.

On the overhead speaker and over the noise created by the false wind of the doorway, they heard it: the steady beeping of Everett's transponder. Smiles were exchanged all around the technical area at the surreal spectacle of the windblown doorway and the haunting signal that pulsed through the air.

Moira looked at the monitor and there it was. Sandwiched between a red line and a green. The monitor changed views and a series of numbers started to be placed on the screen by Europa, who was calculating longitude and latitude of the signal. The amazing Blue Ice system of Europa started to use her NASA and European Space Agencies star charts and her own time and distance tables to calculate where and when the signal originated. She accomplished this by using strength of signal versus known star positioning and then she figured the closest area by mere inches as to the location of the pod. Finally the coordinates appeared and steadied. All eyes went to the second monitor and the view of the computer center in Nevada. Morales was there and he was smiling.

"The odds just went down . . . it's Antarctica calling back. She's calling collect, but she is calling!"

A cheer erupted and even Niles Compton smiled through his discomfort, and then he realized that the science fiction of the past had become a sudden reality. Most stomachs in the room rolled as they realized what a potential world changer this could become.

The Einstein-theorized time machine became operational at 0210 hours and forty-six seconds.

The presidential protection clock was still running. And that was one thing the machine could not control.

Jenks tried his best to inventory the team's supplies and at the same time avoid the accusing eyes of Virginia as she glared at him from the sealed-off area where the extraction team prepared. The master chief finally huffed and then removed the cold cigar stub and returned the look.

"You're the one who brought me into this historical menagerie, and now that I might get a boo-boo you want me to back out?"

"You're too damned old for this crap and you know it," Virginia said as she picked up a case of MREs and handed it to a questioning Jenks.

"So you want me to stay behind with the broads and the geeks and let you go in my place?"

"I am more capable of getting the doorway in Antarctica up and running far better and faster than you."

"Well, that dog just won't hunt, Slim. Call me all the names you want, but I will not let someone who I care"—Jenks stumbled—"I won't stay behind and let you go in my place. I don't care if it's what you call, 'not very PC,' but you can go to hell." He angrily placed the stub of cigar into his mouth and then reached past Virginia for the illuminating signal devices and plopped it hard onto the trailer transport. "I suppose you have a retort or whatever you eggheads make for an argument?"

Virginia was silent as she stared into the eyes of the graying master chief. She nodded just once and remained quiet.

"I'm sorry I was too much of a caveman to make it work with us, Slim," Jenks said as he kicked at an invisible object and then angrily tossed the dead cigar away.

The assistant director was taken back by the hastily worded comment. The master chief lowered his eyes and then reached quickly for the next set of signal devices that were wrapped heavily in the manufacturer's packaging. Virginia placed a thin fingered hand on Jenks's own, stilling his movement. He looked into her green eyes and held them for as long as he dared.

"After all of the degrees I have gathered, the accumulated knowledge of centuries, I have come to one immutable fact of life, Harold, and that is that you are allowed two great loves in the span of one's life. We just happened to be two people who loved not only each other but also the work we do. No ones' fault, but the love is still there regardless."

"I . . . I . . ." Jenks stalled.

"When you get back to this dimension, we'll have to make a choice, Harold."

"But—"

Virginia leaned over and kissed the gruff old master chief.

Jenks watched as Virginia turned away but then hesitated.

"Besides, I want to see if you can follow the directions on the doorway's instruction manual. I personally think you'll be like a father trying to put his son's bike together on Christmas Eve." Virginia waggled her fingers behind her in farewell as she left hurriedly.

"Damn, she always has to have the last word."

The master chief continued to load the transport but at least for the time being the gruff old engineer was smiling.

———

"Will we have any problem maintaining a locking signal on the beacon until the doorway is constructed in the past?" Niles asked for the second time. He was showing his doubts and concerns in the past twenty minutes by grilling everyone in the conference room. Asking the same questions over and over to the very same people.

Virginia looked at Niles and simply shook her head as her thoughts remained on the master chief and his age. This mission was not for him and she knew it. SEAL instructor or not, he was just too old and too damn stubborn to admit that fact. Morales answered for her when she remained mute.

"The signal as of this moment is very strong."

"Target area—they aren't going to be put down in the water or released twenty thousand feet into the air, are they?" Niles asked as he was furiously writing down notes.

Morales again spoke up from Nevada. "The comp center has pinpointed the exact location and according to the British geological survey of 2014 it's right on the edge of the newly named Durnsford Sea, approximately six hundred and twenty feet from the suspected edge of the inland shore. We'll compensate by a mile east of the sea; that should be a safe guess as to a landing area. Equipment and men will be prepared for a mis-landing regardless. Heady, especially since the sea level landing is at this moment two miles below the surface of the ice. Europa says she can do it plus or minus one millimeter in height."

On the large monitor Europa was projecting the star chart used to determine the exact time and location of the jump. Niles reached out and struck the button that activated the installed holographic system. Around the conference table the room illuminated with a ceiling full of star constellations. They revolved, stopped, and revolved again as Europa triple-checked her own figures. It was like the Event Group was sneaking a peak at the supercomputer's arithmetic. The stars would expand outward from the time they suspected Everett had disappeared into the wormhole until they settled into their current position. Again and again Europa ran her model and she came up with the same results.

"Europa knows that lives are on the line," Morales volunteered from the desert.

"Excuse me?" Niles said with a jolt, looking from the simulation and into the large monitor.

"Europa has learned the hard lesson of human loss. It had never been explained to her that her work could possibly send men and women to their deaths. I have since explained it to her. She knows what's on the line now; she never did before."

Niles thought that their new personnel move might have come a little too hastily as he listened. It was Alice who reached out with her hand and placed it on top of Niles's and stilled him from questioning the new computer genius too harshly. He relented and moved on.

"Now, where is my missing geological specialist and our little Anya Korvesky?"

Coincidentally timed, a moment later the door opened and standing there were the two missing women. Sarah's eyes went to Jack and then to Niles as she started to apologize for her sudden departure. She had several items in her hand as Anya accompanied her inside the conference room. They all noticed the way both Sarah and Anya made eye contact with Moira before sitting down.

"You know we are desperately short on time and you decide to take off without so much as a good-bye. You broke protocol by shutting down your cell phones' geo locator. If you think we—"

Sarah cut Niles short. "I think we should get the entire story from Madam Mendelsohn about just how many people know about the existence of the doorway."

Niles looked from Sarah toward the Traveler. He refrained from saying anything more about broken procedures as he studied the old woman. He didn't have to broach the subject of security to a woman who had understood the need for it since 1942.

Sarah slid the disturbing charcoal drawings she had found inside the incinerator to the middle of the table. Charlie Ellenshaw stood and spread them out so all could see. Before Charlie realized it his hand moved quickly away after seeing the drawings in their half-incinerated state.

Niles raised one of the drawings and examined it. The depiction of children inside a concentration camp was vivid, unlike most camp drawings Niles had ever seen before inside the Holocaust museums. The detail was as if the artist was picturing the scene from memory. The one problem with that was the dates were handwritten by the artist in the lower right-hand corner.

"Nineteen seventy-one," Niles said aloud.

"Nineteen sixty-seven here," Charlie said as he was unable to touch the drawings again.

The images were stark and black. Children crying. Other children being led away to their deaths made most wince at the scenes all done in very disturbing charcoal. Anya turned away, knowing that this was her heritage being shown to her by the memory of some child who had lived through the nightmare.

It was Jack Collins who stood and turned the pictures over on the tabletop. Jack was one of those soldiers who found anything concerning the holocaust far beyond the imagination of a professional American soldier. The images always made him furious as to how a modern society or soldier could ever allow that to happen.

"How many did you bring back, Moira?" Anya asked. "How many children did you smuggle out when you couldn't find your brother?"

Moira smiled as she looked at the faces around her. "All that I could. I know I changed the destinies of so many, but then again, Albert Einstein never had to look into the eyes of children on their way to mass slaughter. Yes, hundreds." She braved the shocked looks of those around her. She saw no meanness in those looks, but one of awe and understanding . . . to a point.

Niles swallowed and calmed his scientific wariness at her actions but it was then that he realized the Event Group was about to attempt the same thing, on a smaller scale perhaps, but no less guilty of changing the destiny of one of their own.

At that moment an Air Force sergeant walked in and gave Niles a message and then made his way out. Compton read the note and then his good eye found the Traveler.

"This is from our contact in the FBI. It seems your entire board of directors has had a mishap over the East River tonight. They were all killed."

Moira stared at Niles for the briefest of moments, not really understanding.

"How many of your board of directors were children of the Holocaust?" Virginia Pollock asked.

Moira didn't have to answer as all of them saw it in her face. She lowered her head.

"They all grew up at your privately funded orphanage, didn't they?" Sarah asked.

"Yes." She looked up and the briefest of sad smiles crossed her lips. "Can you imagine the magic they believed brought them out of those camps? We intercepted the largest contingents from transports, but most had already seen the insides of smaller camps, so they knew for the most part what the Nazis had in store for them. As I said, most were very, very bright."

"Now some of those brightest are dead. Perhaps you better enlighten us as to why and who would want that," Jack said as he waved Ryan over and told him quietly to make sure the outside watch was aware of the situation. Ryan quietly left.

"I don't know who this could be. The board always had complete autonomy to act in the best interest of the children and their security."

"We're not real big believers in coincidence," Niles said as he turned to Jack. "Colonel, I'll leave it up to you for a go, no go. This was clearly an assassination at a very inopportune moment in our plans. This could bring those other sister agencies charging in and I don't think the president can stop the avalanche."

Collins looked at Moira and decided she didn't know anything more than what she had said. The only thing Jack figured her guilty for was being human enough to save kids from a fate worse than what history had planned for them.

"Master Chief, Henri, Charlie, I can't order you to go."

"I didn't bust my ass building that thing and then nearly come to blows with Slim, er, uh, Dr. Pollock here, not to go. I figure whoever is out there threatening this thing is going to act regardless if we go or not," Jenks said as he avoided the stark eyes of Virginia.

Ellenshaw looked up from the table and then slid the glasses back up on his nose. He looked directly at Niles. "I have to go."

"If this is the only way I can get out from under the thumb of this Group, what choice do I have?" Farbeaux said as he shook his head at Ellenshaw and his weak answer to a life-or-death question.

"If it's a question of volunteers, I don't—" Sarah started to say but Niles cut her off as he examined the clock on the wall.

"It's not. Dr. Morales, is Europa ready?"

Sarah angrily looked from Niles to Jack, who just shook his head, angry that once more she tried to bully her way onto the team. He was going to have to put her in the same drifting lifeboat as Ryan.

"Okay, Jack, get your team ready, we go in thirty."

The meeting broke up with the individual departments crowding around Jack, Henri, and Charlie as they sent a myriad of intelligence on ancient Antarctica their way. No one approached Jenks as he stood with Virginia. Instead of barraging him with warnings she simply placed a hand on his broad chest and patted him lightly.

"Keep an open mind out there, Harold."

"I'll just be another old fossil where we're going, Slim. Besides, my carcass is too tough for anything to chew on for too long. I'll just wait them out."

"Listen, animal life back then is probably a little more patient than any current species."

Jenks winked and then looked over at Collins, who was shaking hands with Niles.

"Good luck, Colonel. Bring him back if you can, but lose no one else, or this whole thing is for nothing."

Collins nodded. He had no intention of losing anyone else. He turned and he faced a smiling Henri. He half turned to Compton as he was about to say that he couldn't guarantee all of them were coming back, but just smiled back at Farbeaux instead.

"Jack, er, uh, Colonel?"

Collins and Farbeaux stopped and turned and saw Sarah standing with Anya.

"You two are on my shit list . . . again," he said as he eyed McIntire exclusively. "Now, I have given orders to Ryan to beef up outside security. Since you two don't seem to perform a duty around here, and have time to saunter off on a Nancy Drew mystery tour, you will be assigned a post by the commander. We're a little shorthanded. I hope it's not too boring for you amateur sleuths."

Sarah fumed but turned and left with a stuttering Will Mendenhall close behind.

Anya stood her ground. "Thank you for doing this, Colonel."

Jack stared at her before edging past the former Israeli agent. "I'm not doing it for you, Anya."

Henri smiled at the dark-haired woman and nodded. "Complicated, isn't he?" Farbeaux left the office.

The activity inside the newly and hastily renovated conference room slowly drizzled to nothing until only Alice Hamilton and Niles were left inside. Compton looked up into the large monitor and saw Xavier Morales looking at them. The activity around the computer genius was bustling as the comp center made ready for the dimensional shift of the doorway. Niles reached out and studied one of the disturbing pictures in charcoal. He let it slide through his fingers. Alice remained silent as she knew the director was debating something in his thoughts. It was these meanderings that etched a sad crevice of doubt on his lined face.

"A morality play is at work."

Compton and Alice both looked up at Morales, who continued to see them from Nevada.

"The right to change one's destiny. I suspect that is what the director is concerned with."

Niles shook his head. "You would have liked Pete Golding," he said with a small but sad smile. "You're a lot like him." He then looked over at Alice. "Only far less timid about voicing his opinions of my psyche."

Morales smiled. He knew some thought him far-thinking beyond his years, but he knew it was nothing more than a young man's exuberance in experiencing everything he could inside of his limited and paralyzed world.

"Sorry, but you never asked my opinion. I thought I would voice one."

"Voice it, everyone's opinion is valued here," Alice said as she was curious as to what someone so young could think about the changing of destinies.

"Morally, I think we're wrong. Just because we have the power to change things, do we have that right? Don't we learn from the harsh realities thrust upon us through adversity? I believe deep down that we could very well lose our humanity if we allow this as a viable practice beyond this one experiment. When I saw what those children had survived through those horrible pictures, I, like most in the room there or inside the comp center here, wanted to save them all. We have the power as I said, we could go back and stop it from ever happening. Colonel Collins seems like he would be more than capable of going back and placing a bullet into that maniac Hitler's computer, simply avoid it all. But what will we have learned from that barbaric little man? After all, we have the power to do that, don't we— the very power to change the world forever."

"Thank you, Doctor. What would you do in my place?" Niles asked as he slowly stood and with the help of Alice limped to the large observation window and the active scene below.

"I'm easy, Director Compton, my world consists of this chair and my work. I would go in a split second if I could, morality play or not. I would go and get our man. That is why I disqualify myself from the problem of morality plays and leave it in your capable hands."

"Yes," Niles said as he glanced up at the monitor before returning his good eye to the rush of personnel on the floor below, "you'll fit in nicely round here." Niles turned and limped from the room.

"I will?" Morales said as Alice gathered her paperwork. She paused and looked at the monitor.

"Yes, you fit in because you, like everyone else in our Group, would do anything to get into the field."

"He's right on that point."

Alice smiled. "Thus the morality play in full bloom, Dr. Morales."

"What do you mean?"

Alice placed her paperwork in her case and then looked up one last time. "Pete Golding was killed in the field, but Niles knows he cannot save him, even if he could. He's not lost, Carl Everett is. Morality plays are a little more hellish and real than you thought, aren't they, Doctor?"

Xavier Morales watched Alice Hamilton leave. He now understood better just why the director of Department 5656 had slumped shoulders—he had the weight of all world history upon them.

Jack checked out Henri's suit and helmet. Charlie was already wearing his and Jenks looked him over.

"Now don't worry here, Nerdly, if we walk into a pocket of methane or somethin' as delectable as that, your environment monitor in your sleeve there won't allow your helmet to unlock. The colonel issued you this." He held up a nine-millimeter semiautomatic pistol and slammed it home into a holster that stretched across Ellenshaw's back and covered the front of his jumpsuit. "Guess he doesn't relish the thought of a nerd with an M-4. You have extra ammo in the packs. Just remember to point it at anyone but me."

"Got it," Ellenshaw said as he was tempted to pull the weapon and examine it, but saw the master chief looking at him to see if he would make that kind of stupid decision.

Jack turned and made sure the packs were secured properly to the trailer and then checked if the four-wheeled John Deere tracked vehicle was ready. The rugged all-terrain vehicle was pulling six of the five-by-five trailers. The secondary doorway was safely ensconced in shrink wrap and boxed inside of protective polyurethane containers. The power source was bolted to the second trailer. If they lost any one part of either the doorway of the portable power storage unit they wouldn't be coming back from this little jaunt. The rest of the team was issued tents, camping gear, signal devices, and defensive measures that were top of the line. Altogether they were taking over a ton and a half of supplies with them. Jack then adjusted his helmet as the sliding door started to rise and they heard the spinning doorway for the first time. The light changed inside the ready room as the door exposed the Wellsian Doorway. Each man looked at the miracle of quantum physics and were frozen to the spot for a moment.

The last thing Jack thought about before entering the large chamber was the fact that he had left Sarah behind and his angry last words to her rang in his memory. He wished he had said good-bye but he just couldn't face seeing those eyes and their accusing glint. Everyone would sit this one out. He looked at Charlie Ellen-shaw, the only member of the team who was there for purely psychological rea-sons—he had to save Carl for the simple fact he hadn't been able to save his best friend Pete Golding. He hoped this would help the old cryptozoologist to return to the Charlie they knew and loved.

The loudspeaker came to life.

"Return signal is holding strong. Doorway is at fifty percent power and is also holding at nominal levels. The *Los Angeles* is reporting her reactor board is in the green."

In front of Jack, Jenks, Henri, and Charlie, the Wellsian Doorway spun in its revolving arc and the colors were brilliant as they reflected off their visored hel-mets. The activity of personnel heated up as technicians started to clear the platform floor.

"Time till displacement, ten minutes and counting."

15

BARCLAYS CENTER, BROOKLYN, NEW YORK

The cleaning crews were just finishing the long night of clean-up after a raucous concert earlier that evening. Many of the concertgoers were still mingling around the exterior of the new arena. Most didn't pay any attention to the step van that eased into the loading dock at the back of the large venue. It backed in and several men emerged and started using a bolt cutter to snap the exterior lock on the roll-up door.

"Hey, there's no deliveries this late, it's nearly two thirty in the morning, you need to—"

That was as far as the security guard and his partner got in questioning the delivery drivers. The silenced weapon was quickly put away and then two bodies unceremoniously moved to the side as the large loading gate slid up. The brand-new soda machine was quickly wheeled inside. The five men vanished into the darkness and then returned a moment later. With one last look around they en-tered the step van and then they slowly pulled out.

The second set of guards had just come from the front where they had tried to get the early-morning concertgoers to move along when they spied their two downed brethren. The first started to raise his radio to his mouth but the words were never allowed to escape his lips. The bomb hidden inside the soda machine detonated. The two guards were blown free of the loading dock and tossed like rag dolls into the alley beyond.

The rear portion of the brand-new arena blew outward and flames erupted into the night.

Ten minutes later the parties responsible made their announcement to the news media. It seemed terrorists had made a statement in the heart of Brooklyn and soon every policeman and federal agent in the five boroughs was rushing there. The Russian ploy to isolate the doorway had successfully diverted police and federal attention from other areas of Russian concern.

The Brooklyn Navy Yard was now fully exposed and the Event Group was on their own.

Alexi Doshnikov pulled up the sleeve of his expensive coat and looked at his watch. The frightened family watched his lips move as if he were counting down the seconds. After a few tense seconds a deep rumble was felt through the thick frame of the limousine. The night sky was illuminated to the east and that was when they saw their Russian abductor smile. He lowered his arm and looked at the family. Benjamin and Natalie Koblenz, their son-in law and daughter next to them with a sleeping baby in the mother's arms, and he smiled. His bearded face held no humanity for the frightened family.

"It seems our little road show is officially open." He looked at the family across from him and then looked at his man in the seat next to him, and nodded. The bodyguard picked up a phone and spoke into it. The large limousine started to move forward with no less than six Ford Explorers following.

"Why are we here? Where are you taking us?"

"A poker game. And you five are the chips that will allow us a seat at this very exclusive table."

The four frightened members of the kidnapped family saw the gleam in the man's eyes. He looked at the oldest member and smirked.

"Your Madam Mendelsohn is about to make me a very, very wealthy man."

ANTARCTICA, 227,000 B.C.E.

The earthquakes, other than a few stomach-rolling tremors, had subsided as the brief glimpses of the fantastic starfield showed itself for one of the few times since his arrival. Carl was resting his back against the small cave opening that he was currently calling home. It was elevated and looked down upon the game trail three hundred feet below him. He had traded in his homemade bow and arrows for the rigid Roman bow and iron-tipped arrows of the old Ninth Legion. He had to string new rabbit gut for a bow string, but other than that he had far more confidence in hitting something with the meticulously designed weapon. It and the large quiver of arrows sat beside him as he stared up at the brilliant star-strewn sky. Then his mood changed when the rolling ash cloud once again covered them and the large rising moon of the distant past. He felt his confidence shake everytime he lost sight of something familiar such as the night sky.

Sleep was hard to come by as the night sounds of prehistoric animals came alive as the ash cloud once more covered the central plain of Antarctica. He had watched for the past several days the run of animals big and small from the growing danger of the volcano. Erebus had put Carl on notice that there was not much time left. He once more looked at the sky and then closed his eyes.

"Anytime, Jack," he said as he drifted off to sleep.

He didn't know how long he had been asleep. He knew he liked dozing outside the cave during the nighttime hours for the simple fact the former SEAL hated to be caught in a dead end if a wandering animal was also seeking shelter for the night. He also didn't know what it had been that made his eyes flutter open. He lifted his head from the rock facing and looked around. His fingers touched the Birch-wood bow and he waited for the noise to come again. Carl saw that dawn was getting ready to break over this savage land. He adjusted his back and stretched without any noise. That was when he heard the screeching of an animal below him. He looked down into the diffused light of the day. Falling ash obscured a lot of the game trail below. It was because of that whitish-colored ash that he saw what had awakened him. His eyes widened and he inched back closer to the cave's outer wall.

"What the—" he started to say, and then stopped short when the feathered creature broke cover. It was soon followed by two more from opposing directions. The three animals had cornered a fourth. The frightened creature at the center looked like a small tree sloth that had wandered too far from its home. His eyes widened when he examined the three feathered birdlike animals that had its prey surrounded.

The three birds were lizardlike in movement. Their two arms were long and feathered and what made Carl's breath catch in his throat was the fact that these creatures had articulated hands and fingers. They were outstretched as they circled the sloth. He saw the yellow eyes as they watched every slowed movement of the fur-covered tree dweller. The animals were large, standing just about four and a half feet. The feathers along their arms were sparse but brightly colored. These feathers were long while the light down feathers covering their muscular bodies were short and moved with the rising breeze. Instead of the hard beaks of the feathered world, they had lizard snouts, and he could see even from that distance that they were filled with small, sharp teeth. The heads were clean of feathers with the exception of the bright red and blue ones crowning their heads and ran from their crown to the tips of their tails, which moved in dragonlike slowness as they forced the sloth into the center of the game trail.

"Holy shit," Carl mumbled as the hunters and prey squared off. The sloth with its elongated claws used for climbing sliced the air in front of the three Velocirap-

tors, keeping them at bay with loud hissing and squeaks. The three prehistoric car-
nivores circled, infuriated that the small koala bear–looking sloth was actually
going to put up a fight.

Suddenly a thing happened that blew Carl's natural world to bits. The larger
of the three raptors moved quickly off into the bush. This animal was far more
brightly colored than its two smaller compatriots. It vanished as the others continued to keep the sloth in check. The lead raptor reappeared and this time it held
a long stick in its flexing hand. Everett's hackles rose as he was witness to an animal using a tool to possibly kill with. The leader squawked out orders, which scared
Carl even more than the makeshift spear that the beast carried. The alpha raptor
hissed and barked again and the circling animals stopped. The leader slowly raised
the long stick upward and then jabbed at the frightened sloth.

"Run, damn it!" Everett hissed from his high perch.

Without notice the activity stopped. Carl knew he had voiced his concern too
loudly when the leader looked around and its scaled muzzle went into the air and
it sniffed. It turned. Its yellow eyes, with quick, jerky motions, looked up and saw
the man high in the rocks. It hissed.

The sloth, seeing its break, ran off to the nearest tree and vanished. The other
two raptors joined the first as they all looked up at the man. They were quiet as they
examined this new element in the morning's hunt. The alpha raptor barked three
times and then it seemed to shake its makeshift club at the man who had so interfered with its breakfast.

"Uh-oh," Carl said as he gathered up his bow. He started to stand up but his
boot caught on some loose rock and he slipped. He thought he could catch himself before he came too close to the edge but his other foot got caught up in the
quiver of arrows. He knew he had lost and started a fast slide down the incline
that had protected him from the night's terrors. He slid down until the breath was
knocked from his body as he finally came to rest just off the game trail. He shook
his head and then looked around him. His bow was broken in two and his arrows
were still in their quiver fifty feet above him. He quickly scrambled to his feet as
he saw the stunned raptors looking at him.

"I know, not very graceful, was it?" Carl said just to hear the sound of his voice
over the three intakes of breath from the birdlike creatures. Everett slowly withdrew his sheathed survival knife. He eyed the birds as they didn't exactly know
what to make of this large animal that had intruded. The two lesser raptors looked
to the alpha for guidance. The eyes and head flicked about as the raptor studied
Everett. Then it barked twice and its two companions broke and ran to either side
of Carl. The surround game was on again. Carl held the knife out to the leader
and spoke. "Well, asshole, let's do this," he said as the raptor eyed him with fast
blinks and head tilting when he spoke.

The alpha raised the large stick and that was when Carl knew that it wasn't
just a club. The raptor had altered the broken limb for combat. The sharpened end

was as pointed as anything he could have whittled. Suddenly the game was changed and Everett knew he was looking at something that shouldn't be. The animal barked again and then stepped toward the larger human. The spear was held out as it started poking it toward Carl. He heard the other two raptors behind him in the bush. Their ragged breathing was almost as frightening as the vision of these out-of-place animals.

One of the smaller Velociraptors charged Everett from the rear. Carl spun as fast as he could and caught the raptor in the throat and then he cut left to confront the other one hidden behind him. That was when the alpha charged with its spear out in front. Everett slammed the knife down deflecting the weapon as the raptor's momentum swung it wide of Carl. The second raptor surprised him and came on from a direction he didn't suspect. It jumped from a tree and then its weight slammed Carl to the ground and that was when he knew he was in trouble as he heard at the same moment the alpha recover from its aborted attack and turn. The one that had knocked him from his feet recovered and then turned, hissing on Everett. He brought the knife up just as Carl raised his weapon. He didn't realize until later that he wasn't using the knife to kill, but merely to use as a shield against the snapping teeth. The animal's jaw came down on the blackened steel of the K Bar knife. It hit and the animal screamed. Then Carl saw his chance and pushed the knife down the half bird, half lizard's throat. The animal tried to scream again but managed only to spill hot blood down Everett's arm as it stumbled backward. It fell and then started its death spasms as Everett tried to stand. He was too late.

The alpha broke from the brush once more, this time with a powerful leap into the air with the spear raised high. Carl tried to bring his arms up for some sort of defense but knew his move would be too late and the knife would never stop the weight and height momentum of the raptor before it sunk the makeshift spear deeply into his chest.

As Everett braced for the searing pain he knew was coming, a miracle came from the same area where the tree sloth had disappeared to. The raptor's flight toward Carl's prone body was snatched away at the last moment by a blur of white, yellow, and red feathers. He rolled away and saw that the raptor's trajectory had been altered big time. He shook his head and then focused on the commotion in front of him. The alpha leader of the Velociraptors was in a quandary as it it hissed at the large roc confronting it. The great bird was now the one doing the circling. Its small wings flapped as it cawed and screeched at the raptor, daring it to charge. The large talons of the roc were scratching away the undergrowth as it was preparing to charge like a bull. Still the raptor held its ground as it hissed out raptor epithets at the large chickenlike bird.

"I'll be damned," he mumbled when he saw that it was the same roc that he had saved the previous month. The deep scratches that the giant panther had etched into its large beak were the telling factor in his identification. The deep gouges were now a blur as the beak opened and then the roc screamed and attacked.

The raptor knew it was outmatched fighting alone. It threw the spear like an Olympic athlete and, like the terrorists of Everett's own time, it ran away from superior firepower—that being the enormous, sharpened beak of the roc. The large chicken knew not to press its luck with pursuit. It had the instincts to know that the alpha raptor had many friends in the jungles and one roc against a flock had no chance. The roc skid to a stop as the raptor vanished into the bush lining the game trail.

Everett had a hard time getting his heart to slow after the close call. He watched the roc as it scratched the earth with its giant talons as it mocked the flight of its mortal enemy. The giant turned to face Everett. Its yellow eyes blinked in rapid movement. The long neck of the bird craned higher to get a better look at Carl. The rooster took a few tentative steps toward the man who had saved its life. The small wings flapped twice as it stopped only feet away. Everett sheaved the knife and then ventured a step closer to his savior. He stopped when the roc suddenly chirped. Everett's eyes went wide for a moment as he didn't know if that was a greeting or a warning that he was getting too close. The long legs and powerful thighs of the roc remained still as Carl held out a hand toward the scarred beak. The roc leaned over and Everett gently touched the deep gouges that had been close to a death sentence from the earlier confrontation with the large panther. The roc blinked its yellow eyes as Carl's hand came into contact with the hard surface of the beak.

"Well, I guess thanks are in order," he said as his large hand slid easily over the rough surface of the roc's large and menacing beak. It opened its mouth and then it squawked lightly as its head bent lower at Carl's touch.

Erebus took that moment to awaken from its nightly slumber and announce that it was now fully awake. The explosion of ash and rock flew from the mouth of the crater, and three other smaller mounts close to Erebus did the same. The ash cloud formed immediately and slid down the facing of not one, but four volcanoes. The earth moved and then quickly settled as the ashfall became heavier.

The large and curving beak of the roc nudged its equally large head against Everett's hand. The man smiled and then patted the giant on its head as the world became darker around them. They heard other frightened beasts of the eastern and southern plains as they stampeded away from the death and destruction falling from the skies over their heads.

"Looks like we won't have very much time to sort out this new friendship we have here, my friend."

The roc squawked again and then nuzzled Everett's hand even harder than before. Then, as the ash cloud grew heavier, the giant raised its head to the sky and screeched. The sound initially came out high-pitched, but ended in a deep bass sound that reverberated against the stark skies. Carl smiled as the roc looked back at him, its red-feathered head dipping to his hand once more.

"You sound like an old-fashioned foghorn, you know that," he said as he scratched at the roc's feathers on the side of its head. He laughed when he realized he had just come up with a name for his new friend. He pushed the roc toward the game trail.

Erebus rumbled and her three sisters did the same.

"Come on, Foghorn Leghorn, let's find some cover."

BROOKLYN NAVY YARD

Xavier Morales watched as the tractor slowly moved onto the floor of the makeshift laboratory. He saw Jack Collins and Henri Farbeaux at the front as Collins controlled the tractor and its six-trailer load by remote control. Henri stood opposite him with Jenks and Charlie Ellenshaw bringing up the rear near the first trailer. He saw that all but Ellenshaw had M-4 assault rifles slung on their packs. Their white environmental suits gleamed in the multicolored brightness of the powered-up doorway. The procession halted as they came within fifty feet of the doorway. The steel door slowly closed behind them. He watched as Collins looked first at the large monitor and Morales as he viewed from Nellis, and then he glanced up at the observation room where the gathered department heads watched on nervously. He looked but knew Sarah wouldn't be there and his hindsight regrets doubled. Niles nodded and Alice gave them a small, sad wave of her elegant hand.

"*Los Angeles,* this is Group control, we're ready to power up to one hundred and fifteen percent. Are we a go?" Morales asked as his team of technicians excitedly watched from Nevada.

"Group, we are green across the board, ready on your command," came the reply from the submarine laying tied up at the dock.

"All observers, please lower your eye protection," Xavier ordered. Sunglasses were placed on faces throughout the observation room and the platform area. "Dimensional Raiders, lower your visors and prepare for power-up."

Collins shot a look at the monitor and Xavier at the mention of the moniker Raiders, but lowered his visor anyway. Charlie smiled as he secretly loved the new nickname.

"Inject the nitrogen into the doorway," Virginia ordered from her station as her eyes settled on Master Chief Jenks, who glanced over at her and then nodded his helmeted head. That was when they all heard a frightening sound as the large pumps injected liquid nitrogen into the spinning doorway. The noise was overpowering as the coolant spread through the system to cool it while the lasers cut a dimensional path through time and space. Without the coolant the team would walk into the power of the sun.

"Begin collider sequence, five thousand RPMs first." Alice closed her eyes in the scientists' silent prayer of, *God, I hope we know what it is we are doing.*

Inside the large spinning wheel of the doorway the trapped atoms started racing around the interior of the wheel and then another from stream of protons from the opposing end. Both came on at the speed of sound as they passed each other. With every revolution the two particles came closer and closer together. It was only the sheer brilliance of Europa that timed the sequence perfectly and kept the two from colliding before the doorway was fully open. They needed the power of the colliding atoms and protons to punch a hole large enough out of this time dimension and into the desired target of Antarctica of 227,000 years ago.

Inside the observation room some of the department heads turned and they had to smile as Will, Sarah, Anya, and Jason entered. The director looked their way and nodded. He knew he would never be able to keep them out anyway. They had to know if their friends made it through the doorway and he couldn't blame them in the least. He turned and saw Jack and the others looking up at him. Collins saluted and then nodded that they were as ready as they would ever be.

"Dr. Morales, you have my permission to initiate sequence. Note that it was upon my order. Log it into Europa that I am solely responsible for the parameters and of the results of this mission."

"Noted, Doctor," Morales said with a faltering smile as he turned to his technicians. "Gentlemen, let's open the door. Colonel Collins, good luck to you and your team, sir."

Jack and the others braced themselves. Henri felt the reassuring weight of the mini M-4 on his back and was sorely tempted to unsling it and be ready for a charging rhinoceros or whatever terror was waiting for them.

For the first time since she had known him, Alice watched as Niles Compton offered a silent prayer as he closed his good eye and lowered his head. The director had never been a religious man, but she knew that after the recent war he had changed—they all had.

"*Los Angeles*, one hundred and fifteen percent power. Europa, expand the bandwidth and lock doorway on to target area. Let's bring the particles up to light speed."

They all felt and heard the electrical whine coming from the outside as *Los Angeles* ramped up her powerful and highly experimental reactor. The power coursed through the thick lines and soon they all heard the particle accelerator inside the doorway start to charge with an ear-splitting whine.

Virginia Pollock sat down at her station as Jenks looked over at her through the protective glass. Even with her goggles on he could tell she had been crying. She smiled and then started her procedure.

"Injecting the core material. Bring revolutions to five hundred thousand RPM, please."

The doorway started spinning faster. The noise was tremendous and then the sudden heavy vibration almost knocked Jack and the others from their feet. Up above Moira Mendelsohn had never beheld such raw power before. She had had a limited supply and had to use it very judiciously back in the day.

Virginia found she couldn't give the last command. The lights in the room dimmed as the doorway brightened as the opposing particles of atoms and protons finally achieved the speed of light inside of their protective cocoon. The colors were swirling faster than they could track. It was Xavier Morales who noticed her dilemma.

"Heat is holding, start the laser system," he said from the large monitor overhead, knowing Virginia was hesitant to send the team off.

Ringing the doorway's frame, the 162 lasers fired. The green and blue beams of light cut a swath of brilliance through the darkness until it struck the lead-lined wall beyond. The rounded sphere of laser light held steady.

"Europa, please bring lasing system to full power—watch your eyes, gentlemen," he called out as Jack and the others lowered their gaze from the doorway. Suddenly, the intensity of the green and blue lasers heightened to where no one could view them until their eyes adjusted. "Okay, final RPM boost in five, four, three, two, one, initiate power surge."

The scream of the revolving Wellsian Doorway cracked the viewing glass in the observation deck from the audible assault from the platform, forcing those inside to back off nervously with not just a few nervous chuckles. Sarah gripped the windowsill that much tighter as she watched Jack far below.

The doorway hit its revolution limit and a powerful roar filled the air inside the room as she came to full power-up. Europa sounded a warning tone that pierced even the noise of the doorway.

"Collider is at one hundred percent," Europa said with her Marilyn Monroe voice as calming as ever, and believe it or not to most that was comforting to them. "Matter infusion in three, two, one, infusion initiated."

Inside the rapidly spinning doorway the world exploded outward as the atoms and protons inside the collider mated at the speed of light, the collision producing the power surge needed to penetrate the dimensional rift and exploit it. Before anyone realized it, their world of knowledge and theory flew from their minds as the most amazing thing they had ever witnessed began. The laser lights started to bend backward toward the doorway as if a powerful suction were bending them. A human-made black hole was forming, powerful enough to bend light. At the speed of light the lasers shot back and into the Wellsian Doorway and at that very moment, the impossible happened. Never again would the Event Group doubt any science that Albert Einstein had theorized.

The lasers penetrated the doorway and the room exploded with the fantastic spectacle of light as the pressure wave of lasers sent back a hot, humid shot of air. Inside that brief moment of converging times all of the eyewitnesses would later say they all smelled another world as it invaded their own.

Before them, Jack and his team saw the lasers vanish over and around them until they were covered in a tunnel-like corridor. The lasers vanished into a swirling vortex of bright white light. They had their external air valves shut down and were on their limited thirty-minute supply of suit oxygen; if not, Jack Collins would have smelled the ancient savagery of the strange world they were about to step into.

"Tone signal has locked, you will be entering at ground level one and half miles east from the rescue beacon." Xavier Morales could say no more as he anxiously watched the brave men almost two thousand miles away. It was now up to the team leader.

Below, Jack started the tracked vehicle. The train of men slowly and hesitantly entered the Wellsian Doorway and vanished.

The age of time travel had officially arrived for the United States.

PART THREE

THE LAND THAT TIME FORGOT

Morality is of the highest importance—but for us, not for God.

—**Albert Einstein**, from
Albert Einstein: The Human Side

16

The pain, though less than the unprotected nonceramic construction of the earlier German and Mendelsohn doorways as reported by Madam herself, was still enough to make Collins and the others bend over. It was as if their very marrow were being assaulted by molten lead. Farbeaux would worry much later about the long-term effects of such substantial exposure to neutrons, protons, and atoms that flew through air at the speed of light. If it were not for the tractor and its ability to continue to transit the corridor between dimensions, they all feared they would have faltered and stumbled inside the hurricane of light and sound. Charlie closed his eyes against the pain and nearly crumpled to a knee. The light was blinding and it seemed the very atomized particles of this strange transitioning passed directly through their suits and bodies—which in actuality did just that. The team was essentially disintegrated and then their own DNA was reconstituted as they entered the dimensional plane of a new time.

Jack and Henri were the first to feel the sudden difference in their footing as each halting step brought them even more of the assault to their pain centers. The hardness of the old concrete floor of the naval warehouse was gone as their specialized boots were now walking upon a soft, spongelike footing. The pain eased and the team slowly recovered as they walked, each step more pain free. They thought they were through the worst of it when the wave of nausea gripped each man. It quickly passed but was replaced by dizziness that threatened once more to send them sprawling. A blinding flash of light illuminated the air around them and then the brightness vanished and the sound exited the new world with it. They soon found themselves in utter darkness. Charlie clicked on the light that was affixed to his right shoulder and his helmet.

"Shut it down, Charlie," Jack said through his com link just as he raised his tinted visor. He looked skyward and the night slowly started to take shape around him. "Your eyes will adjust. Look up and concentrate on the stars. You can see a few of them through the canopy and the—"

That was when they all noticed the heavy fall of black and gray ash as it fell upon them. Even as they looked the dark ash cloud blotted out the remaining stars. Charlie still did as Jack had ordered and shut off both lights.

All four men heard the heavy breathing and just assumed it was Charlie. It wasn't long before they realized that each of them was the culprit. Jack released the toggle on the tractor's remote and the small train came to a stop. He turned and looked back at where the doorway had been. He saw ash-covered jungle in the darkness as his eyes slowly adjusted. They seemed to be in a small thigh-high grass clearing. He once more looked at the sky and the moon was just sitting in this strange land, that and the ash clouds of angry elements was why the night was so dark. Collins looked over at Henri just as Jenks and Ellenshaw joined them. The master chief still had to have a handhold on the tractor as he steadied his shaking body.

"Well, we made it someplace," Jack said as he looked around them and the stillness of the green canopy they found themselves under. The moon vanished low in the northern sky and then the ash had a complete hold on the night. The darkness became even more still than it had been just a moment before. They all knew it was the total absence of light that played tricks on their minds.

"Yeah, so far anyway," Jenks said as he looked at a small box he held in his hand. "Wherever we are the oxygen level is off the chart." He looked up from his readout. "Twenty times the content of our atmosphere at home. No pollutants other than this." He reached up and caught a handful of hard ash as the pumice-like material fought its way through the thick tree canopy above them. Jenks turned his hand over and allowed the ash to slide off his glove. "Heavy ash particulate. It looks like your volcanoes are acting up big time, Colonel. This isn't from just a smoking cauldron, it's activity that's carrying some weight to it. This stuff is being ejected far from the caldera." Jenks looked to the south and that was when he saw the clouds in that direction were tinted red and flashed heavy electrical activity.

"We only have four hours' extra supply of O2 in the trailers, we're bound to run out. Can we breathe this stuff?" Jack asked.

Before Jenks could answer they saw Henri reach up and slide his locking mechanism on his helmet. He waited a moment and then looked at Collins. "We may as well find out now rather than later if we have to pack up and get out of here." He lifted the helmet free and then slowly took a breath.

Charlie couldn't help but take a deep breath while he watched the Frenchman, as if he were willing the air to be good.

"One thing we must do before we leave this place," Henri said as he took another deep breath, "is to bottle as much air as we can to sell on the black market back home."

Jack smiled and then removed his own helmet. He was happy not to hear the warning alarm for a bad environment sound in his ears just the same.

Before long each man had to sit in the darkness as the air was so heavy and oxygenated that they became momentarily giddy with an overdose of something none of them had ever breathed before—unpolluted air from a world producing such an abundance through the ancient plant life. It was impossible for them to fully comprehend its purity.

"This clearing seems good enough to get our bearings. Master Chief, can you get our precise location?"

"Yeah, I'll break out the sextant," Jenks joked.

Jack cleared his eyes and took a shallow breath as he tried to limit his intake as much as he could. He looked at his gloved hand and then unzipped it and peered at the illuminated dial on his watch. He was shocked that the timepiece made it through the electrical hell as they passed through the doorway. He again glanced up but was unable to see anything beyond the canopy as the falling ash came down like a winter snowfall.

"It should be daylight soon enough. We'll forego camp and make ready to move at first light. We'll set up in a more defensive position when we can see what the hell we're doing. I don't relish the idea of flashing a bunch of lights around without knowing what may be watching."

The stillness of the night was shattered by the scream of a large cat somewhere in the distance. Each man froze as the cry echoed against some far-off obstruction and bounced back.

"That was not a normal large-cat call. I've heard them all and believe me, that's something that hasn't walked the Earth for well over ten thousand years," Charlie explained excitedly.

Jenks, Farbeaux, and Collins looked at Ellenshaw as if he had just reverted back to his old, ditsy self. However, it was the Frenchman who put things into perspective once again as he removed the small M-4 from his back and made sure to charge it.

"I'll say this once again: You people never cease to amaze me in your unlimited and imaginative ways you have for trying to get me killed."

As if in answer to Farbeaux's observation the unseen beast roared again, and this time it was answered by a second, far closer call before the echo of the first had faded to nothing. As they listened a heavy rain came and started cleaning the jungle around them of the white and gray ash. Still, the sound of the animal life of the Antarctic continent 227,000 years ago told them they were indeed a long way from home.

The strange new world they found themselves in was starting to awaken.

BROOKLYN NAVY YARD

Sarah waited as long as she could as the doorway slowly started to power down. She swallowed her fear as Jack had vanished into a wall of light. She felt part of her rapidly beating heart go with him. She felt Anya beside her and she looked up and saw the sympathy in her eyes. The Israeli agent knew the exact anxiety she was feeling.

"Come on, ladies, waiting around in here won't hurry things up any. Let's get some air," Mendenhall said as he nodded toward Ryan, who was speaking with the director and Alice. He soon joined them.

"I don't know about you people, but I've never felt so damn worthless in my life," Jason said as he held the door for the two ladies and Will.

The four walked outside and took in the stillness of the night. The fog had actually worsened in the past hour. The scene was eerily reminiscent of the open Wellsian Doorway in that all sound was absorbed by the fog. The strange light the fog produced made Sarah feel uneasy.

"Peter to Paul, we have a vehicle approaching from the main gate," came the call from one of Ryan's men at the perimeter. "Looks like a limo, over."

Jason raised his brows at the other three who heard the call. He raised the radio to his lips and pushed the transmit button.

"Stop and detain," he said. He lowered the radio and then started to raise it again but stopped. He waited.

The radio finally crackled to life. "Driver says the party is expected by Madam Mendelsohn, over."

"Number?" Jason asked, not liking this one bit. He nodded at Will, who quickly vanished into the night after retrieving a small case from the dock area. Sarah raised a questioning look at Ryan.

"I count what looks like a family of four plus infant." The radio went silent for the briefest of moments. Then it awoke once more. "Two well-dressed men plus the driver, over."

"Will, are you in position?" he asked.

"Yeah," Mendenhall said from the high vantage point he had taken. It was one of the many streetlights he had rigged earlier for climbing. He was using a new scope delivered the past year from Bushnell. The infrared lighting system cut through fog like it wasn't there. Will could switch the system to read heat signatures as well as cold spots. "Oh, it looks like they brought company. They're hanging back just beyond the gate. Lights off. Six large Explorers. Infrared says they're full of very large sacks of meat."

"Copy. Let me know if they move."

"You got it," replied Mendenhall.

"Let them through, then blend into the night and wait for Captain Mendenhall to make a call on those cars. Positions three and four close on the main gate."

Ryan was quickly answered by just three clicks from each man watching the buildings. "Sarah, you and Anya get out of sight for now until we see what these folks are up to. Dr. Pollock, are you there?"

"Pollock," came Virginia's quick response.

"Inform the director we have company, supposedly at Madam Mendelsohn's request."

"Copy."

Sarah didn't question Ryan as she and Anya vanished into the fog next to the USS *Los Angeles*, which now sat dark and silent under the camouflage netting.

"They're moving to your pos, over."

Ryan made sure his own pistol was charged. He stepped forward to greet their visitors and raised the radio once more. "Dr. Pollock, I'm sending Sergeant Hernandez in. He's to stick with the director, who is to remain secured inside the observation room."

"Copy. Also, Professor Mendelsohn was not expecting company. She says she's in the dark."

"Roger," Jason said as he finally saw the long limousine appear through the rolling fog. Its approach was slow as it made its way to the front of the building. Ryan stepped forward and held his hand in the air. As he did he got what the colonel called a jolt to his hackles as he felt the trouble before it actually appeared. He watched as the driver emerged from the front seat and stepped easily to the rear and opened the door. A man eased himself from the car and adjusted his ankle-length coat and then he saw Ryan. He smiled, his teeth even and white. His beard was immaculately trimmed and the navy man immediately took the guy for an asshole.

"Thank you for allowing us to visit," the man said with a slight taste of Russian accent, which brought Ryan to full attention.

"This building and area are closed for the time being. Stems from the trouble this afternoon." Ryan watched the man closely. "Perhaps you heard?"

The man stood his ground and then his smile grew as he looked to his left at the former dry dock area and saw the camouflage netting covering the long shape of the *Los Angeles*. He turned back to face Jason.

"I must admit that whoever you are, you have access to the most amazing resources."

Jason remained as still as he could while his eyes slowly took in the man and his driver, who still hadn't moved from the open rear door.

"It is cold and damp out here, so I will state my business." He gestured to the driver, who leaned in and said something to the people inside the darkened interior and then stepped back. "Inside the car are some particular friends of Madam Moira Mendelsohn. Very close, you might say."

"I don't know a Madam Mendelson and as I said before this section of the navy yard is closed. No one goes inside."

The man looked Ryan over and smirked at the garish tattoo. He stepped aside as he was joined by an older couple and what looked like a young family of three, including a baby. The family looked frightened.

"I insist."

Jason Ryan didn't move or gesture in any way as the three laser beams struck the man and remained unmoving upon his black coat right over where his heart would be. For emphasis a red beam of light struck the bearded man on the forehead. The laser beams were clearly marked as they cut a swath through the fog. Ryan just raised his brows as he waited for the Russian to continue on his insistence to enter.

"Very well," the man said as he took a step back. Ryan didn't like the fact that the Russian did this without fear of being shot. He pulled the young mother forward and then raised the blanket covering the sleeping baby. Jason tried not to react when he saw the plastique and electrical wiring. His eyes went to the well-dressed man, who released the blanket and allowed it to once more cover the explosive-covered baby.

"Barbaric perhaps, but it is an attention-getter, is it not?" The man saw something in Jason's eyes he didn't like. "I assure you there is enough of a charge attached to that child to not only kill us all, but to flatten enough of that building to bring in the authorities. Neither of us can well afford that, can we? Wellsian Doorways are a little hard to come by."

Ryan knew the man had the advantage and no matter what firepower he brought to bear this man held all of the cards at the moment. He couldn't risk damage to or the discovery of the doorway, or they would lose everyone. Ryan gestured toward the building. He raised the radio and informed Virginia about the situation and she also knew they had very little choice.

As the frightened family and the three Russians moved toward the building and the doorway beyond, the six Explorers entered the navy yard and also made their way toward building 117. The remaining Event Group security posts could do nothing about it.

ANTARCTICA, 227,000, B.C.E.

As the sun rose, Jack felt more in control. The jungle surrounding them was lush and green now that the hard rains had washed the greenery clean. With the ash-fall turning to a fine dust, Collins could see the jungle had a youngness to it, a beauty none had ever seen. The flowers were large and colorful. The insect life was active with mosquitoes the size of large houseflies. They had started making their way toward the inland sea and hoped to exit the greenery before too long. The electric drive on the tractor made little noise as the group finally broke into the clear and they saw the diluted, shrouded sun for the first time. The angry ash clouds to the south were far more visible now. Even as they examined the dark sky they felt the movement of the earth beneath their feet.

"Here's something for the books," Jenks said as he had pulled the atmospheric analyzer from the trailer nearest him. He shook his head at the readings. "We just went from a balmy and humid ninety-two degrees to a low of sixty-seven in less than three minutes." He looked up from the analyzer. "Air current shift from the northeast. Cold air front." He again looked at the readout. "We're back up to ninety-two degrees."

"What do you think?" Jack asked Jenks.

"Hell, your guess is as good as mine, Colonel."

"The great freeze has begun," Charlie said as if speaking to himself. He then looked around and saw the team looking his way and he realized he had spoken aloud.

"Go ahead and keep it to yourself, Doc," the master chief quipped.

"Sorry, but it seems the activity of the four or five volcanoes are interacting with the freeze that's occurring in the northeast. Sarah's geology department in conjunction with atmospherics say that we have just entered the opening rounds of the climate change that leads to Antarctica being buried in ice. Perhaps the volcanic activity is retarding the process." He looked at the confused master chief. "Slowed it down. At least for now. But in the end it is the activity of so many volcanoes that they are the ultimate culprit in sending this continent to the same frozen hell as the rest of the world."

"There's a small rise right over there." Jack loosened the high collar of his camouflage BDUs. "It has a clear field of fire for about two hundred yards. I say we start this show right there. I don't relish traveling too far away from the beacon but also don't want to have a sea at my back in case we have to get the hell out of there fast."

"The sooner the better," Henri said as he looked around him. The sudden stillness rankled his calm. "I don't know if you've noticed but we have eyes on us," he said as he pretended to adjust something in the first trailer.

Without comment and believing every word just uttered by the Frenchman, Jack started the tractor forward, its tracks digging deep into the soft soil.

The deep rumbling beneath their feet started and they assumed at first it was the movement caused by the rumbling mountains to the south. But it wasn't Mount Erebus and her sisters. Jack stopped and they all saw the giant herd of bison as they rumbled no less than two miles away. They sped past the four men, moving the very ground they stood upon even at that extreme distance. Collins watched the hairy bison, the likes of which had vanished long ago. The sight amazed him. Charlie was beyond himself as he took in the scene. He quickly removed a small digital camera and started shooting the extraordinary view. The only one who wasn't watching the scene in the distance was Farbeaux. He was busy looking at the jungle they had just exited moments before.

"What in the hell are those things?" Jenks asked as he raised a set of field glasses to his eyes.

Behind the large herd of bison, several smaller animals could be seen running at a strange gait. The smaller creatures would dodge in and out of the herd as if they were driving them toward something. Several more of the animals emerged from the jungle that ran parallel to the frightened bison. The herd started to turn toward them and then back again when the small creatures waved long, feather-covered arms in the air as if they were scaring the frightened animals back toward the center of the large plain.

"Doc, you're the expert, what in the hell are those things?" Jack asked as he lowered his own field glasses.

"My God, they're raptors of a sort. I've never seen anything remotely that size in the fossil record. They must be close to five feet in height. Look at the feathers, how colorful they are!"

"Charlie, I am beginning to believe that that particular fossil record you scientists keep referring to is vastly incomplete," Jack said as he again raised the glasses to his eyes.

Suddenly the men were startled as in the distance one of the birdlike animals raised a right arm and then threw something at the closest bison. Jack's eyes widened when he saw that the raptor had thrown a rock. The animal fell, sliding to a stop as three of the raptors jumped upon its thrashing body. More rocks were thrown to still the injured beast. The raptors then circled the dying animal.

"Tell me, Nerdly, what does the fossil record say about large chickens that use weaponry to kill its prey?" Jenks said as he looked over at the stunned cryptozoologist.

"This is impossible," was the only thing crazy Charlie could come up with.

Henri ducked and warned the others as a long and sharpened stick flew from the jungle only thirty yards away. He brought his weapon up but Jack gestured for him not to shoot. Instead Farbeaux pulled the long polelike object from the ground where it had embedded itself next to him.

"Dr. Ellenshaw, perhaps you can enlighten me as to how an animal with a brain no larger than a walnut can develop such tool-using capabilities?" he asked as he again examined the spear. He broke it and held it high toward the dark jungle it had come from.

"I'm at a loss," Charlie said as he watched Henri toss the makeshift weapon away.

"Look, I don't particularly wish to stay here and get skewered by a pissed-off hungry chicken. May I suggest we egress to said hill and make a defense of some sort?"

"I must concur with our rough friend here," Henri added.

To punctuate the statement another, although smaller, stick flew from the greenery and ricocheted off the last trailer.

As Jack moved off he hoped Carl had survived in this backward world.

The large herd of bison had moved off after losing seven of their number to the hunters. Jack and the others had been amazed at the efficient way the raptors had disposed of the large carcasses. Instead of feeding in place, the birdlike animals dismembered, butchered, and moved the meat off with very little left behind. They had nervously watched as they set up the camp. They had just finished when the sun started to set. The raptors had not made an appearance since the hunt, and the jungle only a quarter mile distant had remained unmoving. Even Henri felt the eyes were no longer upon them.

"I thought we would see more animal life than we have," Jack said as he reached over and threw a switch that activated the automated laser defense pod he had just installed. The camp was now ringed with the high-tech weaponry. The six modules were perched on their high posts and were aimed outward. The weapons looked like nothing more than a small black box with a glass ball in its casing. Each pod was capable of firing two thousand high-voltage radar-guided laser bursts. It should be enough to frighten anything that may come upon them in the night.

Master Chief Jenks made sure the doorway was secure inside the last trailer. He would start to build it during the lighted hours of the morning. He hated losing the day but they had no choice if those chickens decided to visit during the night. The camp was efficient. They set up a small cookstove but refrained from putting up their shelters. The tents would only keep them from knowing their surroundings and give them a false sense of security, and Collins wanted them all in one place and alert. The five trailers and tractor had been dispersed so as to give them some sort of cover as they watched the terrain below them. Jack knew the makeshift barrier looked like covered wagons and they were the settlers. He stood at one of these and examined the darkening terrain. To the south the earth rumbled and they could see the glow of Mount Erebus. Every now and then a deep explosive jolt would course through their feet as the great volcano rumbled. As they waited for nightfall the night became cold. Yes, the deep freeze was slowly coming to the last land on the planet to know warm sunlight.

"This place has a decidedly dark edge of doom to it, don't it?" Jenks said as he prepared to send the signal balloons up. He adjusted the strobe light that would flash inside of the white aerial device. He quickly filled the balloon with helium and it shot skyward. As it rose into the air the flashing beacon shone brightly in the night sky like a magical orb.

"There, I hope we attract the attention of Toad and not some monster out of a nightmare," the master chief said as his eyes watched the round balloon sending out its flashing beacon. "I've noticed that in my time with you people you seem to attract a hell of a lot of monsters," he said as Henri nodded in agreement. Jenks repeated the process two more times until three of the balloons rose a thousand feet into the air.

"Now look up, Carl," Jack said mostly to himself as his eyes took in the bright luminescent balloons overhead that blinked their magic against the most brilliant star field they had ever seen. Then the night sky was slowly blotted out as a large ash cloud rolled over the area, cutting off the signal from above.

Five miles distant other eyes were trained on the strange sight that filled the night sky, and the ancient world slowly came alive with menace.

"What in the bloody hell is that?" Henri asked as he spit out the mouthful of food as he attempted the impossible task of not allowing it to touch the inside of his mouth. He figured his tongue and taste buds had already been lost.

Jenks smirked and then spooned his own tasty mouthful.

"Uh, enchilada casserole I believe the package said," Ellenshaw said as he examined his own MRE packet.

"Beats the hell out of the old C-rations we used to have to force down," Jenks said as he ate some more of the casserole. "Back in 'Nam we would have sold our souls for this crap. The only good thing the old 'rats had was cheese and crackers."

"I would gladly take your cheese and crackers over this," Henri said as he tossed the casserole free of his plastic spoon. He slowly placed the open package into the plastic bag they were using to keep the animal life from snooping around for food. He spit again to clear his mouth and then drank some water.

"We have enough of the damn MREs to last three months," Jack said as he sniffed his own package of roast beef. He reclosed it and decided to try again later.

A soft tone came from the remote panel Jenks held on his lap. The master chief placed the MRE package down and raised the small plastic console. The holographic map displayed the radar information the portable defense system was acquiring. The first station coordinated with her sister units and that gave Jenks a complete 360-degree view of their surroundings and anything that moved within.

"We have major movement close to the tree line."

"Which one?" Jack asked as he raised the night-vision scope to his eyes and started scanning the trees to his left no less than three hundred yards away.

"All of them," Jenks said as he saw multiple targets moving in and out of radar range. He switched over to infrared and his eyes widened. "Targets are too numerous to count." Jenks leaned over and switched on the main acquisition program on the weapons control. "Laser system is now armed." He looked up at Collins. The light-colored ash was now falling heavier than a moment before as the skies to the south were a deeper red in the night sky. "What fail-safe point do you want the safeties placed on, Colonel?"

"Zero," Jack said as he lowered the nightscope. "I don't intend to wait around here and allow something to get close enough for us to identify it." He turned to a nervous Charlie Ellenshaw. "Doc, you said the odds of the local animal or human-oid life escaping Antarctica's frozen future are a basic zero, right?"

"Yes," he said as he wondered what Jack was thinking.

"So we won't be altering the destiny of any living species occupying this land?"

"That's just a theory, of course, but the anthropological departments and also natural history concur. Europa reported that all the animal life here at this time will perish."

"Good. Master Chief, give me a three-hundred-round spread just into the tree line on all sides. Let's see if our visitors' interest in us is a motivated one."

"Right," Jenks said with a gruff chuckle.

"Very scientific of you, Colonel," Henri said as he lowered himself to form a smaller target just behind one of the empty trailers.

Collins raised the glasses once more and saw that the white blurry targets were gradually easing themselves closer to the first line of trees. The jungle floor hid most of their bodies from view.

"Thirty-five three-thousand-watt bursts from each laser should make our chicken friends think better about dropping in on us without calling first."

"If that's what's out there," Ellenshaw said as he hunkered next to Farbeaux.

"You just add the most wonderful elements to any discussion, Doctor, you know that?" Henri said, looking at crazy Charlie as if he had lost his mind.

"Ah, you ought to be used to me by now, Colonel."

"That's what's worrying me—I am."

"This shouldn't hurt us too much with the system's portable battery. Here goes nothing. Firing sequence—now!"

The six long poles with their strange little black boxes affixed to their tops ac-tivated and started tracking the closest moving targets inside the tree lines on all sides of the camp. As one target was picked by one weapons system its sister tracked the next in line and then the next, all the while feeding their own targeting infor-mation to the base system controlled by Jenks. The targets were then prioritized as to threat and all of this happened in less than a microsecond. The lasers started their silent destruction. The sound of a small battery-powered generator fired, giving the laser its umph. Small pinpoint beams of light burst from each weapon with an audible pop as the argon laser cleared the glass apertures of the black boxes. The shots were faster than the speed of light and the green dot of burning energy was hard to pick up in the glow from the south. But soon the pace of fire was so rapid that it looked like a science fiction war. Beads of light struck trees and other things that cried out in the night. Like tracers from low-caliber weaponry, the lasers punctured the initial line of trees and jungle. Then all was silent with the excep-tion of the animal cries in the jungle beyond.

Jack examined the black boxes housing the lasers. They were hot but looked as if they had operated as designed. He leaned over and looked at the battery drainage from the light assault. Down only two percent.

"My God, they sound like the screams of children," Charlie said with horror written across his features.

As much as Henri didn't want to agree with Charlie, he was right. The wounded animals sounded like children and it was damn-well unnerving to the Frenchman.

"I hope we didn't screw the pooch here, Colonel," Jenks said as he laid the targeting hologram down. Jack looked and nodded at the device. "All activity with the exception of a few blips have all gone. Listen, the cries are fading. So at least we know one thing."

"What's that, Master Chief?" Charlie asked, but it was Jack who answered with a concerned look.

"Whatever they are, they carry off their wounded." Collins looked at the darkened and quiet tree line. He then faced the men. "Doesn't sound like an animal to me." The colonel raised his M-4 and made sure the weapon was charged and safed. "Okay, two on, two off. Fifty percent alert. Charlie, you're with me. Jenks, you and Henri get some rest, we have a hell of a lot of work to do tomorrow."

With that note, the camp had a very lousy sleep.

17

BROOKLYN NAVY YARD

As Ryan held the door for the unwelcome visitors, his radio crackled to life.

"One, this is main gate, the six vehicles have turned off the main drive and have gone beyond my view. We've lost them, Commander."

"Roger, make your way back to building one-seventeen, consolidate what we have." Ryan lowered the radio and saw that the small group was waiting on him inside the old reception area.

"Problems?" the Russian asked with a mockingly concerned look on his face.

"None at all." Ryan again raised the radio to his lips. "Five, this is one, copy?"

"Copy," Will said from outside.

"Inform the local authorities we may have a security concern."

"Roger," came Mendenhall's reply, and then the radio was silent.

"A wise precaution, my friend. Wise indeed."

"You know, I've always noted the comic book ways you guys talk, a much more precise language, trying to be more sophisticated than you are, when in the end you are nothing more than those pathetically depicted comic book villains."

The smile faltered for the briefest of moments and Jason could see that his words had angered the Russian. He smiled and gestured that they should follow him.

Joshua Jodle directed the first Explorer in line to the south side of the navy yard toward the original building 114. The windows of the building were dark as all of the activity had shifted to building 117 a quarter of a mile away.

"The tunnel better be there."

The small man looked over at the brute who was wearing a black leather jacket that didn't do much to hide the small automatic weapon he held.

"Of course it's there. I supervised the construction myself," he lied. "How do you think we could move about from one building to the other while reengineering the doorway without being noticed by the navy yard staff? It's there, it goes directly to the subbasement of building one-seventeen."

The man nodded and then opened the door. He removed the Israeli-made Uzi from his jacket and then waited for his fifteen men to join him.

"Remember, once we are in, there is to be no firing of weapons. I am informed that there is some very delicate equipment inside that does not react well to gunfire."

The other men nodded and Jodle cringed as he saw the explosive firepower of the Russian mob firsthand.

The former concentration camp survivor moved the men into the darkened building where the first doorway had allowed much more honorable men to invade the heart of Nazi Germany not many years before.

But tonight his task was not so noble and he felt guilty as the men made their way to the basement and the tunnel that would lead them to the time machine.

Sergeant Hernandez stepped in front of Director Compton when he tried in vain to move past him and the meeting just outside the observation room.

"Step aside, Sergeant," Niles ordered as calm as he could.

"No, sir, can't. Commander's orders, sorry," Hernandez said, and truly felt bad. He realized he just told the man in charge of Department 5656 and secretly one of the most influential men in the world that he couldn't do something. "After the reaming we took from the colonel . . . I mean . . . can't you see we're on thin ice here?" The sergeant looked for help from the only other person in the observation room, Moira Mendelsohn, but she only shook her head. *No help there*, he thought.

"Sergeant, the bite of Colonel Collins is nothing compared to mine. I swallow military personnel whole, now open that door," Niles said so calmly that the large army sergeant took an involuntary step back. After all, he had never once spoken to the kind, scholarly man before. And now here was that same kindly and scholarly gentleman threatening to swallow him whole. He reached out and opened the door—as far as the sergeant was concerned it would be a pleasure to get court-martialed by Ryan. At least he didn't have to look into the scary one-eyed visage of the small director. Compton took the wheelchair's handles and bypassed the battery system of Madam's chair and they left the office together.

"Ah, there she is," the Russian said as Niles limped behind the chair and both he and Moira entered the reception area where the ghosts of World War II secretaries gossiped over the latest Cary Grant film sixty-five years before.

Virginia looked angry as she took in Niles. She should have known he would pull something like this. The man hated being told what to do. This Group had spoiled their own boss too damn much. The assistant director wanted to throttle the man.

"I was just telling this asshole here that this is a private concern and that he can go fuck himself. Do you have anything to add, Doctor?" she said as her eyes bored into Compton's only good one.

"No, sounds like a good position to me," Niles said as he made his way over to a chair and sat down. Moira was silent as she took in the scene before her. Her eyes sadly found the Koblentz family and she wanted to call out to them but she forced herself to remain still. Then she saw the small baby wrapped tightly against the night. She had heard a few days before that the mother had gone into labor. She had always insisted on being informed when the offspring of one of her children were born as each child received a full scholastic scholarship. But now it looked as if all of that were over for her and her extended family.

The Russian half bowed and then looked at the small balding man who had just taken a seat. The portly man was in poor shape as the Russian soon discovered. He was scared and had a limp and an arm that didn't seem to work quite properly. All in all these people were not the meek scientific types he had expected. They would bear watching.

"Alexi Doshnikov." He straightened after the brief protocol of the bow.

Virginia and Niles had heard the name and they could see by the look on the Traveler's face she had heard of the mobster herself. It also looked as though a small smile eased across her lips. Compton looked up and he could see one of the outside monitors in the reception area and saw the face of Xavier Morales appear and then disappear almost as fast. Suddenly he saw that Europa had shut down all of the monitors inside the building. Even the cell phones died in the Group's pockets. Europa had pulled the plug. At least he knew they were being monitored by an outside source.

"The police have been called," Ryan said as he looked angrily toward the director. The act of defiance started here at Group right at the top of the heap and worked down.

"Oh, that," Doshnikov said with a sad smile on his face. "The local authorities have a small terrorist act on their hands, nothing major I assure you, but it seemed to be directed at Brooklyn's pride and joy of an arena, so it looks as if any response time from the police may be an extended and lengthy proposition."

"See what I mean about talking as if you're a sophisticated villain," Ryan said angrily, but kept his smile from reaching his eyes.

"My friend, your little quips of humor have a decidedly harsh and mocking edge to them, and I am growing tired of it. Out of respect for the Traveler, I will not have you shot in front of her, but keep in mind there is no help coming and that mouth of yours is a severe liability to the survival of this innocent family."

The door opened from the outside and Will Mendenhall, Sarah McIntire, and Anya Korvesky walked in as if they were unaware of what was happening. Jason noticed none of them were carrying the M-4 rifles they had had earlier, but at least all of them played the role well as their eyes widened in mock surprise as they slowly raised their hands into the air.

"These are the two that were on top of the building this afternoon," one of the larger men said as he stepped forward and frisked Mendenhall. Will had to smile when he saw the melted nylon of the man's coat pocket.

"Have a little accident there, Ivan?" Will asked as he nodded at the man's pants where the confiscated cell phones had melted down. The Russian angrily tossed Mendenhall against the wall and made a far more thorough and rough search of the captain. Ryan winced as he realized Mendenhall was trying his best to provoke these men.

"Where are my four men?" Doshnikov asked as he stepped menacingly toward Ryan, who held his ground.

"It seems we left them in the loving arms of some very motivated Italian folks. You might know them since they ran these neighborhoods a hundred years before you were born, Stalin."

The backhand to Ryan's jaw caught everyone but the navy man off guard. Jason shot Will a look to let him know that he just took the heat off of him and for the captain to knock off antagonizing these assholes. That was his job and he prided himself on doing it well.

"I will deal with our Italian friends another time. For now you will take us to see this marvelous machine you have stolen from our poor Madam Mendelsohn. If you do this, we will utilize this golden ticket"—he nodded at the young family and the baby the mother held close to her chest—"one time and one time only. And then you can return to rescuing Jews or whatever it is you people do. I couldn't care less. I need one night only, one trip only."

"What do you hope to accomplish?"

All eyes turned and faced the Traveler. She was leaning forward in her chair and waiting as if a patient teacher had asked a backward student a question.

"A great many things, Madam. They may not be the noble endeavor you and your associates have planned, but one that will benefit this great city very much. One that I might add benefited your own company very much indeed. Ah, don't tell me you are unaware how your board of directors made their fortunes, are you? Come now, who's being the naive one here, Madam? Yes, we have a far less noble, but yet beneficial endeavor."

"And that endeavor is?" Moira asked just as patiently as before.

A warning look from Alice Hamilton failed to still the questioning by the brilliant scientist.

"Alas"—Doshnikov looked from Alice then back to Moira—"I'm afraid my quest is one of avaristic value alone, just as your board of directors before me. Only I won't be nickel-and-diming, as these Americans like to say. I'll be making my moves all in one night, and the special thing is, and I mean very special, is the fact that other than the use of this magnificent doorway, it will all be completely aboveboard and legal. You see, I plan to be running this city this time next year and I plan on having the financial backing to do it." He smiled and stepped closer to the wheelchair-bound Moira. He patted her old hand and then turned over the wrist and saw the tattoo: 674392. "And your miracle of science is going to supply me with that opportunity."

Moira only smiled as she pulled her arm free of the man's grip. Then she turned and gestured for the new mother and held out her hands for the baby.

"That is not recommended," Doshinikov said as he stepped between the mother and the Traveler. "As the child has yet to be burped, and we wouldn't want that, would we?" he joked, and then saw that the tattooed Ryan wasn't laughing.

Niles nodded that they should adjourn to the observation room. He waited until it was just him, Virginia, Alice, and a Russian guard before following. He nodded descreetly toward the darkened monitor. Both Virginia and Alice knew then that Xavier Morales was knowledgeable of their situation.

But could the new computer whiz do anything about it?

As the Russian took in the stirring sight of the Wellsian Doorway and the many technicians who were preparing for the return dimensional shift when and if the signal was received, they could not prepare themselves adequately for the size of the operation. Seeing the many angry-looking technicians made Doshnikov momentarily hesitant about the size of his task. But seeing the doorway eased the problems to the back of his limited brain.

"Everyone is just so busy, a stirring sight indeed," he said as he placed a manicured hand onto the shoulder of one of Virginia's female operators. The specialist recruited from George Mason University but five weeks before turned her body away from the man's cold touch.

"We aren't going to allow this, you know that, right?" Ryan said as he nodded at the director to hurriedly escort the young science tech from the room.

"Oh, I think we can come to an understanding," Doshnikov said as he nodded toward the baby and the closing door where the female operator had just left.

"We won't be killing the baby, you will, along with the doorway," Ryan said as he didn't want the director speaking directly to this man.

The Russian looked at his watch as he again stepped to the window.

"Oh, we will be killing far more before we even get to the child." He turned and smiled as the noise was heard from below through the speakers on the observation room wall.

Ryan stepped hurriedly to the glass and saw that the room had filled with many men and all of them were carrying automatic weapons. They had bypassed external security somehow and entered through a portal the Event Group had no idea was even there. The plans for the building didn't include another exit.

"Oh, these dramatic shifts in circumstances always give me that comic book thrill," he said, smiling, and with mock excitement as he took in an even angrier Ryan. "Or is that too wordy for you?"

Below on the platform floor, the Event Group technicians were rounded up and forced against the wall and held there.

"Now," Doshnikov said as he turned and faced the people in the room, "let's see if we can make this expensive slot machine pay off." He pushed Ryan toward the stairs. "Shall we?" Jason made eye contact with Niles on his way out. He silently pleaded with the director to not antagonize these men. As he told Will earlier, that was his job to keep the black-hearted men off balance.

Below them the doorway lay dormant. In Nevada Xavier Morales wondered just what he and Europa could do to help because if they could not resolve the situation sooner rather than later, Colonel Collins might not have a way to come home again.

Director Compton said he would face excitement even inside the complex, but thus far in his limited experience with Department 5656, this was just plain ridiculous. Xavier hit the emergency switch located at his desk and the warning chimes sounded throughout the complex. The Event Group was now on alert for a possible hostage rescue in Brooklyn.

With the exception of Niles, Alice, Moira, and two of the larger Russian guards, the group was led down the stairs. The three were left behind because of age or infirmities, along with the outright thought that the three could cause no harm, even if they somehow escaped. But in all reality Doshnikov just didn't have the time to get them down the stairs and ensconced in the large elevator.

The Russian immediately left the group after stepping from the stairwell. The rest were being brought down by the freight elevator. He wanted to gaze upon the doorway by himself. He saw his fifteen men had secured the technicians safely—after all, they would be the ones to help him achieve his goals this night.

He turned and saw the doorway as it sat silent and still, steaming like a hot iron. The lasers were being cooled through the conduit system that was currently being flushed with liquid nitrogen, which made a loud and ear-piercing noise as it struck the hot system. The Russian didn't even flinch at the loud noise as he was mesmerized by the sight of the ceramic-covered doorway.

The radiation warning lights were flashing their yellow cry of danger as the system was being rebooted. When Virginia reverse-engineered the doorway she was only guessing at the turnaround time. Moira had explained that at the height of their dimensional jumps they had a twelve-hour turnaround time to reboot their systems and to recharge their antiquated laser platform. That was when she realized how painful Moira's trips were through the German Doorway before the advent of the advanced lasers of today. It was a wonder the girl child had survived even the four experimental jumps back in Germany.

Doshnikov saw something just beyond the doorway and stepped up to the platform. He cautiously ran a hand through the air to make sure nothing vanished on him. Then a loud scream sounded and the Russian almost screamed. He turned angrily at the intruder to his thoughts. It was the man they called Ryan. He had screamed as soon as the elevator doors had opened wide enough for him to see what he had been doing. He intentionally made the Russian look the fool. Jason was brutally pushed forward as he and Mendenhall laughed at the fright he had put on the mobster.

Doshnikov returned to what had attracted his attention. He grimaced and then stepped through the front portal of the doorway. He took five steps inside and then reached down and felt the cold steel. He then reached over and retrieved something from the deck. He straightened and saw that it was dirt and some form of moss. The entire entryway to the doorway was covered in what looked like ash. He looked down and the trail vanished after only a few feet. He brushed the dirt and ash away and slapped his hands together and then turned to face the others. He moved over to the glass partition where the Event Group technicians sat stoically, not moving but not frightened either. Most were defiant and just waiting for Commander Ryan to lead the way and tell them what to do. They had come to learn the colonel's security department was always one step ahead. They all turned when they heard a grunt and saw that Jason Ryan had been clubbed on the head pretty good by one of his captors. The reality of knowing they may not be one step ahead didn't frighten them as much as anger them. After Overlord, it was pretty damn hard to scare people from Department 5656.

"Perform your duties well and you will soon be set free"—Doshnikov gestured around him—"to go about doing whatever it is you very strange people do. Do not perform them and I'm afraid there will be repercussions. Starting with that small child. And I know how you Americans can be so aghast when harm befalls children." He gestured toward his men. "Take the family Koblenz to the observation room. Give me the detonator."

The detonator to the explosives strapped to the baby's carrier was passed to him and the family was moved back into the elevator once the threat was made and understood. It was then that a groggy Ryan looked at Mendenhall and then his eyes found the small detonator device in Doshnikov's hand. Will nodded but at the moment there wasn't anything he could do about it. Anya and Sarah were also watching and examining the detonator. The key here was to make sure that the baby and family were left unharmed. To every man and woman in the Group, that was now the priority, even beyond the safety of Jack and his team, Everett or themselves. Niles had explained time and time again: what they did was not worth one innocent life in their pursuit of historical acumen. Ever.

"Now, Mr. Jodle, please step forward."

In the observation room Moira saw the traitor for the first time. Joshua Jodle. She had known the man was a weasel and the only child she ever regretted bringing out of Germany. Ambitious was a mild word for the cruel child. He had learned from the Nazis just how to get things done through intimidation. Sad that was the only lesson the boy had learned in the camps. The board had warned her of the man's ambitions.

"Are you prepared?" the Russian asked.

Jodle held up an aluminum case. The prize was held chest high and the Wall Street genius nodded.

"If I may ask?" Ryan said as he rubbed the bump on his head and angrily looked at the guard who had delivered the blow. The tattoo made the Russian thug wary of the much smaller naval officer.

"Ah, finally some curiosity. Actually I was hoping you would ask. Inside this case"—he reached out and tapped it lightly on its top as the smiling little rat that held it did the same—"is the future, or should I say the past. This is the mythical Pandora's Box and it is filled with the key to riches beyond measure."

As Moira listened to the men speak through the speaker system, she cringed as she realized just what the traitor Jodle and the Russian were about to attempt. The thought that all of her wealth that her board of directors might have accumulated in the same manner over these many years made her physically ill.

"What are they up to, Moira?" Alice asked.

"They are simply going to change their destiny. I suspect that inside that case is a stock portfolio from sometime in the past, perhaps an exact copy of Warren Buffet's. Or perhaps corner the market on Microsoft stock. My bet would be on Buffet or Gates."

"Can they do that?" Niles asked.

"Yes, but they would have to use the doorway from building one-fourteen way back when it was operational, and since time and the dismantling of the doorway from building one-fourteen means nothing to the quantum jumper, it could be done. They would lock on to the signal during one of our operations just as you did tonight, and then they can travel all the way back to 1968 if they wanted. But they wouldn't have to go back that far. I would guess they would shoot for the door-way's last operation, when we brought back that little bastard Julien."

"Industrious, I'll give the poor bastard that," Niles said as he eyed the monitor in the corner. It was still dark but he suspected that Xavier was there along with his entire staff. He was hoping he was thinking the same way that he was at that moment. Niles nodded at the monitor and the two Russian guards thought he had gone into some sort of spasm. Again he nodded at the monitor and then moved his head to the side toward the glass that separated the observation room from the doorway below. Compton quickly and deftly ran a finger across his throat.

At that moment both Alice Hamilton and Moira Mendelsohn knew what Niles wanted Xavier to do. The two Russians conversed in their native tongue at Compton's strange behavior and that was when Alice broke the silence since the guards wouldn't know what they were talking about anyway.

"What about our people?"

Niles shook his head.

"That's just it, they're our people and they will know what to do."

Alice and Moira both looked at each other, knowing the director might have just ordered the death of all in that room.

The camera system had remained on but was set only as a one-way link. Xavier could see them but they couldn't see him. Morales could hear them but knew the director was limited as to what he could say in the open. What Compton did manage shocked and astounded him. There was only one thing he could do to achieve what the director wanted and he hoped he was thinking along those same lines.

"Gentlemen, I need your attention and your expertise," he said as he turned his wheelchair and looked out on the computer center floor. His 112 techs looked over at their new department head and listened.

"What do you need, boss?" Harvey Anderson from photo intelligence asked before the others could. The men and women had managed a growing respect for how fast the twenty-five-year-old thought.

"We cannot make adjustments to the settings from here, they can only do that in Brooklyn. But we can do something else."

The large center waited as he thought a moment. He hoped beyond measure it was the same thing the director was thinking.

"What, sir?" Anderson asked.

"We can turn the doorway on. And do it on full power. We can't adjust the settings from here, as I said, but we can sure as hell make that doorway burp a little. I need a direct link to the *Los Angeles*. We need that boat on standby for emergency power-up."

"At full power that doorway will create a hurricane force inside that building, and then it will suck anything in front of it through to another dimension." Anderson looked around him at the other techs that were just as shocked as he.

Xavier smiled. "And hopefully right into the waiting arms of a very pissed-off Colonel Collins."

The light slowly dawned on the technicians' faces and they knew that this man had just as much if not more brass balls than that had been demonstrated by none other than Dr. Peter Golding.

"People, let's get ready to send this Russian jerk-off into a world he didn't expect. Someplace his stock portfolio does little good."

Joshua Jodle examined the new and improved design of the doorway. He went from the rectangle lining the doorway to the technicians' stations behind the glass partition. One of the Group's younger electrical engineers from UCLA watched the man and shook her head. He caught sight of this in his peripheral vision and turned on her.

"What is the minimum reboot time for this system?"

"You got me there, fella, they don't tell me diddly around here," she said in all seriousness.

"Unlike my Russian partner over there, I do not like to use threats, but you must know that they are not beyond my capabilities, young lady." Joshua turned to face the girl and her colleagues sitting against the old brick wall. They all seemed to be enjoying his lack of knowledge.

"Yeah, we're going to cooperate with a bunch of lowlife bastards who just strapped explosives to a sleeping baby." The young blonde looked to her left at the other young technicians. They were all of the same mind and it was at that moment most realized just how much their chief of security had rubbed off on them.

Jodle looked through the glass at the waiting Doshnikov and shook his head. The Russian just nodded once and one of his guards went to the first tech in line and stood the young man up. The defiance in the kid's bespectacled face was evident to Ryan and Mendenhall, who stood with Virginia, Sarah, and Anya. The boy's eyes momentarily flicked to those of Ryan for the bravery he would need in the next few moments.

"I believe the question was what is the turnaround cycle for the doorway," Doshnikov asked with an exasperated intake of breath. His eyes bored in on the young tech, who swallowed as the larger Russian took him by the lab coat's collar menacingly.

"That's enough," Jason said as he took a menacing step away from the center of the room, but only made it two feet when an old-fashioned six-shot Colt .45 Peacemaker was put into his face. Ryan raised his brows when he saw that it was the head man who had produced the weapon. The end of the barrel looked like a cannon's bore. Will followed suit and the gun moved minutely to the right and stilled him. Doshnikov nodded that his man should continue the questioning.

Ryan had decided to move again when he caught sight of Alice Hamilton in the observation window above them. She had her hands on the windowsill and he barely saw the small gesture of her hand waving him off and the small shake of her head. Then one finger went up, two fingers went up, and then finally the third finger.

The gathered Russians flinched when the doorway started its slow revolutions. The lasers were off but the coolant chambers were still charged with nitrogen and that stored liquid vented through one of the ports on the side of the rectangular mainframe of the doorway. This loud noise made the Russians jump back as the revolutions increased, creating a small onrush of air as the doorway gained momentum. Doshnikov looked first at Jodle, who was also watching with interest, and then over at Ryan, who gave the Russian a sad look as if his earlier question had unintentionally been answered by the doorway itself.

"Ah, it has completed its cool-down cycle." He looked over at Jodle, who meekly agreed with a nod.

The technicians who lined the wall exchanged knowing looks that the doorway did not require a cool-down period before a second attempt could be made. They hoped what was about to happen didn't occur until at least their friends were out of the line of fire.

Jason, Will, Sarah, Virginia, and Anya all saw Niles Compton as he stepped to the glass and stood beside Alice. Niles Compton closed his good eye and then nodded his head. Ryan swallowed when he realized that the scenario facing them was a simple one—they had to get the Russians and that detonator out of the building, and there was only one way to do that. He didn't know how they would get the Russians to voluntarily step through the doorway, but Jason was willing to go on faith. Before he turned away, Commander Ryan nodded back at the director. He then looked at the darkened main monitor where Xavier would have been. Ryan raised his eyebrows in concern for the plan. He knew it was a silent plea that asked the young computer whiz if he knew what he was doing.

"Oh, shit," Virgnia said as it just dawned on her how this plan had only one way of working.

"What?" Sarah asked as quietly as she could as the Russian admired the spinning doorway in front of him.

"There's only one way to get these dickheads through that doorway without asking them to do so—Xavier's going to flood the system and open the doorway with a surge burp."

"A what?" Sarah hissed in questioning.

"It's a theory, but should work." Virginia's features soured somewhat. "Damn, this is going to be something."

EVENT GROUP COMPLEX, NELLIS AIR FORCE BASE, NEVADA

"A what?" The young computer specialist asked as he listened to their new boss's plan. The other specialists were just as confused.

"When we studied the plans for the German doorway and the more recent apparatus from Madam Mendelsohn, we discovered their earlier mistakes that cost them a few innocent lives in the process. It seems it happened a few times when the doorway was brought online too fast. The surge, or burp, as Madam Mendelsohn called it, is a backwash of energy that rebounds in the opposite direction of the doorway's intended path when the system's lasers are started too quickly. The light refuses to bend until the doorway is at full revolutions. Until that speed is achieved the light has no place to go except to bounce off the incomplete doorway path."

"I don't follow," the young man said as he knew he was listening to another computer boss that was light-years ahead of all of them.

"The power of the dimensional shift will bounce back into the room." Confusion still reigned on most of their faces. "You know, where the bad guys are currently standing."

It dawned on most at the same time and they realized the Russians were not the only people in the line of fire.

"By the time the burp backfires into the room those people will think the gates of hell have opened up. Madam Mendelsohn claims it's an enclosed hurricane that sucks everything and everyone into the vortex before anyone knows what's happening. The RPMs on the machine are at max power and they have a one-way ticket—target, Antarctica—and hopefully a helping hand in Colonel Collins and his team. I hope they're ready for this."

The faces staring back at him were worried and Morales knew why.

"It's the only way we can protect the bulk of the Event Group staff and the doorway. We have to disable those explosives and removing the only way to detonate them is the only way we can achieve that. We just have to hope Mr. Ryan knows what's happening. So, let's remotely get this thing started before that Russian asshole decides to kill everyone there."

The computer center came alive with frightened but determined activity.

BROOKLYN NAVY YARD

"Okay, you can shut it down now, Joshua," Doshnikov said as his hair was beginning to be tossed by the increasing revolutions.

Joshua Jodle stepped from behind the technicians' safety glass, shrugged his shoulders, and hurried over to the spot where the artificial wind was starting to move Doshnikov's heavy coat.

"I said you can shut the doorway down now. We must prepare for your journey."

"I didn't start the cycle. I assumed it was on a timer and after she cooled down it would automatically reboot. As you can see it's just the centrifuge turning, no lasers." He now had to shout to be heard and that made the young stockbroker concerned as he turned and looked at the spinning doorway. That was when he looked up and saw that little balding man with the eye patch. He could swear the man was moving his lips as he was saying something. It looked like—

"Good-bye."

Jodle turned and saw that Doshnikov felt the same thing they were all feeling—the electrical charge coursing through their bodies had increased five-fold in seconds. Jodle found he couldn't move his lips or voice his warning.

Ryan reached out and grabbed a hold of Sarah's belt. She did the same with Anya. Will and Virginia huddled together, following suit. The room was erupting as the fifteen Russian guards quit paying attention to their charges and their strange behavior. Doshnikov's heavy coat was almost ripped from his frame as the revolutions increased.

Before anyone realized it, the large monitor sprang to life and the face of Xavier Morales filled the screen. The overhead speaker blared to life and that was the only thing everyone in the laboratory heard as Morales spoke.

"I owe you one, Commander Ryan, I will get you back home, I promise, so . . . hang on!"

The lasers burst into life. Without the required revolutions and the collider still dormant, the green and blue light burst from the spinning circle of the doorway, shot into the room, hit the far wall, and then an amazing thing happened—the lasers reflected off the old brick and burst backward through the doorway and smashed into the laboratory where the hurricane winds threatened to tear the people and the doorway apart. The electrical charge froze all and they spasmed and jerked. The handholds that Ryan and the others had were not quite enough and they were ripped from one another. The lights burst into a multicolored flash that engulfed the Russian and then the doorway came up to the dimensional-shift speed it needed. The entire room exploded. The guards watching the technicians collapsed into the cowering men and women, and the men next to Doshnikov felt their bodies being swept through the doorway.

Niles froze as the view below was distorted by the blinding light as the Wellsian Doorway burped and then, like a fishing net, a bright circle of light surrounded all and a sparkling sensation filled the room. Before anyone could blink, the sixteen Russians, Joshua Jodle, Jason Ryan, Sara McIntire, Will Mendenhall, Anya Korvesky, and Virginia Pollock vanished as they were pulled into the shift with battering harshness.

The Wellsian Doorway started to wind down as the main coolant lines erupted.

In the observation room Niles Compton turned from the window and saw the two guards staring numbly at the spot where a moment before their boss had been standing with twenty-one other people. Some loose papers still swirled and floated and the static electricity seemed to make anything made of metal glow with light blue haze. The two guards were in shock at the sudden disappearance of Doshnikov and the others. Their mouths were gaping in disbelief. Compton excused himself as he easily reached past Moira and then grabbed the radio before the two Russians could gather their wits, and then the director simply clicked the transmit switch three times in rapid succession. As he did he hoped he had remembered the right number of clicks that Jack had explained earlier.

The two guards turned and knew they had been had when the door burst open and two men—Sergeant Hernandez, who had lost himself in the shuffle and confusion when the intruders had herded everyone down below, and one other from a posted station outside—were on the two before they knew they were being attacked. The two powerful tranquilizer darts hit simultaneously and before the men could grab their chests where they had been struck, two more of the Pfizer chemical–supplied darts hit the men in the neck and shoulders respectively. Their vision clouded and their muscles froze and the paralyzing agent completed the cycle by momentarily cutting the oxygen supply to the brain, dropping the men cold within 1.2 seconds.

"The *Los Angeles*?" Niles asked.

Sergeant Hernandez rolled the first Russian over and then looked at the director.

"The sudden turn for one hundred and fifteen percent power from a standstill fried a few of her circuits, but other than a small fire in the power transfer cable, the crew says she will be good to go in two hours."

"Thank God Xavier timed that right. Without the power we would have fried everyone inside that room." After checking the family Koblenz and after Hernandez and the Marine had safely removed the baby carrier with the explosives, Niles went to the window to check on his other people.

The technicians had all stood and started running for fire extinguishers, and the lone Russian left guarding them could only watch in stunned surprise after the shock of the dimensional displacement. As he tried to close his mouth his weapon was removed from his right hand. The Georgian gangster slowly turned with his toupee askew and saw the young blonde girl from UCLA holding the Glock nine millimeter in his face. Her smile never met her gorgeous green eyes.

"What did you people do?"

"Oops," she said as she jabbed the taller man in the ribs with the weapon. The young technician was thinking that she could very much get used to this. It was preferable to monitoring gamma radiation readouts.

18

ANTARCTICA, 227,000 B.C.E.

Jenks cursed at the tight fit of the last laser emitter to be installed. It didn't help any that Charlie was having a difficult time holding the ladder still as he tried in vain to check its wobbly movement on the uneven ground.

The doorway was almost completed and it wasn't noon on the second day yet. It would have gone faster if they had the help of Collins and Farbeaux, but since the colonel, on Jenks's own recommendation, had shut down the radar-operated defense system to save precious battery life, necessitating a fifty percent security awareness around the camp. That didn't stop Jack or Henri from cringing every time the master chief let out a long profanity-laced tirade at poor Ellenshaw.

"There, damn it, that's the last one," Jenks said as he eased himself from the shaking ladder. He hit the ground and produced a cigar from his jacket pocket, then lit it with his lighter, the whole time staring a hole through Charlie. Once it was lit to his satisfaction he spit and then looked at Ellenshaw and was about to tear into him for trying to fling him from the ladder when he stopped himself. "Well, I guess I've had far worse assistants." He chomped on the cigar and moved off toward the lone trailer in the center of the camp.

Charlie smiled at the false praise heaped on him by Jenks and allowed the ladder to wobble until it tilted over and hit the centrifuge on its way to the ground. The master chief looked up and shook his head.

"Almost got it, Master Chief?" Collins asked as he and Henri walked into the middle of camp drinking water.

"Yeah, if Crazy Charlie there doesn't send the whole thing rolling down this hill."

Jack looked at Ellenshaw as he struggled to get the ladder up. He nodded at Farbeaux, who reluctantly went to assist.

"Yeah, yeah, I know. The doc's had a rough go of it." Jenks removed the cigar and looked up from the interior of the trailer as he rummaged for the last two items to complete the doorway. "Hell, I'm used to losing soldiers and seamen. I have to remind myself that civilians don't react like us old salts."

Jack nodded, knowing he didn't have to say anything beyond what Jenks had just explained.

"Is that the portable power unit everyone's so paranoid about?" Collins asked as he finished his water.

"Paranoid? Yeah, you can say that, Colonel. There are two in existence. This one and one that NASA and General Electric keep close to home. But even more important to our little science experiment is this." He raised a small foam-encased box and opened it. Jenks held the box out to show Collins. "That is the electrical transducer. It transfers the power from this box"—he slapped the five-by-six-foot generator/storage unit—"to our doorway. Without this you may as well be in Europe with American electrical plugs. You're shit out of luck. I don't want to even ask the director how he managed to snag these babies since together they're worth about the cost of an aircraft carrier and her fighter wing combined."

"Director Compton has his ways," Jack said as he turned and looked at the sky. The ash cloud had thickened since morning and the white ash was falling at a far steadier rate. Jenks followed suit.

"That's another little development. I didn't want to say anything to the doc, but that's why he couldn't hold the ladder straight, I just like yelling. But if you hadn't noticed, fearless leader, the damn earth is moving in rather peculiar ways since about nine this morning, and the winds have shifted as you just saw. The bulk of the ash cloud is now coming from the southwest, directly from Erebus and her little bitch sisters, and, oh, by the way, the temperature has dropped by twenty-one degrees in the past two hours."

"Anything else, you sour bastard?" Jack asked as Henri and Charlie approached after hearing the last of Jenks's wonderfully delivered report.

"Yeah, there is," Jenks said as he looked from face to face. "Since I've been standing here shooting off my big mouth we've seemed to have gathered an audience. About five hundred yards to your south."

Jack turned and saw several creatures gathering just outside of the protection of the jungle and the trees. He quickly raised his field glasses and took in the scene. Charlie and Henri followed suit.

"It's them!" Ellenshaw said loudly. "Raptors. *V. Mongoliensis.*"

"Vamongo what?" Jenks asked as he saw the gathering of about fifteen of the small animals.

"*Mongoliensis,* a Velociraptor." Ellenshaw slowly lowered his own glasses and looked out at the scene before them. The look on his face made Collins take a second look at Charlie. "They shouldn't be here."

"What do you mean?" Henri asked as he saw the creatures just standing there and looking at the camp in the distance.

"They died off sixty-five million years before our current time frame." He looked at Jack. "They should not be here. Plus the feathered raptors supposedly died off before the more modern version we are used to seeing in the movies. But here they are, almost as if they reversed their evolution."

"They don't seem too damn reversed to me. Four of them evil buzzard-looking things are carrying sticks long enough that you have to qualify them as spears."

Jenks was right—four of the small brightly colored raptors held long poles like the one that flew into camp earlier. As Collins studied the curious group, he noted the feathers were somewhat thicker and more colorful on the winglike arms and the tail, where they ended in a graceful plume like an at-ease peacock's.

"Uh-oh," Charlie said as he saw what the animals were doing.

"Are they pushing those others out into the open?" Farbeaux asked, amazed at what he was witnessing.

In the distance the group as a whole were using their strange humanlike hands to push two of the raptors from their cover. One of them even used one of the sharpened sticks to encourage the two chosen guinea pigs forward.

"What the fu—" Jenks started to say.

"Did I just see that?" Charlie asked incredulously.

Collins was amazed as two of the raptors forced spears into the hands of the chosen two. "Henri?"

Collins heard the charging of an M-4 as an answer to his inquiry.

"Should I turn on the defense system?" Jenks asked.

"If this is just a probing action, no, I'm not ready to ascribe to your smart-chicken theory, Doc, we can manage without the lasers." He lowered the glasses and looked at Jenks. "But stay by that damn switch in any case."

"Here they come," Henri said as he lowered his own glasses and brought up the M-4 and sighted on the lead raptor as it charged with wings hanging low to the ground. Its spear was in its left hand and was only inches from the ground as both raptors came on at close to forty miles per hour. Jack also brought his weapon up and started sighting.

"This is beyond anything we know about their behavior. They're just not supposed to be here and they surely shouldn't be able to use tools!" Charlie's fear and excitement grew as the two animals charged the camp.

"That's it, they're not slowing," Jack said as he took aim at the raptor on the right. He fired a single round. The birdlike animal stumbled and then fell, skidding to a halt and blurring the twin experience of the second colorful raptor as the Frenchman struck his mark. The dust slowly settled. Collins raised his field glasses and looked again. The scene was getting darker as the ash fell heavier than just ten minutes before.

"I have four, looks like they're pumping themselves up."

Jenks was right as the others soon saw. Four of the raptors circled the group of eight and were bobbing their necks back and forth, raising the long sticks up and down. Then they broke from the pack and their group watched on in interest from near the tree line. They charged as the first two had.

This time the example was made far earlier as Jack and Henri made short work of the second set of attackers.

"Jesus!" Jenks screamed as he turned just in time as four of the raptors broke through the camp from behind. They had drawn the attention of the team while others maneuvered around them and then attacked using stealth. Jack was stunned at the sudden problem-solving skills exhibited by the once-extinct creatures.

Charlie was quicker than anyone would have thought possible as he fired his Glock nine millimeter at the closest raptor. It fell but tried to rise again as Charlie shot it three more times.

A spear, this one smaller, struck the trailer next to Jenks and pierced the aluminum. He turned and quickly fired. The weapon was on full auto instead of the three-shot burst. The powerful rounds almost cut the raptor in half. Still, the grasping gray-scaled hand reached for Jenks's leg. The master chief fired once more into the upturned, ugly face of the lizardlike muzzle. And even after the bullet struck its head the jaws still snapped at empty space as the nerve center kept firing even after death.

Jack turned and saw he was going to be too late for the third attacker as it hopped into the trailer and hissed at a startled Charlie. The creature poked at the cryptozoologist with its sharpened stick, actually stabbing Ellenshaw in the side and drawing blood. Ellenshaw yelped just as the fourth raptor jumped into the trailer alongside the first. This one screamed a horrible sound that raked their nerves. The beast raised the spear and threw it. Henri stepped away at the last second as the sharpened shaft hit the earth at his feet.

"Son of a bitch!" Charlie screamed and shot the first raptor, sending it flying from the trailer and Henri finished it with a quick three-round burst.

The last raptor hissed and spat angrily at the four men and then quickly reached down and grabbed something with its hand. With colorful wings spread wide the raptor sprang from the trailer and hopped over the remaining perimeter trailers and sprinted for the tree line to the north just as a multitude of sharpened spears came flying into camp. They managed to dodge the high-arcing weapons but by the time they recovered, the last raptor had vanished into the falling haze of white ash and jungle beyond their reach.

"That was just a little bit beyond probing our defenses. What in the hell was that all about?" Henri asked as he ejected his magazine, checked the loads, and then popped it back in.

"At West Point they discussed the Viet Cong tactic of attacking a spot to cover the real objective, and they didn't care how many they sacrificed to do it."

"Well, they had a goal, all right, and if they knew what they were doing they couldn't have hurt us more, buckos." Jenks cursed as he slammed the empty Styrofoam box back into the trailer. "That smart-ass chicken just made off with our power coupling, and they even managed to cut our tethers to the signal balloons."

"And this means what?" Henri asked, afraid of the answer.

"It means, Froggy, we're screwed as far as getting home goes or even signaling Everett that friends are here. As I said, truly screwed."

Jack cursed and then reexamined the perimeter with his field glasses. He knew then that they had to go hunting in a land where they could quickly become the hunted.

"If they stole that thing with the intention of coming back for the doorway, tell Compton that I quit. First Russians and now buzzards with an attitude and smarts."

"For once, Master Chief, I am in total agreement," Farbeaux said angrily as he glared at Collins, who would more than likely succeed in getting him killed after all.

"That just makes my day, Froggy. I'm so happy to have you onboard my way of thinking."

Henri ignored Jenks, who was showing his fear and frustration.

"Big, crazed chickens and Frenchmen—what's next, a friggin' asteroid?"

At that moment the trees to the south were illuminated with a bright flash of brilliantly colored light and then the jungle and dense tree canopy where the team had originally shifted to erupted in flame and noise.

It wasn't an asteroid.

The pain was almost merciful as it caused such a shock to their systems that they lost consciousness. The last sensation Ryan felt was his hold on Sarah's belt as she was ripped away from him with a force that made his strong grip seem like a child's. The noise was ear-shattering and the light blinding. The electricity popped through their bodies as if firecrackers were being set off in their very bone marrow.

Jason felt the impact as the large group was ejected from the doorway. All sound, light, and sensation had vanished and all felt as near death as any had ever felt.

Sarah was the first to shake off the effects of the displacement. She felt herself smoldering but for the life of her she didn't know what it was she was supposed to do about it. The heat started on her arm and was slowly working its way up. She knew her eyes were open because she had the sensation of her lids moving up and down. She heard a loud pop from very far away. Then another.

"Oh, crap!" came the voice Sarah immediately recognized as Will Mendenhall's. Because of the heat and the pain in her arm her eyes finally cleared and then opened. That was when she saw Will with blood on his face as he started slapping at her. At first she was shocked by his actions until she felt the heat and pain on her arm lessen to the point that she regained some of her lost composure and senses. Suddenly she heard more loud popping noises. Sarah rolled over in time to see Anya and Ryan as they seemed to be wrestling with someone. Finally, as Mendenhall lifted her to her feet, she saw that they had removed a weapon from a severely burned man on the ground. The pistol Jason held was still smoking. Sarah again looked at the man who must have been spasming and firing his pistol off through pure instinct. The Russian stopped moving as his smoking corpse settled and finally gave in to death.

"My God," McIntire mumbled aloud. She looked around at the men that were slowly picking themselves off a semi-darkened ground. Fires were everywhere and the screams of shocked travelers filled the air. Several of the Russians were clearly dead.

Virginia Pollock was magically standing in front of Sarah. Virginia quickly snatched at the blood streaming from her own nose as she leaned over and checked Sarah's arm. She tore away the burned sleeve and then nodded. "Nothing too bad," she said as she looked around nervously. Her features suddenly sank.

"I'll have . . . that if . . . you don't mind," came the voice of Alexi Doshnikov.

Sarah cleared her eyes once more and saw the Russian holding the large Colt Peacemaker to Jason's head.

"Glad to see you made it, Ivan," he said as Doshnikov angrily pushed Ryan toward his four companions.

The mobster quickly removed his smoldering greatcoat and tossed it on the ground. He gave himself a quick health and welfare check and saw that other than being a little singed and having a broken nose from where he had rolled into a rather large tree, he would survive. He was shaking and was having a hard time regaining his senses beyond the ability to keep the American from gaining a weapon. He looked at several of his men as they were in various states of wakefulness. Then he saw others that would never awaken again. He counted five of these that lay smoldering and burning on the ground. He realized then that these were his people who had been on the periphery of the doorway, closer to the lasers and the centrifugal heat caused by the spinning collider as they passed through. Unlike the survivors who had been in the center of the room. This was cause and effect no one, not even Virginia or Xavier Morales, had foreseen as a consequence of the dimensional burp.

"Oh, man, that's something you don't see every day," Mendenhall said as he tried to brace Sarah for the sight.

Fifteen feet away Joshua Jodle was half in and half out of a large tree. He had phased into this existence in entirely the wrong place. His hand was still holding the aluminum case that had all of Doshnikov's plans and dreams. As a shocked group watched on, the case slowly slipped from the dead man's fingers.

A stunned Doshnikov turned and faced Sarah, Jason, Anya, Will, and Virginia and was amazed they had basically made it through unscathed. In his childish mind he thought it extremely unfair that this was the case. Even as they all stood in a semicircle the earth shook so violently that they almost lost their footing. The earthquake subsided and then the world became silent once more.

"What have you done?" he asked as he gestured for his men to cover the Americans.

"You wanted a trip through our little dream maker, and you got one," Ryan said, not being able to stop the smile from coming. He disliked most Russians out of habit.

"Tell them to turn it back on, immediately," he said with spittle flying from his lips.

Now Jason wasn't so sure he should have been antagonizing the man. He looked a little unstable to say the least. The Colt was shaking in his hands.

A loud crack and a flaming branch came down and the Russian shot it twice before he realized it wasn't a threat outside of the flames. He nervously looked at Ryan, the man who was his antagonist since he had seen him that very afternoon. Ryan was to blame for this, Doshnikov didn't know how, but he was sure of it.

"As soon as you tell me how to go about that, Chief, but in case you haven't noticed, you're not exactly in Kansas anymore."

Again Doshnikov looked around and saw a burning primordial forest he had only seen in museum dioramas. He was finding it extremely hard to draw a breath. No, that wasn't quite right, he thought. He was drawing too much. He had to place his free hand on a smoldering tree to steady himself as his head spun as if drunk.

"The effect you are feeling is over-oxygenated air. You're used to smog, particulates. This is a clean, unmolested environment, with the exception of volcanic fallout . . . exhilarating, isn't it?" Virginia said as she nodded at Ryan that now would be a good time to leave these people before they regained all of their senses. Then she lost hope as she felt the pure oxygen effects also. She clung on to Sarah, who was down to a knee. Ryan was about to say something when he too became dizzy. To his horror he saw the Russian and most of his men straighten from their own discomfort and start shaking their heads. It seemed they were recovering far faster than he thought they would.

"I think . . . I will start with . . . the small woman . . . first," Doshnikov said as he took a menacing step toward the five. "Then we . . . will see if the mutual . . . cooperation we had earlier . . . returns. I want that . . . doorway turned back on!" He screamed the last two words. He raised the Colt revolver toward a kneeling Sarah McIntire.

Jason was just getting ready to move his shaky body in front of Sarah's when the scene was shattered. First came the roar and then the scream of men as a blur of orange, black, white, and gray burst through the flames of the trees and into the midst of the Russians.

Virginia's eyes widened and Mendenhall nearly lost the contents of his bladder when they saw what had sprung at them from the unsettled jungle and burning forest. The saber-toothed cat was at least a thousand pounds of bustling muscle and sinew. The eight-inch incisors were snapping at the men who were so shocked none of them made any move to fend off the giant lionlike beast. The scream of the animal was horrifying to say the least. The claws of the saber-tooth swung and caught the first Russian across the chest area, ripping his still beating heart from his body along with a section of breastplate and ribs. Doshnikov regained his senses first and fired two shots into the cat but that only increased its fear and hatred of the men it had cornered. It hunched its back and sprang at the next man in line.

Before Ryan really knew what he was doing, he picked McIntire up and started pushing the other four away from the scene just as more shots rang out from the

Russians, who were fast recovering from their shock after they had just witnessed their companion being eviscerated.

They heard another shot, then another as they ran for the jungle undergrowth, but the still-burning fires made their silhouettes stand out and Jason feared that made them excellent targets. Then to cement his opinion he felt the bullet fly just past his right ear and slam into a giant fern plant as they finally made it to the undergrowth.

Behind them the cat screamed and men died before silence once more filled the world.

Jack used the binoculars but the thickening ash made viewing the four miles difficult. He lowered them just as the sound of distant gunfire came to his ears. That distinctive sound made even Jenks stop his cursing over the power coupling's loss—momentarily.

"Carl?" Charlie asked with hope lacing his question.

"No, that was more than one brand of weapon. I counted no less than three different calibers," Jack said as he looked over at Henri for his opinion. The Frenchman just nodded his concurrence. Collins raised the glasses once more. "Master Chief, we were going to conserve the batteries on the two drones until we had the doorway up and running, but I think now is the time to get them in the air. We need eyes out there."

"Well, I hate to be the stick in the damn mud here but we have another very serious concern," Jenks said, drawing the attention of the others. "Unless we track that damn chicken-lizard down we're going to be sending out change-of-address cards to the post office. Now what do you suppose we do about that?"

Jack shook his head as he looked over to the master chief. "Well, I guess we have to go and get it back, don't we, you grumpy old bastard?"

"When was the last time you tracked one of those Velocipedes?"

"Actually it's called a Velociraptor, there is a distinct—"

The look coming from all three of his companions shut Charlie up.

"This will be my first raptor hunt, Master Chief," Jack said as he tossed Jenks the binoculars he had been using. He caught the glasses and then almost dropped them. "Now, do you think you and Charlie can get those two drones up and then arm the laser defense system and possibly keep those damn things from stealing any more of our toys?"

Jenks didn't respond with anything other than a huff.

"Actually, I don't think there was a devious attempt to thwart us," Charlie said. "I mean they are smarter than any animal in the fossil records, even their direct ancestors, but they are still animals."

"Come on, Doc, what in the hell are you saying?" Jack asked as he retrieved a field pack and then tossed it to Farbeaux, who was listening to Ellenshaw.

"I mean to say that I believe the raptor stole the coupling because it was shiny. The stainless-steel housing had to look awful tempting to the animal. They are after all part of the avian family, or so the theory goes anyway. So I think this one acted just like a raven, or crow, it likes bright shiny things."

"So?" Henri asked as he changed out the magazine on his M-4.

"I am saying that if you are to track them, keep in mind that they will act like an animal at first, don't give them time to think things out. It's like telling Pete Golding a riddle, at first he will be stumped, but give him time to think and you're had."

Collins looked from Ellenshaw to Farbeaux. The poor doc hadn't even realized that he had invoked Pete Golding's name. It was as if Pete hadn't died in Chato's Crawl. Jack lowered his eyes as he concentrated on situating his own field pack.

"Just water, Henri, we'll travel light."

"That's fine with me as I would rather eat bugs than that MRE disaster you Americans are so proud of."

"Before this little foray is over you may be wishing for some of that crap. Ready?" Jack asked as he slung the M-4 over his shoulder and gathered his scopes and night vision equipment.

"Remind me again why you insisted on bringing me out of your president's forced retirement of my services?"

"Because you're expendable, and for the decidedly more important fact that you owe *me*, not the president. After all, you're no longer a wanted man in the United States," Jack said while producing his only smile of the day.

Farbeaux watched as Collins nodded his farewell to Jenks and Charlie as he left the center of the camp.

"In case you have failed to notice, my dear colonel, we're not *in* the United States."

Jack glanced back just before he stooped over and examined the tracks made by the thieving raptor. "Just think of it as Central Park after midnight, Henri." Jack looked back at the raptor print and then started out.

With a last look at Jenks and Ellenshaw, Farbeaux followed the crazed colonel.

"You don't suppose all of this is an adverse reactionary hallucination to all of those inoculations they gave us, do you?"

Master Chief Jenks looked at Charlie as if he had truly lost it.

"Exactly how many acid trips did you go on in the sixties, and how many resembled this prehistoric menagerie?"

"Well—"

"Never mind, Doc, your answer would probably scare the hell out of me."

19

Jason and his wayward travelers finally broke out into the open. It looked like they had traveled south, but Ryan knew that was very misleading. In all directions in Antarctica you traveled north. No matter your position, and no matter what directions you thought you were traveling in, you were always headed north, there just simply was no other way to travel. All roads led north. He stopped running as his lungs cried for relief from the purified oxygen of the times. The ash cloud was now so heavy that he was fearful of breathing in some of the volcanic particulate that would eventually lead to his death.

"Get down!" Mendenhall screamed as he pushed Anya, Sarah, and Virginia to the thickly ash-covered ground.

The bird missed Ryan's head by mere inches as it swooped out of the sky. Jason hit the dirt and then saw the shadow of the giant condor as it pumped its twenty-three-foot wingspan to regain altitude. Ryan had felt the tremendous rush of air as the five-hundred-pound bird nearly swept him up.

"Holy crap!" Will said as he hustled the women to their feet.

"Let's take cover over by those rocks," Ryan yelled, and made sure everyone was on the same thinking track as himself.

Once they were hunkering around the large boulders, they saw the enormous condor swoop low again some distance away. They then heard the sound of rapid gunfire once more, thankfully quite some distance away.

"I guess those Russian assholes have met Tweety bird," Mendenhall said as he winked at a frightened Virginia.

"The ones that survived Sylvester the Cat, you mean?" Sarah said, not wanting to but smiling nonetheless.

"Exactly," Will agreed. He looked at a shaken Jason Ryan. "What now, boss?"

"If the colonel and the others were close by, they had to have heard the gunfire. We have a choice here: hide, or go and find them."

"Speaking for myself, I think I would prefer to stay in the open and not hunker down as you Americans like to say."

"Yeah, open sounds good to me," Will agreed.

"I think you're right."

"Smell that?" Sarah said as she looked around the best that she could through the falling ash cloud. The earth continued to rumble beneath her feet.

"What, the smell of primordial terror?" Mendenhall asked. "Well, I'm afraid to disappoint you, but that's me. I may have had an accident in my drawers."

Sarah ignored Will's foxhole humor and then stood up and looked to what she assumed was the west.

"No, I'm smelling chlorine in the air. Something else."

"What—" Jason started to ask.

"Methane and sulfur." Sarah sniffed the air again. "Mount Erebus and the others are getting ready to blow."

"Damn Niles and his theory about Erebus setting off a chain reaction in the climate parameters of this time frame."

"What theory?" Ryan asked, not liking the sound of Virginia's voice.

"That the eruption of Erebus and her sister volcanoes brought on one of the deadliest ice ages in natural history."

"Okay, that should give us a little time, right?" Ryan asked hopefully, but his hope was dashed as soon as he saw Virginia's face go slack as the earth rumbled and shook.

"Before the ice comes, Jason, it is preceded by fire. Lots and lots of fire, earth shaking, mountains exploding, basically nature saying enough is enough."

"How long?" Anya asked for the others.

It was Sarah who answered. "Hell, as far as timing goes, we couldn't have picked a worse time or place to go sightseeing." The earth shook harder. "We're already on borrowed time, and the tax man is at the door."

Ryan looked around and decided on a course. "That way," he said.

"Why that way?" Mendenhall inquired as he assisted Virginia to her feet.

"Because it's in the opposite direction of that." He pointed to the sky many miles distant.

At that very moment a hard wind moved the ash particulate away and they all saw it. Erebus's smoke plume was as red as Hades and as thick as any they had ever seen. For emphasis the ground shook again, almost knocking them from their feet.

"Atom bombs, crazed Russians, alien invasions, monsters in the Amazon— when are we going to get a library research gig?" Will asked, turning to see no one.

The others had already started following the commander, and Will cursed and hurried to catch up.

Ryan pulled up when he managed to briefly spy the small rise of rock just ahead through the irritating ashfall. In just an hour the ground had been covered by over a foot of the abrasive particulate.

"There, we'll hold up and rest. I don't know about you people but my system is used to a little more pollutants in the air I guess. This clean stuff is killing me."

"I agree, we need to collect our bearings before we run into something we can't escape from," Virginia said as she quickly checked Sarah's scorched arm. She smiled at the diminutive geologist as she studied her worried face. "Don't worry, I think Jack can outsmart any big pussycats."

Sarah smiled and shook her head. "It's not Jack. I was thinking about all of those lectures in school about the many theories of how the major ice age was brought on. I'm afraid I have to ascribe to the nutcase theories that Erebus was the cause of it all. It just happened to freeze the rest of the world before its own home turf."

"Fascinating, but can we move to a little higher ground for defense before we discuss further the shortcomings of modern science?" Ryan asked.

"Defense?" Will asked as he followed Anya and the others.

"Yeah, I think we may have to start making some bows and arrows."

"That's what I like about working with the best organization in the world: we have all of the high-tech gadgets at our disposal."

The two drones separated just short of the large canopied forest. The round, four-engined drones were capable of ten hours of continuous flight but the limitations imposed on her viewing systems were worrying the master chief. Capable of infrared or night vision, telescopic or laser-designated targeting, the drones were state of the art and had been constructed by the mechanical engineering department at Group.

"I'm going to put number one on hover just west of the black forest there. That damn ashfall is retarding the efficiency of the plastic propellers."

"I can handle flying that thing, Master Chief," Charlie said as he spared a look from the radar system of the defense pods.

"You just concentrate on keeping those refugees from Colonel Sanders from getting too close. I'll play flyboy."

The two remote viewing systems were designed by Niles Compton's special projects division, the very same division Jenks himself was to take over, if and when he survived this ordeal. They came equipped with night vision, three different telephoto lenses, infrared detection, and laser targeting. A little redundant in Jenks's experience, but he had to admit the drones were very nearly self-flyable. Jenks followed the compass heading that was currently giving him erratic readings, forcing him to position the drone by eye, which was growing increasingly difficult because of the thick ashfall.

"Well, the infrared systems work, there's the colonel and Froggy."

Charlie chanced a wrathful rebuke by Jenks and leaned over and saw the aerial view of Jack and Henri as they made their way slowly across the small savanna toward the area where the explosion was seen. He even saw Henri look up at the passing drone. He smiled when the Frenchman shot them the bird.

"Damn French have no respect," the master chief mumbled as he ordered the drone forward. The second drone was taking up a preprogrammed station to the opposite side of the large wooded and jungle area.

They watched as the second drone slowly crept in on the smoking site at over three hundred feet. The monitor showed small fires still burning, which ignited a white blur on the camera lenses. Jenks switched to passive viewing. He hovered just inside the woods and over the tree canopy. Once he was over the site he used the telephoto lens to try to penetrate the sparse areas where the giant trees didn't shut off their view.

"Damn it, this is like to trying to catch a glimpse of a hot woman getting dressed through a keyhole."

Charlie looked from the monitor and at the master chief with concern. He adjusted his wire-rimmed glasses.

"Oh, don't give me that look, it's not like you never tried to peek at a good-lookin' lady through a keyhole."

"I most certainly have not. Why, I would—"

"Whoa, someone screwed the pooch," Jenks said, cutting Charlie's indignant response short.

Ellenshaw looked at the monitor and saw the small opening through the canopy and the three mangled bodies on the ash-covered ground. The red blood soaked through the ash, giving them a clear idea of their condition.

"Looks like whoever they are they ran into something that didn't like them being there."

"Stop joking, we know who has the only access to the doorway back home. Those can only be our people down there," Charlie said as he raised the radio and called Jack. He informed them of what they saw and were ordered to cover them as they entered the forest.

"Look, Doc, since you're not a military man you don't understand the humor of scared men."

Charlie realized what the master chief was saying and then slowly nodded. "Sorry for biting your head off."

Jenks laughed as he adjusted the hover mode on the second drone. "Is that what you call biting my head off, Doc? Looks like I'm going to have to give CPO training on how to talk to people. No one can chew ass like a chief petty officer."

"Yeah," Ellenshaw said, still leery about the master chief.

Suddenly the static picture on the monitor went wild. The view skewed from a still shot of the tree canopy to a wildly spinning shot of the ash-colored sky, and then the ground and the sky again. Jenks fought with the toggle in an attempt to control the spinning drone.

"Doc, get the other drone up higher in altitude so I can see what the hell's wrong with this damn thing."

Ellenshaw quickly turned the control knob on the hovering first drone and the view on the second monitor rose with the plastic craft. He didn't have to adjust anything else as the machine rose to three hundred feet.

"This is ridiculous!" Jenks said loudly as he spit his cigar stub from his mouth.

On the screen both men watched as a giant condor with a wingspan of a Cessna dove once more for the drone. The bird missed on the second pass as Jenks moved the drone out of the giant's path. On the second monitor it showed the wings nearly miss the flying craft. The vortex shook the drone and almost knocked it from the sky.

"Damn chickens have an air force, too?" Jenks said as he dipped the rounded nose of the drone over and dove for the tree canopy below. He would try to get her close, too close for the large bird to follow. "Hit return on that panel. We don't need to lose both drones out there."

Charlie did as he was told and then he watched the view of the first drone move away and then start back toward the camp. Meanwhile Jenks was watching for the return of the great bird.

"Do you mind telling me what in the hell that was?"

"It looked like an exact duplicate of the species of California condor that is close to extinction in our time. Only much, much larger."

"Well, they look pretty damn healthy to me in this one."

On the monitor the giant flew close over the drone and then vanished high into the falling ash overhead.

"Inform the colonel he not only has to watch for chickens, he's now got something real freakin' big in the air large enough to carry both him and Froggy away."

The earth shook far more violently than ever before as Charlie made the radio call.

Jason had managed to wedge everyone into a crevice on the rock face of a small hill. The area was covered by giant trees and had good ground cover. He and Will had cut up small branches and made a small stockade area that covered them from the ashfall, which had blanketed them all until they were a sickly white. Once they were all inside the makeshift fort, Ryan sat hard on the grass and ash-covered ground. He shook his head and the ash flew from his dark hair. He took a deep breath, not really wanting to go into how desperate their situation was.

As he looked around at not only the people he was responsible for, but who were also his very close friends, he knew they could all handle the situation without losing their composure. Will, Virginia, and Sarah had actually been in worse situations, and Anya was a trouper who faced death every day in the Middle East. No, he was worried about how he was projecting his command. Thus far he had managed to get everyone out of harm's way for the moment, but as for a plan, he was at a loss. Maybe the colonel was right, maybe he was destined to always be an Indian and not a chief. That thought used to give him comfort, but since being around Jack, Carl, and Will, he had become someone he never used to be—a responsible officer. He wanted the chance to prove that those good men had rubbed off on him.

"Water?"

Jason didn't know Mendenhall was speaking as he sat and thought. His tired brain was worn from the dimensional shift and he was slow to recover—he wondered if the others were just as affected.

"Hey, fearless leader, our first priority has got to be water, right?"

Jason finally looked at Will and then realized he had been asked a question. He slowly nodded.

"Yeah, but no one else is going back out there. Will, you'll stay and everyone had better start sharpening some sticks. Let's just hope water is close by."

"Jason," Virginia said as she stood and walked over to him. She leaned in close so the others couldn't hear. They were busy collecting some of the leftover cuttings from their fort making. "Look, we can just lay low. The colonel is bound to find us. After all, I think we made quite a spectacle on our arrival."

Ryan shook his head. "No, we can't assume anything. First order of business is to make sure we'll be alive if and when they do find us." He started to move toward the small opening they had left as a doorway.

The gun in his face stopped him short. He took a step back and then held Will Mendenhall at bay as he too realized they weren't alone.

"Oh, look, it's Mr. Wonderful and his band of cutthroats."

The pistol's barrel hit Ryan in the chest, forcing him back into the makeshift cover.

"Not exactly the Ritz, my friends, but as they say, any port in a storm," Doshnikov said as he and four other men made their way inside the makeshift shelter. "Very industrious in such short order, it makes me suspect you have had superior training for situations such as this." Each of the five was armed and each of them showed signs of their tangle with the saber-toothed cat. "Sit down," he said, waving the Colt Peacemaker menacingly. Jason backed away and slowly sat with his friends. The other four men looked grateful to be out of the elements. "I must apologize for my earlier hysteria. I'm afraid your little trap confused me for a moment. It is now obvious we need each other." He saw Ryan eyeing his men. Doshnikov wiped some blood from his still-bleeding nose and then looked at Jason closely, the gun still pointing menacingly at his face. "I see the arrogance of military training in you, my friend, so let me warn you. I have four more men waiting outside, so you see, even if you got by us my four more ruthless employees would handle you."

Ryan threw his first plan to get out of the enclosure with the knowledge that Doshnikov wasn't as stupid as he first thought. He settled in and watched as the Russians started tending to their wounds. He noticed along with the others that his men were no longer watching their boss in awe. They now looked at him with trepidation as to how the man could have gotten them into this mess. Ryan would have to take advantage of that if he could.

Doshnikov eased his aching frame to the ground and then allowed the hammer of the old Colt to slowly release. He looked at Ryan and then Virginia.

"You were one of the doorway's designers, yes?"

Virginia looked at Ryan and he nodded that it was all right to talk, after all this was no big military secret. They all knew they were truly screwed.

"No, I didn't design the doorway, we reverse-engineered it, as you well know."

"Semantics, my dear lady."

"Awful big word coming from you, dickwad," Mendenhall said as Sarah and Anya cringed at Will's blatant insult.

The Russian snickered. It was more of a laugh that conveyed the joy he felt at having survived the transit to this time, but also the fact that he had survived something out of his worst nightmare—an animal he had only seen pictures of in books.

Doshnikov looked at Mendenhall with not anger but with a small degree of admiration. "I will not blame you for your views on us Russians, my friend. The lie that we are all dumb peasants is widely perpetuated by your unfair news media, but I assure you that some of us have had all of the training you have, maybe even a measure more in other deadlier areas. But I believe that yours is now the correct attitude we will all need to escape our predicament. So I will ignore your attempt at an insult and at pushing me into a corner as what to do with you. I think you know the answer to that, my friend."

"Listen, pal, we're going to need more than that. We have another team out here somewhere, and guess what, our boss is with them and he's not going to take it too kindly that we're here. So if you want to make like friends, I suggest you give us two of those weapons and start doing exactly what this lady here tells you."

"Cooperation, yes, weapons, no."

Ryan only smiled. "Okay, fearless leader, water—we need water and we need it now, and to get it we need those weapons. Unless you want to volunteer to go and get it yourself?"

Doshnikov smiled his own crooked grin and then slowly stood up as he again raised the Colt and then replaced two spent shell casings from the cylinder. "You think me a coward? My men, cowards?" He laughed this time. "Where we come from we have to fight to survive every day, not like you people who have had everything given to you. No, we are no cowards, and no, we are not fools either." He pointed the weapon at Jason and then moved it to Mendenhall. "Shall we go and find that water, gentlemen?"

Jack surveyed the scene after the three-mile trek back to their original landing area. He couldn't believe what it was he was seeing. Men were lying in pieces. He counted at least ten men in varying states of dismemberment. He leaned over and turned a body skyward. The man had both arms missing and it looked as if something had taken a large bite from his neck and back. He examined the face.

"Who in the hell are these people?"

"Judging by their dress, I don't believe this was a planned trip for these men."

Collins looked over in time to see Henri toss him something. He caught it and looked the blood-splattered shoe over. On the bottom in gold script was the brand name Gucci.

"Pretty expensive camping attire, don't you think, Colonel?"

Jack tossed the shoe away and looked the scene over.

"What in the hell happened back in Brooklyn?" he mumbled as he gestured at Henri to follow.

"Where to now?" the Frenchman asked as he looked around nervously.

"This way," he answered, looking to the west as he saw the tracks. He glanced up at the canopy overhead and hoped the drone he was hearing over the trees could follow.

That was when Henri saw the second and third set of tracks. One set led off in the opposite direction as them, and he could tell it was some sort of large animal, a cat possibly. The second set was unmistakable as they had seen these before.

"I suppose you noticed our little feathered friends are hunting again?"

Jack turned and looked at Farbeaux. "No, Colonel, we're now the hunters, and I have a very bad feeling here that we may be in for a surprise as to who exactly is out here."

"What are you referring to?" he asked.

Jack knelt by a set of smaller prints. Farbeaux followed suit but kept a wary eye on his surroundings and as he did so the colonel saw an impression pressed into a bloodstained carpet of white ash.

"A woman?" Farbeaux asked incredulously.

"Yeah, wearing Group-issued combat boots. Size six."

Henri stood first as his heart skipped a beat. He looked at Collins as the colonel stared off into the jungle where the prints vanished.

They both knew only one person who wore Group-issued size six combat boots. Jack kicked at the thick ash and then raised his M-4 to his chest and moved off mumbling.

"Damn you, Short Stuff!"

The thought of leaving Sarah, Virginia, and Anya behind with the four Russians made Ryan angrier than being prodded along by Doshnikov and his five goons, who he noted were rather large. It was also clear why these brutes survived the giant cat attack—they were just too damn big to die. The one assigned to Mendenhall towered over the captain by a good foot and a half.

The ash cloud had shifted and the skies, while not clear, had at least allowed small snippets of sun to burst through. His guess was that they were headed in the wrong direction to find the colonel, Farbeaux, Charlie, and Jenks, that they were instead heading in the exact opposite direction from rescue—they were headed toward the great inland sea.

After an hour of travel they were hit with a freezing breath of wind that came in from the south. The next wave of air was warmer and that was when Jason realized that Sarah had been right—this continent was going through changes that had never been recorded in history. The very last continent to fall under the spell of death that Erebus had cast upon the rest of the world.

The seven men made their way through the heavier undergrowth but had to skirt the more impenetrable bush, which made their zigzag pattern time consuming.

"Look, we can't be out here much longer. We don't know when the sun goes down here and one thing I do know is that we don't want to be caught out here in the dark," Ryan said as he stopped and leaned against a large tree.

"You are worried about your women back at the shelter?" Doshnikov laughed. "I despair when I imagine what it is that you have heard about us Russians. Do you think us barbarians?"

"Not all Russians, no. As a matter of fact the last Russian I dealt with was one of the bravest men I have ever had the privilege of fighting alongside."

Will nodded his silent agreement as he remembered the battle for Moon Gap during Operation Overlord and the Russian naval captain who had given his life in that fight.

Doshnikov went silent when he didn't know what to make of the secretive comment.

"At any rate, your women are as safe with my men as—"

"Don't move," Ryan said easily as Doshnikov saw his men freeze and the black man back off a few steps. That was when he felt the movement behind him in the thick jungle.

Ryan felt his mouth slowly fall to the open and stunned position as he saw the creature looking through a clustered bramble of vines and branches. The yellow eye blinked and then the head tilted and the eye moved left and then right. The beak alone was wider than an old catcher's mitt and its yellow-gold eyes moved in rapid motion as it studied the men before it. Doshnikov slowly turned his head without moving his body. His eyes widened when he saw the yellowish-brown beak slowly open.

If it wasn't for Ryan's quick movement and action the Russian would have had his head snapped clean off. Jason hit the Russian and both men went flying just as the giant roc fought to clear itself from its entanglement of vine and brush. The jaws of the giant, flightless bird missed Doshnikov's head by three inches as the long-legged grounded avian screamed and clawed in anger as it missed its target. Ryan rolled onto his back with wide eyes as a vision from an old horror movie tried desperately to get at the seven men.

The roc stood at over six and a half feet. The powerful legs were far stronger than any bird species ever to roam the world. The giant snapped and hissed as it tore at the vines holding it back.

Several gunshots rang out and then the world around them went silent as the roc was sent crashing into the undergrowth with bullet wounds in its chest and head. Jason looked over at the two large Russians who had dispatched the large predatory bird. The men looked pleased with themselves.

"Let's get the hell out of here," Will said, not liking the fact that he and Jason were the only two unarmed men in the most hostile world he could ever have imagined.

"We need water," Doshnikov said as he picked himself up from the ground. "We have to or we'll dehydrate and—"

Again he was cut short as one of the men who had fired on the roc screamed as something rushed at him from the undergrowth. They saw a blur of black feathers, shortened wings, and powerful legs as the second roc slammed into the man and then ripped at his upturned face. Instead of helping their comrade, and preceded by their fearless leader, the men ran, even leaving Ryan and Will behind in their haste to escape the feathered nightmare. Mendenhall looked at Jason, knowing this was their chance to get away. They saw the second roc look up from its meal and eye them with that chicken look all avians have. The tick-inspired, quick glance and rapid eye movement took them in. They both decided that accompanying the Russians was probably the best recourse for the moment. They too ran as even more rocs came flying through the jungle after smelling blood in the air.

The simple foray for water had turned into a complete disaster.

Sarah allowed Virginia to look at her arm once again and found the pain was becoming far less tolerable than before. It was declared that she would live to see the dawning of a new day. Then Virginia turned and looked at the face of one of the younger Russians who sat near the entrance and tried to get a makeshift dressing on a large gash that had been administered by the saber-toothed cat. The nuclear physicist eased herself over to the kid and raised her brows. The Russian lowered his weapon and nodded that it was okay. She started wrapping the torn sleeve dressing far better than he had.

"You know," Virginia said as she smiled at the frightened Russian, "none of us have been inoculated for this little safari into Adventure Land. There's no telling what diseases are floating around here just waiting to attach themselves to us."

The four Russians who had been left behind by their boss exchanged looks of discomfort.

Sarah remembered laughing at Jack and the others as they had endured a series of shots that made their arms go numb from the puncture wounds. Now it looked like Jack would get the last laugh.

"As a matter of fact I would venture to guess that—"

The roar made their hearts freeze as something tore at their feeble enclosure from the outside. Sarah immediately thought the giant saber-toothed cat had tracked the Russians here through the smell of blood. But the roar of the beast outside was far more deep sounding, not a cat's call at all—a roar that was unbelievably more terrifying than the enormous cat. The bass sound alone shook their eardrums as the animal tore at the branches enclosing their shelter. The eight-inch-long claws reached through and a fur-covered arm swiped at the men as the women were quick enough to duck away. One of the Russian guards was not quite so lucky. The long claws caught the man mid-torso as he attempted to dodge the knifelike weapons of the giant towering over them. The young Russian tried to stand but was knocked down by the body of the first as the top half of the man struck him and sent the kid reeling.

Sarah and Anya waited for Virginia as she fought to assist the kid she had just helped to his feet. As she did, the animal outside tore away a goodly percentage of the branches covering the small crevice. Anya and Sarah's eyes widened when they saw the muzzle of the largest bear they had ever seen outside of a natural history museum. The cave bear swiped and roared at the intruders to its lair. The second and third Russians never stood a chance as they tried to squeeze past the women to get to the opening. The set of claws hit the first across the throat, sending his head flying half on, half off as he continued to fight for the doorway. The sight froze the second man as he saw his friend dispatched right before his eyes.

Sarah hurriedly reached for the running and headless man's Glock nine millimeter but the headless man continued into the open and then finally collapsed into the collected ash of Erebus. The roar of the enormous cave bear shook the world around the women as the bear started to lower its spittle-filled muzzle toward the cowering Sarah, Anya, Virginia, and the only Russian guard who was left. All they could do was cower as the cave bear moved its fifteen-foot body far enough to block their only escape route.

They leaned as far away as they could as the giant roared with bloodlust. The prehistoric bear crashed into the enclosure and the world exploded with blood and fur.

Jenks finally got the second remote unit under control. The nightmare-sized condor discovered something far less maneuverable and vanished into the now-clearing skies after the wind had shifted the ash cloud. The master chief cursed and brought the drone to a much higher altitude. As he watched the monitor he saw the distant outline of the bird as it made its way to the south.

"Damn, Slim should have put a mini-gun on this damn thing," Jenks hissed as he spun the remote 360 degrees to see if there were any more surprises waiting for his robotic viewing pleasure.

"Master Chief, you better look at this," Charlie said.

Jenks placed his drone in a hover over the canopy as he leaned over and looked at what Ellenshaw was viewing on drone number one's viewing screen.

"What in the hell is that?" he asked, knowing well that the cryptozoologist had no idea what it was they were seeing.

"Well, the telephoto lenses are at full capacity, maybe thirty-five miles or so, but they're close enough that I can tell you beyond a doubt that not only are we seeing a large contingent of mammoths, but the largest herd of bison ever dreamed about in North America. Millions of them are flanking the mammoth families at the center. They seem to be migrating toward Erebus," Charlie said, his excitement growing while his eyes took in the magnificent sight.

"You can see all of that?" Jenks asked, looking at the way Ellenshaw perched his glasses on his head as he closely viewed the scene on the monitor.

"Oh, yes. See how easily they move? This looks like a natural migration." Charlie looked over at the master chief, who was staring at the monitor. He turned and gently lowered the cryptozoologist's glasses to his eyes.

"My point being, Doc, if you can see all of that why can't you see the dust clouds rising to either side of this mass migration?"

Ellenshaw looked closer at the monitor. He scowled as he saw what the former navy man was referring to, but not his point. He faced the master chief.

"There. About the middle of the pack and toward the front. Watch closely."

Charlie finally saw the movement Jenks was seeing. Every few seconds a number of the bison would roam farther from the giant herd after smelling greener grass, and as they did they ventured closer to the valley walls where trees of prehistoric size lined the trail. At first he saw a shadow break quickly from the cover of the tree line and make straight for the wandering beasts until the animals stopped and were scared back into the fold. The same thing happened toward the front of the migratory animals. Another small, darkened shape shot from the trees as some young bison and even a small baby mammoth strayed too close from the herd and stopped and ran a very fast circle around the frightened animals until they too were turned back.

"Uh-oh," Ellenshaw said under his breath as he reached out and pushed replay on the small screen. The high-definition scene rewound until the small creature had just burst from cover. It was one of the small raptors that had attacked them. As Charlie pushed the play feature, the camera began a live streaming of the migratory herd once more. He zoomed in on the line of giant trees that encompassed most of the ancient game trail. Then his heart froze as he saw the enemy of both man and animal—thousands of the brightly colored raptors were following both herds and that led Ellenshaw to believe the same thing was happening on the far side of the game trail also.

Jenks cursed something under his breath as he turned to his own monitor and saw that the second hovering drone had lost Colonel Collins and the Frenchman. The master chief knew any attempt at finding them would be a waste of battery time, and this new development had changed priorities, at least as far as the base camp was concerned.

"Think you can fly that drone back here without cracking it up?"

"But we need to keep an eye on this, and what about the colonel and Farbeaux? We need to stay in contact with them."

"That's why we have radios, Doc. Now get that drone back here so we can recharge it for when we really need it."

An angry Charlie waited the briefest of moments until the master chief looked up. He returned the look. "Listen, do you see that Ferris wheel–lookin' thing over there?"

Charlie saw the doorway in its incomplete state. "Yes."

"The priority is that damn thing, not keeping an eye on two men that know how to take care of themselves. We need to know when those murderous chickens start getting too close, is that clear to you, Doc?"

"Yes, but I don't like the fact that I feel we are abandoning our friends out there, Carl."

"One more thing while you're so damn worried about everything else, there's a missing piece of that Ferris wheel and those damn raptors or whatever they are have it. We need to see where they have taken it before the whole damn thing becomes a moot point. And in case you didn't notice, we are sitting right in the middle of that damn game trail."

Without another word Charlie started guiding drone number one home. He still couldn't shake the feeling that they were abandoning Jack and the others when they needed their eyes the most.

Without knowing it, Ellenshaw was mirroring the master chief's very thoughts.

20

The giant cave bear's claws missed Anya's head by mere inches. The blow was so close that it cut clean a long lock of her black hair. She cursed in Romanian and then in Hebrew as she scrambled backward on her behind just as the branches covering the small crevice came crashing in upon all of them. The enormous but blunted snout of the brown and black fur–covered behemoth roared as it leaned in to swipe at the branches covering its intended targets. The young and wounded Russian managed to slide by Sarah and Virginia and partially raise his weapon up and through the large leaves of their cover. That was a major mistake as it acted like a marker for the monstrosity fighting to get in. The boy screamed as the beast moved like lightning and took the man's hand, but instead of biting through the light meat, sinew, and bone of the man's wrist, the bear pulled the Russian up and out of the collapsed enclosure. Sarah and Virginia tried for his flying feet but missed.

The man screamed as he was thrown through the air to crash into other trees. The bear turned to move toward the easy meal.

Before anyone realized it, something had drowned out the roars of the enraged bear. Gunshots sounded outside and then their hopes soared as they realized that the colonel and his team had found them, or at the very least that bastard mobster had returned with Ryan and Mendenhall. Three more shots were fired and the roaring animal vanished from the enclosure. Sarah, Virginia, and Anya scrambled to push the debris of the shelter away as they struggled to take advantage of the brief respite. McIntire was the first one to break through and it was like a drowning swimmer breaching the surface for some much-needed air, only this particular sensation was brought on by fear. Anya popped up next to her and then Virginia with a halo of leaves garnishing her brown hair.

The animal screamed again and they saw the beast as it charged something that was blocked from view.

"Why aren't they still shooting it?" Anya yelled over the din of the charging cave bear.

That was when they saw a fur-covered form break cover and dodge the charging giant. The man-shape moved quickly and took up station just to the animal's exposed left flank as the beast crashed into the undergrowth where their savior had been in cover. Then they were amazed when the fur-covered figure fired a large arrow into the confused bear. Then another arrow was quickly nocked and fired without hesitation. Then the figure was again on the move just as the enraged animal turned to confront its attacker. The dark figure moved fast and before the women knew it the attacker had launched two more arrows at the bear.

"What in the hell is that asshole doing?" Sarah asked as she fought further to free herself from the roof of the enclosure. "Arrows?"

The bear had had enough. The giant roared one more time at the pesky animals that had thwarted its meal. The cave bear rose once on its hind legs and then screamed its outrage. It flopped onto all fours and vanished into the thick growth.

Sarah finally managed to free herself totally and then helped Anya and Virginia. They turned, and with their hearts still threatening to beat right out of their chests, they saw the fur-covered hunter move quickly toward the downed Russian. The man's pulse was checked and the person or whatever it was lowered his head. Then their new company looked up toward them. There was no movement for the first few seconds as they waited to see who or what had come to their rescue. Finally, without rising from his crouched position, a gloved hand was raised and the fur hood was removed.

Even at the distance Anya saw who it was and her heart froze. Sarah and Virginia laughed aloud and even clapped their hands as the blond man finally rose. The beard was thick but even from that distance they saw the man's eyes and there was no mistaking Admiral Carl Everett. He slid the large bow over his shoulder and smiled. Yes, it was Mr. Everett, and Sarah felt the tears come to her eyes as Anya ran forward. Virginia placed a hand on Sarah's shoulder and they took in a reunion that had never been dreamed of until Moira Mendelsohn had been discovered. She jumped the last four feet and flew into his fur-covered arms. Carl took her in, fearing his own voice would fail him. As it turned out he didn't need his voice at all.

Sarah looked at Virginia and saw that the older woman was crying. For Sarah it was a rerun of her reunion with Jack during the Leviathan mission . . . she knew the joy. Sarah's smile said it all.

"We beat the damn odds, didn't we?" she said as she watched Carl Everett embrace Anya for the first time since his once-upon-a-time death.

Before the embrace and the joy faded, the odds had shifted again for the worst as Mount Erebus rumbled and belched burning-red boulders from her caldera, and this time she and her sister world-killers didn't stop.

The radio coming to life made Jack cringe. He hurriedly pulled it from its holder and lowered the volume. The noise in the silent jungle was not conducive to avoiding some of the pitfalls he and Farbeaux were made aware of by the screams of cats and other species that seemed to want to eat everything they came across. Collins could see that Henri was coming a little unglued, and he had to admit to himself that he was faring no better. You could only search in a scary place for so long before you start to hear monsters behind every bush you see.

"Collins," he said into the radio as he hurriedly tempered his angry response, after all it wasn't the master chief's fault he had left his volume up like a rookie.

"Colonel, we have a serious problem," Jenks said from five miles distant. "It seems we have an assorted selection of wildlife heading straight for us, and they have some disturbing company herding them. Doc says that they are migrating toward Erebus while the rest of the wild kingdom is heading the other way away from the volcano. The group heading our way is being herded by our feathered friends, over."

"Our raging peacocks again?" he asked as Henri stopped beside him with an open bottle of water from his pack. Collins shook his head and then waited.

"Oh, yeah. The smart little bastards are keeping a massive migrating herd of bison and some damn big, ugly elephants." Jack and Henri heard Charlie Ellenshaw's complaint in the background that they were called mammoths before he was cut off.

"How long?" he asked as the exasperation and hopelessness of the situation was starting to wear on him.

"Doc says they're traveling leisurely, but even if they stop at Denny's we're lookin' at no more than twenty-four hours until they amble right over us and the doorway. Over."

"Master Chief, do you see any indication of where these raptors may be clustering? Maybe they have a nest or something."

It dawned on Jenks and Charlie at the same moment they heard Jack's question.

"No, but I see what you're getting at. Any leadership cast or whatever social, or pecking order"—they heard the master chief laugh if only briefly—"that may be where they stashed our little coupling."

"My train of thought exactly."

"Okay, we have our orders, we'll use both drones and see what we can see. Any luck finding out who the assholes were that started the fires?"

"Negative, there wasn't that much left to view."

"I see, Jenks out."

Jack lowered the radio and looked at Farbeaux, who had recapped the water and then wiped his brow. He looked from Collins toward the setting sun.

"The winds are bound to shift again and bring that damnable ash cloud back. Are you sure you want to use both drones to search for the coupling? Without at least one we'll have a hard time tracking our new team members, whoever they may be."

Collins knew not dividing up his two remotes limited his chances of finding Sarah and whoever else was sent through the doorway and into this hellhole of a continent, not to mention the fact that recovering Carl had become a distant part of the mission.

"You know who's out there, don't you?"

"Yes, I had my suspicions when you and I both saw the boot size that only one woman we both know wears. So, if you're asking me if we should continue the search, yes, as a matter of fact, Colonel, I insist." The Frenchman smiled, irritating Collins to no end.

"You want to take five?" Jack asked as a way of challenging Farbeaux. He returned the smile.

"No, but when I rescue young McIntire I fully expect for you to keep the word your president gave me when I fulfilled his recent, black request. I want to be free of you and your people for all time." He smiled wider. "Or I'll accept the offer of dear Sarah in return. Your choice."

Jack started moving off without comment at Farbeaux's desires. He then slowed to face the Frenchman. "The odds are that we'll remain right here, Henri, so if we somehow manage to get out of here, and if I don't kill you for any more remarks about Sarah, yes, when and if we get back you're free to go."

Farbeaux failed to see the humor in the comment as Collins laughed and then continued to follow the tracks in the fallen ash field. Then he realized it was so simple—if they got back.

"I truly despise you, Colonel."

They were lucky to have only lost the one man. Doshnikov went to his knees after they had stopped running as did most of the others. Jason looked at Mendenhall as both men were not really winded but very much over-oxygenated. He shook his head at the captain.

"We have to ditch these assholes."

"I agree, but in case you failed to notice, my backward navy friend, they have things they call guns. And we of course do not have said apparatus as per our usual circumstance."

Before Jason could retort at his friend's smart-ass observation they were joined by Doshnikov and two of his remaining men.

"If you think you can escape, by all means, I will not try to stop you." The Russian looked around him nervously. "I don't know where you fools have sent us, but this is not a very nice place."

"If you only knew half of the places we've been, buster, you would crap yourself."

Everyone looked at Mendenhall, who was deadly serious.

"Now, I'm sure you have an extra cap gun hidden away somewhere and me and my buddy are feeling a little exposed out here."

"Listen," Ryan said as he finally straightened from where he had his hands on his knees. He tilted his head as Will and the others fell silent when they saw he was trying to hear something. He tilted his head in the other direction. Then he froze, and before the Russians or a startled Mendenhall could say or do anything, Ryan started trotting away. The others hurriedly followed.

Doshnikov almost bumped into Ryan before he realized the American had stopped abruptly. He watched as Jason reached out and pulled some screening plants out of his way. The filthy Russian smiled and pushed past Ryan.

The river was fast flowing and blue as the gorgeous waters of the Caribbean. The smell of freshness after the dense jungle and forest was heavenly to Ryan. The others saw what he had smelled and pushed past him.

"Leave it to the navy to accidentally stumble onto water," Will said as he slapped Jason on the back on his way past. Ryan smiled and followed. At least they wouldn't die of thirst before some beast had their teeth-savvy way with them.

Ryan could see that the twisting river had worked its way down from the slopes surrounding Mount Erebus. He could even see fish as they jumped in the fast current. His smile vanished as he watched the Russians and Will drinking at the water's edge. It looked as if they weren't concerned about how potable this ancient waterway was, but of course he knew that the colonel's team had all of the purification equipment and chemicals to make assurances of anything.

He started to join them when he saw that the river vanished over the small cliff in front of them. He was looking at a waterfall. He advanced slowly and was still wary of the animal life that he knew also used the waters to drink from. He eased slowly to the edge and then his mouth fell open when he saw where the river vanished to.

"Holy shit."

When Will finally joined him with Doshnikov close behind, they found the navy man sitting on the ash-covered grass overlooking the falls and the greenest valley they had ever seen not far below. Mendenhall was about to say something when Ryan pointed to the valley and they saw what had stunned Ryan and sent him to the seat of his pants.

"If you have not lied about what time frame this is supposed to be, and if every schoolmaster in my life were not the most wonderful of liars about history, maybe you could tell me what in the hell that is doing here?" Doshnikov asked as his mouth dried up even after the thirst-quenching trip to the river.

Below, entangled in vine and undergrowth, was the remains of a wooden stockade. They could even make out the remains of watch towers at each corner and at the centerline of each fence. The jungle and forest had taken over the wooden structure and they could clearly see that it was deserted from their high vantage point. Inside the rectangle of stockade they saw deteriorating huts and other makeshift buildings. They saw sally ports along the high walls.

"You know what that looks like?" Mendenhall asked as he slowly looked at Ryan.

"Even I know what this is, and I didn't go to school in America." The Russian brushed past Will and examined the fort below.

Ryan stood and joined the others. He looked down at a sight they had no right to see in this distant epoch.

The Roman-style encampment was complete with a dried-up moat surrounding it. It looked to have been abandoned for a century at least.

Will laughed aloud and then turned to face the others in their lost band of idiots.

"This is going to throw a major kink into a lot of brilliant minds back home."

Mount Erebus exploded as an exclamation point to the most bizarre discovery of that very long and trying day.

Carl smelled atrocious and as Sarah finally pulled back from her hugs and kisses so Virginia could get her shots in, she turned to face an exuberant Anya Korvesky. They hugged.

"I won't even ask how," Carl said as he held Virginia at arm's length after her battery of welcoming hugs and kisses on his bearded cheek.

Everett allowed Virginia to move away as he reached for the dark-haired Gypsy woman and took her in his arms again. Finally it was Anya who couldn't take it any longer. She pulled back from Carl and held her nose.

"I tried to be a stand-up trouper, but my God that cologne!" she said as she laughed as did the others who had been too polite to point out the fact that the admiral smelled so sickening that it was hard not to gag on the stench.

Everett acted as if he were hurt for the briefest of seconds, and then he broke out laughing also. He removed the longbow and the quiver of five arrows from his

back and then pulled the bear coat off of his large frame. He tossed an empty shortened version of an AK-47 away as he did.

"Sorry, but to get around out here you have to smell like something bigger and
badder than anything else—I find saber-tooth lion pee-pee the best." He laughed
as the women recoiled in horror.

Sarah saw the nine millimeter strapped to Everett's filthy and ragged flight suit.
The suit had once been white with red trim, but was now unrecognizable with the
exception of the small American flag on his left sleeve and the Overlord mission
patch on his chest.

"I guess saving us was worth only six shots? I take it you wanted to practice
your Robin Hood thing?" Sarah joked with her right brow raised.

Everett smiled and then removed the Glock from its holster. He tossed it to
Sarah. "My last bullets were fired over a month ago. I was lucky to come across a
rather gruesome scene a few miles back and found that." He kicked at the empty
AK-47 at his feet. "It only had what you heard in the magazine. After that I had to
use my superior mountain-man skills."

"How long have you been living like this?" Virginia asked as once again Anya
was on Carl like a lost puppy.

"A thousand rounds of ammunition were gone within three days. The damn
raptors took my MREs the second day, and those damn condors flew off with my
enclosure with me in it on the third. That was a close one, I can tell you."

Sarah lowered her head and then swiped a tear from her eye just thinking what
this man had to have endured in the six months he had been here.

"Okay, you've kept me in suspense long enough. Where's Jack and those two
low-ranking idiots I call friends and colleagues?"

Anya pulled back from Carl and then looked at him closely. "We haven't seen
the first team since we arrived. We don't even know if they made it. Jack, Master
Chief Jenks, Charlie, and Colonel Farbeaux—we can only hope they're still alive."

"Team? Then just what in the hell are you guys, then?"

"We're an accident thanks to some outside Russian mob interference. They're
the ones who brought that." She indicated the automatic rifle. "And as a real
kicker that's exactly who is holding your two low-ranking friends at the moment."

"I'm not following one little bit." He turned to Virginia and Sarah, who tossed
the empty nine millimeter back to Everett.

"Longer story than the first," was Sarah's answer. "Right now we have to get
Jason and Will back."

Carl looked around and then leaned down and retrieved the stinky bear coat
from the ashes covering the ground. He looked toward the erupting Erebus and
shook his head. "Not now, the sun's getting ready to go down and we can't chance
getting caught out here with only one bow and five arrows for artillery." He looked
at Anya and kissed her on the lips, his red-tinted beard itching her nose. "Unless
you have a rocket launcher under that blouse?" Anya blushed like a schoolgirl and

then looked embarrassingly at the two knowing women. "No, no rocket launcher? Then I have a place we can hang our coats until daybreak."

"Where is that?" Virginia asked as she stepped into the small line of retreat from the forest primeval.

"This time it's you who won't believe it," he said as he eased his found charges off into the jungle and the river that flowed not far away.

As the world around them started to come alive with the terrors of the night, Erebus belched smoke and flame and then settled into an uneasy slumber.

BROOKLYN NAVY YARD

Niles Compton limped toward the phone that was held out by Alice Hamilton. He set his demeanor to one of defensive confrontation as he took the receiver. Alice nodded, knowing he had to be firm.

"Mr. President?"

"What in the hell is going on in Brooklyn, Baldy?"

"No 'Niles,' no 'hello,' not even a 'how are you doing, my very good friend'?"

"Do not, I repeat, do not act like it's just a coincidence that a possible terrorist action in Brooklyn happens the same day you find it necessary to raid the Brooklyn Navy Yard. And also at the same exact time you seem to have been avoiding my damn calls. Your commander-in-chief! Now what gives, Niles? I have agencies screaming from here to the Potomac about some mysterious group of people running amok in New York. I can't cover for you if you don't keep me up to date. The hundred hours is nearly up."

"Jim, you agreed to a one-hundred-hour window before we report oversight. We have forty of those hours remaining. If I told you that we had nothing to do with the terrorist action at the Barclays Center, will you stick to our agreement?"

"Don't you dare hold me over a barrel, I am not one of those schoolkids you have at Group. I happen to be the President of the United States, who is right now getting ready to send the Marines over there and shut you down, among other things. This is getting messy, Niles. How am I going to explain the terrorist action in Brooklyn?"

Niles remained silent as the president, his friend, the best man at his wedding, exploded when he realized Niles was protecting his office over his express orders to keep him in the loop.

"Do we still have our time?"

The quiet on the other end of the phone was telling. Niles felt the sheer heat coming from his friend's anger at what was possibly going on. He knew as long as the president had full deniability he would be protected.

"Jim, the terrorist action weren't terrorists at all. It was the Russian mob and thanks to them you have a culprit. Allow the FBI to do their job and that should give us the time we need to complete our mission."

"Niles, tell me the truth: Are you making headway in bringing Mr. Everett back home?"

"Very much so. Enough progress to say that we should be finished within your time frame."

"Okay," came the voice at the other end of the line. "I can cover my ass on this end, but no more buildings are to be blown to hell. I have the press screaming bloody murder.

"Niles, where is my submarine?"

Well, that did that. So much for hoping the president had suddenly ceased being smart. He looked over at Alice, who was listening to the speaker phone across the room. She smiled and shrugged her shoulders.

"Uh, yes, the *Los Angeles*. Assistant Director Pollock needed an alternate power source since the explosion and subsequent police response two days ago. She was close by in Groton so I made a few calls. That is in my new directives, along with the proposed allotted oversight time frame."

"Do not quote to me the very policy that I wrote, damn it!"

"Do we have the time?"

"Of course you still have the time. Congressional oversight can only crucify me once."

The line went dead. Niles looked at the phone and then sat heavily into a chair. Alice stood and slowly walked over and removed the receiver from his hand and placed it in its cradle.

"It won't be the first time a president has yelled at the director of this department, I can assure you of that, Niles."

He half smiled and then shook his head. "I hate placing my best friend in this situation."

"It's a situation he agreed to. After all, Niles, Carl is one of his men as well as yours."

"We may not have a mission anymore, and may have also lost even more personnel and friends than just Carl. We may have single-handedly sunk a hundred years of departmental history. The Group may not survive this if the president is caught lying to his own agencies. I've placed my best friend in an impossible situation."

Alice patted his arm and then turned on the monitor to check in with Xavier Morales. She turned just as the computer center back at Nellis came into focus.

"If we can get back our people, who gives a damn in the end? The president is still the head of this agency and one of us."

Niles Compton smiled for the first time in two days as he realized that Alice had just refueled his desire to get his men and women back in one piece and save the president the indignity of having to explain something he had little to do with.

He knew his friend would go down, just like the presidents before him, in safeguarding the secret that is the Event Group.

"Xavier, let's start working to get our people home."

On the screen Morales was there with his many computer techs.

"Yes, sir, we are assuming that they are alive and have been working to get the return doorway operational. We are beginning the signal now and will continue until we get an answer."

Niles looked at the clock on the wall and then shook his head.

The director had a bad feeling that the clock here was not the only one running down as his thoughts quickly went to the threat of Mount Erebus and her murderous sisters.

21

Carl had given Sarah the combat survival knife and appointed her point man. He would guide her from the back of the small line as they made their way down the falls side of the steep ravine. Everett felt far easier with his new charges because he knew the terrain was much too steep for the local animals to feel comfortable hunting on. Still, they made slower time as the ash cloud once more arrived with the winds, and this time it was mixed with a harsh blend of sulfur and pumas that was starting to irritate their throats.

Carl had allowed them all to quench their parched throats at the wide river. The newcomers to his world were faring far better. Everett was still having a hard time believing they had come for him.

"Oh, my," Sarah said as she spied the Roman stockade for the first time as Carl had led them down a trail that was hidden from view, just in case the Russians they had told him about followed them. He knew Jason and Will would have no problem giving them the slip if they hadn't already.

"Okay, I give up on the whole history thing," Anya said as she and Virginia saw the old ruins through the falling ash.

"Someone is going to get an earful when I get back," Virginia said as she stepped toward the long dried-up moat. The trench was over ten feet deep and the opposite side was spiked with old spears that shot off at angles toward the moat. "The whole of history may have to be rewritten."

Everett chuckled as he realized the others had not figured out the little puzzle. He would let them stew on it awhile.

"You have to slide down on your asses I'm afraid, I didn't think it would be wise to build a two-lane highway to my only sanctuary."

Virginia snorted as if his concern for their femininity irritated her to no end. She sat and went sliding down the ash-covered slope of mote. Sarah also shook her head at Carl's concern and then followed suit. Carl took Anya's hand, looked down at her, and frowned when he saw her returning his look as if he had kicked her puppy.

"What?"

"I'm still extremely pissed at you for dying on me."

Everett scratched the itchy beard and looked consternated. "Well, then, I guess I have to make it up to you."

"Don't think it will be that easy. I'm a Gypsy, remember?" She smiled and then plopped down unceremoniously and then gently and adeptly slid down the slope.

Everett knew that no matter what happened, he could be happy with Anya anywhere in the world, or at any time.

The three were shocked at the equipment that had been gathered up by Everett in the six months he had been in Antarctica. Sarah had to stop and examine the Roman shield. The red leather had peeled away exposing the wood beneath. She saw the outline of an emblem or insignia that had long ago left the ghost of a shield.

"Just wait, you're really going to like this," Carl said as he pushed aside some giant elephant ear plants and pulled out something they couldn't see. He had to laugh again when he saw their faces as they turned a shade of red he could clearly see in the mounting dusk and ashfall of the false evening.

"I understand now," Virginia said just as Sarah and Anya realized the true nature of the strange finds. The Rising Sun battle flag of the Japanese army was unfurled. Even though it was tattered and worn out in many places it was still spry with the colors of red and white. Virginia reached out and raised the old wooden shield that had once been covered in dyed-red leather and adorned with tacks that made the shield enduring in thought and memory. "The legendary Ninth Legion," she said as she smiled over at Anya and Sarah.

"The Iranian power plant tests. From their test records the timing fits. The year the legion vanished was in the time frame of their sixth test. Tell me, Carl, was there any Chinese battle gear found?" Sarah asked, hoping to lay the theory to rest.

"Not yet, but then again I wasn't keen on going out and looking for any either.

"They all vanished through a wormhole not intended for them. They were trapped and went through the same rip in time that I did, only many hundreds of years separate," Carl said almost sadly.

"What happened to them?" Anya asked, very much afraid of the answer if he had one.

Everett looked away momentarily and was about to answer when he heard the movement behind him.

"Yes, I would very much like to know the same thing."

They all turned as one and Virginia dropped the Roman shield when she saw

Doshnikov as he and his four men pushed Ryan and Will out in front of them as they left the first enclosure only yards away.

Everett saw the armed intruders to his inherited domain and then his eyes went to Mendenhall and Ryan. Without any regard to what would happen, the three men stepped forward and shook hands. When that wasn't enough they hugged and slapped each other on the back. The whole time Sarah, Anya, and Virginia smiled and the Russians didn't interfere.

"I should have known you two hard-asses would have already infiltrated the enemy camp and taken hold of the situation," Carl said with a broad smile.

"Yeah, we were just getting ready to make our move," Ryan said as he finally released Everett's hand. "Besides, I fully expect a royal ass-chewing if we ever get out of this."

Carl finally turned his attention to the man Sarah had told him about in their trek back to the stockade. The man was looking far worse than his people and that made him smile at the Russian.

"What's your story?" Everett asked as he made Will and Jason step back.

"I am a man not to be trifled with, as your friends can attest."

Carl looked from the Russian's eyes to the old Colt in his hands. Doshnikov saw this and then lowered the weapon and gestured for his men to follow suit.

The Russian turned to face the man that looked like one of the old pictures of his countrymen who lived in the wilds of Siberia, or the mountain men of the American West.

"Yeah, I understand you like to wire explosives up to children."

"No, not children, small babies and their mothers to be more precise. And being a businessman I am willing to negotiate a deal. I will say this in absolute assurance, I will kill every one of you if you do not do as I say. You will get us to that valley and that new doorway these rather strange people built and you will get us back home. I can start right now with this one," he said as he once again cocked the .45 and aimed it at Anya.

The silence after the threat was palpable even over the rumbling of the erupting volcanoes. Sarah and the others watched as Carl remained silent as he stared straight ahead. They all became concerned when they saw a smile creep across his face. The Russians even became uneasy at the strangeness of this man's reactions. Then the world once again froze in time. The ash seemed to fall slower and the earth shaking under their feet slowed as did their own heartbeats when Everett spoke.

"Jack, you have the most outrageous sense for the dramatic. What in the hell took you so long?"

The automatic fire opened up and tracers stitched the ground in front of Doshnikov and his four men. They jumped back as the glowing red tracers arched into the stockade from somewhere the men couldn't or didn't have the time to see as they dove for the soft, hot ash. As the bullets continued to fly, they stood and ran for the far wall of the stockade. A few tracers followed them with no malicious intent other than to scare the fools off.

Carl waited as the others willed their shock away. Walking toward them after only a minute the outlines of two men took shape. Everett laughed as did Ryan and Mendenhall when they recognized the large silhouette of Colonel Jack Collins.

"Piss-poor shooting if I may say so," Carl said as he stepped forward, recognizing Henri Fabrbeaux.

Collins stopped and took in the surprised faces staring at him and the Frenchman.

"I was torn between who to shoot, these people or those Russian assholes."

Jason, Sarah, Will, Virginia, and Anya looked at one another, not one of them knowing at what point to start the tale of what happened.

"But since we have a time machine to play with, I can shoot them anytime, I guess. Then go back and do it again, again, and again."

The two men, and even Henri Farbeaux, shook hands while the others took a deep religious breath at their sudden reprieve and deliverance from the Russians.

Now their problems were narrowed down to a few things. Like finding their stolen power coupling and dodging every horror-story creature God could have thought up, until they left here in a reengineered doorway they weren't quite sure would work.

Yes, Jack Collins had worries other than his anger at all of the new company in this Lion Country Safari family experience.

An hour later while sitting around a small fire Everett scarfed down some of Jack's and Henri's MREs, wishing many times instead that he was eating one of the complex's masterful corned beef sandwiches from the departmental mess. They had briefed all parties on the predicament they found themselves in. Ryan found it shocking that the colonel didn't chew his ass off anyway, but only nodded when briefed by Virginia. What that meant, Ryan wasn't exactly sure.

"I don't know which is hardest to believe, the fact that we find ourselves in the biggest jam we have ever been in, or the fact that we have prehistoric, out-of-time Velociraptors trying to outthink and outfight us."

"What can you tell us, Carl?" Jack asked, leaning forward after finishing the first meal he had had since arriving two days before.

"Hell, after six months of trying to piece things together, I think I've only scratched the surface. I do think with all of us putting our heads together we can at least make some sense of this strange-ass continent."

Everett waited as Will and Farbeaux returned from a thorough perimeter patrol. Henri unslung his M-4 and sat, shaking his head vigorously at the offered

MRE. Instead he started eating a giant berry he had found on the patrol. Jack shook his head.

"We believe now that when the continents separated it took the existing animal life with it. This continent developed totally on its own seven hundred million years ago." Virginia looked at Sarah and she nodded. "Dinosaurs evolved differently and many more of them may have survived extinction by that separation. Maybe not the larger dinosaurs, but the smaller, avian breeds we have come to know from the movies. Left alone they developed rudimentary tool-making capability. In essence they took up where their larger relatives left off, unabated. I suspect that this is a recent development, maybe a hundred thousand to two hundred thousand years. Eventually those small birdlike raptors will learn to make more sophisticated weapons."

"I do not know about you, my American friends, but I think the spears alone are pretty damn sophisticated." Farbeaux tossed the remaining large pit from the fruit away. "And how long did it take humans to think of throwing a rock to defend himself?" Henri said, putting a damper on things as usual. "No, there is more to this than mere evolution."

"Perhaps so," Everett said as he looked deeply into the fire. They all could see that the many months of isolation had taken its toll on their friend. "You asked earlier about humanoid life." Everett ceased staring into the flames, stood, and turned to look up at the falling ash and then toward the red glow of Erebus three hundred miles distant. "I've found fields of bones. Early man, Neanderthal, Cro-Magnon, even the little species we know as Lucy, at least from what my limited education into those fields can tell me. Thousands upon thousands. Entire species of anything that could threaten those raptors." He looked at his rescuers. "You also asked about the Romans, the Japanese, and Chinese soldiers. All dead, massacred to the man. Three modern armies, all taken down by those feathery little bastards. They nearly had me more than once until I figured out how to get around them."

"Do you know anything about the migratory animals?" Anya asked.

"A little from my observations. It may be a yearly trek to get at the richer volcanic grasses near Erebus, I'm not sure. But the animal life that lives around the volcanoes permanently have decided it was time to get out of Dodge. Why one set goes one way, why the other goes a different direction has me stumped. I guess the large herds of mammoths and bison just don't know anything other than that their migration they have been following for thousands and thousands of years is just too hard a habit to break."

"That makes sense," Sarah agreed.

"But one thing I did notice. There are millions upon millions of bones lining that game trail. I believe the raptors actually herd them, or at least take extreme advantage of the migration to kill and eat. There's no end to the smarts of those ugly little bastards."

Jack's radio suddenly sprang to life. The sound, though loud, made Carl feel like he was part of the modern world again. It did no harm to the psyche of the others either.

"Colonel, Jenks here."

Jack looked at Virginia and saw the relief in her face when she heard the gruff man's voice.

"Collins," he said into the radio. He had yet to inform the master chief they had found Everett and the others. Jenks wasn't even aware that Virginia was there. Jack couldn't wait to tell him and hear the cursing start to fly.

"Negative on any roost those damn things may have. We searched until we drained the batteries on both drones. We're recharging now."

"Good, Master Chief. Is Charlie close by?"

"Yeah, he's right here."

"We have Mr. Everett."

The radio was silent as the others around the fire smiled at what must be happening in the camp.

"And a few others that we found picnicking in the woods. One may wish to say hello to you."

"Wait, damn it, is Toad all right?" came the hurried voice of the master chief. Sarah got up and joined Jack. All the while Henri watched her as she moved. She saw this and then looked at the Frenchman and her eyes told him that she was appreciative of him, but that was all for the moment. Jack tossed Virginia the radio before she could react.

"Oh, your precious Toad is just fine, he saved all of our asses. Maybe you should worry about me, you gruff bastard!"

"Slim, what in the holy Sam hell are you doing out here? I told you to keep your skinny ass out of—"

Virginia turned down the volume on the radio and smiled at the others. "That will keep him occupied for a while." She tossed back the radio to Jack and he caught it with a grin.

Collins held the radio and then looked at Carl. "You see, everyone missed you so much that I bet you can't wait to get back and deal with your old buddy on a daily basis."

"Don't you dare tell me that," Carl said as he turned on Collins. "Did everyone lose their damn minds while I was gone?" He paced around the fire. "The director would never allow that man anywhere near his precious collection," he said in his final defensive denial.

"When you're discussing and designing ways of going into hell," he explained, looking around the horrific world, "you sometimes have to deal with the devil, Swabby, you know that. And without Jenks we would never have had the chance."

"*I am going to kick everyone's asses on this deal, let me tell you.*" They caught the final threat of the master chief as Jack turned the volume back up.

"She's happy to hear your voice, too, Master Chief," he said with mock seriousness.

"She's all right? The others?"

They heard the belated concern in Jenks's voice.

"Everyone's still breathing."

"Okay, I'll deal with her when you people get your asses back here, and that little event better be soon."

"Why is that?"

"Because those raptor things are increasing their attacks on the animal herds and they are starting to move far faster than we realized."

Collins lowered the radio in wonderment as to their ability to catch a break.

"We'll send all nonessential personnel back to you. We have to continue on until we find out what those things do with their spoils of war."

"Roger. Get them back so I can bounce some ideas off of Slim's head."

"Watch out for those Russians, they're loose out there and they're scared. They may make a move for the doorway."

"Let them try it if they want to get their asses sliced in two. The laser system is working just fine. But they or the power won't hold up to a full-scale onslaught of those rock-and-spear-chuckin' chicken bastards."

"Roger, Collins out."

"Jack, what was it you were saying about a nest, or lair?" Carl asked.

"It may be nothing, but the off chance that the raptors collect things of beauty, shiny objects, just like other birds, we're hoping, or at least Doc Ellenshaw was hoping, that they took it there, wherever that is."

They saw Everett thinking. He pursed his lips and that was when he turned to them. "I may know where that lair is."

Collins stood with the faint hope that Everett may have an answer. Then he felt his heart skip when he saw the look on the admiral's face.

"It's close by. About three klicks out. But, Jack, you in particular are not going to like it."

"What is it?" he asked as the others came near.

"First, I have to feed my chickens, we're going to need them."

"Chickens?" Mendenhall asked, not liking the sound of anything that had to do with birds of any kind.

"Yeah, I like the eggs, and they like being fed without hunting for their meals. It's a mutual thing. They need me and I them." He saw the strange looks being directed his way as if he had truly lost his mind. "Hey, you guys try living alone out here and not talk to strange birds."

"I do not like the sound of this at all," Will said as he and Ryan exchanged looks of dread. They all made their way to feed Admiral Everett's chickens.

Charlie watched the small radar screen that controlled the automatic defense system. The miniscule blobs of light would appear and then vanish just as quickly. It was as if the raptors on the camp's periphery were testing their defenses.

"They're a little leery after getting their asses kicked the last time. They're just trying to get us to react," Jenks said as he looked through the lens of his night-vision scope that zoomed in three hundred times power. He chewed on the dead cigar and hissed under his breath.

"Do you hear yourself?" the crazed white-haired Ellenshaw asked as he kept his eyes on the scope and the surrounding countryside.

"What?" Jenks asked as he lowered the scope.

"My God, we're actually worried that these abominations are merely trying to get us to react to them. Like they are hoping for a desired plan to take shape."

The silence coming from the master chief was enough to unnerve Charlie.

"How many can we get with our limited supply of battery power?"

"Enough to probably piss off the remaining three or four thousand of the damn things when we're all done." Jenks smiled at Charlie, who had finally turned away from the screen in abject fear.

"Just think Little Big Horn, if that's easier for you to grasp, Nerdly."

The seven novice adventurers were stunned at the makeshift pen Everett had set up toward the rear of the stockade where the Romans had stored other animal life in their short tenure as rulers of this horrid land. What was inside the pen was far more shocking to them. Pecking the ground and scratching at its ash-covered surface were about fifteen of the giant rocs. The huge ostrich bodies were well over ten feet, far taller than a horse. The heads were large and the beaks terrifying in hooked deadliness. These rocs looked different to Ryan and Mendenhall. The killers they and the Russians had run into were multicolored with red and gold and black feathers, where these fifteen were white with red highlights. Their small, stubby wings flapped every once in a while when their beaks came into contact with some crawling thing making its way through the accumulated ash. They were calmly scratching for food as the humans watched them.

Carl went over to a large barrel that looked as if it were a thousand years old. He lifted out a large wooden bowl full of what looked like grain. He walked quickly over to the fence and then he opened the small gate and reattached a rope made of vine twistings. He approached the first roc as the others held their breath.

"You are one crazy son of a bitch, Skipper," Ryan said as his blood froze when the roc looked up at Everett's approach. "Will and I saw one of those tear a man's head off not five hours ago."

Carl turned and smiled. "Yeah, I've run across those guys too, they're not friendly at all. These here? I think they may have been on their way to being domesticated by the Romans, Japanese, and Chinese soldiers before they were wiped out." He turned and put his hand out to the roc. They were shocked when the giant bird nuzzled at Everett's hand. The three long gouges in its beak told the newcomers this particular roc had seen trouble and survived. The head of the rooster was colored in bright red feathers that ended in a curlicue at its top. They could also see the obvious affection Carl had for the large, frightening animal.

"This one is my friend, we each saved the other's life. His name is Foghorn."

"Just when you thought this day could not get any stranger," Henri said as he leaned on the rickety fence that wouldn't have kept in a small bunny, much less the five-hundred-pound monstrosities moving toward their handler.

Everett turned and looked at Henri and his smile widened. With the beard it made the brevet admiral look quite insane, especially in the torchlight.

"You haven't seen strange yet. You still have to saddle your transportation."

"Transportation?" Jack asked, looking at Sarah, who also had no clue as to what Everett was talking about.

Everett took the grain and tossed it wide in an arc and the giant chickenlike rocs went wild as they started to feed on the sweet grain.

"Yeah, I just fed 'em, but you have to saddle 'em yourselves."

The old saddles were not saddles at all. In the real sense it was a strap of leather that was butt wide with bridles and harnesses. There were no stirrups to speak of.

"I can only assume they're Roman. God knows they're hard to ride on, but it beats the alternative of having those course feathers poking you in your ass." Everett laughed when he saw his friends' faces. Farbeaux was in particular despair. "When you get on, be sure to put your feet and legs under its wings. It helps to hang on. Their gait and angle of run can be a little disconcerting from time to time."

They had watched on in complete and abject horror when Carl placed his hands near each of the roc's mouths as they pecked at the grain thrown to the ground. Everett easily placed a bridle on each, securing the beak with a leather strap that looked as if it couldn't control a small donkey, much less a Rodan-sized creature. Each of the eight rocs Carl selected as being the most docile of the group were bridled, saddled, and anxiously awaiting their riders. The yellow eyes flicked back and forth and made them all nervous with the eight sets of predator eyes watching them.

"Okay, you two have your orders. You take one of the M-4s," Jack said as he unslung his own weapon and handed it to Will Mendenhall, "and one of the Glocks. We'll take one M-4 and we have Carl's Glock and extra ammo." He smiled and looked at an anxious Carl as he looked into Anya's scared eyes for the briefest of moments. "And of course we have Robin of Locksley's bow and arrows."

Carl looked at Jack with raised brows. "I was hoping my archery days were behind me."

"We can only hope. Okay, let's get a move on before the sun comes up and the saber-toothed lions, tigers, and cave bears start to awaken."

"Don't forget the wooly mammoths and the giant bison," Virginia joked as if to rid herself of the fear of the great roc she was currently sitting upon with shaking hands holding the leather reins.

Sarah leaned into Collins but Jack refrained from hugging her. Instead Jack just winked. She was relieved that his attitude about their sudden arrival had softened to that of Mount Erebus.

"You kids get straight home, don't stop for Cokes and a burger anywhere," Carl said as he assisted Anya up onto her feathered mount. He turned serious as Will and Ryan both fought to climb onto their skittish birds who each turned in a wide circle making the men run alongside until they had enough leverage to jump up and onto their frightened animals. Will went over on his stomach and was bounced roughly until he righted himself. His eyes were wide as he looked at the others like he had meant to do that.

"Find that coupling," Sarah said to Jack as he climbed onto his own roc while having the same difficulty as Ryan and Mendenhall only with a more dignified ending. Once aboard Jack had to laugh at the Frenchman as he sat astride his roc with his elbows sticking straight out to his sides as he held the reins like a poorly trained cavalryman.

"Stick to the game trail, the rocs will let you know in advance if anything is stalking you. Their sense of smell is like that of a great white shark," Carl said as he leaned over and kissed Anya. "See ya, Gypsy girl."

She smiled, even though she really didn't care for the great white reference, and then she lightly kicked her giant roc into motion. She almost fell off backward as the long-legged animal started to trot toward the far gate of the stockade. Jason, Sarah, Will, and Virginia hurried to follow using their rocs like out-of-control and headless chickens. Will's mount went in circles before hitting the open gate and then almost threw him from the makeshift saddle until he finally gained control and went after the rest of his team.

Collins turned to a white-faced Henri, who waited patiently and acted as if he rode rocs all the time back in France, even though his stiff frame and wide eyes betrayed the fact of the matter quite differently.

"Ready, Colonel?"

There was silence as Henri found he didn't want to make any noise and frighten the very large and carnivorous bird he found himself sitting upon.

"Shall we go and try to retrieve the master chief's little toy?"

"By all means," Everett said as he kicked his own roc, Foghorn Leghorn, not too gently, making the enormous and already skittish bird elicit a wild, cawing scream as it broke at full speed for the gate. Jack's roc followed and then Farbeaux's as he tried desperately to stay in the old saddle of Roman design.

Everett's exhilarating scream of "Hi-ho Silver" reverberated even over the rumblings of Erebus.

At sunup the first probing attacks began in earnest. An exhausted Charlie Ellenshaw almost didn't react to the warning tone sounded by the small radar system installed in each of the sixteen lasers pods. Each revolution of the small self-enclosed dish told Ellenshaw that what he was seeing was real. The defensive system went into action without having being told to do so.

The first sizzle and pop of the eastern-most laser pod startled a slumbering Jenks to full wakefulness. He never hesitated in sending up one of the recharged drones to get a bird's-eye view of what was taking place along the tree line.

Ellenshaw watched as the faster-than-light laser burst into the far-off trees. He didn't know if the accurate system hit anything other than wood. Then before he could contemplate more, a second and third shot sounded and the bluish-green bolts of laser light shot out, reaching for the unseen raptors as they tested the range of the defensive measures they employed. The thought of how smart these animals were made Jenks's head hurt.

All sixteen of the lasers went off simultaneously as the raptors made a bold move and actually broke the cover of the trees to expose themselves. They flapped their flightless wings and screamed into the air and then ran back into the cover of the trees.

Jenks got the number one drone remote to the desired altitude and his blood froze as he saw the bison and mammoth herds moving much faster than before. When he examined the edges of the enormous migratory herd he saw the reasons why—a hundred raptors charged and then retreated, making the animals start to flee in panic.

"Crap, it looks like those bastards are making their move." Jenks reached for the radio.

Charlie Ellenshaw watched as the raptors were no longer interested in hiding and playing games—they were coming on and they meant business.

Above him the lasers started firing off at intervals that told Ellenshaw and Jenks that they now had precious little time remaining.

The lightning in the morning sky overhead lit up like the old footage of London during the blitz. The lasers would fast drain at this rate and they both knew it.

The five miles were covered in bone-jarring speed by the three rocs as they ran free for the first time since Everett had corralled them six weeks before. They were free and the large birds sensed it. Their speed and maneuverability over the uneven jungle floor was amazing. They would smell something that might be a danger to them and automatically shift gears and turn in another direction. Then they would eventually reroute to their original course. Enough so that Jack was beginning to suspect that every animal in this crazed land was intelligent enough to instantly adapt to any quickly changing situation. The men were quite scratched up by the time the three rocs finally broke into the open. Everett was the first to rein Foghorn in, and Jack and Henri were grateful when their rides followed suit.

"It's right over this ridge. Tie up and we'll walk the rest of the way."

Jack and Henri did as instructed and then they started off through the thinning brush of the outermost jungle. Carl was kneeling only feet away.

"I thought it was going to take forever to get a favorable wind."

"Their sense of smell is that good?" Jack asked as he and Henri kneeled next to Carl, who only nodded his head in answer to Jack's query.

As Everett parted the bushes they spied the small valley below. The first thing they saw made their eyes widen in awe as they thought they'd never see one of the damnable things again.

Inside the small clearing was the downed saucer. It was smashed and ancient. Large sections of its round housing were missing and the upper dome of the saucer was smashed and open to the elements. But it was what was crawling all over the ancient crashed vehicle that held their attention. They were even lying casually in front of it on the ground. Several young raptors were playing with one another until one or the other started snapping. Some of the feathered raptors looked to be larger than the ones they had seen earlier. These meandered in and out of the once powerful ship. Jack despaired and turned away and sat heavily into the tall grass.

"The saucer looks to have been dead for at least a million years. Hell, it may even have been the first one to open up a wormhole over Antarctica. But as you can plainly see, it has new tenants now."

Collins shook his head. "How are we going to get inside?" he asked.

"We don't have to—look," Carl said as Jack and Henri tried to see what it was he was indicating in the far distance. "Near the small river running by the saucers starboard side." He looked at Henri. "That's the right side for you landlubbers."

Henri gave Carl a withering look in return.

Jack realized that the quirky Carl was just having the time of his life knowing full well that no matter what his fate would be, he wouldn't have to face it alone.

"See it," Carl said, pointing once more.

Jack removed the cased binoculars from his pack. He adjusted the focus and then scanned the area on the starboard side of the ancient crashed saucer. Then he finally spied what Everett was pointing at. Near the water's edge was a debris pile that several of the raptors hovered around. One would retrieve something and then another would hiss and then throw a rock to get the first to drop what it was holding. As he adjusted the image and brought the large pile of debris into sharper focus Jack saw that it was a collection of detritus that held one thing in common—

they were all shiny or extremely colorful. He saw Roman helmets, banners from the Chinese, and even several shiny sixth-century gladius swords. God help this backward world if the raptors ever started using the weapons they had scavenged.

"If they have it, it's in that pile."

Jack lowered the field glasses and then pursed his lips.

"Recommendations?" he asked both men.

"Do we have a choice? How many of those feathered lizards are there?" Farbeaux asked.

"Maybe a hundred."

It was Jack who faced both men. "Then we have to scare the hell out of them long enough to examine their little collection."

"And how do we go about accomplishing that?"

Jack smiled, although only briefly. "The old cavalry way. We charge into the camp and run off the tribe. I figure we may frighten them off for the chance at seeing the coupling."

Carl nodded but Henri did not. "Are you insane?"

"Yeah, I am."

The Frenchman watched as both Jack and Everett made their way back to their waiting rocs.

"I'm truly starting to hate you two gentlemen."

22

Sarah saw the encampment from a mile off and the sight made her freeze. The roc she rode smelled the violence in the air and balked at continuing forward. The five of them watched from the highest hill surrounding the center of the game trail where Jenks and Charlie were waiting for them. The vision that greeted Ryan was chilling as he watched the defensive laser system crisscrossing the cloud and ash-laden sky like bursts of diamonds that streaked to their targets. In the distance they could see the many thousands of animals as the dust cloud they created blotted out the sky, but they could still see the small shapes that ran in and out of the migrating animals. The massive weight of both mammoth and bison herds shook the very earth beneath them.

"Damn it!" Ryan said as he had trouble controlling the roc, which wanted very much to leave the area through its serious sense of smell. It knew what was hunting the bison and mammoth herds. "I figure Charlie and the master chief have about a half hour before they are trampled underfoot or them raptors get to them. The way that laser system is firing off they won't have much juice left in the batteries before those murderous things are on them." He looked at his frightened companions. He didn't need to ask what they should do because as one they kicked the giant rocs into motion. The enormous birds were hesitant at first and then the frightened avians broke cover. It wasn't long before they found out what changed the rocs' small minds—the raptors came at them from the rear. They had somehow worked their way around them, or this had been another group that came in from a different direction than the main assault. The first raptor screamed and leaped at the roc that Virginia was astride and missed her by mere inches as Will didn't hesitate to shoot three times from the Glock into the stumbling raptor. With that fight closely won, they charged down the slope and through the screening trees in front of them.

The five people and birds shot down the hill narrowly missing trees and raptors that sprung from behind cover. They dodged three of these attacks with only Sarah's roc coming up bloody as a raptor had managed to strike the roc in its hindquarters. The bird was able to keep its feet only after careening Sarah and itself from tree to tree, momentarily threatening to dump the diminutive geologist.

Jason found his path to the valley blocked by three of the hissing reptilian creatures that displayed their plumage as if this alone would dissuade Jason from fleeing. Just before the first of the three bent over to spring, it was stunned and frightened by the incredible roar of Erebus as she blew her caldera. The expanding gas and ash hit and rolled down Erebus and her sisters like a tidal wave of scalding fury. The pyroclastic phenomena had one intention—to kill the continent of Antarctica, the last landmass free of the ice that covered the entire world.

Sarah and Anya flew past Jason as the raptors blocking their path fled before the onslaught of noise and thunder. Jason, Virginia, and Will were not far behind as the choices had become clear to all—face the four giant volcanoes' wrath, or run the gauntlet of voracious raptors.

Above, the sky filled with black smoke and the rain consisting of fiery coals started to devastate the surrounding landscape.

They charged headlong into the first great battle between Mother Nature and her smartest animal life, and one thing was looking foregone—both man and animal were going to lose this fight.

The coincidence of Erebus erupting at the exact same moment of Everett's disappearance was not lost on Sarah or Virginia. The wormhole effect had done something to trigger this event but they had precious little time to contemplate as to why. It seems the history of this world had been shaped by beings other than any who ever called this planet home. Human destiny had been in the hands of others all the way from the beginning.

The world of 227,000 years ago was coming to an end with fire, and then miles upon miles of ice.

Henri could not believe what it was they were attempting. Did these men have a death wish? He saw the excitement in both Everett's and Collins's faces. It was as if they actually looked forward to the challenge. The Frenchman, although thoroughly motivated to find that power coupling, was equally anxious not to be knocked off of his giant chicken while riding into the very nest of raptors they normally would have avoided.

"Gentlemen, shall we sally forth?" Jack said. He raised the Glock nine millimeter as his large roc pawed at the earth, irritated by the sulfuric smell emanating from the south. Carl raised his own weapon and then they both looked at Henri, who unenthusiastically raised the M-4 in mock bravado.

"By all means, let's ride off to our deaths, because by the look of Erebus, we're out of time."

"Boy, he's a real killjoy, isn't he?"

"Yes, he is that, but he's French, what can you do?" Jack said as he kicked the roc into action. Everett smiled at Farbeaux and with a return look expressing his incredulity, the former French black operation commando reluctantly followed the two crazed Americans into the valley of the shadow of death—*or something akin to it anyway*, he thought.

The batteries were draining so fast that Jenks had to adjust not only the rate of fire from the sixteen weapons, but also the distance to engage the target. He tapped in the new parameters and then placed the laptop down and tossed Ellenshaw another thirty-round magazine for his M-4.

"Okay, Doc, we need to supplement the lasers. Start by firing into the front of that bison herd when they get within two hundred yards. Maybe we can turn this stampede into going another direction."

"Shoot the buffalo?" Ellenshaw asked, horrified about shooting such a magnificent animal.

Jenks inserted his own magazine into his weapon and then charged it. He finally spared Ellenshaw a look of frustration. "Look, either we turn them now or wait until them hairy-ass elephants are crawling up our butts."

Ellenshaw finally understood. He turned and aimed, waiting for the bison to come within range.

The attack from behind caught both Jenks and Ellenshaw off guard. As Jenks turned and saw the four raptors jump upon the outer trailers of their defensive line, he quickly fired, hitting one of the brightly plumed animals, dropping him into the empty bed of the trailer. Charlie wasn't as fast and managed to stitch the sky with tracer rounds as the three remaining raptors jumped from the green-painted trailers into the center of the camp. The first sprinted, feathered arms outstretched for balance as it tried desperately to avoid the bullets striking the ground at its feet. The master chief cursed again when he saw the animal crash into the ceramic and steel doorway. It rebounded with half of its scaled, reptilian head sliced open and dangling. It quickly shook off the blow and started to charge the doorway again.

"Son of a bitch!" Jenks said, and fired ten rounds into the running raptor just as the next two charged the doorway. One had a large rock that it threw, not at the doorway, but at the master chief's head. It narrowly missed as Jenks fired five more rounds hitting the red- and yellow-colored feathers at the creature's neck, sending him into a sliding crash next to the doorway.

As Charlie took aim and easily dispatched the last of the intruders, Jenks had time to figure out the horrifying fact that the raptors had somehow found a gap in the laser system's radar coverage. How they found one was far beyond him.

"Oh, oh," Ellenshaw said as he saw the blips on his own screen. Five targets were emerging from the forest line to the south and six more not far ahead of them. Two distinct groups were charging the camp simultaneously.

Jenks swallowed and wiped sweat from his face as he studied the radar scope on the laser control panel. He shook his head. "We can't cover all fronts here," he said as he hurried away and gathered up his two recharged drones. He yelled something at Charlie that the doctor couldn't hear, and then the master chief started pulling access panels from the two air force drones. Ellenshaw saw the ordnance box next to Jenks and grimaced, afraid of what the navy man was up to. His attention was taken away by the loud hissing as the five raptors in the first group finally broke cover and charged the camp just as the first set had done. Charlie fired but his aim was off and he knew at that moment that at least four out of the five would make the trek into their camp.

Once again Erebus belched flame and fire. The plume blotted out what was left of the sunlight and a surreal landscape came into view and it had a nightmare quality about it—like the world had turned a sepia color. The ground shook so hard that the front two raptors stumbled and fell as the other three easily hopped over their fallen comrades.

"Look out!" Ellenshaw shouted as three spears—sharpened sticks is a more accurate description—came flying through the air and dug themselves into the ash-covered ground near the doorway. It was almost as if the reptilian beasts were out to destroy it. But Charlie knew this couldn't be, they were just afraid of it and wanted it gone.

He fired and then his M-4 jammed. The second set of three raptors were on them, but just a second before the first of them could leap the trailers they were using as a camp barricade, several shots brought it down. Then more shots rang out over the roar of the distant mountains.

Both Jenks and Ellenshaw heard the shouting as the giant rocs broke through the cover of the trees. Charlie couldn't believe his eyes when he saw the prehistoric birds had riders perched upon their backs. The rocs screamed and the riders charged through a screen of raptors, the huge taloned feet of the running rocs decimating the aggressive little dinosaurs as they crashed through their ranks.

"It's Jason!" Charlie shouted as he tried to clear his weapon of the jam. Jenks looked up from his tinkering and saw the commander as he fired point-blank into the back of a raptor's skull, dropping it like a sack of potatoes. To Jenks and Ellenshaw the point was now moot about the impossibility of anything surviving an age it wasn't supposed to on this messed-up continent. So, raptors outlived their brethren a mere sixty-five million years, but now they were actually witnessing Jason Ryan of the United States Navy riding a giant feathered roc like a charging cavalryman. "It's Virginia, Sarah, and Anya!" Ellenshaw screamed, causing Jenks to fumble the C-4 charge he was handling. Cursing, he looked up from his task and saw Virginia as she kicked brutally at the giant bird's hindquarters to get it to jump the first trailer. Then Jason, Sarah, and Anya broke through the gap in the defensive trailer line and skidded to a stop. Jason immediately ran to Charlie and slapped him on the back.

"What are you guys doing here?" Ellenshaw asked as Ryan fired his smoking nine millimeter into the line of raptors that now threatened to break through the tree line in force. Ellenshaw suspected they awaited the herd of bison and mammoths to crush them first.

"Never mind that, Doc, what's up with that dust cloud?" Jason asked as Sarah and Anya joined them at the firing line. The rocs had decided that they could be in a far better situation than the one they currently held. As one, their mounts deserted them.

"The raptors are using the bison and mammoth herds to stampede our position. They have been herding them for two days now."

"Raptors? Mammoths?" Ryan asked, looking from Ellenshaw to Anya and Sarah.

"You know, those lizard-looking chickens you just shot up," Charlie said as he, Anya, and Sarah turned back to look at the animals they had assumed were just small rocs laying dead and dying in the fallen ash.

"To tell you the truth, I was really hoping that Carl was a bit touched in the head when he told us about them things," Sarah said as they continued to look at the nightmarish advanced evolutionary form of an extinct Velociraptor.

"What in the hell?" Ryan asked as he stood, because he had to see this.

As the others looked on in amazement, they saw a larger-than-normal raptor stride easily from the trees. It stood directly over the raptor that was wounded and writhing on the ground. Ryan would swear later that the brightly colored feathers of the six-and-a-half-foot reptile plumed out from its long and flightless wings and rose along its spiny back. It seemed to be posing for the humans who watched it. Then to their amazement the sharpened spearlike stick came down into the wounded raptor's chest. It suddenly stopped moving and lay still. They would swear later that the raptor never looked away from them as the spear came down, its bright yellow eyes challenging the humans.

"Okay, it's official, I don't like this place," Jason said as he lowered himself to a kneeling position.

Virginia had slid to a stop and jumped from her roc. She saw the wide eyes of the master chief as he realized just what it was she had been riding. The roc screamed and then ran off just as Will Mendenhall made it over to the both of them.

"Glad to see you're still alive," Virginia said as she knelt beside Jenks and his dismembered drones. He continued to work as Virginia pecked him on the cheek.

"Nice horsey you had there, Slim," Jenks commented as he tore a set of wires free from a drone.

"Yeah, a little hard on a woman's ass, though," she said as Mendenhall silently agreed.

"What are we doing, Master Chief?" Will asked as he hurriedly tossed his and Jenks's M-4s to Sarah and Anya before turning back to the frantically working navy master chief.

"Slim, slide the blasting cap into that wad of C-4 in drone number one. Captain, do the same on two. I've got to rewire this telephoto lens to send the charge through."

"What's the plan here, Harold?" Virginia asked as her slim fingers easily pushed the inch-long cap into the block of C-4.

"In case you failed to notice, Miss Nuclear Sciences, we have a herd of giant bison and even larger Frankenstein elephants charging down to the camp, which so happens to include the doorway. We have to turn them before they get here."

"Master Chief, the raptors are all out in the open, they're forcing the bison and mammoths to charge!" Charlie called out as he started to follow Jenks's last order to him. He emptied the full load of tracer rounds into the fast-moving bison herd.

"Jesus, we may as well be shooting at a brick wall," Jason said. "Jenks, we're out of time here!" Ryan also started firing in hopes of scaring the frightened animals even more than the raptors pushing them.

Jason, Anya, Charlie, and Sarah watched the trees come alive as thousands of raptors slowly broke from cover alongside the racing animals, adding to their terrified panic.

"Okay," Ryan said as he stood up to see the full picture. "That is a lot of raptors." He watched as the bison were now only a quarter mile away. "I'll never laugh at another made-for-TV movie again."

Behind them the first of the two drones flew skyward and quickly vanished in the increasing ashfall.

The initial shock of Jack's planned attack went off with spectacular results. The raptors that were caught playing or lounging were taken by surprise, probably for the first time in their lives. They saw the charging rocs and the men who sat upon them. Collins, Everett, and Farbeaux fired into the running raptors, not really caring if they hit anything at all. The object was to scatter the nest, so to speak. They needed the time to search for the coupling. Even the fatter, older raptors thought it better to retreat and reevaluate the strange behavior of the rocs, the raptors' only natural enemy. It was by sheer luck that the rocs had been chosen to carry the men. But as most professional soldiers will tell you, battles are decided by a healthy dose of that particular charm—luck.

Henri and Carl would stay mounted since Jack was the only one of the three to even know what the coupling looked like. As he ran toward the raptors' booty pile, a single feathered menace, who had not had a chance at running, turned on Collins and charged. Jack, while looking over the large pile of colorful and shiny detritus, raised his nine millimeter and quickly dispatched the charging raptor as he was far more interested in the impossible task ahead of him: finding the coupling in this mess before the raptors found out they had been had and returned with a little payback.

Carl and Henri rode to the ancient and crumbling frame of the downed saucer and fired blindly into the trees surrounding the nesting area of the raptors.

Jack almost had to turn away from the smell as he kicked at the first pile of treasure. That was when he saw the arm with a bright and shiny wristwatch upon it. It was obviously one of the Russians who had been taken as a spoil of war. He grimaced and started in earnest to pull items from the large stockpile of absconded items. Seeing a colorful stone that had obviously come from Erebus, he also saw there was five MRE packets, their mylar wrap shiny to the raptor eye. He was looking at a near impossible task to accomplish before the nesting raptors found the courage to return. Still, he went crazy looking.

Henri felt the presence of the raptor before his roc recognized the smell of the animal, turned, and was so taken by surprise that rider and bird fell to the floor of the nesting area. The ash plume rose and hid the Frenchman for the briefest of moments, but not before Carl saw what had scared the roc so bad. There, standing inside the damaged frame of the million-year-old saucer, was the largest raptor they had seen. This one was over six feet tall and stared down at the men as if they were intruding on its home. Everett hurriedly tried to correct and fire at the same time but his roc also screamed and fell backward. Carl was able to maintain his precarious hold on the bird but he lost his nine millimeter in the process. As he corrected the fall of the roc his eyes caught on something shiny in the clutched digits of the raptor's left hand as it surveyed the chaos of his nest. The world shook but the raptor only stared out as if the men and rocs were but a minor inconvenience. This one was not to be intimidated.

"Jack!" Everett shouted as he frantically looked for his lost weapon, but it was now buried so deep in the fallen ash that he gave up. Henri was just getting to his feet when he saw exactly what Everett was yelling about.

Collins kicked at a smelly pile of collected objects when he heard Everett's shout. He turned and his eyes immediately fell upon what the roosterlike raptor was holding in its tightly clutched right hand—the shiny stainless steel power coupling. Evidently it was his prize and his alone. As he watched, Farbeaux quickly moved toward the saucer. He saw the raptor's eyes turn his way and knew that he was had before he ever made the twenty feet. The raptor's eyes went wide and its feathered arms flared outward and its neck's down feathers went to full attention. It hissed again as the Frenchman came on, firing the M-4 as he did so. The raptor screamed as a round nicked its winglike arm. The creature opened its slim jaws and the teeth were apparent as it leaped from the skeletal remains of the downed saucer. Instead of sizing up the Frenchman it charged him. Suddenly Farbeaux realized that the elongated twenty feet wasn't that long at all. The rooster was upon him.

Jack moved but he knew it would be far too late. Henri was about to be torn apart right in front of them. Still, he raised the pistol and aimed.

Everett, who was also moving, saw that neither he nor Collins was going to be early enough to save the Frenchman's life. The raptor screamed in triumph as it leaped into the air, clawed feet coming at Henri like a small set of arrows. With Jack's and Carl's bullets striking near it, the raptor had no other route to land except right in Farbeaux's lap.

The blur of brown and black caught the raptor right before its leap connected with Henri. He was shocked to see the raptor suddenly vanish in a rush of falling feathers. The world turned to a slow-motion movie as the saber-toothed lion tore at the stunned rooster only feet before they both struck the ground and rolled. As Jack looked around he saw other large cats, bears, and prehistoric antelope as they charged away from the burning woods behind them. Erebus was running the population of animals away from its slopes. The frightened lion quickly tore at the soft orange- and red-tinted down of the rooster, who was struggling to free itself from the teeth of the massive cat.

Farbeaux felt his bladder nearly explode as the cat and raptor went flying right over his head, close enough that he actually smelled the musky odor of the saber-tooth as it sped past. He then felt the searing pain as something struck him hard in the area that most men dread. He felt his breath explode outward and immediately felt the bile rising in his throat as he was momentarily incapacitated. He fell backward as the world spun. He didn't even realize that the pain had caused him so much consternation that he actually rolled right into the biting and scratching cat and raptor.

Both Carl and Jack slid to a stop and almost cringed as Farbeaux wasn't even aware of his dire situation. It looked as if he were just lying there not caring about much at all. Finally the lion snapped the neck of the raptor and with a giant paw on the lizard's chest, the great cat roared in triumph. It leaned over, smelled death as it claimed the rooster, and then in one motion the beast bit deeply into the raptor's neck and leaped into the trees and was gone. Jack and Carl ran to Farbeaux, who was lying there moaning in pain. Next to him was the object that had struck him right dead center of his groin—the power coupling. It was barely visible through the mounting ash deposit covering the ground. Collins reached over and retrieved the vital part of the doorway.

"Now that was impressive," Jack said as he ruthlessly pulled the Frenchman to his feet where he wobbled and almost fell backward. Carl slapped him on the back and then one of the most ruthless men in the world vomited. He swiped angrily at his mouth and vomited again as the pain slowly started to subside from his groin as it worked its way up and out of his body.

"If you ever"—he spit out some ash-colored bile and then looked at both Americans—"I mean ever, mention this in mixed company, I swear I will track you both down and kill you." Henri bent at the waist and yelled an obscenity. Jack smiled.

"You see, Frenchmen know what to do with their sex packages. I told you he would come in handy," Collins said with insulting intent.

Again, Everett slapped his back. "You sure did."

"Now, before I throw up again, may I suggest we get that part back to camp and get the hell out of here as I don't relish the thought of fighting all of them off." Henri was pointing back to the destroyed and ancient saucer.

"Oh, damn," Collins said as he and Everett slowly pulled the Frenchman backward as they spied the two hundred raptors that studied them from the highest point of the vine- and vegetation-covered ship.

Carl quickly caught the two remaining rocs. They tossed Henri up on one and Jack jumped in the makeshift saddle in front of him. Henri screamed as his crotch settled into the harsh leather saddle.

"You better take it as easy as you—"

Jack spurred the giant roc forward and its bounding gait made Henri scream in pain once again. As he threatened Collins's life for the hundredth time in his long and illustrious career, Everett joined up with them on the back of Foghorn Leghorn, and the trio sped away before the raptors could regroup.

Ryan's eyes were on the center-most part of the bison herd where the charging mammoths crushed the poor buffalo-like animals into the ground. As he watched with trepidation he saw that the thousands of raptors lining the edges of the stampede had actually slowed and then stopped as they looked to be gathering things off the ash-covered ground.

"What are they doing?" Sarah asked, having to scream over the roar of the charging beasts combined with the eruption of Erebus and her sisters.

"I suspect they are gathering missiles for their final assault after the herds are finished with us." Charlie smiled when he saw the horror on their faces. They hadn't seen these smart creatures in action before. "They seem to like rocks and sharp sticks as their preferable mode of killing."

Jason, Anya, and Sarah looked at Charlie as if the old hippie professor had lost his mind. Jason was about to explain to the white-haired professor just how he felt when the zip of the second drone sounded behind them. Virginia and Will soon joined them behind the wall of empty trailers.

"I think you can inform that mean bastard that we can see our deaths coming rather vividly. I don't think we need the drones to tell us what's coming."

"He's got a little more planned than idly watching, Jason," Virginia said as she and Will exchanged knowing looks.

They heard the first drone cease its hovering inside the ash cloud. As it was joined by the second drone, they heard the two automated systems scream off toward the charging bison and mammoth herds. They saw the giant animals were now only a hundred yards to their front and were not going to veer away for some small insignificant humans.

"This is going to hurt," Ryan yelled as he pulled Virginia and Anya down to the ground, hoping for some relative cover of the John Deere trailers, but they all knew the mindless fear of the animals would assist in crushing the trailers like tinfoil. The lasers above them continued to fire. With dawning horror Mendenhall hit the earth beside his friends. At least twelve of the laser pods had ceased shooting. They were out of battery power.

The forward line of bison started to jump over the fallen as they came within a hairbreadth of breaching the camp perimeter.

Suddenly the world exploded in front of them. The earth shaking of the Erebus eruption seemed tame in comparison to the rolling and rocking that Jenks's little surprise caused. The combined eight pounds of C-4 plastique detonated after the drones it was attached to reached an altitude of five hundred feet. Jenks had nosed the drones over and sent them at 150 miles per hour downward. The first struck the ground only fifty feet in front of the first line of bison, sending at least two hundred of them to their doom. The mammoths were knocked from their feet as the explosion sent an invisible shock wave outward. It struck the trailers they hid behind and they rocked on their wheeled frames. The John Deere tractor lost its hold on the world and went flying, coming dangerously close to striking the doorway. Ryan was struck in the face by a dismembered hoof of one of the bison.

Jenks flinched as he clenched the cigar in his teeth and was pleased to see that the raptors had not been expecting that. The five or six thousand of them toward the front beat a hasty retreat back into the safe cover of the trees.

"Just a tad more advanced than chucking rocks and sticks, huh, you ugly sons of bitches!"

The master chief sent the second drone down into the midst of the animals themselves at the front of the stampede. The detonation rocked the game trail and sent both mammoth and bison skyward.

"Yes!" Charlie screamed in triumph when he saw that although the first detonation did little to sway the frightened but determined beasts, the second convinced them another route was more preferable to the noise and carnage in front of them. The animals turned right and then they turned left. The raptors that had ran before the powerful explosions stared on from the tree line as their well-laid plan of stampede fell apart right before their menacing eyes. Mammoths and bison slammed into the milling thousands of feathered lizards.

The rumbling of the two herds dwindled as the screams of the raptors escaped the trees. Charlie stood and smiled over at a grinning master chief.

"Where in the hell would you people be if I wasn't here to save your pansy asses?"

Virginia stood and, with a womanly casualness, brushed her clothing as she approached Jenks, who was expecting a big wet one on the lips for his heroics. Instead he saw that her eyebrows were raised as she approached. She was even beautiful with her hair covered in ash and her face in mud.

"Do you think for one damn minute that any one of us couldn't have thought that little idea up? Do you think we were helpless before you came along . . . Harold?"

Jenks was taken aback but only momentarily. He dropped the drone remote box, tossed his cigar away, and kissed the assistant director hard on the lips, then released her.

"You're welcome, Slim," he said, and then walked away.

"Hey!"

Jenks turned and saw the filthy black face of Will Mendenhall. He raised his chin, wanting to know what the young captain wanted.

"I thought your plan was pretty cool."

Jenks was about to chew the captain's ass off when he glanced at the warning Virginia gave him. Instead the master chief just nodded and with one last look at Virginia he walked toward the doorway to inspect it for damage. They all realized at the same exact moment that the two had to be the most bizarre couple imaginable. Jason, Sarah, Anya, Will, and Charlie turned to look at an eye-batting Virginia, who was fawning at the retreating master chief. She then turned and smiled like a high school girl.

"Ain't he something,"

The laser system was out of power with the exception of her radar system, which was being heavily scrutinized by Jason and Will. The look that crossed their faces was not one to make an observer comfortable.

"Is it Jack?" Sarah asked as she approached with a bottle of water as she attempted to keep the heavily falling ash out of her eyes as much as possible. She looked around at the dark sky above that was streaked with red light as Erebus ejected five- and ten-ton boulders from her guts.

"Uh, no," Ryan said as he fixed Sarah with a look. He stepped aside and allowed the lieutenant to scan the radar. She saw the gathering blobs of light as they once more gathered just inside the tree line. Since the detonations of Jenks's little surprise, the raptors had laid low for forty-five minutes but were now starting to gather their courage once more. Jason had to admit they were a determined bunch even after losing their screen of fifty thousand animals.

"Oh, that isn't good at all," Sarah said as she handed the water bottle to Will, who splashed his face with the remains.

"I swear when I get back I will never eat another chicken or turkey again, the scheming bastards," Mendenhall said in all seriousness as he tossed the empty bottle away. The earth rolled and they heard Master Chief Jenks yell as the doorway rolled with the ground it was anchored to. The master chief was nearly crushed before the doorway stilled and the anchor pins held. He hurriedly went back to work.

"We have movement to our rear," Charlie said as he grabbed hold of his M-4, which he had become very attached to.

Jenks stuck his head up from where he laid on his back making an adjustment to the particle collider. He looked at Virginia as she was in the process of handing Jenks a torque wrench.

"What is it?" he asked.

"They may be attacking again."

"Or it's them damn Russians, don't forget them."

As they watched to the south they saw a bright red flare burst from the trees and then quickly vanish as it reached the low-hanging ash cloud. Sarah lowered her head when she realized it wasn't raptors, but Jack and the others—hopefully.

Ryan's radio crackled to life.

"Popping color," came the voice of Jack Collins, which made Sarah go weak in the knees.

Ryan raised the radio to his lips. "I see a red flare, over."

"Coming in," came the tired voice.

Sarah ran to the far wall of trailers and was biting her lip as Anya joined her. They both wanted to gasp when the first roc exited the smoldering trees. They saw Henri Farbeaux as he and the roc he sat upon came out of hiding being led on the ground by Jack. They were followed by a second with Carl onboard, and that sight made Anya smile. The matter of the recovery of the power coupling was far from their minds even as they knew it shouldn't be. They were soon joined by all, including Jenks and Virginia.

"Well, I guess those chicken bastards didn't get their afternoon snack," he said without realizing the others weren't laughing.

Ryan and Will moved one of the wheeled trailers out of the way and Jack led the roc inside as Mendenhall assisted Farbeaux down from the giant bird. Everett was next as he allowed his weary body to slide off the back of Foghorn.

Sarah hugged Jack and Anya repeated the process with Carl.

"Well, the gang's all here, but did you find the golden egg?" the master chief asked, a little more than curious.

Jack pulled away from Sarah and then reached into his pack and unceremoniously tossed Jenks the power coupling. He caught it and smiled at Virginia.

"How about it, Slim, you want to get the hell out of this screwed-up Disneyland?"

"I was ready about three days ago."

With the exception of the master chief and Virginia, who were busy connecting the coupling to the nuclear-powered battery system, the rest were scavenging the radar systems of the laser defense pods to back up the signal enhancer. Only Henri was off by himself recovering. All of the others gathered around the two remaining rocs as Carl slid the old Roman saddles from their backs. He slid a powerful arm around them both and they looked as if they wanted nothing more than the man to stop choking them. He patted each on the enormous beaks and then slapped them both on the tail feathers, sending them through the circled trailers. Then Everett went to the redheaded rooster he called Foghorn. He patted the animal on the neck and Foghorn nuzzled the man's hand. Carl stepped back and then waved his arms. The giant roc, with one last look at Everett, jumped the trailers and was gone. The three enormous birds trotted easily away without looking back. Carl watched them go with a hint of sadness to his slumping frame. Anya walked up and placed an arm around him as they watched the three remaining rocs vanish into the trees. Everett turned to look at Sarah, who was putting a field dressing on Jack's arm.

"My birds aren't going to make it, are they?" Carl asked Sarah, who slowly shook her head.

"Today, tomorrow, or even next month, everything on this continent will be dead and will soon be covered by two miles of ice."

"Get attached?" Jack asked as he flexed his arm.

Everett looked momentarily embarrassed. But he managed a smile. "Foghorn Leghorn wasn't the best conversationalist, but him and the others were the only buddies I had in this part of the world." He lost his smile as he looked over at Ryan and Mendenhall. "At least they never talked back but listened to everything I said without complaint."

The two men only smiled. They were in the mood to tolerate a lot of guff from the admiral; after all, they each considered it a miracle they were looking at him at all. Everett ceased his joking as he glanced at the doorway as it was about to be powered up. He looked at the faces around him. The kind look even extended to Henri Farbeaux as he joined the group.

"I don't know what to say," he said, as he felt he couldn't face the people who had gambled so much in their attempt to bring him home.

"You're a navy man—why is that so surprising? You guys never know what to say," Collins said with his brows raised, meaning for Carl to knock off the thank-yous.

"Regardless"—he looked at his friends and then his eyes settled on the Frenchman—"thank you. All of you."

Farbeaux noticed most of that was directed at him, but the Frenchman couldn't bring himself to say anything. He was resentful of the fact that these men and women made him examine his life, and he did not like that at all. He only nodded in response to the debt of gratitude.

"Okay, everyone better cross their friggin' fingers," Jenks said as everyone turned and watched as he crawled out from underneath the circular collider after connecting the main power source. Jenks nodded as the others shied away, making the older navy man laugh out loud. "Oh, come on, the least that will happen is that this magical erector set explodes and fries us all just like that volcano will do eventually, so what in the hell are you afraid of? Hell, I would be more afraid if this thing doesn't work and we are left here with the Colonel Sanders army chasing us until Erebus blows her top." He looked at his watch as a joke. "Which should be in about thirty minutes by the feel of the ground." He saw the others relax. Maybe he was gaining some humanity—who knows?

"Uh, would you mind ceasing with the jokes and start that damn thing up?" Ellenshaw said as he turned away from the trailers. "We have a lot of company heading our way."

The others walked over and saw what Ellenshaw meant. In the veil of falling ash they watched as the raptors came out of the trees by the thousands. They pushed, screamed, hissed, and fought each other as they came. A large rooster was in the front and it held what looked like one of the ancient Roman spears at its side.

"Yes, now would be a good time," Jack said as he turned to Jenks.

"Okay, Slim, let's see if we can jump-start this damn thing."

Virginia mentally crossed her fingers as she reached into the last trailer and raised the clear plastic cover of the world's most expensive portable power source. She closed her eyes as she flipped the red switch.

They all felt the ozone in the air as the battery generator kicked in. Its small reactor core sent an electrical charge through the very ground as it slowly amped up in power. As Jenks turned to the doorway he cursed as the collider didn't move. Then he mentally kicked himself and ran to the collider and released the static pins holding it in place. It was only a second longer that the large collider started to slowly rotate on its axis.

"Start with fifty percent power only, Slim, until we get a return lock-on signal from Europa."

"Right," Virginia said. She was soon joined by Sarah.

As they watched, the doorway started to spark and hiss as it revolved faster and faster.

Master Chief Jenks sniffed the air and then cursed himself again. He was screwing up in his anxious state to get the hell out of there. He turned to Virginia. "Release the coolant reservoir, slowly. She's starting to sizzle a little."

Virginia did as ordered and then crossed her fingers as she watched Jenks go to the main control panel in the trailer. He adjusted the audible signal and turned the knob all the way up. At first they didn't think it was working, then they all felt the minute irritation of the signal as it penetrated their eardrums.

"Signal is broadcasting," Virginia said as the others gathered around and watched the sparkling doorway slowly open to another dimension with eye-hurting brilliance.

Virginia wanted to jump when the needle on the return signal pegged out in the red.

"Europa is on the line!"

Before any of them could react to the good news, the world exploded in flame and shrapnel.

23

BROOKLYN NAVY YARD

The return team was shocked as the warning alarm on the doorway sounded three times, almost breaking the monitors along the technician's stations.

Niles went to the window where Moira was sitting in her chair. Alice bit her lip as she was confused as to how the return trip would work. They watched as the young technicians ran to their various stations. The activity was vivid and exciting as they speculated on the success of the mission. Most though worried about the missing security team that had deported with the Russians. Xavier Morales was most worried about that fact since it had been him who had so unceremoniously sent them away.

"*Los Angeles,* we need fifty percent reactor power," called out the young UC Berkeley grad who was now in charge of doorway operations.

"*Los Angeles* reports her board is in the green. Going to fifty percent."

"Open the collider and send out the return."

The doorway slowly started its revolutions. The sound was piercing as most placed the headphones over their ears. They had learned that fact the last time—it was painful when the audio tones began.

"Signal acquisition at twenty-two thirty hundred hours and twenty-two seconds."

The loud cheer went up inside the control room and at the science labs at Nellis.

Niles nodded his head as the first hurdle was jumped successfully. He turned and looked at the large monitor where Xavier was sitting, patiently and nervously waiting with the rest of them.

"What are the chances of us accidentally bringing something back that we don't particularly want?" Compton asked. Moira had not thought of that. The worst thing they had ever feared bringing back was a batch of angry Nazis, not monsters from a long-dead world.

Morales smiled. "Group locators will tell us; even our French friend was fixed with a tracking bug. We injected him the day before his departure." Xavier watched as Niles clearly understood.

"You can stop an intruder from entering based on their transmission signal?"

"Yes and no. We can't stop them from transiting once they are through the doorway, but we can redirect an undesirable to another location if we prefer."

"Where's that?" Niles asked, but as he looked at the Traveler he could see by her smile that she already knew.

"There are only so many operational doorways emitting signals, Doctor."

Compton fully understood then.

ANTARCTICA, 227,000 B.C.E.

Jack shook his head and tried to clear the fog that clouded his memory. One minute he was standing next to Sarah as they were both exhilarated that a return signal had been acquired, then the world went crazy. He felt a sharp sting in his back and Sarah's small fingers digging into his skin. He hissed as she pulled out a smoking piece of metal shrapnel. He slowly looked up from his prone position and saw the others as they recovered and started moving. Charlie had his hair in his accustomed state, but he was bleeding from a large wound on his forehead. Others were tending to people who were slow to get up from the devastating explosion. The first thing a bleeding Jenks did was check Virginia, and when he saw that other than a broken nose she hadn't taken a big shot, he immediately crawled to the still-spinning doorway. He looked and saw that it was still functioning. He was about to turn and tell Virginia the good news that it hadn't been the doorway that exploded, but the gun pointing in his face explained the real reason behind the shocking and brutal attack. Doshnikov was standing over him. Jenks slowly stood on wobbly legs and saw the other four torn and battered mobsters as they held the team at bay with their sidearms.

"I am so disappointed you were going to go home and leave us behind without at least saying good-bye," he said as he pushed the master chief hard into Virginia's arms, who stayed his fall while giving the Russian a withering hate-filled glare. He gestured with his Colt .45 for the others to stand. "I am sure you won't mind if we go first this time?"

Jack rocked back and forth as Sarah stilled him. Charlie Ellenshaw helped Farbeaux to his feet and Will and Ryan were still trying to gather their senses. Carl was on the ground with a bleeding Anya lying prone with her head in his lap. Everett was watching the Russians with murderous intent. The dark-haired Gypsy moaned and they all felt relief as she batted her eyes. Everett looked down—his relief was most visible.

"Now." Doshnikov stepped forward and then reached for little Sarah. When Jack tried to stop him, Doshnikov shot the colonel in the upper thigh, sending him crashing to the ground.

"You son of a bitch!" Sarah said as she fought the hold of the Russian.

Ryan and Will ran to Jack but another shot rang out and ash and dirt flew from the bullet striking just inches from their feet.

"Another foolish attempt to stop us will result in us leaving one of these behind as we pass through the doorway." He raised something he held in his left hand and easily tossed it up and down. It was an old grenade. "It seems you were right in your theory about others coming here before us, Colonel," he said as he watched Jack hiss as he struggled to sit up. "We found two of these inside the pack attached to the skeletal remains of a soldier. We couldn't tell if he was Japanese or Chinese, but I must say it was indeed fortuitous that we came across him in our flight from your treachery."

"There he goes using those big words again," Jason said as his anger was just about to boil over. He would rather die here and now than take a chance at his friend being left behind in this whacked-out menagerie.

Doshnikov turned and looked at Ryan. He pointed the .45 at his head and pulled the trigger. Click, the hammer fell on an empty chamber.

"Your luck is holding, my friend." He eased the old and rusty pin from the grenade and smiled as he held the handle in place and turned to the master chief and Virginia. "Now, start the process and get me and my men out of here."

Jenks looked at Virginia and winked. She didn't understand why Harold was taking this so well. He stood on wobbly legs and made his way back to the trailer. He looked at Jack, who was watching while holding his wounded thigh. Of all people it was Henri who was applying pressure and a dressing to the bleeding hole. Collins fought his building anger with every ounce of willpower he had as the Russian reached out and took Sarah by the arm and steered her toward the still-spinning doorway.

"Remember, all I have to do is drop this inside of there and your dreams of a future are done—am I understood?"

Jenks smiled but it was brief and only Virginia saw it. She bit her lip, wondering why the gruff bastard was taking all of this so well.

"Behave and you just may see this lovely young lady again; misbehave and she will die a horrible death and you can stay here and contend with the animal life."

"Master Chief, send this man to where he wants to go," Jack said as Henri assisted him to his feet.

"Yes, sir," Jenks said as he started the collider rolling at full RPMs. "Slim, stand by on the lasing system."

Virginia saw Jenks switch to another tone setting on his control panel and made sure the volume was down when the return signal arrived. Her eyes widened when she realized what he was going to do. She looked at Sarah and then hurriedly back at Jenks, who winked.

"Start the lasing and get the collider lined up."

Doshnikov heard the orders and, remembering this was where they were tricked back in Brooklyn, roughly brought Sarah to his side.

Henri made as if to move on the Russian but Jack forcibly stayed him. They exchanged looks and then Farbeaux knew the Americans had other plans for Doshnikov.

"Let's just cut to the chase—no countdowns, no fact-checking. Either this damn thing works, or it don't." He smiled at Virginia and then nodded. "Bring the collider online at full power, Slim."

Without even looking at the panel before her, Virginia did as she was told. Sarah looked over at Jack with fear in her eyes. Jack nodded at Jenks, telling her to concentrate on him. The master chief looked at the small woman whom he had come to like immensely.

"You trust me, Shorty?" Jenks asked as Doshnikov forced her to the doorway's opening. Sarah could only nod that she did. "Then tell everyone we'll be along shortly." She nodded and Jenks smiled, relaxing her as much as he could.

As the other Russians came forward to join their boss, the doorway went into full-power mode. Suddenly the lasers reached the correct frequency and the burst of pure atomic sunlight exploded from the circling laser apertures, sending out a brilliantly illuminated perfect tunnel of spinning light. Doshnikov turned and smiled at the Americans. He halfheartedly saluted them as he started forward through the vortex of wind and multicolored light.

"Short Stuff, remember: that asshole doesn't have a Group security clearance," Jack yelled above the din of noise.

The dawning look of understanding filled her face. She smiled as she realized what was about to happen.

The five Russians along with Sarah stepped into the doorway.

BROOKLYN NAVY YARD

The doorway went to 115 percent power and the world inside the building started to shake and rattle as the dimensional doorway opened before them.

"Dr. Morales, we have six targets coming through, only one has a transponder."

"All right, Europa, cull the herd down to size," he said as he watched on from Nellis.

"Separation of signals commencing," came the call as the explosion of light bathed the old building in a myriad of color. Before they saw the doorway start to power down they heard it.

They heard a woman's yelp of pain as the vision of the technicians returned slowly after having their retinas fused by the brilliant lasers. When they cleared they saw a lone figure standing on the far side of the doorway as the lasers shut down one at a time.

"*Los Angeles,* cut power!" called out the lead tech as she stood and ran to the latest traveler.

"Damn, that hurts!"

Niles smiled when he recognized the small form of Sarah McIntire. And then that smile was replaced with a look of concern for his missing nine people. He started to open the intercom to get his people moving again, but Xavier Morales was ahead of him.

"Get the doorway back up!"

As Sarah was assisted from the pad, she looked around in confusion and was wondering through her pain just what in the hell happened to her traveling companions.

DORTMUND, GERMANY,
MAY 16, 1943

Heinrich Himmler smiled as the young Jewish lab rat, as he referred to her, stepped through the doorway and vanished. He smiled as her brother was led out of the lab and the doorway started to slow.

Many Nazi officers smiled and congratulated the Reichsführer on the success of the Wellsian Doorway.

"How soon can we transport the doorway to Berlin?" he asked, but was soon cut off.

"Doorway is coming back online!" called out one of the German techs.

Down below in the laboratory, Professor Thomsen's mood went from one of triumph to one of confusion.

"I didn't order the doorway to be reopened yet. We have to recharge in order to bring the Traveler back."

In the observation room Himmler saw the confusion below as the doorway started spinning faster and faster. Suddenly the room filled with bright light as many of the German technicians dove for cover, thinking the Wellsian Doorway had exploded. They were even more confused as twenty uniformed guards broke in and pointed their weapons at them, thinking they had something to do with the malfunction.

"What is happening?" Himmler asked.

Then the doorway opened. Doshnikov shook off the pain of the transit as he stepped into far cooler air. He smiled as his eyes adjusted to the dim lighting. His relief quickly faded as he realized that he wasn't back home at all. As his four men joined him, the German soldiers rushed the strangely dressed travelers. He started cursing in Russian and that really got the party rolling. Gunfire erupted and Himmler high above in the viewing room stomped his feet as he thought the doorway had been compromised by their enemy, the Red Army.

As bullets started flying, Doshnikov cursed the Americans for tricking him again. He decided upon the best course of action after seeing the uniforms the troopers were wearing. He smiled as he tossed the grenade just as the automatic gunfire cut him and his ragged group of time travelers down.

The German foray into time travel had become very confusing indeed.

BROOKLYN NAVY YARD

The Wellsian Doorway started spinning and coming up to full power.

Above, Niles Compton placed his hand on the shoulder of Moira Mendelsohn as they waited. It didn't take long. He met the eyes of Sarah McIntire as she sat next to Alice Hamilton and drank a glass of water. Niles nodded.

"We have a signal coming through," Morales said from the complex in Nevada. Then everyone heard the new computer genius laugh out loud as the other computer specialists started cheering and clapping him on the back. Xavier looked into the large monitor and made sure Dr. Compton was watching. "Nine transponders coming through. The team is accounted for, including one wayward admiral!"

The cheers continued as Niles sat hard next to Moira, who patted the director's hand.

"Thank you, God," was all the director could say.

The homecoming was a rather raucous scene as everyone hugged anyone who had anything to do with the most harrowing mission Department 5656 had ever been involved in. Carl was in tears as they all hugged and offered congratulations.

Above, Niles Compton sat heavily into a chair next to Moira as Sarah dashed from the room to see Jack and the others.

"Thank you for this," he said as he patted the old scientist's hand.

The next day as the Event Group made ready to depart Brooklyn, they were surprised to see six very large and very black Ford Explorers come screeching to a stop just outside of building 117.

Niles, who was standing on the front steps of the building, was leaning on his cane. He smiled over at Jack, who winked in return. Sarah, Will, Ryan, and Carl saw the two men standing there stoically as ten federal agents calmly walked up to the old concrete stoop. The lead agent produced a badge as if Jack and Niles didn't know who these men were.

"Dr. Compton?" the lead agent asked.

"Yes," came the answer.

"Agent Freeman, Secret Service."

Jack and Niles exchanged looks as they had expected the FBI and a whole lot of questions. The agent saw Collins's wrapped leg wound but decided not to ask.

"Sir, as you know the president is still recuperating from his surgery in Los Angeles and he wanted me to pass this along." He handed Niles a small parcel. "He would have done it himself but said you would understand his rather busy schedule with the problems incurred in the past few days." The agent gathered his men and they quickly exited the navy yard.

"What is it?" Jack asked.

Niles opened the package and smiled. He held the object out to Collins, who had to laugh at the gift.

In Niles Comptons's hand was a small item he recognized. It was a large, mouth-watering corned beef sandwich. He looked at the note written in the president's handwriting.

"*We're even, Baldy,*" was all the note said.

On the large dock where the others waited for the laughing director of Department 5656, the remaining members of the strangest mission ever conceived by the Event Group gathered. They watched as the sleek black hull of the USS *Los Angeles* slid out of the birthing area for her trip back to Groton.

"Where is Henri?" Virginia asked no one in particular.

"The last we saw he was being checked out by medical," Ryan said, and Mendenhall agreed.

Virginia nodded just as alarms sounded inside the building where the last of the doorway was currently being dismantled. Ryan and Will shook their heads at the irony just as one of the engineering techs opened the door and stepped out.

"Dr. Pollock, we have an entire case of industrial blue diamonds missing."

Virginia closed her eyes just as the sound of a large outboard motor was heard coming from the river. They looked up in time to see a waving Colonel Henri Farbeaux as he gunned the speedboat forward, heading toward the open waters of the bay.

Virginia was the only one who didn't look stunned. "What is the value of the case?" she asked.

"About eight and a half million dollars," the tech said.

Jenks whistled.

"You want us to go after him?" Ryan asked as he was smiling so wide that it was almost scary.

"No, I don't think we need to do that," Virginia said as she turned and looked at her people. "After what we put him through I'm sure he could use some walking-around money. Besides, who here thinks Henri is out of our lives forever?"

No one spoke.

"Then let it go," she said as she turned and watched the speedboat blazing past the U.S. Coast Guard. Henri was still waving.

Ryan and Will exchanged amused looks. Jason started down the steps.

"Good for you, Henri."

EPILOGUE

DISCLOSURE

We the people are the rightful masters of both Congress and the courts, not to overthrow the Constitution, but to overthrow the men who pervert the Constitution.

—**Abraham Lincoln**

EVENT GROUP COMPLEX, NELLIS AIR FORCE BASE, NEVADA

Virginia and the newly demoted Carl Everett, wearing his old silver eagles of a captain on his blue jumpsuit, waited by the cargo elevator descending from gate number one. The giant lift slowly slid down to level five and then stopped. The two exchanged looks as the doors slid open.

Niles Compton and Jack Collins stood and waited for the Secret Service team to step out. They were immediately joined by the President of the United States.

"Captain, I am truly happy to see you again," he said as he released the captain's hand and then turned to look at Compton and Collins. "Shall we proceed?"

Virginia gestured for the president to follow them. Carl was formal as he greeted Jack and Niles, but they all soon fell into step behind the assistant director and their boss. They made their way to one of the interior elevator banks and entered the air-cushioned ride. The doors closed and the car remained silent as it descended into the most secure facility in the world.

"Dr. Pollock, I assume you received my approval for the replacement personnel for the Group?"

"Yes, sir, we did."

The president waited for the assistant director to expand on her answer but there was nothing forthcoming. They soon found themselves inside the large conference room.

After coffee had been served and the small party was alone he half turned to Compton next to him.

"This Wellsian Doorway, you refuse to turn it over to my people."

"That isn't true. The doorway was destroyed and we cannot recover it nor re-engineer the science."

The president slapped his hand on the tabletop in frustration, knowing his friend was lying to him.

"The technology can never get out in the open. We have seen firsthand how greed takes over common sense. The doorway's destruction was a godsend, because we were tempted to use it for what we thought was right. We have friends that we lost in that damn alien war and we wanted to get them back and had the means to do so. But when we start changing what was meant to be, we start dismantling who we really are. Without the pain of loss there is no commitment to be better than what we ever could be."

"Yet you saved Captain Everett from his fate."

This time it was Niles who slapped the tabletop and leaned forward even farther.

"We went and retrieved a man we sent off knowing he was not going to come back. We, you and I. We could have changed his destiny by not allowing him to go, but we decided we didn't have that right to change what we knew was meant to happen. We adjusted that way of thinking by using the doorway to correct that decision."

Niles stood with the assistance of Jack, who was very proud to know the man who faced down the president. Both men limped as Niles spoke.

"I have known you all of my adult life and I love you like a brother, but I cannot allow you to shame yourself by bending to the very temptations that you yourself despised about the big office before becoming the president. Your handling of Overlord was the greatest achievement ever conducted through the office of the presidency, ranked only with Lincoln and Roosevelt. No, you are better than that. We always play by the rules, we are the good guys. Remember saying that to me?"

The president sat stock-still. "The Constitution, Niles, we evaded the Constitution in not informing Congress what we were up to."

"When I heard you on television that you were caving into the men that scare this nation on a daily basis because it helps keep us alert through fear, I knew that it wasn't you talking. It was that injured man at Camp David. The man that lost friends and sent boys off to a fate that you knew they were not coming back from."

"That's what happens to soldiers, Niles."

"My people are not soldiers for the most part, but they died anyway. It doesn't matter to me if my people wear a lab coat or a uniform, they are mine. They are also yours, and now I think you need to meet a few of them as you never have before."

Niles and Virginia walked to the door and Jack waited for the president to rise from his chair. He buttoned his coat and reluctantly followed Compton to the large cafeteria. They entered and the president saw that the entire Department 5656 was present. They were silent as the four strode into the room and seated themselves in the back.

"What is this?" the president asked Compton.

"This is the Group's way of saying good-bye to our friends. We wanted to wait for the memorial until we recovered Captain Everett. Charlie Ellenshaw organized it."

The president blinked when he saw the pictures on easels at the front of the cafeteria. The president closed his eyes at the soft refrain of Mama Cass Elliot as she sang the slow ballad, "Dream a Little Dream of Me."

The president recognized far too many of the young faces in the blown-up photos. They lined the far wall on both sides and went all of the way to the front. Two hundred photos in all. He blinked when he saw the pictures of a scowling Garrison Lee, a smiling Matchstick, and Gus Tilly, Pete Golding, and Denise Gilliam and the many other military and civilian techs lost in Event Group field actions. He swallowed hard as Charles Hindershot Ellenshaw III stood and made his way sadly to the front. He placed a hand on the portrait of Pete and stood for the longest time until a wheelchair-bound man approached and tugged on Charlie's lab coat. The professor looked down and saw that it was Xavier Morales, the man who replaced Golding. They both nodded and then slowly left the crowded cafeteria.

As they sat long enough to see everyone slowly file out, the president nodded at Sarah McIntire, Jason Ryan, Will Mendenhall, Carl Everett, Anya Korvesky, and finally Alice Hamilton. They all just nodded as they passed by and the president felt he had no right to meet their eyes. Soon they found themselves alone. Only Virginia, Jack, and Niles waited.

Finally the president stood and buttoned his coat again, reached for his own crutch, and nodded his head at the three.

"That was low, Niles."

"Yes, I believe it was. Cold. But you have to put the names to the faces, Jim. The soldiers and sailors of the nations that fought in that war are honored in public, but these people are anonymous. No one knows they ever existed and died for their world, their country, knowing that no matter what they did, no one would ever know about it. No one says thank you, no one can even mourn them because of who and what we do. If we do anything to change that and become just another tool for men to keep and hold power, what are we? Technology such as the Wellsian Doorway can never be controlled by men in power, even you, sir. Sometimes, as you once told me not long ago, we have to give the damn Constitution a rest."

"Sometimes we in power become blinded by the need to protect those who can't do it themselves." The president lowered his head.

Niles and the others nodded at the man who had just been forced to look into the mirror and didn't like the face of the man who looked back. Compton could never allow the Event Group to become the personal pawn of the presidency. Technology had to be controlled. He knew the president's approval of the mission had been based on discovering time travel that could be used for the betterment of the

United States, but Niles was smart enough to know that tech like the doorway was nothing more than what the Nazis had invented it for—that of greed and power. He had to protect his friend.

"That's why you need people like these," Niles said as he gestured sadly at all of his dead people memorialized in frames. "Mr. President, they can help you in protecting those that can't do it themselves, but we have to do it legally and above-board. These people, and many more thousands just like them, are your technology. Trust them, they do rather well when called upon."

The president looked down at his friend and nodded. "I hate it when you become my conscience, Baldy. You're brutal, even more so than my wife."

"Well, as Alice will tell you, I have the very same shortcomings myself."

"Speaking of which, does that old woman still have the key to Lee's wet bar?" Jack took out a key and tossed it to Niles.

"No, but I do. Come on, I'll buy you a drink," Niles said as he turned and faced Jack and Virginia. "Join us?"

Virginia smiled and claimed she had never in her life turned down a free drink. She joined the trio.

"Jack?" the president asked, hoping the colonel would join them.

"I'm afraid I have something I have to take care of, Mr. President," he said, and left the empty cafeteria.

Collins found himself alone on level seventy-two. He waited with the electric truck brimming full with Styrofoam-packaged materials. Finally Sarah showed up. She kissed him, knowing there were no cameras down here and not even Europa could spy on them.

"Ready to see the real wonderland?" he asked.

"I am surely not cleared for this level," she said nervously. Jack only smiled.

Level seventy-two was the deepest level of the Event Group facility, the very farthest level from the top. It was the only level to house vaults that no one, not even the highest-ranking department heads, knew about. The black files were kept here and as Jack smiled he slowly pushed the crated material in and gestured for Sarah to follow. They deposited the Wellsian Doorway into the vault area. Jack explained that he just had to allow Sarah to see the strange items inside that would never, ever be exposed to the outside world. After an hour Sarah left the newly discovered level with her face showing the shock of what the Event Group had discovered throughout its long history—items that were so dangerous to the human race's existence that the level would never be visited by even those in power. After smiling at Sarah's shock, he then closed the heavy door and sealed it with his security badge. He turned and whistled as he and Sarah left the only operational time machine in the world, locked away from the greed of men.

Sometimes, as Jack and Niles had agreed upon, you had to give the United States Constitution a rest, just as the president had said those many years ago.

It was two weeks later when Jack, Carl, Sarah, and Anya stood inside the luxurious foyer of the expensive apartment on the Upper East Side of Manhattan. As they waited they saw the many pictures on the wall of students long since gone but raising families of their own.

Moira Mendelsohn wheeled herself into the foyer and smiled as she greeted the guests she hadn't seen since she had been whisked away by Group security before the federal authorities arrived in force at the navy yard.

"It's so good to see you again," she said as she accepted the hugs from her new friends, the people who knew how to keep secrets.

"We thought we would stop in and see how you are doing, Professor," Jack said as he studied the picture of a young child on the wall. He turned with a questioning look. "Boy, there's a resemblance there, isn't there?" Jack said.

"Oh, yes. That's my brother. It was taken three days before our family was rounded up in Poland," she said with a sad look on her face.

"The boy you failed to find in all of your time travels?" Sarah asked as she joined Jack by the wall.

"Yes, I failed to save the one person that all of that was built for."

Jack nodded at Carl and Anya, who stepped over to the front doors of the apartment and waited.

"Madam, on behalf of our Group, we would like to say thank you for everything that you did. As you know we have a computing system that basically has a mind of her own."

"Oh, yes, that wonderful Europa. I realized that she wasn't your typical laptop." She smiled.

"Well, she's damn good at digging. She found an older gentleman who lives in Battle Creek, Michigan, of all places." Jack nodded that the doors should be opened. "Moira, you failed to find your brother because he was never in Germany after that night. Well, as you know we had that little mishap with the Russians and sent them back to Germany, where it is obvious they met a well-deserved fate. According to Master Chief Jenks and Virginia we screwed up the time line but good. We brought you the results of that screwup. It seems your brother in all of the confusion escaped Europe and made his way across the border, where a French family sheltered him until the war's end. He immigrated to the United States in 1949 and became a citizen two years after that. His name is Peter Chumskey."

Carl and Anya gestured that the man should enter.

Moira's eyes widened as she recognized a boy in a man's body. She started crying and Sarah and Anya could not help but follow suit. The old and tired man rushed to the wheelchair-bound Moira and collapsed at her feet and hugged her legs.

Jack nodded at the others and they quietly left the apartment as the two siblings learned how love spanned even the ravages of time.

The Traveler and her only living relative were finally home.